X θ

USA TODAY bestselling and *RITA*® Award-winning
author **Marie Ferrarella** has written more than 300
books for Mills & Boon, some under the name Marie
Nicole. Her romances are beloved by fans worldwide.
Visit her website, marieferrarella.com

Discover more at millsandboon.co.uk

GOING ROGUE IN RED RYE COUNTY

KATIE METTNER

CAVANAUGH JUSTICE: DETECTING A KILLER

MARIE FERRARELLA

MILLS & BOON

First Published in Great Britain 2023
by Mills & Boon, an imprint of HarperCollins*Publishers* Ltd
1 London Bridge Street, London, SE1 9GF

www.harpercollins.co.uk

HarperCollins*Publishers*
Macken House, 39/40 Mayor Street Upper,
Dublin 1, D01 C9W8, Ireland

Going Rogue in Red Rye County © 2023 Katie Mettner
Cavanaugh Justice: Detecting a Killer © 2023 Marie Rydzynski-Ferrarella

ISBN: 978-0-263-30715-3

0223

MIX
Paper | Supporting
responsible forestry
FSC
www.fsc.org
FSC™ C007454

This book is produced from independently certified FSC™ paper
to ensure responsible forest management.

For more information visit: www.harpercollins.co.uk/green

Printed and Bound in Spain using 100% Renewable Electricity at
CPI Black Print, Barcelona

GOING ROGUE IN RED RYE COUNTY

KATIE METTNER

To my husband.

For picking me up when I fall, dusting me off and
reminding me that the stories I tell matter. Your
unwavering faith in me is the reason this book exists.
I love you.

Chapter One

Mina stole the gun from the safe while he slept. Smith & Wesson. A .38 revolver. Small. Point-and-shoot. That was all that mattered when she tucked it under her waistband. She patted the inside of the safe, pleased to find extra rounds and a stack of hundreds Nathan had been saving for a rainy day. Someday, she'd make it right, but for now, she'd have to owe him one. Hell, if it helped her get out of this alive, she might owe him her life.

On her way to the front door, Mina paused and pulled the curtain back from the living-room window. Dim headlights swept across the lawn as an old pickup truck swung around the corner. She ducked her head back. That was the third time she'd seen the same battered pickup since dinner. It was trying too hard to fit in here in Chester. Her trained eye said it stuck out like a sore thumb. Mina had to wonder how long it had been casing the place. She didn't know, but its appearance told her one thing—time was running out. Correction. Her time had run out.

Another peek out the window showed her neighbors having a party on their front porch, and while they'd be good noise cover, if they spotted her, they'd tell the person driving the truck exactly when she'd left and what direction she'd headed. She couldn't let that happen. Her only escape was out the back, where she had her route planned through the trees, if she wanted to avoid the road and whoever was in that truck.

She bit back a strangled snort as she plastered herself against the outside wall of the laundry room. As if she didn't know who was in that truck. She knew, and they weren't Boy Scouts. Maybe she should say they weren't Girl Scouts. Nah, there was no way The Madame would send girls. The Madame would send thugs who she knew without a shadow of a doubt Mina couldn't beat.

She'd have to go it on foot for now. She paused for a moment to make sure Nathan hadn't awakened. Fat chance of that happening considering how many sleeping pills she'd dumped in his beer the second time she saw that truck in the neighborhood. Guilt lanced through her, but she didn't have time to dwell on it, so she grabbed her go-bag from the laundry room, slung it over her shoulders and grasped the walking pole waiting at the door. It was now or never. Her heart pounded, and the blood rushed through her veins at the idea of stepping out into the open. She had twenty feet of open space to clear before she'd meet the tree line. Twenty feet was nothing if you could run, but it was an eternity when you couldn't. And Mina couldn't. She could barely walk and was held up by nothing more than a carbon fiber leg brace, the sturdy walking pole and a lot of determination.

A glance through the curtain on the back door and a deep breath in gave her the strength to turn the doorknob and step out to the concrete steps. She paused and picked her way down the steps carefully. Falling this early in the game was a guaranteed death sentence. She took her time, but when her feet hit the grass, she dug the pole in for all she was worth and half ran, half limped toward the trees. Those trees were the reason she rented a room here. The long oak fence on each side of the property blocking the neighbors' view helped too. It gave her cover to her surefire escape route. Surefire if the men looking for her didn't know about it, that is.

She hesitated on her next step. Did the men who were after her know about the woods? She couldn't say for sure, but she would have to assume they did. All of that said, her choices were limited. The street left her wide open to the people in the truck. At least the woods gave her cover, and she knew them better than anyone. She'd mapped out multiple escape routes through the underbrush—routes others wouldn't know existed. If they tried to follow, she'd hear them crashing through the underbrush, and that would give her time to change direction.

Finally swallowed up by the dark branches of the trees, Mina let out half the breath she'd been holding. She quickly found the first stash of supplies she'd tucked under a tree for an emergency. She knelt, but old habits kicked in, and she glanced up at the tree canopy. She'd lucked out. The stars were hidden behind heavy clouds, giving her a chance to escape unseen. The weather could buy her hours. Hours she'd need to get out of this one-horse town. It wasn't going to be easy, and she knew it, but Mina had little choice in the matter now. The sands in her hourglass had run out much quicker than expected and left her questioning everything—including her roommate's allegiance to her.

Mina forced her mind to calm. "You've been trained

to escape dangerous situations," she reminded herself as she shook out her shoulders. "You might be a little bit dented and rusty, but it's like riding a bike. Trust in yourself."

Her pep talk over, she felt around for the stash hidden inside the hollowed-out tree. Mina's backpack only held her personal items that wouldn't raise her roommate's suspicions should he check the bag. She always knew if she had to run for the trees, a different set of supplies would be needed to survive. She dropped her backpack and slipped her tactical chest pack on, immediately hiking the backpack over it and strapping it on. She moved the gun to its rightful spot on her hip and ran her hands over the chest pack, making sure everything was in place.

Binoculars, compass, spare burner phone, emergency shelter, knife, protein bars, water and maps of the topography of North Dakota. She was as ready as she'd ever be.

The walk to Bismarck was going to take a full three days, and that was if she could walk the required miles each day. Chances were good that wouldn't happen. Her foot had been getting worse instead of better, and it was going to make traveling through the woods nearly impossible. Regardless, she had to stay hidden as she worked her way toward the storage unit outside of Bismarck, where a car, a new name and a new life waited for her. That was how it had been for the last year. A new car, name and town every three months, no matter what. This time, she got lazy. When she made it two weeks past the three-month mark, she stayed. She was tired, and the safety she'd found in Chester gave her hope she could stay another few months, even if in the back of her mind she knew she was playing with fire. She just got burned. Hopefully, she had time to put out the flames before they got her for good.

Her back plastered against the tree, Mina took a calming breath and shook out her legs. "You got this, girl," she muttered to herself.

That had been Mina's mantra all her life until her injury. Now, a year later, she was still dealing with the fallout from it, and it was going to get worse before it got better. She would need every ounce of strength she had to survive.

"Clear your head," she chanted, her breath making little puffs of white in the cold October air. A deep breath in squared her shoulders naturally, and she pushed off into the darkened forest. It was time to move if she ever wanted to see the light of day again.

ROMAN PULLED THE rumbly truck over to the curb and put it in Park. He doused the dim headlights on the old truck, which had more rust than paint but was forgettable in a town like Chester, North Dakota. He had to be forgettable, for his partner's sake. Special Agent Wilhelmina August had been his partner for six years, and as far as he was concerned, she still was.

He eyed the neat-as-a-pin two-story home across the street from where he'd parked. He couldn't picture Mina August living there. At least not the Mina August he knew a year ago. The Mina August of today, he didn't know a thing about, and that was what drove him to this tiny town on a Sunday night.

Roman tipped his head side to side to force the negative thoughts away. He was here to make right what he'd done wrong, but first, he had to convince Mina he wasn't here to hurt her. That would be his biggest challenge, considering their last encounter. She was a federal agent, but she was also a scared woman who was alone, on the run and in pain. Guilt ripped through him as swiftly as wildfire. She was alone because he hadn't prepared for every scenario. She was running for her life because he hadn't mitigated the threat before it was too late. She was in pain because he failed to do his job. They both knew it, which was why Mina would shoot first and ask questions later. The phrase *trust no one* was ingrained in them at the academy, and Roman had no doubt Mina would trust him least of all.

Taking a few deep breaths, Roman calmed his mind and focused on the task at hand. Getting Mina somewhere safe. He climbed from the truck and approached a group of people sitting on a porch next door to Mina's rented room. He'd been driving around the block every thirty minutes, hoping to see her outside, but it hadn't happened. He could wait no longer. He'd thought about sneaking around the back of the house to see what was there, but with his luck, it would be a Doberman. He wasn't in the mood for a trip to the ER. He had tracked Mina to Chester after a full year of searching, and he wouldn't let her get away now.

"Hey, is Caitlyn around?" he asked, approaching the sidewalk with nonchalance. He just needed to confirm her location.

"There ain't no Caitlyn here, man," a dude said right before he spit a wad of chewing tobacco over the porch railing.

Classy. Roman fought hard against the eye roll threatening his composure.

"Shoot, she told me she was 1897 North Bradford

Street," he answered, making a show of looking at the house number.

A woman hooked her thumb over her shoulder. "That's next door. This is 1895. A woman moved in there, but we don't know her name. Not super friendly. She rarely leaves the place. I'd go crazy myself but to each their own." She took a long draw on her cigarette like it was life-giving oxygen.

"Oh, I'm sorry," Roman said, lacing his words with contriteness. "Well, here," he said, jogging up the sidewalk with a picture in his hand. "That's my friend Caitlyn. Does she look like the woman next door?"

"Sure does," said the dude before spitting more tobacco out the side of his lip.

Roman glanced to his right and shrugged. "House is dark, so she must be gone or sleeping. I'll stop by tomorrow. Thanks for the help." He raised his hand in a wave and jogged back to his truck. He rolled halfway down the street before he flipped the headlights on and rumbled out of the neighborhood. Something didn't feel right. If Roman had learned one thing after the fiasco in Red Rye, it was to follow his gut. His gut told him to turn left and make one last pass around the property.

He'd gotten confirmation that Mina lived there, but there was no point knocking on the door when it was buttoned up tight and no lights were on. With the neighbors outside, he couldn't sneak into the backyard either. Roman knew her as well as he knew himself, and if she noticed his truck circling the house, she'd be gone. Tomorrow he'd knock on the door, and she'd either be there or she wouldn't, but at least in the daylight, he might avoid getting shot. The deep bass of his laughter filled the truck.

"As if, man. The first thing she's going to do when she sees you darken her doorstep is shoot. She won't even bother asking questions."

Probably true and rightly so. As far as his partner was concerned, he'd let her down, and while she didn't know the whole story, the part she did know looked damning. He wasn't the guy she thought he was, and that bothered him. He'd spent the past year looking for her just to prove he wasn't heartless enough to let her get hurt on purpose. Or worse yet, that he was working for The Madame. If she believed he was the reason the operation went sideways, he'd never get within ten feet of her. The guilt raging through him forced a grunt from his lips. They'd been partners for six years, and he prayed Mina knew he'd never compromise an operation for his own gain.

Darkness had fallen since the last time he'd turned down the old dirt road that made up the back half of the property Mina rented. It wasn't a block so much as it was three streets and a gravel road through the forest. It would make a perfect escape route, and he had no doubt that was why she'd rented that house. He tapped the brake and pulled the truck over to the side of the road before he doused the lights.

An escape route.

A fence protected the backyard on each side, and Roman would bet his shield the back door led directly to the tree line. She'd be prepared to run. He didn't even question the truth of that statement. The problem was, knowing what he knew, how was Mina going to go it on foot? She'd need a vehicle sooner rather than later. Roman disabled the dome light and slid out of the truck. He walked a bit until he'd lined himself up with the back of Mina's house.

Wait. No. She wouldn't do that. She'd work those trees to her advantage and cross the road somewhere else. She would walk this grove of trees halfway down the block, cross the dirt road in three steps and be back in the trees. That was what he'd do. Staying in the grass off the edge of the road, Roman searched for any sign of footprints. They wouldn't be solid proof she was on the run, but no one was going to be walking on this road in the rain for fun.

He walked another quarter of a mile before he noticed a tumble of gravel off the edge of the road. The heel depression told him it was manmade. Or, in this case, more likely made by a woman. He flicked his flashlight up onto the road and noticed three prints, the left one with a drag on the toe. The sole pattern, and the word *Vibram* stamped in the dirt, gave her away. Mina wore one specific brand of boots, and he'd spent enough time following her footprints to know the sole pattern intimately. He'd found his partner. Well, he found where she had been. Now, the search reset.

Roman shook his head as he pulled himself into his truck. He hadn't been this close to Mina in a year. He wasn't going to let her slip through his fingers. A light mist was on his windshield when he got back inside the truck, and he ran the wipers. He had to find her before The Madame did. He'd spooked her, which he expected, but he couldn't let her get away. The night would be long, but if he could track her down, it would be worth it.

With the rain falling, he'd easily be able to follow her footprints through the woods, but he'd likely get shot before he could say his piece. Roman only saw one option. Find where the trees ended and be waiting for her there.

It was a chance he had to take.

Chapter Two

Why *wouldn't* it start raining? As if Mina didn't have enough to deal with as it was. Now she had to worry about staying dry. She had three shelters along her route that would provide resting spots, but she would have to cover her miles each day if she was going to utilize them. Since she had to bug out in the night, she wouldn't make the first shelter before dawn. That meant she would have to keep her eyes open for someplace she could hide during the daylight hours tomorrow.

She would go as fast as she could, but the rain was going to slow her down simply because her foot hated it. From what she'd read, that was common with an injury like hers. When your foot was shattered beyond repair, there wasn't much that would help the pain. Whenever it rained or snowed, Mina turned into a cranky old woman in need of a heating pad and some menthol rub. She didn't have either of those things out here, so she'd have to put it out of her mind and push on. Her life likely depended on it.

Mina had found the river quickly enough, but the long hike through the trees in the dark was treacherous. Walking exposed out on the road wasn't an option, even if she wished it were. There were too many farms along these roads. There was too great a chance one of the farmers would remember the woman in a combat vest hoofing it down the highway with a heavy limp. Her only choice was to move about under the cover of darkness and trees.

She kept her head pointed down at the dim light strapped to her walking pole. It lit her path without lighting up the entire night. Traveling without it under the heavy canopy of trees was too dangerous, so it was a risk worth taking. There would be only so far that she could push her foot, and falling would only hurt her, literally and figuratively. If she could find a secure shelter, she could sit it out another night just to give herself a fighting chance at making it to Bismarck.

She'd spent the last two hours meticulously running the last four months of her life through her head. She analyzed every move she made, trying to determine which one had been the wrong one. She'd come up empty-handed. Mina was positive she hadn't left herself vulnerable to any outside forces. Nathan, her roommate, was the only one who had checked her out, and her story held, so it didn't make sense that The Madame had found her here. She checked her belongings for trackers and never found any, so how did they know where she was? She purposely didn't have a car to avoid being tracked or, more likely, blown to bits when she started it up one day.

Unless her breadcrumbs had finally paid off.

The thought jolted her, and she almost tripped on a log. She hesitated for a moment. Had he found her? She shook her head and forced her feet forward. She couldn't risk stopping on the off chance the person in the truck wasn't out to kill her. She had to get to her car.

She'd bought the car with cash and never registered it. There was no way anyone knew that Caitlyn Carver owned an old, beat-up blue Ford Fairlane. She chuckled, and the sound rose into the trees and fell back down upon her. To her ears, it wasn't amused. She'd spent countless hours locked inside a storage unit working on the car to ensure it would run when the time came. And the time always came. Mina was glad she'd pilfered that pair of plates off an old junker just last week. They were tucked securely in her backpack for when she arrived at the unit. They wouldn't get her far, but they didn't have to. Once she hit another big city, she'd disappear on public transportation, never to be seen again.

"Maybe that was my mistake," she muttered, stepping over a fallen tree. She nearly caught her toe on a branch but saved herself at the last second. With her heart pounding, she stopped and took a few deep breaths to settle it again. She also took a minute to check her map, so she'd know when she had to cross the next open area. The time was coming, and it would require her to cross a farmer's field that was wider than she'd like. If this were summer, she could hide in the corn, but it was almost November, and the corn had long since been picked.

Mina blew out a breath and dug her pole into the soil, the scent of wet earth drifting into her nostrils and sending her back to a time she'd prefer never to think about again, but those memories, they didn't care. They dragged her back to that night every chance they got. The smoke. The screaming. The terror she felt in her gut as a seasoned FBI agent when she realized she wasn't getting out alive. Never in her thirty-five years of life had she felt so utterly helpless as she had the night the flames closed in around her. The eyes. The eyes she recognized but couldn't place as she was dragged to a window, the new source of oxygen fueling the flames.

Her foot caught on a vine, and she pitched forward, running her forehead smack-dab into a fallen log. Mina fell to the ground and fought for air while a trickle of blood ran down her forehead. Once she could think clearly again, she made precise movements with every one of her extremities to ensure they worked before she pushed herself into a sitting position.

"Great," she mumbled, fumbling in her pack for a bandanna. She pulled it out, spun it around a couple of times and tied it around the bleeding gash on her head. At least what she assumed was a gash. It wasn't like she was at the Ritz and could just check the gilded mirror. "Sarcasm. Works every time." Mina chuckled and pushed herself to a standing position, then brushed off her clothes. She checked the ground for anything that may have fallen from her pockets before she took off again. She forced her head to stay in the game and concentrate on the terrain because another injury would mean certain death, be it in the woods or a hospital. The moment Mina was on the grid again, The Madame would take her down.

Her head took that moment to pound once, just to drive the point home. She moaned and then shook away the fog. The Madame would not win this game of cat and mouse. The Madame might have more resources, but she relied on others to do her bidding—others who weren't hell-bent on protecting their own lives. Mina had more skin in the game than anyone on the other team.

As she walked, she forced herself to focus on the

person in the truck. Her head throbbed with the effort it took, but she concentrated on the first time it drove through the neighborhood. It was the truck that stuck out. It was old and rusty but silent, which meant its power was being disguised. A truck that old and beat-up should have chugged like a mother down the street. That was her first clue something was off.

Her mind's eye zeroed in on the driver's side window on the second pass. A baseball cap. Just one. There was no one in the passenger seat. Mina cursed the fall sunset because it was already too dark to make out any features of the driver when he went by at six o'clock. It was a man, though. He had to be a scout. The Madame would never send just one man to take Mina out. She wouldn't leave the job to chance. Her guys weren't trained agents looking to survive the next twelve hours. When your life was on the line, your motivation super-seded anyone else's determination to finish a job.

Blazing white anger filled Mina. Anger at her bosses, who insisted she take the undercover position with The Madame, and anger at her partner for not having her back.

"Special Agent in Charge Moore, you wanted to see us?" Mina stood next to her partner, Special Agent Roman Jacobs, who was just as curious as she was to learn why they'd been summoned.

"Sit, please." He motioned at the two chairs in front of him. After they were settled, he leaned against his desk and crossed his ankles. It was a tell he didn't know he had, so Mina braced herself for what came next.

"I need an undercover agent."

Mina worked hard not to smile. Of course he did.

"You're going to need all of your expertise and experience for this one, Agent August."

"What's the job, SAC?"

He walked behind his desk and grabbed two files off the top, handing one to each of them. "Red Rye, Kansas. The word on the street is the house is a brothel."

"A brothel in the middle of Kansas?" Roman asked, flipping open the file. "Prostitution is illegal there. Why wouldn't the city police deal with it?"

"Because from the outside, it's being billed as a legal escort service."

"Pay the girls for companionship and not sex," Mina translated.

The SAC snorted. "Sure, and the Vikings are going to win the Super Bowl this year."

Mina tried hard not to snicker. There was zero chance of that happening.

"We're in Minnesota," Roman said, pointing out the obvious. "Isn't there someone on the Kansas team who can take this?"

"No," SAC Moore said, sitting down behind his desk. "They're stretched thin and don't have any women who can go undercover inside the house."

"An undercover male could get the same job done," Mina suggested. "A simple john sting is all that's needed here."

The SAC shook his head and motioned at the folders, giving them time to read them. Mina scanned them, but her confusion grew with each page she turned.

"Why can't they find any of these girls in the database?"

"Excellent question," SAC Moore said. "And they think more girls are involved."

"You mean they think there are more houses with more girls?"

"Yes," he said with a nod. "Our Kansas office thinks this may be a branch of a bigger operation. Red Rye is in the middle of nowhere, but it's within driving distance of five or six big cities. Their agents have images and videos of the women in the house, but our facial recognition system is getting nothing on them."

"They're ghosts," Roman said, closing the file.

"So to say. It's hard to be a ghost these days, though. Whether they are ghosts by chance or by choice is the other question."

Mina lifted a brow, her curiosity piqued. "They want me to ferret out if there are more houses and where these girls are coming from."

The SAC answered with a head nod.

"Why Mina, though?" Roman asked, her partner's protectiveness coming through in his tone.

"We need someone with her skills," he said, handing a printed sheet over the desk for them to read. "They're advertising for a receptionist and billing position. The ideal candidate has coding and app-building skills."

Mina glanced at Roman and then at the SAC. "They want to build an app to hide their illegal activities with legal ones."

"Most likely. And you have the skills to build that app and log everything that goes on as evidence."

"Maybe. I'm not sure that evidence would be useable in a court of law since it would have been obtained illegally," she pointed out. "I might be able to write in a backdoor that holds the information on a private cloud, but I still don't know if that's going to help us."

"I've been assured that the data will only be used

when and if a sting needs to take place. Think of it as building a blueprint for the case. Once we raid the house and arrest its leader, we can subpoena the information in the app. That's why we're sending you in to apply. You can write the app while you're inside the house learning the operation and ferreting out if there are more girls involved."

"Wait," Roman said. "You want her to go in as an employee and not as an escort?"

"They aren't looking for escorts, are they?" the SAC asked with his brow raised. "Those girls are being brought in from somewhere else. What they need right now is someone with skills who they can vet but, at the same time, tempt with the carrot of stability."

"They need a girl with skills but one who is living on the edge of society. Someone with no family, no hope and no ties to anything," Mina translated and noticed the SAC nod while she was reading. "They need a girl who is going to jump at a chance like this to have steady housing and three meals a day. The problem is, most girls living that close to the edge don't have the training or skills to build an app. How many have applied?"

"From what the Kansas office tells me, they've interviewed over a dozen but turned all of them away. You've got three hours to read that file and learn your backstory. You've got skills, but no family or friends. Your drug addiction consumed the last few years of your life, but now that you're clean, you're looking for a better life. You've been scrubbed and recreated. Make this happen. The plane is waiting. You leave in thirty minutes."

"What's my role?" Roman asked, standing when Mina did.

"You're her partner," the SAC said, "regardless of where she is or who she is. You're her eyes and ears outside of that house in Red Rye. You'll be briefed if she gets the job. I want you to go with her today, and while she's interviewing, scout the address in the file as a possible home base. Report back when the interview is over, and we'll wait for them to call. New phones and IDs are on the plane. You have an hour in the air and two in the car to learn it."

"Thanks for the heads up," Mina muttered.

"I know there isn't much lead time, but I was given the same courtesy. Today is only the interview. When it's over, you'll have a couple of days to get your affairs in order here before you head back to Red Rye."

"You're rather confident, SAC," Roman said with a slight grin on his face.

"Well, let's just say my people will be in touch with their people, one way or the other. Mina, your disguise is on the plane. A wig today, and dye job tomorrow. You're going in as a blonde, confident, sexy computer coder who doesn't put up with bull but is willing to help anyone who needs it."

"That shouldn't be hard for her then," Roman said, wearing a smirk, "other than the blonde part."

Anger swamped Mina as she pushed through the woods. The guy who was supposed to have her back turned out to be a dirty fink, too. The thought of Roman Jacobs had her stomping across the muddy ground until the sharp pain in her left foot reminded her why she had to tread lightly in life now. She would never be an undercover agent again because of Roman Jacobs.

Her heart paused in her chest at the thought and paused again when it added *right?* to the statement. The memories she was positive were the truth a year ago had slowly lost their authenticity. She realized the dreams, the nightmares, were tangible memories of what happened that night. Those eyes she saw dragging her to the window for fresh air haunted her.

Forcing her mind away from the dreams, she slowed her steps. The pervading silence lulled her into an easy rhythm until she heard something that sent a shiver of fear skittering down her spine. Mina froze in place and tipped her ear toward the road. Tires on pavement. She hid the dim light, not that she thought anyone could see it from the road, but it wasn't worth taking the chance. She moved to a large tree in silence and plastered herself behind it. Waiting. Listening.

The vehicle was on the road to her left. Likely a drunk coming home from the bar, but she'd stay put until it passed. No sense in tempting fate this early in the adventure. Not that anyone could see her in this forest full of foreboding trees, but she had an open field to cross soon, and she couldn't afford to make any mistakes.

She slid down the trunk of the tree and pulled her long raincoat under her butt before she sat. If she had to bed down right there for a few hours, she would, but in the meantime, she'd give her back a rest from the heavy pack. Mina rested her head against the trunk of the tree and closed her eyes. It had been a long day and a longer night. Once the coast was clear, she'd dig out some Advil and water before she soldiered on to her destination. She told herself the Advil was for her headache, but the aching pain that rumbled through her foot made a liar out of her.

Chapter Three

Roman slid into the grass before he shut the truck's door with barely a click. A glance around the area assured him the truck was hidden behind a long row of wrapped round hay bales. It wouldn't stay hidden come daylight, but hopefully, he'd be in it long before the sun came up. He would move forward on foot then double back for the truck once he had Mina with him.

Crouching alongside a hay bale, he asked himself what he was doing. *The right thing*, a voice reminded him. Mina was his. She had been for years, both as a partner and a friend. There was once a time when he thought they could be more. It was a senior agent who stressed that a workplace relationship was never a good idea. He was right, but she still dominated his every thought, even if those thoughts speared him with guilt. Living with the guilt that permeated every ounce of him was exhausting. He had to make things right and, hopefully, convince Mina they could still be partners.

His huffed breath shot a white plume into the air. As if he stood half a chance of convincing Mina to come back to the FBI. He'd be lucky if she didn't shoot him and leave him for dead. Roman distractedly patted his ribs where his shoulder harness hung. He would never shoot Mina, but he was willing to shoot anyone out to hurt her.

Roman's plan to wait for her to emerge from the trees ended when he realized she could run through the woods for hours and never cross the road. He'd regrouped at a gas station just outside of Chester and used Google Maps to get a bird's-eye view of the area. Then he used his knowledge of Mina and his training as an agent to figure out her route. There were abandoned structures in the overhead view perfect for cover during the day. If he were Mina, that was what he'd do. Hide in the daytime and run at night. His only option was to intercept her at one of those buildings. The first one on the map was just up the road a few miles. He couldn't be sure which direction she would go, so he was taking a chance that she was using the woods to head toward a big city rather than push west into the remote forest.

He would choose the big city, and they'd been partners long enough for him to know she'd do the same. He darted across the road, thankful his boots were silent on the concrete. He cursed the rain for soaking him on his dash through the woods, but at the same time, he was grateful it covered the sound of his footfalls. Mina had a jump on him in terms of run time, but he had the advantage of a vehicle for the last two hours. He also had the benefit of two good feet. She didn't, so he'd taken that into account when he calculated the distance between her house and the abandoned structure. He checked his watch. It had been six hours since he'd found the footprints on the gravel road. It was nearing three in the morning, and he was tired, but he wasn't giving up on Mina August.

Running over soggy ground and jumping over mossy

logs had his heart rate up when the wooden structure came into view. The front of it faced the river, which told him it was once someone's fishing cabin. It had seen better days. The windows were grimy, and the ones facing him had holes in several panes. The roof was missing logs, and the building listed a bit to the right. Regardless, it would still hide his partner well.

He paused next to a tree and waited, slowing his respirations and getting his head in the game. The rain was covering every sound now as it pounded down on the canopy of trees. Assessing the building wholly shrouded in darkness, Roman realized his mistake. There was no way to approach it without getting shot if she had a gun. If she didn't have a gun, she'd run. He racked his brain to come up with options that didn't involve him dying at her hands. She likely wouldn't hesitate, given what she believed about him.

It wasn't true.

He didn't desert her. Just the opposite was true. Mina wouldn't be alive if he hadn't been there that night. She didn't remember that part, so he couldn't hold it against her. That self-hatred and guilt filled his gut and head, but he forced it away. There was time for that later. Roman knew he had to find a way to get her to trust him within seconds of their next encounter. He had to act right this minute before Mina took off again. A thought struck him, and Roman took a deep breath, praying Mina was inside the cabin. He clapped his hands together once, kicked a tree twice and clapped again, hopefully loudly enough for her to hear. He waited, but when he got no response, he repeated the pattern. It was the handshake they did every time they signed onto shift together. At least it was before she'd gone undercover.

Was that movement? He scanned the area around the cabin and caught the flash of a black shadow at the last second before it darted into the trees. Roman took off running without worrying about if she had a weapon. He wasn't going to let her get away. He refused to yell and let it be known they were out there to anyone else tracking them through these woods. His mission was to rescue her, not get them both killed.

With his legs pumping hard over the fallen logs, he was on her in a heartbeat. He grabbed her arm and spun her around but blocked her right jab simultaneously with his other arm. "Mina!" he hissed, his voice low and desperate. "I'm not going to hurt you! You don't need to run from me."

Her body was taut and ready to spring. Roman couldn't let his guard down. She would run again if he gave her a chance. That was Mina. Even if she knew she was going to lose, she was still going to try. "What are you doing here, Roman?" Her question was hissed more than it was asked.

The tree branches practically snatched her words into their trunks, and he had to lean in to hear her. "Trying to help you."

"Like you helped me a year ago? Thanks, but no thanks. I'll go it alone."

She tried to wrestle her arm out of his grip, but he held tightly to it. "There are two groups headhunting you, Min. I know you think you can go it alone, but if you want to survive the next forty-eight hours, you're going to have to trust me."

Roman finished his proclamation and stared into the eyes of the woman he hadn't seen in too long. She was gorgeous in a girl-next-door kind of way. Thank goodness she was no longer a blonde, and her golden-brown hair was partially tucked inside a stocking cap. He wanted to pull the hat off just to watch it fall free. That was always the favorite part of his day. The moment they'd finished a shift, and she'd pull that band out of her hair and let herself relax.

Tonight, all Roman wanted to do was regain her trust, and there was only one way to do that. Prove to her what went down that night in Red Rye wasn't his fault. That didn't mean seeing her again for the first time in a year wasn't messing with his head. It was, but he had to keep his eyes on the prize, and the prize was finally in his hands.

"The Madame and the FBI?" she asked, her tone so low he felt the vibration through her arm more than he heard the words. He nodded mutely but kept his gaze trained on hers.

He watched her fight with the two choices she had. Go it alone and face the bad guys down to certain death or trust him and stand a fighting chance of staying alive. He witnessed the moment she accepted her fate, and a tentative smile lifted his lips upward.

ROMAN JACOBS WAS the last person she expected to find her in these woods. He may have been her partner at one time, but if he thought she would trust him blindly for that reason alone, he was wrong. Mina's gaze traveled over him in quick assessment. He was still six kinds of yum sold as a variety pack. She wasn't tiny at five feet eleven inches, but Roman still intimidated her at his six feet three inches. He had enough bulk behind those inches that rarely did anyone resist his requests in the field. They'd had a few suspects try to push back, but they failed miserably against a guy like Roman.

He still tucked his jet-black hair behind his ears, and the curl at the ends gave him a boy-next-door look that softened his physique when he relaxed. The number of times she thought about running her fingers through that hair to see if the locks were as soft as they looked embarrassed her now. How moony she'd been over the guy when he was conspiring against her all along. At least that was what she kept telling herself so she didn't cry at the thought that he'd not only kept looking for her but found her.

His gaze raked her, and his sharp brown eyes were still as assessing and unnerving as they always were. He was a favorite with the ladies everywhere, but he never dated coworkers. That was his cardinal rule he insisted he would never break. She scoffed. His other cardinal rule he swore he'd never break was to always have his partner's back, but he'd epically blown that one last year.

"Let's use the cabin to get out of the rain, and we'll make a plan there."

"How did you get here?" Mina asked, taking a step back. She noticed his grimace but refused to give him the satisfaction of stepping forward again.

Instead of answering, he took her hand and tugged her back to the edge of the tree line. A look left, right and left again was all he did before he dashed for the dilapidated cabin that was supposed to be her salvation. Now she prayed it didn't end up being her grave. She tried to keep up with him, but her left foot didn't allow it. When she went down on one knee, he came up behind her, scooped her up and deposited her inside the cabin in what felt like one motion. He certainly hadn't lost any of his strength over the last year.

Mina snugged herself into a corner and waited while he closed the pathetic excuse for a door. It would keep them dry, but it wouldn't stop anyone who wanted in. Keeping her voice low, she asked the question burning in her mind. "How did you get here?"

"In a truck that I paid cash for in Minnesota. Plates are still registered in the other guy's name. The phone is off and untraceable."

"Where's the truck now?"

He stepped forward, his sweet, brown-eyed gaze eating up all the lines of pain and fatigue she couldn't hide on her face. "About a mile back in a farmer's field behind some hay bales. It's safe until we can get back to it."

"Wrong," Mina said immediately. "That truck is dead to us now. Who else knows you're here? Did you tell anyone your plans or ask for help?"

"No one," he promised, crossing his heart like a third-grader. "The FBI knows I've been looking for you since that night in Red Rye. I told SAC Moore I was burned out and taking a leave of absence. As far as he knows, I never found you."

She pushed off the wall of the cabin and refused to let the pain in her foot bring a grimace to her lips. "We gotta move." When they were shoulder to shoulder, Mina held up a finger. "Correction, I gotta move. You need to go home."

"That's not happening," he insisted. "People want you dead, but I'm not one of them. You have to trust someone before it's too late, Min."

Anger spiraled low in her belly, and fire spit from

her lips. "First, stop calling me Min. I'm not your buddy anymore. Second, trust you? Gosh, you mean like when I trusted you last year?" Her words were more of a snarl than a question. "Thanks, but no thanks, Jacobs. I hereby free you of any guilt or misguided duty you feel to save me from my enemies. They're my problem. Not yours."

"Wrong," he inserted before her last word died off. "They were our problem then, and they are our problem now."

"If they were our problem then, why did you abandon me?" she asked, the satisfaction of finally getting to ask that question tempered by the wave of pain flooding his eyes.

"I didn't abandon you. I never got the green light to go in! By the time I realized something was wrong, the place was already in flames."

She waved his words away. "It doesn't matter right now. This is my battle to fight. Go home while you still can. My life has been over since I first stepped foot in that house in Red Rye. I was a dead woman walking and didn't even know it. Now, I know it. You'd be better off walking away now with your life."

"We all thought The Madame snatched you until we figured out that she was still looking for you, too. How did you escape in that kind of condition?" Roman asked, clearly ignoring her impassioned plea to leave.

Mina relaxed her face and prayed her eyes didn't hold the horrors of those early days on the run. The Madame had hobbled her before the fire and left her to die. While the doctors did their best, they couldn't put crushed bones back together in perfect alignment. It was like a jigsaw puzzle with pieces that were all the same color. The memories of the pain she suffered while trying to stay alive stole her breath away.

"I managed," was all she was able to say. Roman's raised brow told her he would never settle for that answer, but it was all she had time for right now. When he opened his mouth to speak, she jumped in. "Go home, Jacobs. I don't want you here."

He stepped up into her space and took hold of her raincoat, the material crinkling in his tight grip. His heat radiated through the material to warm her head to toe, and she remembered why she had a love-hate relationship with Roman Jacobs. He was either intensely possessive or flippantly aloof, and there was no in-between. Right now, his possessiveness of her was evident, if not a little bit surprising. He had always been hands-off with her, but he certainly wasn't following his cardinal rule tonight.

"Listen to me, Wilhelmina August, and listen good. Since the day I walked into your hospital room and found that bed empty, I've searched for you. Not out of guilt or a misguided sense of duty but because you are my friend and my partner. Partners don't let each other fight alone. Do you understand me?"

Her nod was her only answer. Mina's tongue was too tied staring into his coal-black eyes in the darkness of the little cabin to respond with words.

"Good. Now, let's get to my truck, and we'll find someplace safer than this." Roman released her coat and smoothed it down. "I need to get you somewhere safe and then secure the perimeter before we plan our next move."

Missing the heat of him up against her, Mina swallowed before she spoke so she didn't sound like a needy woman who hadn't been with a man in years. She hadn't been, but that was beside the point. She wouldn't give him the satisfaction of knowing how much it mattered that he was searching for her. Granted, she'd prefer if he weren't here mucking up her plans and putting himself in danger, but she was still touched that he wanted to find her.

"As for your truck, you know, the one you parked behind a hay bale?" Roman nodded mutely, but his assessing gaze had switched to one of urgency. She'd seen it in his eyes so many times on the job. It was always her who pulled him back from doing something stupid to blow the whole case. "I'm waiting for it to hit you that we can never go back to that truck. As soon as the farmer is up to milk the cows, he'll notice it and call the cops. Bet that didn't cross your mind, did it?"

Her triumphant gotcha moment died on her lips when he stepped tight to her again. Anger radiated from his core, but his words were measured when he spoke. "No, because I planned for two scenarios. The first was not finding you here and moving on to the next abandoned shelter I found on the map. The second was finding you, dragging you back there immediately and getting you the hell out of here. What I failed to do was plan for the third scenario, which was typical Mina August obstinance."

Chest to chest, she stuck her finger in his. "I am not obstinate. I'm cunning, careful and precise. You worked with me long enough to know that I think before acting, unlike the person standing before me. You have no right to tell me how to conduct my life, Jacobs. I've been out here keeping my hide alive for a year without your help. Don't think I can't continue that trend now that you're here—"

A loud explosion cut off her words, and they plastered themselves up against the cabin wall. Roman held out a hand, signaling for her to remain in place while he worked his way around the perimeter to the back window of the cabin. A glance through the grunge-covered window revealed the glow of a fire in the distance. He hustled back to her and gave his head a shake.

"I do believe the truck option has been taken off the table."

Mina swallowed hard around the panic in her chest. "Why would someone blow up your truck? Were you followed?"

"I don't know that someone did, but the fire is in that direction, so regardless, a good number of emergency vehicles are about to descend on that location. What say we get out of here? We've got time to work our way out of range of that onslaught and find a new shelter for the daytime hours."

With a nod, she tightened the straps on her backpack and pulled the hood back up over her head. She forced herself to keep her mind clear of anything but the steps they needed to take to get to the next shelter. Her foot ached, and so did her head, but she'd push through it if it meant she could ride out of Bismarck with her life.

Chapter Four

Roman pulled up tight to the cabin door and waited for his partner to fall in behind him. They had an open area about twenty feet wide before they'd hit the tree line running. Well, an open area might be an overstatement. It was more like an area overgrown with weeds, but unfortunately, they weren't tall enough to use as cover.

He was sure of one thing—the fireball he'd seen in the sky was his truck. He was trying to protect Mina's tenuous trust in him and her thin grasp of sanity by being indirect about it. The Madame blew his truck up, which meant someone in their organization had him under surveillance, and he hadn't seen them coming. He was positive he didn't leave any electronic trails, nor was he followed out of Chester. Regardless, he was going to get her out of this alive if it killed him. He grimaced at the thought because engaging with The Madame could end in that result.

"After I give the all-clear signal, stay behind me and follow me directly into the woods."

"I can't run well," she hissed from behind him, and he bit back a sigh before it escaped. That would only serve to make her mad—madder. Besides, the sigh wasn't in anger at her, but at himself for allowing The Madame a chance to hurt her.

"I know. We'll take it slow and easy, but we still can't be exposed for longer than necessary. Ready?"

She grabbed the back of his coat and leaned in over his shoulder. Even surrounded by the fetid scent of rotting vegetation, he could smell the sweetness of her apple-blossom shampoo. It took him back to when they used to smile and laugh together—a time before The Madame.

"What's the plan if we're ambushed?"

"We fight. That's the only move we've got. Do you have a gun?"

"Yes, but using it might alert others to our location."

"Good point. We avoid guns at all costs. I'm sure we have time to find cover, but we have to go now."

She tapped him on the shoulder in a fast one, two, three, and he knew it was time to take that step out the cabin's door. He inhaled and stepped out with Mina tight on his back. There was nothing he could do about the blind corners, but chances were good whatever entity had set the truck on fire hadn't made the mile run to the cabin yet. First, they'd have to know it existed.

Gauging the distance, Roman picked a speed he hoped Mina could keep up with on her damaged foot. She was in pain. He could see it on her face when she moved wrong, but there was little he could do about it until he could get them somewhere safe with a modicum of modern services. He had noticed the dried blood on her forehead and had to fight with himself not to check that injury, too. He didn't have time to worry about either right now. First, he had to get them to the tree line. His head on a swivel, he headed for the dark overhang of branches twenty feet away. He would have preferred they walk back-to-back, but he didn't suggest it. She could barely walk facing forward without falling.

They hadn't taken more than three steps when a shadow stepped away from the corner of the building. The man was dressed in black, silent and packed a hell of a punch. Roman was ready for it, and the quiet *oof* he made was overpowered by the cry of the assailant when Roman pulled his arm behind his back and snapped his wrist. A fast uppercut with his knee to the guy's chin had him dropping like a sack of potatoes to the ground.

A commotion behind him drew his attention, and he spun to see Mina trying to fight off a guy twice her size and doing a decent job of it. She had the guy in a head-lock, but he was about to flip her to her back, and she didn't know it. Roman ran at him, ramming his head right into the guy's kidney and pushing him off his partner. They rolled together on the hard, cold ground in a tangle of arms and legs while Roman tried to gain the upper hand. Mina got it when Roman ducked, and she gave the guy a swift kick to the head with her tactical boot. He dropped over, a trickle of blood running from the split skin at his temple.

Roman jumped up, and they went back-to-back, turning in a circle while they waited for the next threat. When no one else joined in the fray, Mina asked the question he was thinking. "They only sent two?"

"Probably scouts. There'll be more on the way. We need to tie them up and ditch before they arrive."

"Grab his bootlaces." She pointed at the guy she'd just drop-kicked. "I'll get the one with the broken arm."

He heard the hint of laughter in her voice as she broke away from him and made quick work of getting the first guy's shoelaces free of his boots. Roman focused on her and nothing else. The way she moved with such precision always made him wonder what she'd feel like moving over and around him. He shook his head and ducked away, grabbing the leg of the unconscious man in front of him. He had to stop thinking about Mina as anything other than someone he had to protect. She was his mission and his responsibility. If he thought of her in any other way, he was going to get them both killed.

He quickly hog-tied the guy on the ground and was ready to grab Mina's hand to head out when the scout groaned and opened his eyes. Mina had fashioned a gag out of the other guy's hat, and Roman reached down to do the same when she grabbed his arm.

"Wait." She stood over the scout and grabbed his hair, lifting his head out of the dirt. "Who sent you?"

"You have no idea who you're messing with," he croaked rather than answer her question.

Roman bent down and yanked his tied hands tighter to his head, lifting his legs into even more of a pretzel. "The lady asked you a question. You'd do well to answer it."

"The Madame," he said, barely able to get the words out from the compression of his chest against the ground. "New wave coming. She'll never give up."

"Yeah, well, neither will I," Mina promised, then slammed the guy's head into the ground until he went slack. After she shoved the hat into his mouth, she stood up straight. "We need to go."

In one step, Roman grabbed her and swung her up into his strong arms. His long strides ate up the terrain, putting distance between them and the cabin that could have been their grave. He wouldn't let that happen again. From now on, he was the first line of defense whether the woman in his arms liked it or not.

MINA SLAPPED HER hand against Roman's hard chest. "Put me down!" Her words were barely a whisper in the silent forest, but he heard the anger in them loud and clear.

"A little further," he huffed, his steps not slowing even while carrying her one-hundred-and-thirty-pound frame, not to mention all her equipment. If she were honest with herself, being in his arms gave her a few moments of rest, but more than that, comfort. Comfort that had been missing in her life for more than a year. The comfort of home. The comfort of a hug from family. The comfort of a friend. The comfort of her partner in crime. As much as she hated to admit it, the few minutes of comfort this ride offered her, not only to her foot but to her soul, might give her the strength she'd need to push through this to the other side. She just couldn't let him know that, or he'd use it to his advantage.

Roman slowed as they neared the riverbank, the sky still dark even as it neared five o'clock. They would have to follow the riverbank a few hundred feet before they could dodge back into the trees and head toward Bismarck. When he lowered her to the ground, she noticed he took a step back. He was probably waiting for a punch or a tongue lashing. He wouldn't get either.

"Thank you," she whispered, her breath puffing white into the air as the early morning temps hovered in the forties. "For the ride and for saving my butt back there. I'd be dead if you hadn't shown up when you did." A shiver ran through her. She didn't know if it was the cold wind or the idea of death at the hands of The Madame. Worse yet, being a hostage.

Roman rubbed her arms up and down, probably thinking the shiver was from the cold. "Maybe, maybe not. I've learned you never count Wilhelmina August out of any situation. Besides, I might be the one who led them straight to you. I swear no one followed me, and I told no one where I was going."

"They didn't need to follow you. All The Madame had to do was put a tracker on you somewhere. It was common knowledge that you were my partner. They could follow you anywhere without showing their faces."

Roman ran a hand through his thick, black hair and sighed. "I checked everything religiously and never found a tracker."

"What are you wearing from Minneapolis? Anything they could have a tracker in without your knowledge?"

"No, my clothes and boots I bought right off the shelf at the farm store. There's no way there's anything in them. My watch, wallet and phone were in the truck."

"Did you use your phone tonight?"

"I searched Google Maps, but the phone is a burner."

"Did you leave the truck unattended at any point?"

Mina didn't need confirmation. She could see it on his face before he answered.

"I had to a few times to sleep, eat and shower. Once again, I dropped the ball. I didn't think anyone was following me or would know the truck was mine."

Mina punched him gently on the shoulder. "Don't beat yourself up too much, partner. They were going to find me one way or the other. All you did was accelerate the timeline. I should probably thank you for that because moving every three months was a real pain in my backside." She laughed, but he didn't join her.

"I dropped the ball, Mina, again. I'm sorry."

She shrugged and straightened the pack on her back. "We can't go back in time, but we can move forward. That's our only move now. Look at it this way, Roman. If I'm going to survive a resurgence of The Madame and walk out alive again, I'm going to need all the help I can get."

"Why else would I be here?" Roman asked, his shoulders straightening now that he had his breath back.

"To kill me." Mina noticed the three words hit him like bullets. "But since you just saved my bacon back there, I don't think that's why you're here."

"The very last thing I want is to kill you. Lock you up in a room to keep you safe from The Madame is what I want to do. I know that isn't going to happen, though, so I'm following your lead. Where are we headed?"

"North."

"That's what they'll expect, though. Following the river is a dangerous ploy."

"We don't have a choice," she insisted, her breath tight in her chest. "We need to get to Bismarck, where my storage unit is with a car and a new life. Going south only leads us back to them."

"We need to get back to Minneapolis, Mina. There are people there who will help you."

"No," she hummed, sticking her finger in his chest. "I won't set foot back in that city until we know where The Madame is and why no one came to help me that night. Trust no one. I shouldn't even trust you!"

Roman wrapped his hand around her finger and held it patiently. "I hear what you're saying. I understand your reasoning, but you have nothing to fear from me. I want you to be free to live your life without looking over your shoulder. That's the only reason I'm here. If you want to go north, we'll go north."

The air stolen from her sails, Mina hesitated. He was right. The Madame knew their last location, and she'd expect them to go north. If they made it to Bismarck—and that was a big if with The Madame this close—it would take them days. Days her pursuers wouldn't need with a vehicle at their disposal.

"There's no way to beat them to Bismarck now that they know where we are. We probably have ten, maybe twelve hours tops, to get to Bismarck and get back out before they catch up to us again. It's over twelve hours of walking from here."

"And that foot of yours isn't going to last twelve more hours. It's almost daylight, and we are out of options except one. Do you want to hear it?"

"Do I have a choice at this point?"

"Not that I can see," Roman said with a grin, "but I'll wait while you decide for yourself."

She punched him again, harder this time to remind him she could hold her own. "Fine, hit me with it."

"We go east. It's all farmland. Where there are farms, there are…"

"Farm trucks," she filled in, and he nodded once. "Stealing a truck will be tricky. Once we have it, we're still in danger driving down the highway."

"All of that is true, but we only have two choices. We get a truck and drive or start walking and risk running into more of The Madame's merry men."

"If we can get a truck, we could be at the storage unit in a couple of hours. If we get that far, we're home free. The car will get us to a hotel where we can rest and make a new plan."

He pulled a piece of paper from his pocket and held it out, shining his penlight on the map. "I marked all the areas with civilization before I came out. I know this is a farm," he said, pointing at a crudely drawn roof.

"We have to cross the road to get to it, though." Mina ran her finger along the two-lane highway that cut through the patch of trees they were hiding in.

"We're out of time, Min. Just remember, when we get there, we have a vehicle, and you can give your foot a rest. Focus on that."

Her nod was one and done, then she turned to the east and glanced behind her. "Ready?"

"Lead on. I'll follow you anywhere, Agent August."

Mina took off through the trees as fast as she could, and Roman matched his steps to hers. As the wet branches whipped her face and soaked her clothing, all she could think was Roman Jacobs was either her savior or her downfall. She knew him, and she knew his skills. He had been a top-notch agent his entire career until he failed to provide necessary backup to his partner, nearly leading to her death. Before that event, he was the kind of guy she would trust with her life. Mina's gut said that was still true, but she didn't have time to hash out the particulars of that night with him right now. First, they had to dodge the people hunting them. She was out of options, so if Roman Jacobs was the enemy, it was wise to keep him close.

Chapter Five

Something had finally gone her way in this mess. They'd made the trek to the farm in record time, motivated by the idea of a chance to dry out on the ride to Bismarck. Their first bit of good luck came when they found an old farm truck parked behind a barn. It was more rust than metal, but it had plates and was used recently if the hay in the bed was any indication.

Mina flipped the visor down, and the keys fell into her lap with a jingle. She shook them at Roman, who grinned and started pushing the truck through the grass to the old road. Thankfully, it was far enough away from the farmhouse that they wouldn't have to use the driveway and alert the farmer. She wouldn't start the truck until they were ready to pull onto the highway, just to be sure they weren't heard. The rain was working in their favor, too. While they were wet and cold, the cloud cover kept the stars and moon at bay and gave them more time to escape unseen before daybreak. With any luck, they'd be at her storage unit before the sun came up.

After glancing up and down the highway for lights, Roman motioned for her to start it up. He jumped in, and she headed north up the highway, the heater on high to blast out enough warm air to dry them. Mina wanted to close her eyes, but she refused to let Roman drive. He didn't know where the storage unit was, which simple directions could have fixed, but she didn't trust him. He would take her back to Minneapolis, where everyone was a foe, and no one was a friend.

"If you need a break, just say the word. I'm not going to turn the truck around and head back to headquarters. You can trust me."

Her chuckle released some tension in her chest. "You always could read me like a book."

He smirked, and she forced her eyes to stay on the road. If they didn't, she'd probably crash the truck when she got lost in his giant brown ones.

"That's why we worked so well together." He leaned his bulky frame against the door and his head on the window. "We didn't need words to know what the other was thinking, and that saved us a lot of time and saved a lot of lives."

"Until the one time it didn't," she muttered.

Roman didn't say anything. There was probably nothing he could say. He screwed up, and he knew it. Her eyes flicked to all the mirrors, but there were no headlights behind or in front of them. She kept a tight grip on the wheel as they plowed forward into the darkness. She was laser-focused on getting them to Bismarck, dropping the truck somewhere for the cops to find and then hitting the road again. She wasn't happy that she'd have to take Roman with her, but there was no doubt it was better to have him with her than out there leading the monsters to her door. If she knew one thing about him, it was his determination. He would never give up on her, so ditching him now would be useless.

He was going to keep coming back until she let him help her. The problem was his determination could get him killed this time.

The clock said they'd been on the road for almost an hour. When Mina glanced over at him, his eyes were closed. His hair was still plastered to his head on one side from the rain, and he was still the most handsome man she'd seen since this madness began. Mina thought she was over her crush on Roman Jacobs after he nearly got her killed, but it turned out it was an out-of-sight, out-of-mind situation. Now that he was in sight, the crush was back full force.

Her sigh was heavy when it filled the cab of the truck. She should hate him with everything inside her for abandoning her that night. He said he never got the green light to go in. She turned that over in her mind a couple of times. She'd sent the SOS message, so why didn't he get it? Mina was confident in her coding skills, and the possibility that he didn't get the message shook her to the bone. If that were true, then that changed everything she believed over the last year. Regardless of the reason, he wasn't there for her that night.

He's here now.

This time the breath she blew out sounded like she'd been gut-punched. He *was* here now. He had taken a leave of absence to find his partner because that was Roman's code of honor. No man left behind. That was his motto in the army and as a civilian. He was insistent she would do the same thing if the roles were reversed. He wasn't wrong, but the difference was if the roles had been reversed, she would have done her job the first time to ensure he didn't have to run.

But if what he said was true, and he never got the

SOS, that meant the message got hung up in the app, and it wasn't his fault. Her brain kept asking *what if*, but her heart kept refusing to answer. Her heart wanted to believe him with everything it had. If he was telling the truth and never got her message, then what happened that night was her fault. Then again, maybe someone intercepted it. It had crossed her mind that someone in The Madame's organization may have interfered with the message, but she was always so confident in her work that she refused to believe it. In the end, maybe it was her ego that caused the carnage that night.

"Are we there yet?" Roman asked into the quiet cab.

Mina jumped, torn from her musings by the man himself. "Almost," she answered after she cleared her throat. "Keep your eyes out for a place to dump the truck. I want the cops to find it and return it to the farmer."

"You kept your gloves on the whole time?" he asked, motioning at her hands with his chin.

"I'm not new at this, Agent Jacobs."

His strangled snort brought a smile to her lips. "Just checking. The storage unit you have, is it well lit?"

This time it was her sarcastic snort that brought a smile to his lips. "Define *well lit*. There are seven rows of units, and the only lights are at the front. I'm in row seven, which is in the far back and butts up to a field."

"On purpose." She lifted a brow but said nothing else. He wasn't asking a question. "Let's drive the truck to the unit then. We'll need the headlights to flush out anyone who might be waiting. Once it's clear, we'll move the truck to the front and leave it there. Someone will report it."

"That leads them directly to me, though." Mina shook her head. Did he think she was going to do that?

"Not at all. It leads The Madame directly to the storage unit, which knowing you, and I do, is sitting in the middle of nowhere. We won't be anywhere near it when the truck is found, likely a day or two from now. You used a fake name when you rented it, I assume."

"Of course," she agreed with a shoulder shrug.

"We need to protect your foot, Min. If we walk even a mile from where we leave the truck, that's a mile less your foot can do down the road if the need arises."

She refused to acknowledge his words or her weakness. "The Fairlane is packed and ready. Once I swap out Tactical Barbie for Hippie Barbie, we can get on the road."

He was grinning at her like a fool when she glanced at him from the corner of her eye. "Tactical Barbie. I love it. In my opinion, you are the furthest thing from a Barbie a man could find."

The truck was silent for two beats before she opened her mouth. "Did you just imply that I am nowhere near as attractive as Barbie?"

"No," he said instantly, his hands waving in the air. "Not what I meant at all. I just meant that I'm not into unrealistic body images for women. I hate it when people feed me a fake persona. That's all I meant."

"You're saying that, in a Roman Jacobs kind of way, that was a compliment."

"To the highest degree," he agreed. He must have noticed the lights of the town because he leaned forward and swiveled his head around the truck's perimeter. "How far out are we?"

"A few miles. I haven't seen another car the entire

trip. Thanks for being the lookout, by the way." She had to rib him a little bit for sleeping on the job.

"I knew you'd wake me if we ran into trouble. I'll need to drive the next leg, so I decided to grab a few hours. Your turn is coming."

"Like hell," she muttered, slowing for the reduced speed limit sign. She went on high alert when the storage unit came into sight, and she braked as they drove past the driveway. She turned around, drove back and pulled into the gravel drive.

"We'll see about that," he shot back, leaning forward in his seat. "It looks empty. Drive through the rows like a figure eight. We need to make sure no one is waiting to ambush us."

She did as he instructed since she planned to do that anyway, but she bristled slightly. "There's no way The Madame knows about this place."

"I didn't think she was tracking me, either."

The truck fell silent as she concentrated on weaving in and out of the aisles of units until she got to the final row. No one was around, and the place was eerie in the early morning fog. "Let's do this as quickly as possible. I'm going to ditch the truck and work my way back. Give me five minutes. Have the car running."

Mina bailed from the truck, and he waited while she unlocked the unit and flashed her light inside for half a second. All was silent, and she gave him a thumbs-up before she pulled the door down. She knew their reprieve wouldn't last long.

ROMAN EYED THE area around the convenience store, looking for places where The Madame could hide in wait for them. "What's the plan?" he asked the exhausted woman next to him.

Gone was the beautiful brunette he'd known for seven years. She'd been replaced by a beautiful redhead who would have fit right in sitting on the back of an old VW bus on her way to Woodstock.

"I have to use the restroom."

"Same. You go in first. When I know you're locked inside, I'll use the other one. Do not come out until I knock on the door and call to you. After our potty break, we have to decide where we're going."

Mina gave him a nod that said more than words could, and they both bailed out of the car. Roman leaned against the hood of the old Fairlane and watched the woman he'd gone through hell with a thousand times over walk into the restroom. *Walk* was a strong word. *Hobble* was more accurate. A grimace tugged at her gorgeous face with every step until she locked the door and blocked him out. She needed rest and time to heal. There was no question that life on the run the last year had prevented her foot from healing. Hell, knowing Mina, she probably hadn't seen a doctor since the day she left the hospital. He shook his head at her stubbornness and spun around on the hood, his gaze traveling around the area, assessing for threats from any blind corner. He was sure they had bought enough time that there wouldn't be any yet.

The Madame might have teams out looking for them, but they were still searching in the middle of North Dakota. Since they left the storage unit four hours ago, they'd logged enough miles to put them near the border of Minnesota. He suspected she didn't have a plan. She was simply driving in hopes of outrunning the bad guys.

She was exhausted, in pain and not thinking clearly, but she wouldn't go down without a fight.

Roman spied a relic hanging on the side of the old building and jogged over to the pay phone, snapping on a glove before picking up the receiver. He was shocked to hear a dial tone on the other end. He hung it up, jogged to the restroom and took care of business, then knocked on her door. "Ready."

The lock clicked, and she stepped out, her face wet as though she'd washed it, but her eyes told him the real story. The water was to hide the tears of pain that had built up until they demanded release. Roman grasped her elbow, and she leaned heavily on him on the way back to the car. He lowered her to the passenger seat then knelt and rested his hand on her knee.

"You're tired. You need to let me drive, Min. I know you don't trust me, but I trust you, okay? I'll do whatever you tell me to, but I can't let you keep driving in the shape you're in right now."

Her nod was frustrated but agreeable. "I don't have a choice, I know. I'm running on fumes, and the pain has my mind muddled. All I know is once I find someplace safe again, you're going to take this Fairlane and get as far away from me as possible."

"Wrong," Roman said instantly, taking hold of her chin to force eye contact. "We're in this together, no matter what. Listen to me, I have a plan, but we both need to agree on it."

"Then you're a step ahead of me already. What's your plan?"

"I have an army buddy just outside of Fargo on the Minnesota side who we can trust. He has an encampment there that would let us safely disappear for a little while until we can figure out what The Madame wants."

"She wants me, Roman. She wants me." She jabbed herself in the chest with her finger on a grimace. "She thinks I know her secrets, and she won't quit until I'm dead."

He squeezed her knee gently until she quieted. "That may be, but they're only secrets until we tell the world. Your information in the hands of the right people will bring her down."

"You don't seem to understand that I can't trust anyone, Roman. Most especially you!"

"Shh," he whispered, glancing around. "I understand how you feel about that, but just hear me out. The only way we're going to function is to get some sleep. The only way to do that is to be protected. My friend can provide that."

"Your friend with the encampment," she repeated, and he nodded. "Is he a cop?"

Roman's laughter was quiet, but he was sure she could hear the amusement in it. "Not even a little bit. He's private security and…other things."

"Other things that are less legal?"

"He does a lot on the other side of the law, but he does them for the right reasons. That's all I can say."

"How do you know we can trust him? The Madame may have already found him as a contact of yours. He could be compromised."

"Cal is ex–military police."

"So are you," she pointed out on a lifted brow.

"Yes, but I went civilian mainstream, Cal…didn't. If The Madame sent anyone to his camp unannounced, they're already staring at six feet of soil. The things he does on the outside of the law are always for the good guys."

"He's a mercenary."

"He was, but with a code of honor toward his country and his friends. Now he runs a security business with our ex-military brothers." Roman pointed at the pay phone on the wall of the store. "I can call him and let him know we're coming. In less than two hours, you could be in a bed, asleep and protected for the first time in a year."

"Two years," she muttered, her eyes heavy.

"You've been MIA for a year, Mina."

"And undercover with The Madame for the year before that. Do you think I slept with both eyes closed there? Not for a hot second."

"I'd expect nothing less," he admitted with a chuckle "So, what do you say, partner? Should I call him?"

"No. We'll call him. We're putting him on speaker, and if you play any games, I'll use the Smith & Wesson under my belt to put you out of commission long enough for me to leave your sorry, unreliable butt in the dust."

Roman put his hands up and laughed. "I can accept those terms. The pay phone doesn't have a speaker, though. We'll have to snuggle up, and both listen in."

"I have burner phones. Get in and drive in that direction for thirty minutes. Let's make sure we didn't pick up a tail. If we're in the clear after that, we'll find a place to pull over and call your friend."

"I can work with that."

Before she could say more, he lifted her legs inside the car and closed the door then climbed into the driver's side. Once they were buckled in, he started the car and backed out of the spot, pulling onto the two-lane highway. He'd let her call the shots if he got what he wanted out of the deal, and what he wanted was a chance to put The Madame behind bars.

To do that, he had to prove to the woman next to him that he didn't abandon her when she needed him most. He had to prove the mission was compromised long before she tried to send that message. The guilt that filled his chest every time he looked at her had to go. It was killing him slowly from the inside out. The only way to do that was to find The Madame and prove his innocence.

Chapter Six

Mina had been more than a little bit surprised when Roman pulled into his friend's encampment. To her, that word conjured an image of tents and huts spread across an open field of overgrown grass. Instead, they were met at the gate by a guy who could easily have played linebacker for the Minnesota Vikings. He motioned them through the gate onto a sprawling estate with a grand lodge at the end of the long drive. Scattered behind the lodge were smaller log cabins that looked unassuming. Roman had assured her they were hiding bulletproof glass and walls as well as top-of-the-line communications and electronics.

Before Roman could put the car into Park, the door to the lodge opened, and a man stepped out. He was as big or bigger than Roman and close in age to Roman's thirty-five years. He was handsome, but his face showed the hard lines of a life lived doing bad things to help good people. Roman hopped out of the car and grabbed the man in a bear hug. Mina didn't need words to know their relationship went deeper than friends.

Her door swung open, and Roman helped her out of the car, keeping an arm around her waist while he introduced her. "Cal, this is my partner, Mina."

Cal stepped forward and shook her hand, a smile on his face. "Ah, yes, the infamous Wilhelmina August. I've heard many stories about you over the years. I'm more than a little bit relieved that Roman found you. He's been beside himself this past year." He motioned at the lodge behind him. "Welcome to Secure One. Come on inside so you can take that ridiculous wig off and get off your feet. From what I know of your case, you've been going it alone for a long time."

Mina's smile was tentative but accepting. "It's been a long fourteen months. I can't argue with you there."

Roman kept his arm around her waist and helped her up the few stairs to the lodge. She liked having his support too much for her own good, but she'd take it until she got some sleep and had a chance to reevaluate her options. She didn't have many, and without Roman and now Cal, she'd probably be dead. She tried to focus on the men in the woods who had jumped them. She wanted her mind to tell her that she recognized them from Red Rye. If she could link them to Red Rye, she could search the log of men she'd saved in the app's database. Her mind told her it had been too dark, and the adrenaline had been pumping too fast. Simply too tired to make sense of much, she stuck it on the back burner until she was rested.

"I've made up the guest suite for you," Cal said as he led them down a long corridor that sported a beautifully stained hardwood floor and shiplap on the walls. Her trained eye caught the thumb reader keypads by each room and the lights running along the baseboards for illumination in the dark. There was probably an integrated alarm and fire system throughout the entire lodge as well.

"A cabin would be fine," Roman said, smiling at her as he helped her along the hallway. It was barely wide enough for two people Mina's size, so having Roman next to her meant she was smashed up against him, her arm around his waist just to keep from tripping and falling. She could make it by herself, but he didn't seem to want to let go of her. While she liked her independence, being close to someone again hit her in a place she forgot existed. She didn't think it was her heart, either. It was something more profound than that. It was a connection with another soul that she hadn't had in too many years. It made sense she'd feel that way with Roman since he'd been such a pivotal part of her life for so long, but she was supposed to be mad at him for ditching her when she needed him most. She couldn't find the energy to worry about it tonight. Not when he tugged her back into him every time she tried to pull away. Not when she could still hear the words of the guy they'd taken out in the woods when he warned of a second wave. Roman had found them a place to stay, at least for tonight, and for that she couldn't be too mad.

"I'd rather you were buttoned up tight here," Cal said, stopping at the door with his thumb on the keypad. "I don't take chances with family."

"Family?" Mina asked as Cal pushed open the door. To the casual eye, the room behind it was a studio apartment with a small kitchen, two queen beds and a bath. To the trained eye, it was so much more. The hatch in the floor surrounded by a metal cage told her that much without her even stepping inside.

"What? Roman didn't tell you that we grew up together?" He punched Roman in the arm. "I'm hurt, man. Crushed."

Laughter spilled from Mina, and it surprised her. She hadn't laughed with true abandon since the last time she'd had Roman in her life. Even working undercover, he could make her laugh. A silly text or a clandestine meeting under the stars would have her giggling at his goofiness within minutes. She hadn't realized how much she missed laughing until that moment.

"I had no idea," she admitted. "Roman told everyone his family was dead."

"They are," Roman clarified, helping her into the room. "My parents died when I was two. I grew up in foster care until Cal's family took me in when I was five. Cal is my younger brother by three years."

"It's just me and Roman left now," Cal added.

"And Cal is a ghost, so I don't talk about him to other people," Roman explained. "That leads to entanglements that would put both Cal and me in a tight spot."

"I know he loves me, in his own big, bad agent kind of way. But he's right. I prefer to be off the radar if you know what I'm saying." He eyed Mina with a raised brow, and she nodded once in understanding.

"Now that we understand each other, welcome home. Everything you'll need is waiting, including meds for that foot. I doubt they'll fix much, but they might give you a few hours of sleep if nothing else. After you've rested, I'll show you the bunker. From what Roman tells me, you're a bit of an expert at being a ghost yourself. I have some equipment down there that'll help you with your pursuit."

"I'm ready now," she said eagerly. If Cal had a way to end this manhunt The Madame had put in motion, she was ready and willing to participate.

"No, you're not," Roman said, his tone firm. "You

need a shower, food and sleep before you even think about going to the bunker. I know you, and once you get down there, you won't resurface until you've found and mitigated the threat."

Okay, so he wasn't wrong. Mina didn't have to like it, though. The fact was she'd already pushed her body past its breaking point six hours ago. Now, she was running on pure pain and adrenaline. The pain would last, but the adrenaline wouldn't.

Mina crossed her arms over her chest and huffed. "I can't believe you talked me into this. I'm not supposed to trust anyone, and here I am, falling in line behind you two."

Roman stepped in front of her and grasped her shoulders. The way his gaze held hers made her wish she were alone with Roman the man, not Roman the federal agent. "Listen to me, Min. You are not falling in line behind us. You are always in the lead, and as I did for all the years before this, I'll follow you anywhere. We're here because I knew Cal had what you needed to find The Madame and take her down. We're the muscle to make sure you can put this woman behind bars and that you're alive when it happens. Do you understand what I'm saying?"

She nodded, but a memory flickered across her mind's eye, and she tried to grab it. There were those eyes again in that blazing inferno that looked a lot like the pair she was seeing now. Mina shook her head to clear it.

"Shower, food and rest. Then we attack."

"Good," Roman agreed with a nod before he turned back to Cal. "Looks like I owe you another round."

Cal walked to the door with a shake of his head.

"Brother, you know your debts have long been paid in full. Family takes care of family. Shower, rest and share a meal with a friend you haven't seen in too long. Then we'll work. This door locks automatically from the inside. Once I leave, no one is getting in. If they try to smoke you out, you know how to get to the bunker." Roman nodded as he pulled Mina into him again in a sign of protectiveness. It was an action even she couldn't ignore.

Cal slipped out the door, and Mina turned to take in the room. "This is quite the place."

Roman's laughter was everything to her in that moment of uncertainty. When they worked together, that sound always grounded her in the certainty that they had each other's backs. She thought that had been lost to her forever, but now, she wasn't so sure.

"Cal doesn't do anything halfway. This space has all the comforts of home with the added benefit that it's impenetrable. His room is just like this one, but on the other end of the house. The rest of Secure One is staff rooms and a large dining room and kitchen for those staying in the cabins."

Roman pulled her wig off, removed the net holding her natural hair and used his giant paws to smooth it down the way it should be. His smile was tender when he hit her with it. "There's the woman I've been thinking about for a year. I'm so glad you're safe."

Before she could respond, he had her wrapped in his arms, her cheek against his warm chest, and his cheek resting on her head. She leaned into him, his heat a balm to her tired and sore body, but also her tired heart. A friend to help her was what she needed.

"I hope this is okay," he said, tightening his arms a

bit before loosening them again. "I know we're partners, but I've wanted to hug you since that day in the hospital when you disappeared like smoke. I just wanted to hug you and tell you how sorry I was for not being there."

Her arms tightened around him, and she kept her head on his chest. "This is okay," she whispered. It took effort, but she held at bay the tears that wanted to fall at his admission. "I needed a friend. I'm happy you were the one to find me."

"You don't know how glad I am that I found you before those guys in the woods." She felt the shiver travel through him, but before she could speak, he did. "Listen, you're barely upright. How about a shower while I make you something to eat? Then, you get off that foot and sleep for the night. Tomorrow is soon enough to start the hunt."

While that sounded like heaven, Mina had to decide if she could sleep in the same room as Roman. The idea that he was here for any other reason than to help her finish off The Madame was becoming harder and harder to swallow. His actions weren't those of a man out to finish a job. His actions were of a man who was torn apart by guilt. He might be looking to finish a job, but that job wasn't to kill her. From what she could see, the job was to help her get her life back. Her old life, that was gone, but if she could still draw breath when The Madame was put behind bars, maybe she could cobble together a new life from the ashes of her old.

"Mina," Roman caught her arm before she turned away. "I know you must be angry. The one time you needed me, I wasn't there. We're partners, and I made promises I didn't keep."

Mina's sigh bore the weight of that night, and she noticed his lips blanch when he pulled them taut.

"What do you want me to say, Roman? Do you think if I admit that I'm angry about what happened in Red Rye that you'll somehow feel better? That your guilt will be appeased because I'm mad at you? After seven years, I thought you knew me better than that. Did things go sideways in Red Rye? Yes. Was it your fault? Should you shoulder the blame? No, not all of it. I went into the house knowing what the risks were and accepted them as the price of admission. I must bear the guilt and the blame for some of it as much as you. I don't know what happened, but I chose to go into that assignment knowing the risks."

"I should have known something was wrong, Min."

"Maybe, but here's the thing, Roman. Me being angry at you isn't going to make you feel better. You want to believe it will. You want me to scream at you for all your shortcomings so that you can turn that guilt in your gut back on me. I don't know what happened that night. I don't know who I can trust and who I can't trust. All I know is when you showed up in the woods last night, and you didn't take me out immediately, I had my answer. If you were working for The Madame, I'd be dead. At the very least, we'd be on our way to see her."

Roman stood mutely with his jaw pulsing while his hands clenched and unclenched. He was never good at faking emotions. Her partner was always a "what you see is what you get" kind of guy. What she saw tonight wasn't anger but rather self-hatred. He hated himself for what happened that night, and while it made her sad that he had to live with that, it buoyed her at the same time. If he was this upset about what happened in Red Rye, then the chances she could trust him just went up.

"I would never hurt you on purpose, Min. I promised to have your back, and I let you down that night, but I have searched for you every day since. I had to find you and prove that I don't break all my promises."

"Life is what happens between the promises, Roman. You know that. Somewhere down deep, you know my decisions were going to affect your promises. That doesn't make it wrong. It just makes it what it is."

"What is it then?" Roman asked, his words filled with desperation even she didn't understand. "If it's not wrong, what is it? And don't say it is what it is."

"But it is," she said, her lips wearing a sad smile. "We can let it ruin who we are and drive a rift between us we can never bridge, or we can forgive ourselves for whatever we think we did wrong. Listen, it's like this, Roman. I'm thirty-five years old, and I've seen humanity at its worst. Together we've captured some of the most disgusting filth on the planet and put them away for good. I could ignore our past and what we did for six years together. We could both stomp off to separate corners and pout, but in the end, we're too old and in too much danger for childish behavior and miscommunication to be the reason we don't find The Madame. Do you agree?"

"I wouldn't be here if I didn't, Min. You had to know that I never gave up on you. You were my every thought. That's why I'm here."

"No man left behind," Mina said, but his head shook slightly.

"No. It had nothing to do with honor toward a partner

or the job. Finding you had everything to do with worrying that my friend wasn't safe and that she needed me."

"I don't know a lot right now, Roman. I don't know who The Madame is. I don't know how I'm going to find her. I don't know if I'll be alive this time tomorrow, but I do know this. I can trust you." He grimaced, and she rested her hand over his. "You showed up. You put in the effort. You showed me that I was still important to you. So, while I don't know much, I do know that I've lived without you for a year, and it was the most miserable year of my life. I'm going to trust my instincts because they're all I've got. My instincts tell me I have nothing to fear from you."

Mina turned, and this time, her partner let her go.

Chapter Seven

A bloodcurdling scream had Roman on his feet with a gun in his hand before he opened his eyes. The next sound that registered was one he'd heard before from a scared child. Whimpering. This time, the sound came from his partner, and it almost destroyed him. He set the gun back on the table and walked to her bed, lowering himself to the edge, where he whispered to her.

"Mina, honey, wake up."

She was sweaty, and the bedcovers were twisted around her. She must have been thrashing in her sleep. Roman jogged to the bathroom and wet a washcloth under cool water, then returned to her bed. Mina's eyes were open, but her stare was blank. He wasn't sure anyone was home.

"Hey." He muttered the word at a level barely above a whisper so he didn't scare her. "That sounded like a bad dream."

Her chin trembled once before she swallowed. "I have them sometimes."

Those four words were enough to flare that ugly fire of guilt in his chest. He smoothed the cloth across her overheated cheeks and straightened it to rest on her forehead. A shiver ran through her, and if that scream indicated the level of terror she experienced that night, it helped him understand how much pain she must have gone through. He rubbed her shoulder until the shivering stopped and her chest rose and fell once.

"Can I get you anything?" he asked, feeling useless to ease the pain and turmoil he most likely caused.

"Water," she said, her voice scratchy.

Roman jumped up and practically ran to the fridge for a cold bottle. While he was there, he grabbed more of the pain medication that Cal had left at his request. He cracked open the water bottle and returned to the bed to help her sit up. She leaned against the headboard and brought the bottle to her lips, a slight tremble in the motion until half the bottle was gone. He handed her the pills, and she swallowed those before he took the bottle from her and set it on the nightstand.

"Okay now?"

She nodded once before she tried to push the hair out of her face with trembling hands. Roman couldn't resist the urge to do it for her. He tucked her wavy locks behind her ears and offered a smile of understanding and solidarity. "It's only one a.m. I think we should try to get some more sleep. Cal will be up early, but not this early."

Mina held his hand in a death grip. "Don't go."

Roman covered her hand with his other paw and held tight. "You're okay. You're safe here."

"At least for tonight."

"No, forever. I'm not going to let The Madame take you away from me again. Okay? Try to relax."

The sway of her curls around her shoulders when she shook her head made his gut tighten. She was all beauty and grace even when she was tough as nails. She never let down her guard, so to see her this vulnerable and afraid made Roman realize how much she'd been through over the past year.

"I can't relax after that dream."

Another tremble went through her, and in one motion, he scooped her up and rested her on his lap. He wanted to moan his happiness to have her in his arms, but he bit it back. He didn't have that right. He didn't even have the right to hold her, but she needed comfort, and he was the only one here to offer it.

"What do you need, Mina?" he asked, resting his cheek on her head and inhaling the scent of French vanilla. Cal had gone all out when he stocked the room for them. Not only had he filled the bathroom with essentials, but he'd had a new wardrobe waiting for them both, a walking cane for her that Roman knew she'd never use and medication to help relieve some of the pain in her foot.

"I need to find The Madame." Her answer had him pulling himself back to the present.

"You will. When you do, it'll be because you were strong enough to fight through that fire, heal from debilitating injuries and be the one to take her down."

He lowered her to the bed and straightened her pillow and bedsheets. Once it was neat again, he tucked her in and smoothed the hair out of her face. He wished he could do more to soothe her, but he would have to take baby steps until she was sure she could trust him again. He trailed his hand down her arm and turned toward his bed, but she grasped his hand tightly and wouldn't let go.

"What do you need, Min?"

"Sleep. I haven't slept in a year, but I need…"

Her words died away, but Roman didn't need her to finish. He knew what she needed. Comfort. Someone to hold her and tell her she would survive this and have a chance at a new life. He could be that person for her right now. All that mattered to him was offering her a safe place to sleep, be it in an armored encampment or his arms.

Roman squeezed her hand and let it drop, then grabbed a blanket off his bed. He settled in behind her and hugged her tightly to his chest before he pulled the blanket over himself. She was under the covers, and he was on top, ensuring there was no miscommunication about what was occurring.

Her sigh of contentment brought tears to his eyes as she tugged his forearm over her and held on for dear life. "I missed you, Roman. I'm still mad at you, but I missed you more than I ever thought possible."

A smile lifted his lips, and he was glad she couldn't see him. "I know part of the feeling I carried every day during my search was you calling out to me. We've been connected for years, and the miles between us couldn't change that. You needed me, and I was going to find you. That's all there was to it."

"Even though I'm still mad, I'm glad you did."

Roman's chuckle filled the silent room before he pressed his nose to the back of her head and inhaled deeply. "I'll take mad as long as you're in my universe again, Wilhelmina August."

He kept his arm tightly wrapped around her middle until her grasp on his wrist loosened and her breathing evened out. Roman couldn't fall asleep, though. His mind kept turning over the little bit of information she'd shared in the car. She sent a message that he never got.

If he had, he could have stopped the fire and the escape of The Miss, the right-hand woman of The Madame. He wanted to know why he didn't get it and who stopped it, more than she did. His mind's eye showed her limping into the bathroom earlier, and he corrected himself. No one wanted to know why he didn't get the message to rescue her more than she did. He would figure it out, and then he would prove to her that he didn't abandon her. She abandoned him.

MINA WAS ITCHING to see the bunker. If it held the equipment to help her find The Madame, she wanted to be down there now. The last thing she wanted to do was sit across from Roman and eat breakfast while they pretended that they hadn't been wrapped around each other when they woke this morning. She didn't want to admit to herself that waking up that way had been a dream of hers for years.

If she were honest with herself, she was embarrassed. She had shown weakness to someone who had always seen her as strong and unbreakable. If anyone else had been the one holding her last night, she could have separated the agent from the vulnerable woman, but not with Roman.

"Stop." He reached over and grasped her hand. When she looked down, she had managed to push her food around into one big pile but never put any in her mouth.

"I'm sorry," she whispered, lowering her fork to the plate.

"Don't be sorry. And don't be embarrassed about last night."

Mina let out a sarcastic huff that she wanted to be

laughter, but she never got there. "Easy for you to say. You aren't me."

His finger lifted her chin until she made eye contact with him. "That isn't easy for me to say. I know how I would feel if the shoe were on the other foot. I'm an agent. They try to train the emotions out of us, but we're still human at the end of the day. Sometimes, when those emotions get to be too much, we need an outlet. You could find worse ways to deal with it than asking a friend for comfort, especially after being on your own for so long."

"I suppose you're right," Mina admitted, though it almost killed her to do so. She picked at the eggs again, finally taking a bite and washing it down with coffee. She should have been starving, but she was in too much pain after escaping through the woods. She would never tell him that, though. He'd insist she stay up here and rest rather than get to work. He didn't understand that she had to be the one to figure out where The Madame was hiding. If she didn't, she'd never be able to move on with her life.

Roman had gone back to eating, and she watched him from under her brows, taking time to notice him for the first time since he'd found her. He was always a big man, fit, handsome and rugged, but he'd changed since she saw him a year ago. There wasn't an ounce of fat on him anymore. He was all muscle and hard lines, yet when he was holding her last night, he was soft against her back. She wondered how it was possible that the man before her in his black T-shirt, stretched tightly across his hard, sinewy chest, could evoke the feeling of comfort from within her so easily.

"You've lost weight."

"Gained five, actually," he said around a piece of bacon he'd just popped in his mouth.

"Not in fat, Roman. Did you stop eating and do nothing but work out?"

"If I wasn't searching for you, then yeah. Basically, I searched for you for twelve hours, worked out for two and then went back to work."

"Why?" She needed to appease her curiosity, but she suspected it might end up being like that saying about the cat.

He lifted his head and held her gaze when he answered. "The two *P*s, punishment and preparation. Punishment for not getting to you fast enough and preparation for when I found you. My gut told me you were going to need the third *P*."

"Protection," they said at the same time.

"You didn't need to punish yourself for anything, Roman."

"I did, though. I let my partner down, regardless of the circumstances, the how or the why. You can sure as hell count on me this time around. I won't let you down."

"Didn't they put you on another case?" she asked when it filtered through her brain what he'd said his schedule had been for the last year.

"You were my case. The FBI wanted their agent found. My first task was to find out if The Madame had you. Once I learned she was looking for you, too, I knew you'd escaped and were on the run. Trying to track down someone as well trained as you are made it an interesting assignment."

"And you're sure that SAC Moore doesn't know that you've located me?"

He nodded while he swallowed a bite of eggs. "I'm sure. I got the lead on you through a source that has nothing to do with the bureau."

"Every source has to do with the bureau, Roman," she said with a brow raised.

He matched her brow before he answered. "Cal is discreet."

"Wait, Cal found me?"

"Cal has equipment that can do more underground than I can above ground. I didn't want the SAC to know when I found you. I wanted to get to you first to be sure whatever happened next was your decision and not the government's."

"Thank you. I know what would have happened if the SAC had found me. I probably owe you my life, whether it's because I'm not six feet under or locked in a room for years. Either way, I appreciate that you thought of me and not your career. You know it's over now, right?"

"Oh, yeah," he agreed with a toss of his head. "Jobs come and go, but partners are forever." Before she could respond, he pointed at her plate. "Are you done eating? Cal should be ready for us."

Mina's heart raced at the thought of getting inside that bunker, outpacing the pounding that it had been doing after Roman hit her with the partners forever thing. She wanted to tell him she felt the same way, but she held her tongue because now was not the time or the place. There would probably never be a time or a place, but Mina couldn't worry herself with that right now. She had a Madame to find, and he was dangling the key to the search.

"I'm full." She picked up her coffee mug. "Let's get to work."

Chapter Eight

The workspace Cal had nicknamed The Bunker was only accessible from three places on the property: Cal's room, Roman's room and a hidden trap door that came out on the back side of the farthest cabin. That was only an exit, which meant if you left via the tunnel, you'd better be sure you were never coming back. When Roman had helped Mina down the ladder and into the room, he saw the relief in her eyes. She finally had everything she needed to find The Madame and bring her down.

His focus should be on finding the guys who hurt her and making them pay. It wasn't. All his focus was on her. How soft she was snuggled up against him all night, and how good it felt to wrap her up in his arms and not let her go. His heart hurt inside his chest every time she trembled in her sleep, but then soared when a squeeze from his arms had her relaxing back into him. Mina might be an FBI agent, but last night, she was also a woman with vulnerabilities. Those vulnerabilities were partly his fault, and he warred with himself over hiding her away until The Madame was found or helping Mina be the one to find the woman. He knew she didn't want protection, but she also couldn't see how much danger she was facing. It was his job to make sure she was protected, whether she liked it or not. She wouldn't like it, but the guilt that swamped him every time she took a step would allow for nothing else.

The Madame couldn't wait. They had to stop her before she hurt more women and destroyed more people's lives. He would take an exorbitant amount of pleasure in bringing her in and then letting Mina have a little alone time with her. A smile quirked Roman's lips. He would pay good money to watch that exchange on a CCTV.

Mina had done an initial glance over the equipment, but now she spun toward him with fire in her eyes. "Are you ever going to tell me why you weren't there the night of the fire, or are you just going to keep pretending it didn't happen?"

"That's not what I'm doing," he assured her. "I didn't want to split your focus now that you have the chance to find your target."

"Trust me when I say my focus is already split. Please, do tell." She motioned at him with a flourish, and he had to bite back a laugh.

The hatch opened to their left, and they both had their guns pointed at it before they took a breath. Roman lowered his gun when he recognized the pair of boots coming down the ladder. He pressed Mina's toward the floor with his hand.

"Wow, you two are jumpier than spit on a skillet," Cal said, hopping down off the ladder.

"You could have announced yourself," Roman said, tucking his gun back in his shoulder harness.

"The risk of getting shot was worth that display of FBI greatness," Cal said, punching him on the shoulder. "What do you think of my setup?" he asked Mina as he turned to her.

"Top-of-the-line everything," she agreed. "I haven't had a chance to start searching yet, but I should have everything I need now to find The Madame."

"Did I interrupt something?" Cal asked, glancing between them.

Roman lowered himself to a chair and braced his hands on his knees. "I was just about to explain why I didn't respond to her message the night of the fire. You may as well stay. I'm done with the FBI at this point, so telling a civilian about a case can't hurt my career."

Mina sat down abruptly and stuck her left leg out to keep pressure off it. She was hurting, and Roman wished there was something he could do to help her. All he could do was help her find The Madame and put the woman behind bars. Only then would it be safe for her to see a doctor again.

"I don't know what happened, Min. After you met me the night before to tell me something was going down, I gathered the team. We were ready and waiting to go in, but I never heard another word. I sent two messages to you via the app but got no response, so I waited as agreed upon at the beginning of the mission. My gut told me something was off, but I had to trust my partner. I should have at least done some recon around the house rather than wait up on that hill," he growled, squeezing his knees with his fingers.

Mina and Cal were silent, as though they were processing what he said. Finally, Mina responded. "If what you say is true, then you followed protocol and our agreed upon terms, Roman. What I don't understand is how you never got the message. I sent it right before I was…accosted," she said, the last word coming out as a cough. Roman could tell she was trying to hold it together.

Cal spoke to Mina. "How did the fire start? Do you remember?"

Roman recovered and pointed at his brother. "We wondered the same thing. It didn't make any sense that The Madame would burn down the house."

"Unless she'd been compromised," Mina answered.

"Had you compromised her?" Roman asked, his eyes wide.

Mina gave him a finger gun. "Only in the sense that The Miss and The Madame figured out I was an undercover agent."

A word fell from Roman's lips that had him smiling sheepishly at Min. She hated profanity, but, in this case, it applied. "We didn't know the SOS was because you were compromised."

"There would be no way for you to know that if you hadn't gotten the other messages. The panic button just tells you to send help."

"I didn't hear from you at our agreed upon time that night, so I assumed that it was taking longer for you to get whatever evidence you'd referred to the night before. In the meantime, I activated the team. Something in my gut said to be ready, so we waited until it was a full two hours past your check-in time."

"She missed a check-in time, and you didn't go in?" Cal asked. His stunned tone had Roman bristling.

"It wasn't that unusual for her to miss a check-in, Cal. If she was busy with the house, sometimes it would be two or three hours later. We were in a rhythm, and I was used to that, but this time, something was off. I should have trusted my gut."

"None of that," Cal said with authority. "As far as you were concerned, she had the tools she needed to reach you if there was a problem. You had no way to know she was out of commission if the message didn't come through."

"He's right," Mina whispered. "As hard as that is for me to admit. I used my anger toward you the last year to keep myself alive, but I never took the time to consider that you may not have gotten the message. My ego about my coding skills was too big, and I was convinced the app had no weaknesses."

"Everything has a weakness," Cal said with conviction.

"That's what I was starting to think by hour two," Roman agreed, standing and starting to pace. "I pulled four guys together, and we were going to approach the house. As we stood on the hill preparing, we saw the flames light up the sky. I lost my ever-loving mind and just ran for the house, the rest of the team hot on my tail. Then the SOS message came through, and I knew you were still inside but all you could do was push a button."

Roman watched Mina's elegant neck bob as she swallowed hard. She leaned in a bit closer, and he did, too, waiting for her to drop something else on him that would destroy him as both an agent and a man.

"I tried to send a message through the app first because I thought I'd have time to get to you." She shook her head and bit her lip for a moment. "I thought it sent. I was heading for the back door to rendezvous with you when they grabbed me."

"Thank God you saw those flames," Cal said, squeezing Roman's shoulder, knowing he needed a moment.

"By the time you saw the flames, The Miss was long

gone," she whispered, her words swallowed by the terror in the room. It rolled off her in waves, and Roman wanted to take her in his arms and comfort her, but he couldn't. His guilt wouldn't allow him to show weakness in front of her or his brother. "I was dragging myself to the window with the plan to throw myself out when I found the phone. They'd kicked it under the dresser before they tortured me. I remember hitting the SOS button, but I don't remember anything after that until I woke up after surgery."

Roman remembered. He remembered it all. The smoke and the sound of crackling as the flames licked their way up the side of the house. A shiver went through him, and he coughed to force the images away from his mind.

"So, the SOS message went through, but not the original message. I wonder why?" Roman asked, trying to make sense of the whole thing.

"The SOS wasn't a message. It had different coding. If I hit that button, it just sent an alarm to your phone. They wouldn't have had the inside ability to stop it."

"How did you cover who Roman was?"

"I was a client," Roman answered his brother, reaching out and grabbing Mina's hand to squeeze it.

Mina didn't let go of his hand when she spoke. "The first message said, 'There's a change in plans. Be ready in fifteen minutes. We will bring your date to the agreed upon meeting spot.'"

"You were made, and he needed to get the team ready, and you'd meet up with him in fifteen?" Cal asked, and they both nodded. "Was there any way they could have known that he wasn't a client?"

Mina shook her head. "No. There were so many clients that it was easy to hide him as one without raising anyone's suspicions. My job was to make the dates and organize the girls. The Miss never got involved as long as the money was coming in and the girls were going out."

"They were going to stop any message you sent. It didn't matter what it was," Cal assured her.

"If I had just hit the SOS button the first time," Mina said, staring at the floor.

Roman noticed a tremor go through her, and he squeezed her hand again. "No, don't do that. You did exactly what we agreed upon as step one. Storming the place unprepared could have resulted in death for anyone in that house. That's why we decided to avoid it at all costs. You know that."

"He's right. You can't go back and change things, but we can go forward by finding The Madame."

"That's going to be difficult," she said, a shake of her head barely noticeable other than her hair swaying slightly. "They started the fire and thought I'd burn along with the evidence. The evidence burned, but I didn't. To be honest, I don't even know how I got out alive. I don't remember much other than hitting that SOS button."

"The first floor was already engulfed when we got there," Roman explained. "There was no way to get up the stairs. I found a ladder discarded by the garage, but it wasn't tall enough to reach your window. All I could do was break the glass and get fresh air into the room, which was filled with smoke but hadn't started burning yet."

"I keep trying to remember, Roman. Sometimes I see eyes before the moment is gone."

His eyes. Mina probably remembered his scared, pained, worried eyes gazing down at her and praying she was still alive when the firefighters arrived.

"When I saw how much smoke there was, I couldn't wait. I used the ladder and then the trees until I was able to hoist myself through the window. You were already in bad shape. I carried you to the window and started breathing for you until the firefighters arrived. They got us out, but not before you were nearly dead from smoke inhalation."

"Some days, I wish the smoke had taken me, Roman."

"Don't say that, Mina," Roman insisted, his fists clenching. "Don't say that ever again."

The look she gave him was one he had never seen before, and he had no idea how to read what it meant.

"You didn't let me finish."

Cal chuckled, and so did Roman, her words lifting his lips into a sheepish smile. "You're right. My bad."

"I was going to say, 'and then I remember The Madame is still out there.' It's still my job to stop her. It'll be my last job with the bureau, but I will close this case."

"Mina, there's no reason you can't keep working—"

Mina cut him off with a wave of her hand in the air. "I need to dig into the coding on the app. Is it still active?"

"Yes. The SAC wanted it left online in case you tried to contact us via the app."

Cal glanced between them. "Is it risky to dig into the app now? Will that tip off The Madame that you're back online?"

"Remember, I coded it." She shrugged and motioned at the computer panel. "I wrote a backdoor into the code that only I know is there. Even FBI coders won't find it, which means neither will The Madame's. All I need is a computer and a few hours to get into the information I saved there."

"I have a computer, and you have the skills," Cal said. "It's time to end this nightmare for both of you."

"Do I have a choice?"

"You always have a choice, Mina," Roman said. "We can always go back to Minneapolis and let the SAC deal with it."

She was silent for so long he was convinced she would change her mind about finding The Madame alone. "No. If I make that choice, I could get a whole lot of innocent people killed. In this case, I don't have a choice. I have to suck it up and do what needs to be done."

"There's my girl." Roman ran his finger down her cheek and offered her a wink.

He stepped back while Cal walked Mina through the particulars of his computer system. The Secure One computers were vastly different from the ones she used at the FBI. Roman stood behind them, his thoughts forcing him back to that house with the flames licking around them and the woman he was supposed to protect almost dead in his arms. The memories always left his stomach swirling with how close he came to losing her.

"If you need anything," Cal said, "hit this button, and I'll head back down." He pointed at a black button on the console. "We'll regroup after you've had some time to work on the app."

"Regroup?" Mina asked, and Cal squeezed her shoulder.

"You might not have the FBI behind you anymore,

but you still have my men and me. When you have your next course of action, we'll be here to initiate it."

Cal shook Roman's hand and then climbed the ladder, closed the hatch and spun the lock.

"He's something else," Mina said, her hands poised over the keyboard.

"He won't let anyone hurt us here. Family looks after family every time. You're safe. Get to work."

With a grin, her fingers started tapping the keyboard.

MINA'S FINGERS FLEW as she searched the app's code for any breadcrumbs she could use to ferret out The Madame's identity. Too bad she couldn't keep her mind on her work. The picture Roman painted of that night was dark and ugly, but the look in his eyes when he spoke was what did the most damage to her heart. His retelling of having to breathe for her just to keep her alive would remain with her forever. She never wanted him to see her like that. Like this. Weak. Broken. Damaged. She was his partner, and she was supposed to be as strong as he was. She wasn't anymore. She never would be again.

Now she knew they were his eyes that she kept seeing in her dreams. No, in her memories. Her dreams had nothing as comforting as Roman's eyes starring in them. They had nothing but pain and terror. They held the eyes of all the girls she let down in the house that night. Those flashes she'd been getting were memories, and now, thanks to Roman, she could separate the two.

She was so busy thinking about the past that she almost missed what was right in front of her. Her hands fell away from the keyboard on a gasp. Roman, who had been pacing the room for the last hour, was by her side in two steps.

"Did you find something?"

"No." Her head shook as she stared up into the face that had saved her that night. "You said," she swallowed back the fear and forced herself to be the federal agent she'd always been with him. "You said the first floor was already engulfed by the time you got there. Did you get everyone else out? No one was killed or hurt?"

She noticed his slight grimace even in its brevity. "We got everyone, yes."

"Did you get Marlise?"

"Yes." Mina took note of his heavy sigh and waited him out. There was more to the story. His second sigh told her she was about to get it. "We found Marlise overcome by smoke less than two steps from the front door. There was no one else in the house." He motioned at the computer monitor in front of her. "How much longer before you get to that backdoor?"

"Roman." Her tone was sharp, and he snapped his attention back to her. "Was she hurt?"

He knelt in front of her with his hand on her knee. "Yes. By the time we found her, the fire had spread to where she'd collapsed, and she suffered significant burns to her face, neck and left arm."

"They punished her for warning me, didn't they?" Mina asked with her forehead resting on the table where she'd dropped it.

Roman lifted her chin and stroked the hair back off her face and behind her ear. "Min, listen, nothing that happened that night was your fault."

"Of course it was, Roman. If we hadn't gone in and tried to topple The Madame's empire, Marlise wouldn't be scarred."

"No, she'd probably be dead," he whispered as a reminder. "You do remember the river drownings around the country?"

"Yes, that started about six months into our assignment, but Red Rye doesn't have a river." Mina was confused by his train of thought.

"No, and that's what led the Kansas office to wonder if the towns that had a river also had a house like Red Rye."

"Have there been more drownings since the fire?"

"No, and Kansas thought they could connect those murders to The Madame. Especially since the girls who drowned were scrubbed clean of any identity."

"Just like the girls in the Red Rye house."

"Exactly. Kansas is still working it, but they don't have much to go on other than girls with no identity showing up in random rivers across the country. They're never found in a big river in a big city. It doesn't make any sense."

"It does, though. If those girls are from a house like Red Rye, it wouldn't take much for The Miss's guards to load a woman into a vehicle and drop her in a random river. I'm not saying that's what they're doing, but we have to consider it as a possibility."

"That's true, but they could still be unrelated. It's unlikely considering the girls have no traceable identity, but we can't know for sure until we find The Madame." He pointed at the computer in front of her. "If you want to avenge Marlise, that's how you get the job done. Find the information we need to bury The Madame and all her minions."

Mina's head nod was sharp, and she put her hands back on the keyboard, her fingers flying again. Her mind flew to the voices, faces and secrets she'd come to know during the time she'd been part of The Madame's organization. Had she kept girls alive when she was undercover? Why couldn't she remember what she'd learned before the fire?

Without taking her fingers off the keyboard or looking at him, for that matter, Mina spoke. "You said I met you the night before the fire to update you. What did I tell you?"

"That you were close to a break in the case, and that's why I got the team ready for the next night. You said you were meeting with someone the next day who would break the case wide open, but you couldn't give me more than that at the time."

Mina's fingers stopped moving for a moment while she laughed. "And you let me go back to the house with so few details about what the break was? That doesn't sound like you, Jacobs."

His shrug was barely there when he paused by the monitor. "I trusted you. You were the one calling the shots. I was there to support you and feed you information from the outside, but I had to rely on you to get the dirty details of the operation. When we met that night, you were vibrating with excitement, and I'd seen you that way before. You were close to a break, and you assured me you were only days away from knowing who The Madame was and the house of cards was going to fall."

"Why can't I remember!" She meant it to be a question, but it came out as an ugly, guttural exclamation. She rubbed her hands over her face and leaned her elbows on the desk, her face in her hands. "The information is sitting on my tongue, but my brain feels disconnected from it. I can't spit it out, and I don't understand why."

"Min, you were given Special K. That's why you can't remember."

Her hands fell away, and she glared at him. "Ketamine makes you forget the time you're under the drug's control, not days before that."

"If you hadn't run out of the hospital before being properly treated, you would have heard the doctor tell us that you had mild edema around your brain on the CT scan. You were punched, or you hit your head on something a few hours before we found you."

A flash of memory hit her, and she shivered. "They tortured me, Roman." She rubbed her temple and sighed. "I get bits and pieces of memories. Flashes, if you will. It's frustrating, but maybe that means I'll remember more soon. I have to, or we're never going to end this manhunt The Madame has put out on me."

Roman walked behind her and started massaging her shoulders. The sensation shouldn't have been erotic, but parts of her that had been dead for years came to life at his touch. Heat roared through her to all the places she hadn't even thought about in over a year. Now, she had to force herself not to think about them when in close quarters with her partner.

"Then we get to work. We work the case as we know it and follow the leads where they take us. We go back to the start and do what we always did. We problem solve. We were partners for so many years because we solved cases, Mina. That's the only reason the bureau never broke us up. Let's do that now and prove to them we can do it again."

"The Gruesome Twosome."

Roman laughed, and her heart soared to hear his laughter again.

"It's been too long since I've heard you say that, Min," he whispered, squeezing her shoulders. "God, it's so good to have you with me again."

"I won't be for long if we don't make The Madame show her face in the light of day. We go back to the start and work the case," she repeated, her fingers on the keyboard again. "We'll follow the leads."

She typed at lightning speed while he kept massaging her shoulders. "That's my girl. Head in the game."

A shiver went through her again. She could only dream about being Roman's girl. When they finished following the leads and solved the case, their partnership would also end. Being chased by men determined to kill her evoked emotions she knew how to cope with and use to her advantage. Losing the one person who had been a constant in her life for so many years while knowing he was living his life with some other woman, she didn't. In the end, if The Madame didn't kill her, losing Roman would.

Chapter Nine

Roman set a plate down in front of Mina. "Eat this."

She picked up the sandwich without taking her eyes off the screen, took a bite and went right back to typing, all without missing a keystroke. Roman had been watching her work for the last two hours and had never felt more useless. His hands were tied until she found something. Until they had a direction to go, all he could do was wait. It hadn't happened and not for lack of trying, either. He could see and feel how frustrated she was today. Breaking into the backdoor of her program was arduous, which she'd done by design. If it took her this long to get into the app's backdoor, it would take someone unfamiliar with it days, weeks or, hopefully, forever.

It was the frustration of not being able to remember the information she thought was in her mind that was bothering her the most, though. He could see it in her eyes when she asked about Marlise. Chances were good that she'd been chewing over Marlise being hurt in the fire since she asked him about it. He wished he had comforting words for her, but the truth was what it was. Marlise was mixed up with The Madame, and that was a dangerous game to play.

"Did you know that the name Marlise means *wished for child* in Hebrew?" she asked after swallowing a bite of her sandwich.

"I didn't," Roman admitted, leaning against the wall with his arms crossed over his chest. He was going for relaxed so she would too, but he knew that would never happen. Not until they were free of the threat coming at them.

"Marlise used to say it as part of a joke she'd make about herself. Her parents surrendered her at a shelter when she was two days old. She would say, 'More like my name meant *wish this child would disappear.*'" She stopped speaking then. Roman could hear the tears in her voice as she choked up. She cleared her throat and went on. "I do remember worrying every day that she was going to disappear."

"She's okay, Min," he promised, squeezing her shoulders. "The person we were most worried about was you." This time, it was Roman's turn to clear his throat. The emotions of finding her alive kept hitting him in all the places he couldn't protect. The thought that he might never have found her was the second of the one-two punches. "I'm still reeling from the fact that I found you, Mina. God, you don't know—" He stopped speaking rather than make a fool of himself.

"I don't know what?" she asked, her hands going still on the keyboard and her body stiffening.

Roman tilted his head to the ceiling and took a deep breath. "You don't know how many nights I laid awake wondering if you were dead or alive. You don't know how many times I hit the punching bag at the gym out of frustration and terror. You don't know how every time my phone rang, I begged the universe to let it be you. It never was, Min. It never was."

Her left hand came up to cover his right hand on her shoulder. "I didn't know who to trust, Roman. I wasn't just trying to keep myself alive. I was trying to keep the girls who were trapped by The Madame alive, too. They weren't there by their own free will."

She stood up instantly and turned, falling into him until he steadied her. "Some of those girls were bought and paid for, Roman!"

"Slow down, Mina. Tell me what you mean."

"Sex trafficking. That's how The Madame gets the girls."

"We interviewed Marlise, and she never indicated anything to do with sex trafficking."

She grasped her head and twined her fingers in her hair. "I didn't mention it at any time over the year I was undercover that the girls weren't there by choice?"

"No," he promised, his head shaking. "When you briefed us, you indicated the girls were there by choice, though they were hesitant and skittish when they first arrived. They wouldn't talk to you about how they got to Red Rye, but we chalked that up to nerves about the escort service. That said, when the fire happened, you were just getting to the point where The Miss was pulling you deeper into the organization."

"The Miss was The Madame's right-hand woman in Red Rye, but only Red Rye."

"Only Red Rye?" Roman asked on a brow lift.

"Yes… My God, Roman, I remember now. There were other houses full of girls!"

"You told me that when we met the day before the fire," Roman agreed. "If you remember, that's why the SAC initially sent you into the Red Rye house. He wanted you to find out if there were other houses and if sex trafficking was part of the operation. The app was just a convenient way to keep you there until you were indispensable to the organization."

"The FBI knows what cities the other houses were in?" she asked and he nodded.

"Those houses were raided and the women were rescued, but The Madame still escaped capture."

"That's good," Min said with a satisfied nod, "but The Miss didn't know there were other houses until the day before the fire. She wasn't happy because she thought she was leading the charge for The Madame and that the Red Rye house was the beginning of something big."

"Finding out that she was just a smaller part of something bigger made her angry?" he asked, as he waited for her to sort out her thoughts.

Her head nodded as her eyes roamed back and forth as though she were searching her mind for the information. "That was the vibe I got when I overheard her talking to someone on the phone. I don't know if it was The Madame or someone else. I remember now. I was afraid I'd get caught eavesdropping by a guard, so I couldn't hang around to find out who she was talking to."

"Either The Madame kept her in the dark, or she didn't trust her completely yet."

"Could be," she agreed. "Or it could be that there was a Miss at every house, but none of them knew the others existed. You said she was long gone by the time you got there that night?" Mina asked and was rewarded with a nod. She lowered herself back to her chair, and her shoulders slumped. "I remember that I made daily logs on the app. If I can access those, that'll help us unravel the case."

Roman knelt next to her and forced himself not to get lost in her eyes. He'd spend all day gazing into those big, beautiful brown globes if time allowed, but it didn't. He had to concentrate on getting her through this. Only then could he finally let go of the guilt eating him alive and try to find a new kind of normal, even if it wasn't with the FBI...or Mina. "I was always very uncomfortable with the idea of you keeping notes on the app, but the SAC backed you, so I was overruled. Do you think The Miss found your notes?"

"Impossible. I could barely hack it, and I made the app. They figured out who I was some other way."

Roman stood up and motioned for her to continue. She typed and ate for another fifteen minutes before her hands stilled on the keyboard. "I'm in," she said on a breath before her fingers picked up their rhythm again.

His heart raced at the thought that they might finally learn what happened that night. How did The Madame know Min was a plant? They had crafted her persona right down to the last detail of her life. She didn't even look like the woman he knew the day she walked into that house and applied for a job.

"What?" She leaned forward and stared at the computer screen, opening another program and pasting something into a search bar there, pausing while it computed. "See this?" she asked, pointing at the screen.

"It looks like an IP address," Roman said, noting the way the numbers were formatted.

"It is. An IP address from the city manager's office in Red Rye."

"Liam Albrecht?" he asked, his mind trying to follow the trail. "We know he was never involved with the house. The FBI vetted everyone in the local government there."

"I don't know what to say, except that's the IP address that stopped my first message from going out."

"Wait, what?" he asked, his head tipping further in confusion. "Why would the city manager stop your message from going out?"

"I don't know. The second question is, why didn't they use a VPN to hide their activity?" Roman could see the confusion in her eyes.

"Maybe they did…"

Her brow lifted as she stared at the screen. "You mean someone used the IP address for the city manager as camouflage?"

"It's possible. Unusual, but possible."

"We have to assume two scenarios for now. The first is that Liam Albrecht had something to do with the house, and the second is someone else is trying to pin it on him by using his IP address."

"Agreed."

Min stared at the screen while rubbing her forehead. When her hand dropped, her shoulders squared with determination. "I need to talk to Marlise."

"Impossible. We can't leave this compound until we have more information, Mina."

"Then we bring her here."

Roman noted that her words were final, but he wasn't done with the conversation.

"If we make a move on Marlise, we lead The Madame right to our door. You know she's got the girl under surveillance."

"She's not in custody? Roman! You said she was safe!"

He curled his hand around hers and held it lightly, letting her know he was there for her without words. "I know you're scared, but we couldn't force her into custody, Min. She has rights. She refused to talk to us about what went on in Red Rye. She told the SAC she would only talk to you."

"Do we know where Marlise is?" she asked from between clenched teeth.

"She's in St. Paul, and she has an FBI agent assigned for her protection when she goes out. It was hard enough to convince her she needed that, much less convince her to live under the roof of the FBI."

"Get her here, Roman. She holds the key to unlocking my memory. I know it. My gut is telling me she's the key."

"I don't think that's a good idea. I'm certain The Madame has her under surveillance. She'd be dumb not to with what that girl knows. We try to snatch her, and we lead everyone to Secure One's door."

"Fine. I'll go to Marlise. Move out of my way, Jacobs. I don't need your permission to leave here."

Her voice was filled with righteous anger and determination. Roman allowed himself a moment to relish being in the presence of that woman again.

He grasped her upper arms and held her gaze, fierce as it was. "You're correct, but I need you alive, so you can forget about going out there alone. Let me talk to Cal and see what our options are, okay? If we can bring Marlise here safely, we will. You have to give me a little bit of time to do it right, though. We can't jump into a fire again unprepared. We might not make it out alive this time."

She didn't move or say anything for thirty seconds.

Roman could see in her eyes the battle she fought to accept her limitations and agree to his terms. He wished things weren't always so hard for her. She deserved a little bit of calm in her life, but he couldn't give it to her, and that bothered him more than it should. That wasn't his job. His job was to keep her alive until the case was resolved. That had always been his one and only job with Mina, even if he wished they could have been more.

"Do you promise you'll talk to Cal?"

"How much longer do you need down here?"

"Hours. I need to follow the trail of this IP address and see if there are any other messages it intercepted. Before I can do that, I need a break. My head hurts, and I need to put my foot up for a few minutes."

Roman was relieved. He could offer her that kind of comfort. Cal's nurse, Selina, had cleaned the wound on her forehead and closed it with Steri-Strips. She had a bruise and a knot on her head that he was sure wasn't helping her sort through all the information filtering through it. Selina suggested that she had a concussion, but Mina had scoffed at that diagnosis. Selina was probably right, though, so he'd encourage Min to rest as often as she could. She was going to need her wits about her the next time they tangled with The Madame.

"I'll help you up the ladder and get you settled, and then I'll find Cal. You'll be waiting when I get back, right?"

"Of course. I don't have a choice. I'm the only one in this for the long haul. If I can't remember what happened in Red Rye and who The Madame is, this is my life forever."

Roman pulled her into him and wrapped his arms

around her. "It won't be, and you aren't the only one in it for the long haul. You've controlled my every thought for a year, Mina. Even when I slept, I dreamt of you. We're in this together for the long haul. Do you understand?"

The brush of her cheek against his chest when she nodded almost undid him. The vulnerability in that one motion would be the thing he'd keep in the front of his mind until this was over and Wilhelmina August found her confidence again.

THE AIR WAS crisp as Roman walked toward the lake at the back of the property. October was nearing an end, and in northern Minnesota, that meant cold nights followed by sunny days with a strong breeze. He loved his home state, and he was glad to be back with his family after too many years away. When he stood back and examined his life, Roman didn't recognize it anymore. The only thing he recognized was Mina. He recognized her fighting spirit and "don't give a damn" attitude about her own life when it came to protecting the innocent. He respected her and hated her for it in equal proportions. Their jobs required them both to take risks he couldn't be sure were worth it anymore. In fact, he knew they weren't.

I'll never let you down. I've always got your back.

Roman's promise to his partner rang in his ears as he searched for his brother on the property. He'd promised Mina he'd talk to Cal, and he wasn't going to break another promise to her. If he had to walk to St. Paul and fetch Marlise himself, that's what he would do.

"Good thing there aren't bad guys with guns around here. You'd be dead before you knew what hit you."

"I knew you were there," Roman said, spinning and walking backward a few steps while his brother advanced on him. "I just knew I could take you with one hand without spilling my beer."

"I'd like to see you try," Cal said, laughing.

"I was looking for you." Roman handed him the unopened beer in his hand. "We need to talk."

"Let's go to my office." He motioned forward, and Roman turned to follow him. "Where's Mina?"

"She's resting. I've got Mack looking after her."

"I hope the special agent of the FBI doesn't know there's a mercenary babysitting her. I feel like that wouldn't go over well."

"Do I look dumb?"

"Yes," Cal said without missing a beat.

Roman's bark of laughter echoed across the lake as they walked out onto a dock and settled on a bench at the end.

"Ahh yes, the office created by man and occasionally ruined by man," Roman said, leaning over onto his thighs. Lake Citron was a manmade lake that Cal used for various training exercises with his people, from beach breaching to victim recovery. "It's been too long since I've sat here with you."

"Going on two years," Cal said, popping the top off the bottle of beer and taking a swallow. "You had bigger fish to fry."

They tapped the necks of their bottles together and sat quietly for several minutes, just watching the water ripple across the lake as they neared sundown. Roman had spent the better part of the day in the bunker with Min, and now she needed rest, and he needed answers. He hoped his brother had some.

"Mack asked me if Mina had taken a bullet for you."

"Why would he ask that?" Roman asked curiously, kicking a pebble off the dock into the water.

"He figured that was the reason you were so protective of her. That or you're in love with her."

"Tell Mack to keep his nose out of my business."

"I mean, I can, but then no one would have their nose in your business, most especially you."

Roman's eye roll as he took a drink of beer was his only response.

"I assume you haven't been dating lately. Or should I say at all? Like in the last seven years?"

"Cal?"

"Yeah, Roman?" Cal asked with a smirk.

"Shut up."

"You always were a coward. At least that much hasn't changed." Cal's beer bottle went to his lips, and Roman's brow went up.

"That's a bit like the pot and the kettle. I don't see any women on this compound."

"We're not talking about me, Roman. I haven't been in love with the same woman for seven years and been too afraid to tell her. It wasn't me who spent the last year hunting her down like a man desperate for air. I'm glad you found her, but now you have to break that cardinal rule and tell her how you feel."

"She's my partner and friend, Cal. Nothing more," Roman said before he took a swig of beer.

"Sure, keep telling yourself that. I want you to think about this for a moment, though. What if you had never found her? What if you'd found her dead? What if you never got to tell her what she means to you? Could you live with the idea that you spent six years with her and were never able to call her yours? Think about it. That's all."

Roman had thought about those questions more times in the last year than even he cared to admit. He knew the answers, but knowing and doing were two different things. Right now, he wasn't convinced Mina even trusted him, and maybe she shouldn't. He was the reason she couldn't take a step without intense pain.

"I need help with the case."

"I'm listening."

"I need to procure a package in St. Paul and get it back here without anyone following us."

"A package. I assume you aren't talking about a cat or a dog."

"A woman. Age twenty-seven. Traumatized and scarred from the same fire Min was in."

"What's the end game?"

"Mina swears she holds the key to what happened that night. Marlise was the cook at the house in Red Rye. Mina befriended her early in the investigation, and she's convinced if she can talk to Marlise, everything will snap into focus."

"Do you believe that, too?"

Roman set his empty beer bottle on the dock and leaned in over his knees. "I believe that she believes it."

"Well, that's the most talked around no I've ever heard."

"She developed a special bond with Marlise, and from what she tells me, Marlise is who warned her that she'd been made. It is possible that talking to her could jog Mina's memory, so that alone makes it worth it. Bringing the girl here also takes stress off Mina and helps her relax into the job again."

"All of that is understandable. How hard will it be to obtain the package?"

"Government-protection level difficult."

Cal swore and shook his head, his laughter sarcastic when it fell from his lips. "How in the hell do you think we're going to get her away from witness protection?"

"No, not witness protection. She's living in a government-run facility for victims of crimes. She's been treated for her injuries and her mental and emotional scars. We were hoping to hold on to her long enough to use her as a state's witness, but when Mina didn't show up immediately, Marlise clammed up and refused to talk."

"Does she go to work or school? Can we pick her up somewhere away from home?"

"I checked in on her about a month ago, and she was managing the kitchen at the group home where she lives. She always goes out to pick up orders with a helper who has about fifty pounds of muscle and carries a government badge. Other than that, she doesn't leave the house much except for doctor's appointments."

"Again, with muscle?"

"Yep, but he waits outside."

Cal was silent for a few minutes. "It would be easier to set up a secure line for Mina to talk to her on."

"Easier, yes, but if we bring Marlise here, and she opens up to Mina, it might jog her memory about what happened at the Red Rye house. Marlise might be the catalyst to help us solve this case so both she and Mina can be free."

"It's going to be a tough sell if we don't produce Mina when we pick her up. None of my men are snatching a girl for you, so don't even bother asking. She comes of her own free will or not at all."

"Come on, man," Roman said in disgust. "I don't want you to snatch her. We'll send an image of me, you and Mina. You'll also have a letter from Min explaining to Marlise why she needs to see her. That letter and picture get burned as soon as she's read it. Correct?"

"Understood. This might take me a couple of days to arrange."

"Take your time, but hurry," Roman said, a slight tilt to his lips. "We are running out of it. It's four hours to St. Paul one way. That's a day's travel when you factor in having to lose a tail."

"It's an hour by plane. If I can acquire the package, I can be back here in under four hours."

"I don't trust anyone else with this, Cal."

"Understood, brother. Have Mina get the information ready. If I can make it happen, it'll be tomorrow since it's Friday. Doctors' offices aren't usually open on Saturdays."

Roman's lips tipped up into a smirk when he slapped his brother on the back, stood and headed back to the lodge.

Chapter Ten

"Afternoon, Marlise. How's supper coming along?" Mina had taken to the woman immediately upon her arrival in Red Rye. She was dangerously innocent in a place like this and didn't belong there any more than Mina did. The difference was Mina had the power to give Marlise a better life.

The woman calmly turned on the mixer filled with cookie dough, walked over to Mina and stood shoulder to shoulder with her. "You've been made," she whispered into her ear, rushing a shiver down Mina's spine. "I heard them talking. They know you're an FBI agent. You're not getting out of here alive, Agent August."

Then she calmly walked back to the mixer and finished her work. Mina was a trained agent, so she fought back the panic rising in her throat. Marlise knew her real name, and that was cause to sound the alarm. She snagged a cookie from the pile on the counter and bit into it, casually holding her phone in one hand as though checking her email. She opened an app and sent a message, then ghosted the app and stuck the phone back in her pocket.

"Thanks for the cookie, Marlise," Mina said, giving her a wave on her way out of the kitchen. She would sneak out the back door and head to the meet-up point with the team Roman was gathering. It was go time, and she had to go.

She had barely made it out of the kitchen before she came face-to-face with The Miss. She plastered on a smile and prepared herself for battle.

"We need you in the boardroom," The Miss said. "Agent August."

Before Mina could react, strong arms grabbed her from behind. She remained calm since her cries would never be heard through the strong hand over her mouth. With her arms trapped behind her, she had no leverage to break free. She kicked out, her foot connecting with something that shot searing pain through her. She screamed on reflex, but the hand wrapped around her mouth kept anyone from hearing her. God, why couldn't she feel her foot? The strong arms dragged her up the stairs, The Miss following them with a gleam in her eye that told Mina she wasn't done with her yet. Mina calmed the panic in her mind and reminded herself she'd sent Roman that message. He'd get to her before The Miss could do much more damage. She just had to stay alive long enough for him to get the team there.

"I always thought you were too good to be true," The Miss hissed, her words laced with venom. "I love being right." Her arm swung out, and more searing pain engulfed Mina as a scream tore from her throat.

"Mina! Wake up! Come on, baby. You're okay. You're safe here."

Mina's eyes opened as her chest heaved. She stared into Roman's sleepy face. His gaze held fear and uncertainty, and she reached out, caressing his cheek to ground herself. "It happened again, didn't it?"

"If by *it* you mean a nightmare, then yes."

She smiled at his words, even though she wanted to cry from the pain in her foot. She relived the pain every time she had the dream, which was happening more and more frequently now.

"I used to think they were nightmares, but now I know they're more like flashbacks while I'm asleep."

"Your mind is helping you remember when you're in an unconscious state?" he asked, lowering himself to the side of the bed and keeping hold of her hand. She liked that his giant paw swallowed hers. It made her feel safe in a world she knew was anything but safe.

"Something like that," Mina agreed, running her hand over her face. "It's always different parts of my time in the Red Rye house. Tonight, I was dreaming about the minutes after Marlise told me I'd been made."

"Are you sure that's what she meant?"

"Yes, I remember now. She told me I wasn't getting out alive and then called me Agent August."

A curse word fell from Roman's lips that had her raising a brow. "Sorry, but if that was a flashback, then the whole operation was compromised at some point."

She sat up and leaned against the headboard, accepting a bottle of water from him for a drink. "It was real. After she called me Agent August, I took out my phone and sent you the message you never got. As I was headed for the back door to meet up with you, The Miss and one of her goons stopped me. She called me Agent August once her goon had me in a chokehold. I kicked out, and instantly, white-hot pain lanced my foot. The Miss said she knew I was too good to be true and then... I think... Roman, I think she was stabbing me?"

The look on his face told her she was right.

She drank some water and set the bottle back on the table. "I know what happened now." The words were whispered, but they sent a visible chill through Roman. "I can still feel the pain of the knife that went through my shoe and into my foot when I kicked out." She rubbed her left lower calf because she knew better than to touch her foot. "I screamed, but no one could hear me. We were almost to my room when she did it again." The water threatened to come back up, and Mina swallowed several times to keep it down. "Once they got me in my room, they put the knife down and picked up a mallet. Every time I refused to answer a question, they pounded on my foot." Her head fell back to the pillow, and she gulped air just to keep from vomiting at the memories of that time trapped in a room with people who wanted her dead.

"Will you show it to me? I need to understand."

"Show you what?" Mina asked, resting on her elbows to look at him.

"Your foot."

"I don't want to do that."

"I understand that, Min. I know how bad it was when I found you that night. What I need to know is, what is it like now? If we need to run, I have to know if you can, or if I need to cover you."

Her laughter was thin and laced with unrelenting pain. "That depends on the day and the terrain, Jacobs."

"Why do you call me Jacobs whenever you want to put distance between us? If you think I don't notice, you're wrong. I'm here to help you stay alive until we bring down The Madame. That's my only goal, so don't hamper my efforts this early in the game."

Mina's insides quivered at the thought of showing

him how broken she was now. Every time she looked at the foot, it reminded her she would never be an agent again, which meant losing Roman as her partner. A mangled heart would be harder to live with than her mangled foot. At least they could remove the mangled foot to get rid of the pain. They couldn't remove her heart.

She brought her knee up, and he grasped her sock, babying it down over her heel. When he pulled it off the toes, Roman stared at it in silence. His hand took hers on instinct.

"How do you even walk, Min?" he asked, his voice a harsh rasp. "You relied on me to be your eyes and ears, and the one time it mattered most, I failed you."

She grabbed angrily at the sock. "This is why I didn't want to show you!" She sucked in a deep breath to steady herself. "I don't want you to feel guilty. This wasn't your fault. You couldn't have stopped it, even if you got the first message."

Roman held her hand to the bed to stop her from putting the sock back on. "Tell me what happened. They couldn't tell us at the hospital because of privacy laws."

"I think you can see what happened with your own eyes."

Her foot was a cobweb of scars from knives and burns. It wasn't burned in the fire that night, but as a torture tactic to get her to reveal what she'd told the FBI about the Red Rye operation. She refused, and her foot had paid the price. Her bones sat at odd angles, and the fifth toe was gone. The doctors had told her it was nearly amputated when she'd arrived and they couldn't reattach it.

"How do you walk on this?"

"Carefully." She uttered the word ruefully, and Roman smiled in appreciation of her attempt to lighten the mood. "I have a brace I wear to support the foot and the muscles. Without it, I wouldn't walk, much less run."

"Did you get that from a doctor?"

"Not exactly." Her answer was vague on purpose, and he stared her down until she relented. "I bought it off the shelf. It works."

"For now," he said, reaching into the drawer by the bedside. He came out with a tube of ointment and held it up. "Cal uses this for his hand that's been injured."

"I noticed he had several high-tech fingers. What happened?"

"A mission gone wrong," Roman said, his lips in a grim line. "Shrapnel nearly destroyed his hand, but they were able to save everything but his two middle fingers. His hand is still sensitive, so he wears the prosthesis to protect it and improve his grip." He held up the tube. "He also uses this to keep the swelling down and ease the pain. Would it be okay to try it on your foot?"

Mina held her hand out for it, and she read the tube before handing it back. "I've heard about it. It's supposed to work great, but I never had access to it."

Roman opened the tube and squirted a ribbon on his hand, but she moved her foot out of the way before he could touch it.

"No." The one word was punctuated with a finger in his chest. "No. You are not touching it."

"I'm not going to hurt you, Mina. I'll be gentle."

She shook her head while she forced tears back from her eyes. "No. You don't want to touch it. Just...don't."

He rubbed the ointment between his palms to warm

it but didn't speak. He simply slathered the ointment across her skin. She closed her eyes so she didn't have to see his face when he touched her leathery skin and followed the macabre pattern of her bones that jutted out at unnatural angles. She inhaled deeply and shook away the pain of knowing one day she'd lose this man and have to reinvent herself all over again. And she'd do it. She had to survive the onslaught of The Madame so she could keep helping women like Marlise.

Roman's touch was light but warm, as though he wanted to heal her with his hands. Any comfort he could offer her was welcome. She had suffered for a year with unrelenting pain in that foot, so she'd take the five minutes of solace he offered. He tenderly covered her foot with the sock when he finished rubbing in the ointment and then climbed off the bed.

She listened to him wash his hands, and when he returned, he carried a bottle of pain reliever. She had curled into a ball on her side, the blanket pulled up to her chin, and a lone tear ran down her cheek. She angrily brushed it away with her blanket.

"Mina, honey, did I hurt you?" When she didn't answer, he knelt and handed her the medication and bottle of water. She swallowed the pills, but she couldn't stop her hand from shaking while she did it.

"You didn't hurt me. I never wanted you to see my foot, but now that you have, I'm afraid it's going to change everything between us."

"I saw it the night of the fire, Min." He pushed the hair off her sweaty face and trailed a thumb down her cheek. "If I needed more proof that you're the strongest person I know, seeing your foot that night sealed it for me."

She wanted to speak. She wanted to say something smart-alecky or try to downplay it, but after what she'd gone through, all she had left was the truth. "I know I'm not the woman you left the day before the fire."

"You're right," he said, running his hand down her arm to take her hand. "You're twice as strong and twice as beautiful in my eyes. You're also twice as smart. Somehow you managed to stay off the radar for an entire year while dealing with a traumatic injury that has become a permanent disability. I might come off like a bumbling oaf, but I want you to know that I'm proud of you. I know you can hold your own in any fight."

"Not a physical one anymore," she admitted. She rubbed her forehead and avoided eye contact with the man who had just called her beautiful.

"Hey," he whispered. "Would you like to go back to sleep now?"

"No." She shook her head for added emphasis. "I won't sleep now for a bit. I need to let the dream fade away, or I'll be too tense to sleep."

"I have an idea if you're up for it. I know a place where you can reach out and touch the stars. Would you like to see it?"

"Is it a long walk?"

"It's a fair way, but we'll take it slow and stop as often as you'd like. I promise once you're out there, the walk will be worth it."

She tossed the covers back with purpose and scooted to the end of the bed. "If you throw in a bottle of Jim Beam, that will make the walk worth it."

"Done," Roman said with a smirk as he grabbed her shoes and brace and set them by the bed.

ROMAN WANTED TO FORGET, but he couldn't. The destruction of her foot was proof that he'd dropped the ball on the one person he never wanted to let suffer. You could hardly call what she was walking on a foot. It was just a mishmash of scarred flesh and bones in places they shouldn't be. There was no fat whatsoever, and it must hurt like hell. She limped along next to him, and he kept his arm around her waist, helping her over the uneven grass.

"The brace I wear keeps me upright, but it doesn't give me stamina," Mina explained, her voice quiet even in the still of the night. "That's what happened in the woods that night. I had miscalculated how far I could go before resting. The woods had more difficult terrain to navigate than I'd anticipated. I should have planned better. I felt safe in Chester and didn't leave on my normal schedule. I was tired and thought a few extra months in one place wasn't a big deal." Her tone held shame, and Roman hated that she felt anything other than how strong he knew her to be.

"The extra months wouldn't have hurt, except that when I found you, I brought The Madame along behind me. I still won't apologize for tracking you down. How did you even escape the hospital, Mina? I left long enough to take a shower, and there was another FBI guard at your door. You weren't out of surgery twenty-four hours. You had to be in excruciating pain."

Her nod was sharp, and she coughed as though thinking about it still sent her back there. "I was, but that pain would be nothing if The Madame got to me. I wasn't thinking clearly. I was running more on autopilot than anything. At the time, I thought you'd abandoned me in the house, which made me wonder if you were working with The Madame. I knew I couldn't stay there long, but didn't see an escape until the agent they assigned to my door got ill. He took off for the restroom, and I saw a chance. I pulled the IV out and climbed into the wheelchair they'd left in my room. I waited, knowing the nurse would eventually leave the station. Sure enough, they got a code blue on the floor, and off she went. I managed to get to the elevator without seeing the agent again."

"Where did you go from there?"

"I had my bugout bag stashed where I could get to it quickly, along with a car. I managed to get to it, stashed the wheelchair in the back and took off. I found a hotel and laid low for a few days, then moved on until I got far enough away from Red Rye that it was safe to seek medical attention."

"How did you pay for that? Do you have bills outstanding?"

"Some," she answered as the lake came into view. She paused on the next step and sighed. "Look at that view. You were right. It was worth the walk here."

Roman helped her onto the dock, and they walked to the bench, where she lowered herself down. He sat next to her and rested his arm over the back of the bench. He wanted to touch her just to remind himself that she was real and she was here.

"The bureau will cover the bills. You just have to let them know who to pay."

"Maybe," she said. "I'm no longer employed by them, Roman."

He held up his finger until she paused. "Untrue. You're still an active agent of the FBI."

"I won't be for long when they see this foot," she

said with a head shake. "I paid cash for almost everything. I had to dip on a couple of more expensive procedures, which I feel bad about, but the person they treated doesn't even exist. I had cash, but I had to make it last."

"Where did you get the money? Certainly not on what we make a month."

Her laughter filled the night sky, and Roman ate up the sound. She was relaxed for a moment, and he wanted more of that for her. "How true that is. Do you remember when my meemaw died a few years ago?"

"I sure do. She was a sweet lady who raised you right."

"I hope she would still think so," she agreed on a faraway sigh. "Once I sold her house and had all her assets together, I put them in a national bank under a fake name that I could access from anywhere in the country. That money kept me alive all these months, so I didn't have to work and risk being found by The Madame."

"Is the money gone now?"

"Not by a longshot. Why do you think I told Cal to protect the Fairlane?"

Her wink nearly did Roman in. He smiled while he tenderly rubbed her neck until goosebumps covered her skin. "Your meemaw would be glad to know she was able to do that for you. Had you stayed, the FBI would have protected you, baby." The endearment slipped out, but Roman was glad when she didn't bristle.

"I didn't know who I could trust, Roman. Everything went so bad so quickly, and I had no choice. If I stayed and trusted the wrong person, I'd be dead."

"If you trusted me, you mean."

Her shrug was heavy under his hand where it rested

against her shoulder. "Not just you. I couldn't trust anyone until I knew why no one came to save me that night."

"Did you follow the case in the news?"

"In the beginning, when they were still talking about it on the television, but once it was no longer headline news, I couldn't risk checking the net."

"How did you plan to figure out who to trust then?"

She was silent for so long Roman thought she'd fallen asleep on the bench. When she spoke, she said the very last thing he expected her to say. "I waited to see if you'd find me. You know things about me that no one else in the bureau knows, so I left information behind. If you were looking, you'd know to keep following the clues. I guess it worked because here you are."

She grabbed the bottle of Jim Beam from his hand and took a swallow of it.

"Wait, what?" he asked, leaning forward to make eye contact with her. "You wanted me to find you? How did you know you could trust me?"

"I didn't," she answered without pause. "But I needed help, and I had nowhere to turn. If you found me, I was hoping that it was because you wanted to help me and not kill me."

"Mina," Roman said, but the retching of his stomach halted his words for a moment. When he recovered, he took her hand in his. "The mere idea that you thought I would kill you makes me sick. I wanted to find you because you called out to me, and I heard those cries in my sleep. I spent a year as a raving lunatic trying to find you, and every day that passed, I worried I was going to be too late. When I found a hospital that had treated a 'Rebecca Sweet', it was magic. I figured out you were combining names from our cases to use as aliases, and then I was able to get Cal to help me locate you."

"It was a risk I had to take if I wanted you to find me. My only mistake was not considering that The Madame would likely follow you. I put you in danger by leaving those clues."

"No," Roman said, lifting her chin to hold his gaze. "I knew the possibility was there, but I couldn't let it deter me from finding you. I had to protect you, but I couldn't if I didn't know where you were."

Mina lowered her head to his shoulder and stared out over the lake. "I want this to end," she whispered over the sound of the rippling waves. "I'm so tired."

"I know," he said, resting his cheek on the top of her head. "That's why we're here. To make this end for everyone."

"What did Cal say about Marlise?"

When Roman had returned to the room from meeting with Cal, Mina had been down for the count. Rather than wake her, Roman let her sleep, figuring she could get back to work when she was rested. The woman he used to know could work for days on just a few hours of sleep. The woman in his arms tonight could barely work a few hours before she needed to rest. The pain and terror of the last year had worn her down, and he was worried she'd never be the same again. Who was he kidding? Of course, she'd never be the same again. She carried physical and emotional scars of a mission gone wrong, and he was to blame for that. Touching her foot tonight drove home that he didn't deserve to call her his partner, or anything else for that matter.

"He's working out a plan to fly into St. Paul, pick her up and bring her out here. He hopes to have it accomplished by tomorrow night." He paused and shook his head. "Or rather by late tonight. It's going to be risky."

"How will he convince her to go with him? If I were Marlise, I'd be afraid of a bunch of guys Cal's size coming after me."

Roman chuckled and planted a kiss on the top of her head. That was better than planting one right on her lips like he wanted to. "Cal wants you to write her a coded letter with an image of the three of us together to prove that he knows you. The letter won't be understandable until Cal puts it through a special program to decode it once he's with her. After she reads it, the letter will cease to exist. If that doesn't work, Cal will return without her. He refuses to snatch her and take the heat for that."

"No!" Mina exclaimed, raising her head immediately. "I don't want him to snatch her. That would be traumatizing. I'll add things to the letter that only the two of us would know, so she knows it's me and not The Madame. I wish we had another option, but something inside me tells me this is the only way."

"Then we'll do it," Roman promised, rubbing her shoulder to relax her. "I'll do whatever I have to do for you to find peace, Mina."

"It's peaceful out here," she said, her hand motioning at the lake before it fell to her lap.

"Cal calls it his office."

"I can see why."

Roman gazed down at the woman in his arms, and hers flicked to his and held there. The brown in her pain-filled eyes melted away in that moment. "Not nearly as gorgeous as you are, Wilhelmina August. You send me. You always have."

"Send you where?"

"Places I shouldn't even be thinking about."

"But you are?"

He let his eyes fill with all the emotions he felt for her, and before she could object, he captured her lips with his. He kissed Min like he was a man without a home. What he meant to keep languid and light, allowing her the chance to break it off, quickly heated when she leaned into him, latching her arms behind his neck and holding on for dear life. She returned his kiss, which told him that she wanted this as much as he did. The kiss held so much pain and promise that Roman worried his heart would pound out of his chest. She tasted of Jim Beam, pain and redemption, but he wasn't convinced he deserved the last one.

He let the kiss end naturally and rested his forehead against hers while they caught their breath. She was the one to speak. "You just broke your cardinal rule, Agent Jacobs."

He traced a finger down her cheek before he buried the same hand in her hair, holding her close to him. "That rule only existed because of you, Agent August. I've wanted to kiss you for seven long years."

"Was it worth the wait?"

Roman noticed her voice was breathy and wanton, which told him his answer mattered to her. "Oh, sweet Mina. I would have waited seven more years for a kiss like we just shared."

"What if I said I didn't want you to wait?"

"Then I'd say this," he answered as his lips lowered to hers, and he kissed her to the crickets' serenade.

Chapter Eleven

Mina's mind and heart were still reeling from the kisses she shared with Roman last night. Her mind was ticking a million miles a minute with thirty-nine tabs open, and none of it made any sense to her. All she could focus on was the feel of his lips against hers. The warmth of his tongue when it pushed through the barrier to dance with hers. He'd whispered that he'd held himself at bay with an iron will for years, but that disappeared the night of the fire. It was replaced with other things. Things like fear. Desperation. Understanding. Learning how quickly something you want can be taken away.

The computer screen in front of her needed her attention, but her mind kept drifting back to Roman and how he'd held her last night. Protective was an understatement. Possessive might begin to cover the feeling. She noticed when she was in his arms the bad dreams stayed away. He kept the nightmares at bay with the length of his warm body pressed the full length of hers. How many times had she wished for the same thing over the last seven years? Too many to count. But not like this. Not on the run and as damaged as she was. Roman wanted the old Mina, but that woman no longer existed in this world.

"What the hell?" she asked the empty room, leaning in closer to the screen. Roman was helping Cal with recon on Marlise while she hacked into Liam Albrecht's office in Red Rye. "Why would he be corresponding with a senator?"

Okay, so maybe it was a senator for the state of Kansas. That would make sense. She opened another tab and typed in Senator Greg Weiss. In seconds, she knew that wasn't the case. Senator Weiss was from the great state of Maine. She read through some of the emails and shrugged.

"They could just be friends." While true, something felt off, so she flipped back to the other tab to type in the two names together just as there was a knock on the hatch.

"It's just me, Min," Roman called.

He climbed down the ladder with Cal following him. Neither of the men looked happy, and that made Mina's heart tick a little bit faster. "What?" she asked them as soon as they were standing in front of her. "Something's wrong."

Roman raised a brow at her, and Cal grinned. "I guess you win," Cal said.

"Win what?" she asked, aggravation clear in her voice.

"I told Cal you'd know something was wrong the minute you saw us. Listen, Min, there's been a problem in procuring Marlise."

"What kind of problem?" She glanced between the two men, but neither spoke. "Tell me, and don't sugar-coat it."

"She was attacked on the way back from the store outside her house yesterday. They took out her guard and went to town on her, but she fought back."

Mina's heart sank at the news. "That sounds like Marlise. She was always so quiet and meek, but you knew there was anger simmering underneath. Did they take her?"

"No," Roman said, grabbing her hand for comfort. "Her guard came around in time to get in some licks, but he didn't take either of them into custody. The two guys took off, but he couldn't risk leaving Marlise to go after them."

"Where is she now?" Mina asked through clenched teeth.

"At the hospital," Cal supplied. "They beat her up good. She's got a broken arm and nose, busted lip and a concussion, but it could have been much worse."

Mina turned to Roman and grabbed his shirt. "We need to get her out of there. The Madame's men will come for her again."

He wrapped his hand around hers. "We know."

"We have a plan," Cal promised, his voice calm and comforting. "It's still risky, but it's the only option we have now."

"What's the plan?" she asked, easing her grip on Roman's shirt. "I'll do anything to get her out of there."

"You won't have to do anything," Roman promised. "You'll wait here with Mack while Cal and I go pick her up at the hospital."

"How does that even make sense?" she asked, her gaze bouncing between them. "She's not going to go with two guys she doesn't know if I'm not there."

"You're not going," Roman said firmly. "Regardless, she knows me since I've interviewed her several times. She trusts me where you're concerned, Min. She'll believe I found you on my word alone, especially after this attack."

"Roman," she started to say, but he cut her off.

"Min. I can't lose you again. I can't," he said between clenched teeth.

Cal held his hand up to Roman. "I warned you that she wasn't going to go for this. I have a different plan if you'd like to hear it," he said, addressing Mina.

"It better involve me going to get Marlise."

"It does," Cal said with laughter as Roman glared at him with a death stare. "Safely, of course."

"There is nothing safe about your plan, Cal!"

"Safer than having your partner go rogue again to try and beat us there. Have some respect for her, Roman. She's still an FBI agent. She has every right to participate in something that could save her life, whether you like it or not."

"Where do you get off—"

Mina stepped between the two men before Roman could start an angry tirade. "Gentlemen. This isn't helping. I understand both sides here. Trust me. I get it more than you two combined, but Roman," she said, turning to him, "Cal is right. If I'm with you, we stand a better chance of the mission being successful. I can convince Marlise to come with us. I know I can."

She held Roman's gaze and saw in his eyes all the fear that he'd gone through over the last year. She hated herself for it, even though she knew it had been beyond her control. She leaned into him. "I know you're scared to lose me, but if we get Marlise, we get the answers we need to sort out this tangled web of lies."

Roman sighed and gave a slight nod of his chin. "You might be right, but I still hate it. I hate putting you at risk again. Regardless of a disguise, we can't hide the limp you have on your left foot."

"I have a solution for that," Cal said, and they both turned back to him. "If we're pulling this caper off as a medical transport, then you'll both go in as EMTs. I have access to a cast boot she can wear to hide the limp. Do you think you can walk in one of those?"

She nodded before he finished speaking. "That's what I was wearing up until six months ago. It changes my gait, so I can't run, but walking and pushing a gurney would be no problem."

"Let me get everything in place then. We're going in at a shift change, when there are fewer people to notice us. This is unsanctioned. You both know you'll lose your badges for pulling her out from under the FBI's nose, right?"

"No choice," Roman said. "I could take Mina in to get the information from Marlise, but the second we walk out that door, Marlise is dead. The Madame will find her, and her goons will kill her. Probably our agent too."

"Agreed," Cal and Mina said in unison. "Anyway, my badge isn't worth the metal it's printed on," Min added.

"I don't care about my badge," Roman said between clenched teeth. "I care about saving people's lives. I don't care what I have to give up to make that happen."

"Then I'll get the plan in place," Cal said on a nod. "To make you feel better, Roman." He stopped talking, dug in his pocket and pulled out two small black phones. He handed one to each of them. "These phones will only communicate with other phones on the circuit. The only other phones are mine and Mack's. If you get separated from the group, hit the star button twice, and you'll turn on the tracker."

"How is that going to keep me safe?" she asked, flipping the phone over twice. "That'll just lead The Madame to me."

"I can trace the phone from here, but no one else can. If you need to ditch it, snap it in half and toss it. But try not to. They're expensive." Mina laughed as he started climbing up the ladder. "Be ready in twenty. You can change clothes on the plane. Mina, I'll have a wig and makeup for you."

When he closed the hatch, Mina spun back to Roman slowly, her face a mask of neutrality. She couldn't show weakness, or he would try to convince her to stay here where she was safe. Any other time she would, but not when it was Marlise they were trying to save.

"I know," he whispered before she could say anything. "I don't like it, but I understand. She's your friend."

"She may have saved my life. She gave me enough warning to see what was coming, and if my message had gone through, none of this would be happening. I owe her the same dedication since it's the bureau's fault she's living this way."

He shook his head, but his smile was more natural when he flashed it at her. "No, Marlise is living this way because she picked sisters over misters."

"What?" Mina asked with confusion.

"She's protecting you, babe. She has been questioned by the FBI extensively, and she refuses to tell them anything. The only person she'll talk to is you."

"But she doesn't even know if I'm alive."

"Exactly. She's still willing to live with an agent tail-ing her all day, every day on the off chance you are. That means she knows her information will help you find The Madame, and you're the only person she's willing to give it to."

"That sounds like the Marlise I knew," Mina said with a smile. "Let's go get her so we can end this cat-and-mouse game with The Madame and get on with our lives."

"I couldn't agree more." Roman ducked his head and stole her lips. The kiss was gentle and languid, but Mina used it to say everything to him that her words couldn't.

MINA WAS NERVOUS. The plan was solid, but it was still a risk, and she hadn't done this kind of work for a year, much less on a foot that barely responded to her orders. Thank goodness she had the stretcher to push for balance. Hopefully, the boot fooled anyone watching. The blond wig tied up in a ponytail under her Lakeview Transport Team hat would confuse anyone who knew her, and so would the stage makeup applied to give her a scar that ran down underneath the cloth hospital mask she was wearing. Roman was wearing a disguise too, and all she could do was pray that no one asked them why they were wearing the masks.

"Remember the plan," Roman whispered. "Deviating from it is a death sentence."

She nodded and continued pushing the gurney into the hospital to ride up to the third floor, where Marlise waited. She had a new guard on her, thanks to the first guy sporting a concussion, but they had to rely on Mack to make a disturbance to draw the agent away so they could get Marlise out of there. They would have a matter of minutes to convince Marlise to go with them. All they could do was hope that Marlise would agree as soon as she saw Mina's face. The rest of the plan consisted of getting back to the ambulance, where Mack would drive them to the plane parked at a private airport. Cal planned on wheels up in an hour. That gave them enough time as long as everything went as planned.

The elevator dinged to signal they'd arrived at the third floor, and she took a deep breath, glancing at Roman for the encouragement she knew he'd give her. She wasn't disappointed. He winked and whispered, "We got this. We've been through far worse."

His words, and the memories of those times, straightened her spine as the doors slid open. Just as she pushed the gurney out, they heard shouting in a hallway across from Marlise's room. Mina grinned behind her mask as she hurriedly pushed the gurney to room 305. Roman didn't wait for permission. He threw the door open, and she pushed the gurney through before he shut it behind him.

Mina lowered her mask. "Marlise, it's me, Mina."

Her friend gasped and brought a shaking hand to her lips. "You're alive."

"Yes," Mina said, hugging her friend for no more than a second. "But I won't be for long if we don't talk. We can't do that here. Will you come with us? We have a transport ambulance waiting to take us to a plane and a safe place." She motioned at Roman. "This is my partner, Agent Jacobs."

"I know Roman," Marlise said shyly. "He never gave up on you, so I didn't either."

Tears flooded Mina's eyes, and she nodded once.

"I'm grateful that you both knew me that well. Please, come with us?"

Marlise nodded, and Roman strode over, scooping her up off the bed and onto the gurney before she finished the motion. Mina attached her IV bags to the pole on the gurney and covered her with several blankets. She had to take a steadying breath when she noticed the burn scars over the left side of her friend's body. Guilt lanced her, but she pushed it aside to get the job done.

"I'm putting the straps on just to make it look real. Once we're in the ambulance, we'll take them off," Roman explained, dragging Mina back to their present situation.

"That's okay. I might fall off without them. This arm is a problem." Marlise held up her cast, and Mina frowned before she lifted her mask back to cover her face. "We'll get you medical care once we get somewhere safe. Ready to move?"

Marlise lay back on the stretcher and closed her eyes as though she were sleeping. Mina pulled the door open and looked left and right. There was no one in the hallway. All they had to do was get to the elevators, and they'd be in the clear until the agent realized Marlise was missing.

"Come on, Mack, hold him for us," Roman chanted as they pushed the gurney down the hallway.

Without opening her eyes, Marlise said, "Turn right at the next bend. There's a patient transport elevator for moving patients in beds from the ER and OR. No one will see you waiting for it."

Mina glanced up at Roman, and he nodded, turning the stretcher down the hallway just as she caught sight of an agent walking back to Marlise's room, shaking his head. "We have seconds," she hissed as Roman hit the button. They waited for the elevator, both anxious and chanting "come on" under their breath.

"Hey! Where's the patient that was in this room?" they heard a male voice ask with urgency.

"It's almost here. Just wait it out," Roman said, grasping Mina's shoulder. They could see the elevator on the second floor.

"She was being transported," a female voice said. "I've got the paperwork right here."

"Show me," came the angry voice before they heard him speaking into the radio every agent wore when protecting a witness.

The elevator dinged, and they pushed the gurney on. As soon as the doors slid shut, Roman cussed. "They're going to block the exits now. We have no way out."

"There's always the morgue," Marlise said with her eyes still closed. "Put the sheet over my face and take me to the sublevel. Have the ambulance back up to the loading dock."

Mina nodded at Roman, and he pulled his phone from his pocket. While he filled in Mack, she leaned over and took the sheet, placing it over Marlise's face. "It won't be for long, I promise."

"I trust you, Mina," came her whisper from under the sheet.

The elevator dinged its arrival on the sublevel, and Roman slipped his gun under the gurney mattress as the doors opened. Mina knew he would shoot a threat first and ask questions later, so she prayed no one confronted them.

"Mack is pulling the ambulance up there now. We have to move before someone wonders why an ambulance is picking up a dead body," he whispered from behind his mask.

"Anyone watching the security camera would also wonder why we were running with a dead body."

"I know. Eyes on the prize. The Gruesome Twosome unites."

She bit back a snort and picked up a little speed with the gurney, hoping it looked like she was just anxious to get the body dropped off and get back to work. Of course, chances were good security had already been alerted to the missing patient, so if there were cameras down here, it would be obvious what they were doing.

They were almost to the doors of the morgue when they heard a commotion on the stairs. "Time's up!" Roman hissed, taking control of the gurney and pushing it through the doors. Mina followed, her boot thunking against the tile floor as they made a break for the bay where the coroner's van usually sat. Luckily for them, the coroner was out picking up a body.

Mack was waiting with the doors open and his butt planted firmly in the driver's seat. Roman pushed the gurney into the ambulance, followed it in and lifted Mina right off the dock and onto the bench seat in one motion. He grabbed the doors to close them while yelling, "Go!"

He got the doors secured and steadied the gurney when Mack hit the gas and squealed out of the hospital parking lot. "Your blood pumping yet?" Mack asked with a laugh as he spun them to the left. He flipped the emergency lights and siren on, hoping the cops coming at him wouldn't look twice as he went the opposite direction. They didn't, and he kept the lights and sirens going as he worked his way back to the airport over twenty miles away.

Roman lowered the gurney and made sure the wheels were secure in their moorings as Mina flicked the sheet off Marlise's face. "Piece of cake," she said, giving the scared and battered woman a wink. "We got you."

Marlise sat up when Roman loosened the straps and threw her arm around Mina. "I can't believe you're here! I've been so worried about you."

"I can say the same," Mina promised. "Listen, can you walk?"

Marlise nodded carefully but grimaced a bit with the motion. "They broke my arm and my nose, and my head hurts, but I can walk as long as you take this IV out."

Mina glanced up at the bag and made an executive decision. "I'm going to take it out now. We'll have to move quickly from the ambulance into the plane. Once we get back to the safe house, the nurse will put one back in if you need it."

Marlise rolled her eyes. "I don't need this one, but no one was listening to me. Just take it out."

Roman handed Mina the supplies, and she made fast work of getting the IV out. She was glad she'd been trained in basic medical procedures in the field. Now she needed to get this poor girl somewhere safe to talk. She tried to keep her head in the game, but seeing Marlise's face and arm kept sending her back to the night of the fire. Her friend had been badly burned, and while it had healed, the skin on her face and shoulder had finely webbed scars just like the ones covering her own foot. Marlise was injured on her watch, and shame filled her. She'd failed to do her job and—

"We're fifteen minutes out," Mack relayed, breaking into her thoughts. "Cal has the engine running."

"Who is that?" Marlise asked, her eyes wide as she took in the man driving the rig. He made Roman look small, so Mina could see why she'd be scared. "That's Mack."

"Another agent?" Marlise asked, and Mack let out a hearty guffaw from the front.

"Darling, I'm better than an agent. I'm untraceable."

Roman sat on the bench seat across from the stretcher. "Mack works for my brother, Cal. Not my brother by blood, but by life." Marlise nodded her understanding. "Cal is ex-military like me but pro-help when it comes to getting people out of sticky situations. We'll take care of you far better than the FBI did. I'm sorry for what happened yesterday."

"Hey," she said with a rueful smile, "I got some licks in." She held up her arm and turned the cast back and forth. "It's not often you break your hand and wrist punching someone in the head."

Min laughed just as Mack jerked the ambulance to the right, throwing them back against the wall.

"We got company!" he yelled, his erratic driving telling them it wasn't good company. The bullets that hit the rear of the ambulance seconds later were all the proof Mina needed.

"Get her down," Roman yelled while he fumbled for his gun under the gurney. Glock in hand, he busted out the small window in the door to return fire. Mina pulled Marlise down behind the small supply cabinet.

"Stay there! I have to help Roman!"

She pulled her gun and stayed low until Roman ran out of rounds, then she popped up and started firing, getting her first glance at the car that was after them. It was a Dodge Charger. Supercharged. It was going to be impossible for this ambulance to outrun them.

"That's not the good guys!" Mina yelled just as a bullet hit centimeters below the window on the door. She leaned back for a moment then took aim as the car came alongside them.

She saw the snap of the tire before she heard the bullet fire, and she grinned when the driver veered across the road in a fight to get control of the now three-wheeled power beast. Mack hit the gas and drew them ahead, the airport coming into view.

"Driver's-side tire is gone!" she yelled as she ducked so Roman could return fire while she reloaded.

"They didn't call you Eagle Eye August for nothing!" Roman said as he popped up with his gun and unloaded it on the car. "Looks like a bulletproof windshield, but I got a hit on it!"

Mina tag-teamed him and took aim while Roman reloaded. He'd made a spider web out of the windshield, but she had a better plan. She pulled the trigger four times before she made a hit on the front passenger tire. The car, already hard to control, became a sail as it went off the road and into the ditch.

"Go, go, go!" Mina yelled, falling to the floor as a barrage of bullets hit the back of the ambulance.

"We're going to have one shot at ditching this and getting on that plane," Mack yelled over the sound of the bullets pinging off metal. "We have to get in the air before they catch up. You know they aren't alone. If Cal's plane ends up bullet-ridden, he's going to be madder than when the Packers beat the Vikings."

Mina noticed even Marlise laughed at that one.

Roman held watch out the back window for the guys in the car. "There's another car approaching to pick those guys up! Pedal to the metal, man!" Roman yelled to Mack.

Mack's laughter filled the entire ambulance. "Dude, I hit pedal to the metal ten miles ago!"

Min noticed Roman pull away from the window, and he gently lifted her off the floor and onto the gurney. His hand grasped her chin. "Are you okay?"

"I'm fine, Roman." She took his hand down from her face. "Help Marlise."

He lifted Marlise off the floor and back onto the gurney next to her and then knelt to address them. "As soon as those doors open, you run like hell to the plane. There's no time for pleasantries. Grab a seat and buckle up. Cal will be rolling while the door is closing."

Both women nodded, and Roman popped up to check the back window. "Still clear, Mack!"

"Arrival in under one minute," he yelled back.

Mina put her arm around Marlise to steady her as the ambulance took a left at a high rate of speed. Cal's plane came into view, the door opening as Mack raced toward it, jostling them about in the metal rig like popcorn.

"We're going to keep you safe," Mina promised Marlise, but it was as much for herself as anyone. "When we stop, don't look back, just run."

Marlise's eyes were round and terrified, but she nodded just as Mack swore loudly from the front.

"Incoming!" he yelled as his windshield cracked. "Let's keep them in the front. We're going out the back!"

He slid the ambulance to the left and hit it into reverse, driving backward as the car came at them from the other side of the airport. As soon as the ambulance rocked into a hard stop, Roman threw the doors open and jumped out. He immediately lifted the women down and sent them running.

"Mack!" Roman yelled just as the front door of the ambulance flew open. Leaving it open, he used it for cover while he ran for the back of the old cargo plane.

"Go! Go! Go!" Mack hollered, a bullet whizzing past Roman's arm as he headed for the plane. He glanced back at Mack, who was motioning for him to go, so he did, helping Mina and Marlise onto the cargo door and into seats.

The first time Mina saw the plane, she was nervous. It looked like it had been shot down several times and there was no way it would stay in the air. Then she saw the interior. It was state-of-the-art. Cal said he didn't see much point in putting lipstick on this pig when it always ended up with new bullet holes anyway. One thing was for sure, this old girl could easily handle the pathetic guns The Madame's team was using against her.

Roman jumped into the copilot seat. "Go!" He was motioning for Cal to roll just as a bullet hit the front windshield.

"Where's Mack?" Cal asked, pushing the throttle forward. "These guys better get out of my way, or I'm running them over!"

"Securing the doors," Roman answered. "Ladies, buckle up! We might hit a speed bump or two."

Mina helped Marlise fasten the shoulder harness since her arm was in a cast and then did the same for herself. She took Marlise's hand and let her rest her head on her shoulder. "We got you," she promised, her gaze meeting Roman's. Her breath hitched, and she pointed at his arm. "You're bleeding, Roman."

He glanced down at his left arm and noticed the blood, and Mina was already digging through the first aid kit for a roll of gauze.

"It's just a flesh wound. I felt the bullet whiz past me, but it must have caught my sleeve."

Mina wrapped his arm up with the gauze and slapped his right hand over it. "Keep pressure on it until we land."

"Not to worry," Cal promised, pulling back on the yoke as the old bird lifted into the sky. "Selina will patch him up, and then you can play nurse for the rest of the night."

His laughter filled the plane, but Mina and Roman weren't laughing. Mina was trying not to have a coronary knowing that Roman got hurt because of her demands. He was better off without her in his life, and as much as it killed her to admit that, when this was over, she'd have to leave Roman behind for good. His kiss from last night flashed through her mind, and she forced back a whimper. That was going to be easier said than done.

Chapter Twelve

Roman was not dealing well with the events of the day. While Mina was in the shower, he paced the room, clenching and unclenching his fists. Finally, he grabbed a bottle of Jim Beam and poured himself a shot. He hit that one back and lowered the glass to the table. That was too close for comfort. His heart hadn't stopped pounding since the firefight in the ambulance. Why? He knew if The Madame's men locked onto them at the airport, it wouldn't be long before they found them here. He had no other option, though. They had to stay here to get the answers necessary to put The Madame behind bars.

Cal had assured him that his men would stop any siege on the compound, and Roman knew he should trust him, but risking Mina's life repeatedly was becoming more difficult with every passing hour. It was his lack of action that put her in danger in Red Rye, and he couldn't let her keep risking her life. Yes, she was an FBI agent, but she was injured and there was no way she could outrun an attacker on that foot. He had to make a choice, so he made it. Locating The Madame was their objective. It had been that way for twenty-six months, and he didn't want to make it twenty-seven.

Mina would find her, and then together they'd take The Madame down.

The door to the bathroom opened, and Min came out, her hair in curls around her shoulders and her face pink from the warm water. She smelled of green apples, and he wanted her in his arms. In his bed. Roman wanted her no matter what, but he couldn't be selfish and tell her that yet. She was just starting to trust him again, and he had to give her time to know she could trust him in all aspects of life.

"Hi," she said, pointing at the bandage on his arm. "How is it?"

"It's fine," he promised with a wink. "I've gotten worse injuries at the gym. If you hadn't pointed it out, I wouldn't have even noticed."

"How are Mack and Marlise?"

Mack had taken a bullet to the shoulder on his way out of the ambulance. That was one more thing Roman regretted about agreeing to the mission.

"He's been stitched up. It was a through and through, and thankfully, it didn't damage anything important. He's already back on patrol. Marlise is resting comfortably from what Selina told me."

Mina noticed the glass on the table, filled it and took a shot herself. When she finished, she grabbed a second glass and poured two more shots. "To a successful mission," she said after she handed him one.

Roman clinked glasses with her and drank the shot, but he didn't feel any pride in what they'd done. He'd barely kept them alive, and that wasn't something to brag about, in his opinion. "Hard to call that one successful."

"We got the girl," she said sharply. "That was our

only objective. Tomorrow, I'll talk with her, and with any luck, her answers will open my eyes to what I can't see right now."

She walked to the bed, and Roman noticed she was wearing the boot rather than her brace.

"Did you hurt your foot?" He knelt and opened the Velcro to check, but she stopped him.

"It's okay, Roman. The boot lets me move faster than my brace does. Right now, in our situation, I thought it wise to keep wearing it until the risks have been mitigated."

Roman grabbed the tube of gel out of the drawer and loosened the straps. He tenderly lifted her foot from the boot and removed her sock. Gently, he massaged the gel into her skin. "Does it hurt less in the boot?"

"No, but I can go longer before it steals my breath away. I know it's beyond help now, but I can't worry about what will happen to it when this is over. Right now, I have to focus on protecting Marlise."

"Cal will protect Marlise."

"I mean in the future, Roman. If I can't figure out who's behind this operation in Red Rye, all of us will be dead by Christmas."

"Don't say that." Roman spit the words out through clenched teeth. The thought of her dying on his watch was too much for him tonight. "You have the skills to locate her. It's only a matter of time until you find a thread that unravels the whole case."

"I may already have," she said as he lifted her leg onto the bed and propped a pillow under the foot, offering her some comfort for the first time all day.

Roman finished washing his hands and then joined her, sitting on the opposite bed. Sitting next to her, or worse, lying beside her, would result in consuming her from head to toe.

"Why didn't you say anything? What did you find?"

"I had just discovered it when you and Cal came down to discuss the mission. Once we got back, and Marlise was in too much pain to talk, I investigated it more. On the surface, the connection looks innocent, but I'm not sure it is."

Roman made the out-with-it motion. "What are you talking about?"

"Liam Albrecht communicates with a senator in Maine, Greg Weiss. I don't mean once or twice, either. I mean regularly."

Roman leaned in closer. "What kind of communication?"

"I hacked Liam's email account. The emails appear innocuous, but I can't be sure until I have more time to study them."

"They could just be friends."

"Could be," she agreed with a shrug, "but I can't find any connection between them. They didn't go to school together or grow up in the same area. We know that someone with power has to be making these girls' pasts disappear."

"Does a senator have that kind of pull?"

"As a senator, he would have those resources at his disposal."

"We've had eyes on Marlise for a year. We still can't find who she was before she came to Red Rye. We don't even have a last name for her."

"None of the girls in the house had a last name, Roman. Marlise refused to tell you what her name was before she hooked up with The Madame?"

"Marlise was too terrified to speak to anyone but you."

Mina rubbed her forehead and then ran her hands down her face. "I cannot tell you how relieved I was to see her today. Until the bullets started flying and terror filled my gut."

"I think I know that terror better than anyone," Roman ground out, his hands clenching and unclenching. "I was afraid I was going to lose you again when I'd just found you."

"I'm still an FBI agent, Roman." She used her partner voice to remind him, but he heard the waver of it. She wasn't convinced her words were true any more than he was.

"I know, but that doesn't mean I wasn't terrified."

"I get it. Every time you popped up to shoot, I wanted to pull you back down. I'm glad we refused Cal's request to have a team of guys following the ambulance. We barely made it back to the plane. They never would have. This is so messed up," she sighed, leaning her head back on the pillow. "I have the city manager of a tiny one-horse town intercepting my messages. I have a senator from a state halfway across the country communicating with him. I have girls who can't be identified and one who was beaten within an inch of her life yesterday. Did I miss anything?"

"You missed the *we* in there. *We* have all those things. You aren't alone in this, Mina."

"I know, Roman. I've been alone for the last year, and I forget that I'm not anymore. It's no disrespect to you or Cal. I'm just frustrated because nothing makes any sense on the surface. There has to be something I'm missing, and I pray that Marlise has that piece."

"All we can do is keep digging. We already know

someone in Red Rye City Hall blocked your message from getting to me. That means, if someone didn't use their IP address as a cover, they had access to that app."

"Which makes zero percent sense because no one had access to it except the people in the house. Me, The Miss, and probably The Madame wherever her throne sits."

"Wait, what?" Roman asked, standing up and walking over to her bed. "How much access did they have? You said the app wasn't hackable, and no one could see the information we kept in the cloud or the SOS button."

"Which is still true," she assured him quickly. "Other than those parts, which aren't even visible to them, I had to make The Miss and The Madame administrators. The app was written for them to use, so there was no way I could avoid that, which is why I coded the other parts separately. Administratively speaking, they can pause messages from going out of the app. I didn't use the SOS button with the first message. I used the regular app. I thought I would be on my way to you. I didn't expect to get jumped before I got out the door."

"Which is why the second message came through to my phone," he said slowly.

"Because I used the SOS button rather than a message."

"And you didn't do that the first time because?" he asked, his hands squeezing his knees to keep from shaking the woman in front of him.

"The SOS meant rescue with any means necessary. I was afraid if everyone came blaring in with guns, we'd take innocent lives, and the ones we wanted would get away. I didn't have a lot of time to weigh my options, Roman. I was told The Miss was out of the house, so I sent the message and planned to slip out the back door, rendezvous with you and then head back in protected by the team once I knew The Miss was there."

Roman took a deep breath and forced his anger down. She was right. She couldn't have known that plan wasn't going to work, especially if she'd been given false information. If he'd been in her shoes, he probably would have done the same thing. He couldn't fault her for wanting to save lives.

"I can see what your train of thought was now. But how would Liam stop the message if he didn't have access to the app?"

"I honestly don't know. I'm going to dig into it more tomorrow. The Miss could have used the IP address of city hall to throw suspicion on them. I may never know for sure, but with any luck, Marlise can fill in some of these blanks. I hope she's doing okay."

When they'd arrived back at Secure One an hour after they left St. Paul, Marlise was crumbling. She was due for pain medication for her arm, and the adrenaline had worn off halfway through the flight, sapping her strength. Cal had carried her straight to the nurse without a word to anyone. Roman knew his brother called the shots here, so there would be no talking to Marlise until morning.

"I checked with Cal while you were showering. She's resting after the nurse gave her some pain meds and she had something to eat and drink. The nurse said she's stable and just needs time to heal. We'll get together in the morning once you've both had a night of sleep." Roman rubbed his face, the fatigue setting in now that his adrenaline had drained away. "Time for bed. Do you need anything?" he asked, pulling the covers over her before he switched off the light.

"You," she answered, grabbing his hand before he could go back to his bed.

"Mina," he said, but she tightened her hand around his. "I'm already struggling to keep my lips off yours. Sleeping next to you is out of the question. There are things I want to do, and they aren't appropriate for where we are right now."

Her gaze hooded. "Where we are right now? Do you mean the physical place or the emotional?"

"We're safe here physically. Emotionally is another story, Min. If I take you in my arms the way I've always wanted to do…" He shook his head rather than finish.

"It's been seven years," she said, her gaze holding his. "Don't you think it's time we stop pretending that we don't want each other? That we don't care about each other as more than partners?"

Roman set his jaw and sucked air in through his nose. "Min, admitting that I care about you as more than a partner isn't the hard part. The hard part is having you for a few brief moments in time and then losing you again. I can't go back to that feeling in my chest that I carried around for a year."

"Wow, I didn't see that coming."

"See what coming?" he asked harshly. "The truth?"

"Yeah, the truth. And the truth is, you're a coward. I thought I knew just about everything there was to know about you, but I was wro—"

He reacted before he thought. He had his lips on hers and his body plastered along the length of her before she could finish. She met him with the same level of passion and desire, pulling at his lips and pressing at his groin. Her soft moan was too much for him, and he stripped her of the skimpy pajamas she wore. Her warm skin dragged a moan from his lips. He stripped his shirt off, barely breaking the kiss long enough to do so, and then was back to filling his head with the taste of her. She was everything he'd dreamed her to be and more.

"Protection," he murmured against her lips. "I don't have any."

"We're covered," she promised, running her nails up and down his back to draw a shudder from him. "Just don't stop."

"Oh, baby. I couldn't if I tried," Roman moaned, his heart filled with the beauty of her. He wanted to be everything for her at a time when she had nothing.

She lowered his boxers slowly, sending a shiver down his spine. "I've wanted you for so many years, Roman," she whispered as he held himself back from taking her fiercely and with seven years of pent-up desire.

Roman kissed his way down her tender neck to the swell of her breasts, then raised his head to gaze into her eyes while he entered her. "Oh, sweet, Mina," he sighed on a gentle thrust. "My dreams couldn't hold a candle to this. To you. To us, together."

She lifted her head until her lips met his, and her moan filled his heart with a sensation that could only be one thing. Her cries of pleasure tore away at his control until he was primed to fire. He possessed her body the same way she possessed his heart, and when she shot off into the universe on a cry of ecstasy, she cemented herself inside his soul forever.

Chapter Thirteen

They walked down a long hallway to the med bay where Marlise had spent the night. Mina was tired, but she should have expected that when she'd spent three-quarters of the night loving the man walking next to her. Her chest had never felt this light and this heavy at the same time. She wanted him, and he wanted her, but their jobs made that complicated. She knew once they were back in the real world, he'd come to his senses about being with someone like her.

Maybe he already had. When they got up this morning, he went directly to the shower and shut the door. When he came back out, he kept the door shut to his thoughts and feelings about what had happened between them. He spoke as few words as necessary to her this morning, and Mina felt the space he was trying to put between them for what it was. Fear. She understood it even if she didn't like it or feel it. They were partners, and she didn't realize how much pain her yearlong disappearance had caused him until last night when they'd made love. Could she call it that? Could you call it *love* if both people weren't feeling that emotion?

Yes.

Unrequited love was real, but to be honest, she didn't

feel it was unrequited. Roman had been as emotionally invested last night as she had been. He'd taken as much pleasure in her release as he had in his own. Whatever Roman was feeling this morning, she didn't think it was regret. It was fear reminding him of all the things that could happen to her if he let his guard down. She would have to be patient and let him reach his own conclusions about who they could be together. She already knew the answer. He'd given it to her last night when their bodies connected.

"You're quiet," Roman said as they neared the med bay.

"So are you," she responded in kind.

He stopped and grasped her shoulders, turning her to him. "My silence has nothing to do with regrets about last night."

"Mine either."

His nod was comforting, and it told her she wasn't wrong to feel this way. When he leaned down and gently kissed her, it soothed the burning in her soul. "I'm trying to separate Roman the man from Roman the agent. It's not easy, but I know it's necessary if we want to find The Madame. I can hold you when we're alone in our room, but everywhere else, I can't distract you from the objective. We have a job to finish as The Gruesome Twosome."

"No, Roman." She let out a sigh filled with the sadness that she kept buried inside her about her injury. "The Gruesome Twosome ceased to exist the moment I lost function in my foot."

He put his finger over her lips and dipped his brow. "You are still Special Agent August in my eyes. Act like it. Stop telling me you can't and step up. Do your job."

She pushed him away and grunted. "It's that easy, huh? Just forget about all the things you can't do and focus on the things you can do! Well, thank you, Dr. Phil!"

He stood there, arms crossed and his brows up in the air after she finished her tirade.

"Focus on the things you can do," Mina whispered. "Yes. Focus on the things you can do! How far is the med bay?"

Roman motioned down the hallway, and she half skipped, half jumped down the hallway to the door where Roman had to put in a code after scanning his thumbprint.

"High tech," she said with appreciation. "Cal is either incredibly paranoid or incredibly dangerous."

"Both," Roman answered as the door clicked and he pushed it open.

She walked through the door and found Marlise sitting on the bed, nursing a cup of coffee. "Hi," she said, sitting down next to her. "How did you sleep?"

"Like a rock, but I still feel a little hungover. Selina promises it's the concussion, and it'll improve."

Selina winked at them from across the room, where she sat at a desk. Mina admired the woman for working for Cal. She was a tiny little thing, barely five feet tall, but all fire. Selina wasn't afraid to stand up to anyone who wanted something not in the best interest of her patient. Mina had been comforted knowing Marlise was getting excellent care last night, even if she was frustrated that she couldn't talk to her immediately.

"I know you're recovering, so if you need to rest, just tell me, okay?"

"I'll be fine," Marlise promised. "I want to get this

over with as much as you do. I'm tired of being shadowed by guys I don't know or even particularly like. Where does the FBI find these knuckle draggers?"

Roman bit back a snort before he answered her. "You mean the highly trained FBI agents assigned to your protection detail until Mina could be found?"

Marlise rolled her eyes at Mina. "Highly trained might be a stretch. The last one didn't do so hot." She lifted her arm before she lowered it to her lap again. "I shouldn't say too much. He did manage to save me before the guys finished me off. It would have been fitting if they had, I suppose. Considering my life so far, no one would miss me."

"This doesn't have to be the end of your story, Marlise," Mina said with compassion. "When we were living in Red Rye, we talked about what you thought your future looked like, but that all changed when you escaped The Madame's hooks."

"Have I, though?" she asked, her gaze on her arm. "From where I'm sitting, I would say she still has them firmly buried in me."

"That's fair," Mina agreed. "Let's find a way to stop The Madame together, so we can both have our lives back."

"Okay," Marlise said, finishing her coffee. "Where do we start?"

Mina grabbed her writing pad and pen. "The night of the fire. Or rather the day of the fire. All I remember is you telling me to run because they knew who I was. You called me by my real name. How did you learn I was an agent?"

"I overheard The Miss on the phone. She didn't know I was outside the door, but what I heard her say froze me in my tracks. She said we'd been infiltrated. Then she said one of the guards saw Junior Miss— and I knew that's what your nickname was in the house—with a guy the night before. They somehow figured out you were a special agent."

The guards were women in the house who accompanied the new girls on their first dates. Under the illusion they were being protected from violence, the truth was something else entirely. The guards were there to make sure they didn't steal from The Madame. Mina didn't have proof, but she suspected any girls who stole from The Madame would end up dead in a river. The house in Red Rye had been new enough that girls weren't turning over, but Mina suspected it would have only been a matter of time had it stayed open.

Mina glanced back at Roman, who was grimacing. "Hey," she said, grabbing his wrist. "We met once a week for months. If a guard followed me, it was because The Miss already suspected I wasn't who I said I was. This isn't your fault." She waited for his head nod before she turned back to Marlise.

"What happened next?"

"I went to the kitchen so I didn't get caught by one of the guards. I hoped you'd be back soon, so I could warn you. I didn't know they'd act so quickly to get rid of you."

"That's okay," Mina said, gently rubbing the girl's back. "You're doing great. Don't focus on what happened that night. Focus on the whole picture. You told me something a few days before the fire, which was why I had to meet with Roman. I can't remember what it was."

"You didn't tell Roman?" she asked with surprise.

"No," Roman said, his arms crossed over his chest. "She just said she was working on something and would know soon. She said she had to protect you. That's why the FBI questioned you so extensively."

Marlise glanced down at her lap, and for the first time, Mina noticed the shame she wore like a cloak. "I didn't want to talk to those men."

Mina glanced up at Roman while rubbing Marlise's back. He gave her a pained grimace, and she nodded her agreement. "I understand," she assured the woman. "I remember how scared you were in the Red Rye house. You were always afraid the next guy you had to go out with would be the one to hurt you."

Her head still hung when she spoke. "That's why I ingratiated myself as the cook. I was more valuable to them cleaning and running the kitchen than I was working jobs. Men, they didn't want me. They said I was too skinny, shy and dumb."

Anger filled Mina, but she kept her hand on Marlise's back. "Those men were wrong. You were the sharpest girl in that house. You saw everything, processed it all quickly and learned how to protect yourself. Don't ever let those scumbags make you feel bad about yourself. They couldn't land a girl like you if they tried, and that was the reason they had to pay for dates."

Marlise lifted her head and shook it. "I don't think so," she whispered. "The other girls told me there wasn't much dating going on. They were picked up, taken to dinner, occasional sexual favors were performed, and then money was exchanged. The money came back to The Miss, and the girls didn't get their cut for weeks."

Mina turned to Roman and lifted a brow. His expression told her he understood what was going on too.

"When I booked the dates, I had the fee schedule. The law was such that they could not pay for sex. They were only paying for companionship or a date to a wedding or event."

Marlise nearly sucked her tongue down her throat trying not to laugh. "Sure, and if you believe that, I've got a bridge to sell you in Brooklyn."

"You're saying there was prostitution going on?" Mina asked. "None of the girls ever indicated that in the entire year I was there. I dug hard for the information too, but none of them would admit it."

"They knew better. If the girls slept with the men, they got a bonus from The Miss, but it could never be discussed. There were a few who did before you took the job, and they mysteriously disappeared."

Mina's heart pounded in her chest with that information. Girls had disappeared from the house in Red Rye before she'd arrived. If they could somehow tie any of the victims from the river drownings back to the house in Red Rye, they could put The Miss and The Madame away for life. They just needed the evidence. Unfortunately, it wasn't as if Mina could just roll into the FBI files and get the pictures of the girls they'd found in the river. She would have to let her team find the link once they had The Madame in custody. Her team. She had to stop saying that. She wouldn't be part of the team once they made it back to Minneapolis. Capturing The Madame would have to be the final feather in the cap of her FBI career.

"Did you ever sleep with any of these men, Marlise?"

"No!" she exclaimed, jumping backward and nearly falling to the floor. She was caught by strong, tatted arms and set back on the bed.

Mina was surprised to see Cal in the room. She was concentrating on Marlise and hadn't noticed him come in. That spoke volumes about his ability to be a ghost. Cal knelt in front of Marlise and murmured to her. He encouraged her to take deep breaths while Mina got up and walked over to stand beside Roman, shoulder to shoulder.

"I'm not surprised by the prostitution aspect," he whispered. "It was a given that it was going on."

"I suspected but couldn't prove it. It was a high-end call girl service that brought in big bucks. I wasn't in charge of the money, though. The Miss had control of that. You and I talked about how much money I could see coming into the house throughout the investigation. I wonder how much came in that I didn't know about."

"If I had to guess, I'd say millions. We may be dealing with an escort service to cover a money-laundering operation."

"Bring it in, clean it and send it back out. We need the who and the why."

Roman motioned at Marlise with his chin. "See if she knows anything else."

Mina sat beside Marlise again, and Cal moved off to the side, but Mina raised a brow at his protective stance over the tiny woman. She would have to ask Roman about that later. "Marlise, when you went on dates, did the men give you exactly how much the fee schedule said they owed?"

"Oh, no," she said, shaking her head. "They just gave you a bundle of money and sent you on your way. At least they did with me. When I went on a date, they didn't even want to finish dinner. They just gave me the money and told me to go home. They said their plans had changed."

"And you brought the money back to The Miss. Did you count it first?"

Marlise shrugged. "I didn't need to count it. It was always in straps of one-hundred-dollar bills. Sometimes I got one strap. Sometimes there were more. It was never more than I could carry in my purse, though."

"A strap of hundreds is ten grand. That's far more than the agreed upon fee." From what Marlise was telling her, it sounded like money laundering at its finest. The next question might be tricky for Marlise to answer, but she asked it anyway. "Did the men ever give you or the other girls anything else?"

She shrugged but didn't answer. She just stared at the floor with her hair down over her face. Cal knelt again and tipped her chin up to meet his gaze. "We can't help you if we can't find these guys, Marlise. If you tell us everything you know, we'll make them pay."

Marlise sat holding Cal's gaze for a long time. Longer than Mina was comfortable with, but Cal didn't back down. He helped her find the place she needed to be in before she answered.

"The girls," she said, still staring at Cal, "sometimes they brought back drugs." Her words were whispered as though she were afraid they would hear her. "I know they were drugs because where I used to live there were a lot of them."

"Do you know what kind of drugs and how much?" Mina asked, finally pulling Marlise's attention away from Cal.

"They didn't play with the small stuff. It was hard drugs, and I worried most of it was laced. The drugs went to The Miss, too, but we weren't supposed to know about it. Only certain girls went on those dates."

"Ha!" Mina suddenly exclaimed. "That explains why Charlotte, Emilia and Bethany were so busy."

Marlise nodded her head in agreement. "They were the only ones who went on those dates," she said, putting dates in quotation marks. "I'm not supposed to know about the drugs." The tone of her voice went so low they all had to lean in to hear her. "I overheard Charlotte talking to The Miss once while I was cleaning. After I learned that, I started paying attention to when they went out on their dates." Her eyes shifted around the room before they settled on her arm. "I documented it, and I was going to give you the information, but everything happened so fast I couldn't. Then they trapped me in the house with the fire. I tried to get out of the house, but that's the last thing I remember before I woke up in the hospital."

A shiver ran through her, and Cal lowered his hand to her shoulder. "Don't think about the fire. Remember what we talked about before—tunnel vision. The Miss is at the end of the tunnel. That's what you concentrate on."

Marlise sucked in a deep breath and then let it back out. "They used the dresses."

"The dresses?" Roman asked.

Mina turned to him. "Those three girls always took a change of outfit on their dates. I was booking them for large functions and events, often in a different state. They took a bag and a second dress with them."

"They sewed pockets inside the lining of the dress," Marlise said. "No one would suspect the dresses."

"Do you know who The Madame is? Or, for that

matter, who The Miss is?" Roman asked the woman, who was looking paler with every passing minute. "The FBI could not find her anywhere in a database. None of the girls in the house were ever found in the system, including you. It was like you were just sent here as a fully grown adult."

"They were all like me," she whispered. "When they bought me, they changed my name. I think the same thing happened to the other girls."

"Bought you?" Roman asked, taking a step forward, but backing off when Mina held her hand out to him.

"Marlise, are you saying that The Madame forced you to come work for her?"

The young woman nodded her head but then shook it, leaving her confusion evident in the room. Cal still had his hand on her shoulder and knelt before offering her a smile. "You can do this, and as soon as you're done answering their questions, you can rest."

"My real name is Mary, but they changed it to Marlise and made me learn an entirely new history about myself. When I was twenty, I was homeless and living on the street in Phoenix. They looked for women like me, but they never took more than one girl from each city. They pretended to like you. They got to know you. They brought you gifts and paid for hotel rooms. I didn't know that's what they wanted until it was too late, I swear!" she exclaimed, her body quaking with fear. "Please don't arrest me!"

"Shh," Mina whispered, taking Marlise's uninjured hand. "You aren't in trouble. What happened to you is called grooming. The Madame wanted to gain your trust so you'd believe her when she said you would have a better life if you went with her. Is that what they told you?"

Marlise nodded, wiping away a tear with her shoulder. "I believed them at first."

"Who was them?" Roman asked. "The Miss?"

"No, I didn't meet The Miss until we got to the house. There were two women, and they said they worked for an agency. I was dumb. I believed them."

"No," Cal said, his hand firmly on Marlise's back. "You weren't dumb. You were in a situation you wanted out of, and you saw a way to do that. You didn't know they were trying to deceive you."

"That's true," Marlise said on a sigh. "I just knew I didn't want to spend another winter on the streets. I'm going to end up right back out there when this is over, though. I was only working at the women's home because the FBI put me there. I don't know what I'm going to do."

Marlise broke down into racking sobs, and no matter how much comfort Mina or Cal offered, she was inconsolable. Selina came over and gave her an injection, settling her back onto the bed and pushing everyone else away. Mina stood next to Roman with her thoughts spinning out of control. She had to remember what happened, or they were all going to die.

Chapter Fourteen

Mina's fingers moved across the keyboard with frightening accuracy. Her eyes trailed the information on the screen but never looked down at her fingers. Roman was jealous. He could barely hunt and peck his way through a case report. Mina, on the other hand, had magic fingers...in more ways than one. She was one of the best they had in the bureau for coding and hacking. But those hands in bed last night were magic, and Roman wished they were back there. She found his thread and started to unravel it bit by bit until he lost control of himself. He was praying they would do it all over again tonight. Looking at her now, though, he doubted that would happen. That was okay. They had a case to concentrate on, a woman to arrest and their decisions to defend before they could think about their personal lives.

Since they'd left Marlise to rest, watched over by Selina and Cal, Mina had been at the computer while Roman twiddled his thumbs. Okay, so he was doing something. He was running the information through on a different computer whenever she called something out to him.

"I wish I had access to the bureau's files right now,"

Roman grunted. Trying to use Cal's software to run names wasn't nearly as effective as using the FBI's programs.

"The bureau's programs couldn't find who those girls were either, Roman, but there has to be a trace somewhere of who they were."

"Not necessarily. It depends on who The Madame reveals herself to be. If this person has connections, they might be able to wash away any evidence that a person existed."

"Which is why Senator Greg Weiss is my next target."

Roman tipped his head back and forth. "That's a stretch, Mina. We can't find any connection to Liam and Greg other than those emails. Not to mention, Red Rye is Nowhere, USA."

"Exactly," she agreed. "Hiding in plain sight or, in this case, small-town utopia. Red Rye is within driving distance of Denver, Kansas City, Oklahoma City, Albuquerque and, hell, Texas as a whole. I know this because I booked the three girls who worked the big events in all those cities. They're running the drugs out of the cities and using the girls in Red Rye to clean the money and redistribute the drugs. We didn't have that many girls in our house, but if there were the same number of girls in other houses, the money would add up quickly."

"Only Marlise was in the Red Rye house when we got there the night of the fire. Since then, we haven't found a trace of any of the other girls. They didn't fly out using the names from the Red Rye house."

"They didn't have to!" Mina exclaimed, taking Roman by surprise. "They had a private plane they used to transport the girls for events in cities too far away to drive."

"Marlise didn't tell us that when we asked her."

"She wouldn't have necessarily known, and even if she knew, she wouldn't know what airfield they used. I only knew because I had to call the pilot and set up the flights each time. Here," she said, brushing him aside. She started typing on his keyboard, her bottom in his face, and he grabbed her hips, a moan filling the room at the thought of how easy it would be to take her right there the way he wanted to. "Down, boy," she scolded, glancing behind her with a cheeky grin. "We're working."

"All work and no play makes Mina a very boring girl."

She snorted to hold in her laughter, but Roman felt it in the shake of her hips. "Look," she stood and motioned to the screen. "This is the airfield where they kept the plane. We need to find the flight plan and see where they went."

"Do you think The Miss was dumb enough to use the private plane you knew about to get them out of there? Much less file a flight plan?"

"The Miss thought I was burning alive in that fire, but she underestimated Roman Jacobs, and that was her mistake."

Roman stood and pulled her into him, his lips landing on her warm ones and teasing them into a tangle of tongues neither of them would soon forget. "She better hope I never get my hands on her," he whispered with his lips barely off hers.

"Let's find her, and then I'll give you three minutes in an interrogation room with a faulty CCTV."

Roman grinned and kissed her again. "What do you think this is, television? No way that trick would work anymore. Besides, I'd never hit a woman."

He felt the grin on her lips as she kissed him one last time and stepped back.

"You're right, though. The Miss probably didn't file a flight plan. I would suggest we hack the airport's security cameras, but it's been over a year. There's no way they still have footage." She ran her hands through her hair. "I just want to go home."

Roman wanted to take Mina to his home and never let her leave. First, they had to put this case to bed, but they were no closer now than a year ago. "The FBI has run continual facial recognition on every major airport in the country looking for her, but I've known that was futile. If she did fly into a major city, she'd wear a disguise."

"I wish I knew if they took the plane that night. There is no way to know, though."

"What about the pilot? You said you had contact with him."

"I did," she confirmed, her hands flying over the keyboard again, "but I only had his first name. Probably not his real one either, so that's a dead end too."

She fell silent for ten minutes as she typed away, all her attention back on the screen in front of her. Roman was going through flight plans over the last year on the off chance he'd get lucky when the clacking stopped, and she leaned forward.

"Roman," she said, a tremor in her voice. "Do city managers have campaign funds?"

"Usually, a city manager is appointed by the mayor. Only the mayor would need a campaign fund. Why?"

She pointed at the screen. "I finally got into Liam Albrecht's bank statements. For two years, he was making large cash donations to a campaign fund."

"How large?" Roman asked, walking over to stand behind her as she pointed at the screen.

"Between eight and nine grand every week, but never more than nine grand."

"Ahh, yes. Money laundering at its finest," Roman said, his hands on his hips. "Was the campaign fund his?"

"I haven't gotten that far," she said, putting her hands back on the keyboard. "But there's no way a city manager can afford to donate almost forty thousand dollars a month to someone's campaign. That doesn't make sense."

"It does if he's The Madame," Roman said slowly.

Mina spun toward him. "No way. We pulled three times that much money into the house on a bad day, Roman. Just in cash. That's not including the drugs."

"Has to be a cartel. The fund was probably just a front for a cartel. A way to wash the money a few times before it got back to them."

"Could be," she agreed. "The deposits stopped the same week the house in Red Rye burned."

"Convenient," Roman said with his brow in the air. "Can you see if that account is closed?"

Roman knelt next to Mina, patiently waiting while she typed away as if her life depended on it. Then again, it did. If she didn't find The Madame, she'd always be a target. He knew his Mina, though. She'd already found a thread, and she was starting to unravel it.

In ten minutes, she hit the keyboard a final time and waited while information filled the screen. "Look, the account was closed, and the money was transferred to two separate accounts, both of which are campaign fund accounts."

"Which means they know they can't use offshore banking anymore."

She nodded. "At least not for very long. The new regulations require banks to report every quarter, and that's going to send up a red flag if large amounts of cash are dumped in and then pulled out every few months."

Roman paced the small space as she went back to typing. He was waiting for answers, and there was little he could do other than be the muscle for her at this point. She held the power in her hands to solve this case, not him.

"Well, well," she said somewhat sarcastically, and Roman was next to her in an instant. "Looks like The Madame found a new home." She pointed to the screen with an account number and almost a year's worth of the same kind of deposits. "This account belongs to..." she typed some more until she tipped her head to the side. "The mayor of Santa Macko."

"Where the hell is that?" Roman asked over her shoulder.

"Near the border of California and Arizona."

"Well, a mayor would need a campaign fund."

"Do me a favor," she said, but Roman could hear she was distracted and trying to work the problem. "Run Santa Macko through Cal's program. Get me population and how long the mayor has been there."

Roman went to his desk and sat down, entering the terms into the computer. She was already back to typing while he waited for the information to come up on his screen. When it did, he was more than a little surprised. "The population of Santa Macko is under two thousand people. The mayor was elected in an uncontested election two years ago. Benjamin Bartos. He's forty-three and moved to Santa Macko three years ago."

"Just in time to get his residency in place for the mayor's race."

"You think he's a plant?"

"I don't think a mayor who ran uncontested needs a campaign fund of half a million dollars."

She rubbed her hands over her face and sighed. "This whole thing is weird. The Madame's business is still active since they're depositing money, but it was easy to follow the money from Liam to Benjamin, which is also weird. I will have to hack into the housing records for Santa Macko and look at purchase or rental dates for all the properties in the area. It'll be the only way to know if The Madame set up shop to start laundering again."

Roman stood and walked to her, gently rubbing her shoulders. "Not tonight, though."

"Yes, Roman, I can't stop now. We're too close to The Madame to quit."

"Maybe," he insisted, turning her to him. "But even if we are, you're too exhausted. You'll need patience for that much hacking, and that means you need food and sleep first."

"Every day we wait is a day The Madame could slip away," she insisted, her shoulders stiff.

"Min, you know I'm right. There comes the point where your body needs rest. We've reached that point."

This time her shoulders slumped under his hands, and he knew he'd won this argument. At least for the time being. She stood and wrapped her arms around his waist, resting her head on his chest.

"I want this to be over for you and Marlise."

"And I want this to be over for you," Roman whispered, rubbing her back. "You didn't ask for this when you went undercover. You deserve to live your life."

"I kind of did, though," she muttered, and Roman could hear the fatigue of the last year in her words. "I agreed to the undercover operation knowing I was putting myself at risk. I was willing to take that risk to myself to save the girls at the house. All I did was make things worse. Marlise will never be the same, and the other girls are still with The Madame."

"The girls who are still with The Madame are there because they want to be. That's not on you."

"The Madame could still go after Marlise as a pawn."

"She could," Roman agreed, "but right now, the only person she wants is you."

Mina gasped and leaned back. "Then let's give her what she wants!"

Roman cocked his head. "What?"

"Think about it, Roman," Mina said, starting to pace but thinking better of it and resting her butt on the desk. "We know she wants me, so we should give her what she wants."

"No," Roman said as soon as he understood what she meant. "You are not going to be bait for a psychopath. Forget it. You can barely walk, much less protect yourself."

Her temper flared, and she stuck her finger in his chest. "I am not unable to protect myself. I managed for the last year, thank you very much! I don't need a man to push me behind his back and protect me!"

Roman smiled. There was the Min he used to know. She was still hiding in there, waiting to come out. Regardless, she wasn't going to be bait. "Forget it. I just found you. There is no way I'm going to agree to this."

"We may not have any other choice, Roman," she said. The dejection in her tone had him slinging his arm around her shoulder as they walked to the ladder.

"Maybe not, but right now, we still have options. If we don't get anywhere with those in the next few days, we can revisit the idea."

He helped her climb the ladder to their room and closed the door behind them. "For now, you need some downtime so you can look at things with a fresh perspective again."

Roman waited for her to balk and try to convince him to keep working, so he was surprised when she agreed. "You're right. I need a shower, food and medication. My foot is better in this boot, but it's on fire after being down so long."

"Can you shower alone, or do you need help?" Roman asked, grasping her arm to keep her upright.

She raised a brow and took a long perusal of his body. "Oh, I most definitely need help," she said, throwing him a wicked grin. She hooked her finger under his chin, turned and walked to the bathroom, Roman following right behind her just like he always would.

"WE SHOULDN'T BE *meeting like this out in the open,"* Roman said, glancing around the woods they were standing in.

"We're not in the open," Mina said. "I had to see you. Listen, I don't have long, but something big is going down tomorrow at the house."

"What?" Roman asked, locked into the conversation now.

"I don't know for sure, but it may be that The Madame is finally going to show her face at the house."

"Not likely."

"Okay, maybe not her real face, but the vibe I got was a VIP will arrive at ten p.m. tomorrow. If it is The Madame, I'll somehow figure out a way to get prints."

"How do you know someone is coming in?" Roman asked while his trained eye flicked about the trees looking for threats.

"I overheard The Miss telling some of the guards to be ready for a personal car to arrive at ten p.m."

"Is there any way you can get the information sooner rather than later?"

"I don't see how since I'm not supposed to know. I do know this person is bringing three new girls for the house."

Roman's brow went up. "Did you lose girls?"

"Nope, but we have empty bedrooms, and they want them filled. More girls equal more money. Plus, Marlise isn't going out anymore. She's taken on the role of cook and housekeeper."

"I'm surprised The Miss allows that."

"Let's just say that Marlise is never requested a second time by any man. She's too meek and shy. Since she's willing to do the cooking, shopping and cleaning, The Miss sees it as a win. They don't have to bring anyone in from the outside, and it keeps Marlise from leaving the house to give away any secrets."

"I don't think she'd get very far if she tried," Roman muttered.

"She wouldn't make it to the county line before she disappeared. She knows it too. These girls are nobodies, and that's the way The Madame likes it. She can dangle carrots she knows they'll take just to stay alive."

"We need to get this woman, Mina. For all the girls in this house and any other ones. Have you made any progress on the locations of other homes?"

"Yes," she whispered, glancing around the darkening woods. "I know for sure there's one in Seattle, Billings, Atlanta, Dallas, Miami, Chicago, Philadelphia and Washington D.C. Those are just the ones I'm sure about."

"Do you have exact locations?"

"No, if I did, we'd already be out of this one-horse town. I let the powers that be know to look for houses in those cities, but you know that'll take a significant amount of time and manpower. We need to be patient until I can get more information to zero in on the addresses."

"Right, patience. I'm running low after a year of this back and forth. Also, why would they have houses in all those cities and stick one right in the middle of nowhere? That doesn't make sense."

"I know, I was thinking the same thing. If I had to guess, I would say it's because Red Rye is centrally located to the bigger cities. All I know is, they trust me now, and I'm hoping that's why I've been invited to be there. Be ready tomorrow night, Roman. Something big could go down, and I want the team in place. If we're lucky, we get The Madame tomorrow night, but if things go south, I'm going to need backup, and I'm going to need it fast."

"Get back to the house. I'll rally the team and be ready when you say the word."

Mina nodded and turned to go, but Roman grabbed her shirt and hauled her into him. "Promise you'll say the word before it's too late, Min."

"I promise," she whispered, her gaze locked with her partner's. If only he didn't have that cardinal rule, she'd lay her lips on his right that second. She wanted to, but she couldn't handle the sting of his rejection tonight and stay on her game with The Miss when she got back to the house.

"I won't lose you to them, Min. Do not play. If anything feels off, pull the rip cord. We have enough to shut them down already."

"We need The Madame, or at the very least, her real name. You got my back, Jacobs?"

"Just like I always do, and your front and sides," he promised. "Get this woman so we can go home. I'm tired of Nowhere, USA."

"You and me both, but I can't abandon these girls, Roman. They have no idea how much they're being used. They're trading their bodies for the stability they've never had. That's not fair. I won't walk away from them."

He pulled her into a quick hug before releasing her. "I know. That's what I love about you, Min. You never give up on the underdog. Get back to the house now. I'll get the team in place."

Mina woke with a start. *"That's what I love about you, Min."* How many times had the memory of that sentence gotten her through the long nights over the past year? Too many to count. He didn't even mean it in the true sense of the word, but it made her feel less alone to remember that there was a time when she had someone covering her back.

She flipped around and gazed at the man who was wrapped tightly against her while he slept. The lines of worry and fatigue were replaced with the abandonment of sleep. He was relaxed, and she loved the look on him. She rarely got to see Roman Jacobs relaxed, not only now but throughout their career. He took their job seriously, and he often took the job home with him. Some of that was her fault, but a lot of it was just who he was as a person. He didn't like doing a job halfway. It was all the way, or it was no way. That was the reason he hung in with her so long in Red Rye. He understood she couldn't leave those girls to the mercy of The Madame. She knew they weren't there against their will, but she quickly learned that they were willing to give up their autonomy to stay in the house and work for The Miss.

Mina could never understand why until she talked to Marlise. For most of those girls, the house in Red Rye represented something they'd never had before in their lives, even if that meant giving yourself to men you didn't know. Marlise was smart. Early on, she figured out those men didn't like shy, quiet girls who stumbled over their words and didn't make eye contact. She used her natural personality to her advantage. She found a way to stay in the house and keep the stability it offered, but managed to make herself invisible while doing it.

Mina slipped out of bed and strapped the boot on, limping to the hatch door and lifting it quietly. For the last year, all she remembered was the one sentence of that memory. Tonight, she had the whole picture. All she had to do was find one other house on the string, and she'd be able to break the code of The Madame's game. She'd work while Roman slept, and with any luck, by the time he woke up, she'd have the name for the face in her nightmares.

Chapter Fifteen

Mina cursed the pain in her foot for the ten millionth time as she stretched it out to the side of the computer desk. When she got out of this mess, she was going to have to see a doctor. Something told her what they had to say would not be positive. Mina knew there was no saving the foot, but she forced the thoughts of it from her mind and went back to searching for a connection between Red Rye and Santa Macko.

She hadn't said anything to Roman, but she was about seventy percent sure that Liam Albrecht and Benjamin Bartos knew each other. She also suspected that, somehow, they were both tied to Greg Weiss. Nothing else made sense. Not to mention, if someone at the city manager's office were on the payroll, they'd be more willing to convince the authorities not to ask too many questions about what went on at 798 South Hampton Road in Red Rye. That address was burned into Mina's mind forever. She hated that everything went sideways before she could shut down the whole operation. Those girls were still suffering because she couldn't get the job done. Mina didn't care about herself anymore, but she wasn't going to let girls like Marlise suffer any longer.

One glance at the clock told her two hours had passed

since she'd started working. She was waiting for one more search to finish, and then she'd have to give it up for the night. It was nearly two o'clock, and if she didn't get more sleep, Roman would be after her tomorrow about resting.

Her screen froze, and she snapped her attention back to it, waiting to see if it was a glitch or a home run. A picture popped up on the screen that made her heart pound the way it always did when she got a pertinent piece of information on a case. This was a home run.

She needed to show this picture to Marlise, but there was no way to print anything. She couldn't leave it on the screen because she wasn't sure how long it would be before the search timed out. She was about to call Roman when the thought stopped her in her tracks. Call. She still had the phone Cal had given her when they went to get Marlise. She couldn't do much with it, but it did have a camera.

She pulled open every desk drawer until she found the phone. When she snapped it open, she was relieved to see it was still over half charged. She did her best to take a good picture of the computer screen and then tucked the phone in her pocket. She left the picture up on the screen in hopes it wouldn't disappear before she got back, but if it did, at least she had the image on the phone.

Once up the ladder, she closed the hatch quietly and walked to the bed. "Roman, are you awake?"

He grumbled in his sleep, but his eyes never opened. Mina needed to see Marlise now, even if that meant waking her up. If Mina was right, they'd found their thread, and she could finally unravel the mystery of The Madame and her game.

"Roman," she said, shaking his foot, but he snored on, his body relaxed in sleep. The shower they'd shared had probably added to his relaxation, she thought with a smirk. She had to give it to him. He wasn't afraid to love her now.

That's not what this is, Mina, she scolded herself. This is forced proximity mixed with fear. As soon as they were back in Minneapolis, there was no way he'd continue to sleep with her. Not once she addressed the situation with her foot. A man like Roman Jacobs would not start a relationship with a washed-up FBI agent who couldn't walk.

She sighed as she watched him sleep. The truth was painful, but it was the truth all the same. Regardless of what they had to do to her foot, she would no longer be an FBI agent, which meant they would no longer be partners. They both knew it.

The truth was, she didn't want to go back to the bureau. Her stint at Red Rye had taken a toll, and her undercover days were over. Her days of chasing suspects and bringing in the top-ten most-wanted criminals were also behind her. What wasn't behind her was The Madame, and she would see this one to the very end if it killed her. And it might. She would accept that if it meant she saved the other girls in the process.

She grabbed a sheet of paper off the counter and wrote a note before leaving it on the table and sneaking out the door of the room.

Chapter Sixteen

"Everything all right, special agent?" asked the guard, who stood to his full height with his hand on his radio.

"Yes, it's fine," Mina assured him. "I need to talk to Marlise. Will you walk me to the guest cottage she's in?"

"It's almost three a.m., ma'am," he said with his head cocked.

"I'm aware, and if you call me *ma'am* again, Eric, I'm going to show you how an FBI agent takes down a mercenary."

He stifled a snort but couldn't hide the grin. There was no way she was taking down his nearly three hundred pounds of muscle, but he didn't argue with her, which she appreciated. He pressed the button on his radio and spoke into it.

"Agent August is requesting a moment with the patient."

Mack's voice was loud and clear when it came across the radio. "Tell Agent August it can wait until morning. The patient is asleep, and Cal doesn't want her disturbed."

Mina raised her brow. Cal doesn't want her disturbed? Now he was calling the shots instead of Selina? She nodded for Eric to press the button again, only this time, she stepped up. "Consider her told and consider her not to care. Wake her up. We'll be there in ten minutes."

Eric released the button, and Mack responded with a heavy sigh and a ten-four. He knew he would get chewed out by Cal in the morning, but he'd do what she said anyway. After all, she was still the FBI.

Eric walked with her through the lodge and across the rutted grass, keeping his hand under her elbow to ensure she didn't fall. She seriously regretted not bringing the cane with her that was leaning up against the wall in their room. Cal had moved Marlise to the cabin at the back of the property to give her a view of the lake while she recovered, and although that was great for Marlise, it was destruction on Mina's sore foot.

"I'll wait outside with Mack," Eric said as they neared the small, one-bedroom cabin.

She noticed a light burning inside, which meant Mack had done what she'd asked and woken up Marlise.

"When you're done, I'll walk you back. Does Roman know where you are?"

"I left him a note," she explained. "He was sleeping, but this couldn't wait. If Marlise can verify my evidence, then I am one step closer to finding the person behind this."

"Be careful," Eric warned her, helping her up the steps to the cabin. "Those guys meant business the other day at the airport."

"They've meant business since I first ran into them in the house in Red Rye. They mangled my foot beyond repair for funsies, their word not mine, and then tried to kill me by leaving me to die of smoke inhalation. When that didn't work, they came after me in the woods like ninjas in the night. They probably would have succeeded that time if it hadn't been for Roman. Hey, Mack," she said, sliding the greeting in nonchalantly as though they'd been talking about the weather rather than the many ways she could have died in the last few years. "I'm sorry to bother Marlise, but this is important."

"Too important to wait until morning?"

"Technically, it is morning." Mina winked, and Mack groaned while he held the door open for her.

"Don't stay long. She's exhausted, and I'm already going to get my butt chewed out for allowing this."

"I'll take the heat, but this won't take long."

He closed the door behind her, and Mina walked to the bedroom. When she stuck her head inside the door, she wasn't surprised to see the young woman wide awake and sitting up in bed.

"Hey, Marlise. Sorry to wake you up."

"It's no problem. I wasn't asleep. I don't sleep well anyway, but my arm is sore. Selina is going to give me some medicine once we're done talking. Maybe then I can get some rest."

"I'm sorry you're still in pain, Marlise. That's on me. I'll carry that forever."

"Nonsense," she said with a shake of her head. "I was with The Madame long before you showed up. I sold my soul for a chance at a better life, and the soul reapers came calling. I won this time. That doesn't mean I'll win the next time. I'll help you any way I can."

"No," Mina said, gently hugging her friend. "You

didn't sell your soul. You trusted people because you wanted out of a bad situation."

"Only to put myself in a worse one."

"But you didn't know that at the time. There was no way for you to leave once you were there, either. You know that, right?" Marlise nodded, but her gaze fell to the cast on her arm. Mina tipped her chin back up. "I know you don't believe me, and I wish I could have told you this when we lived at the house together, but let me say it now. You were the smartest one in the house. You played the game better than any of them because you learned how to protect yourself. You used your natural talents against them."

"You mean being shy and afraid of my shadow?" Her laughter held no mirth, and Mina squeezed her hand.

"Yes. If I hadn't had you there at the house with me watching my back, I'd be dead. You were so good at not being noticed that you blended in, and that earned you information I would never have gotten."

"I didn't do that on purpose," she said quickly, as though what she had done was wrong.

"I know you didn't, Marlise. I just meant that without even knowing it, you kept me alive. I need your help one more time, and then I can help you in return."

"I'll do anything," she promised, shifting in the bed. She appeared uncomfortable, and Mina wanted to get the information so she could rest.

"You were at the house about three months before I got there, correct?"

Her head shook instantly. "No, I was the first girl The Miss brought to the house, so it was closer to six months before you arrived. I guess she thought she saw something in me that wasn't there when push came to shove."

"What do you mean?"

"She couldn't shine me up like the other girls. I wasn't good at being confident and strutting around on heels. Forget about makeup."

"You're saying they worked with you at the house before they started the escort service?"

"Of course. The recruiters told us we were going to a home where we'd learn to be self-sufficient, take care of ourselves and get a job. I believed them, too. I was desperate to find a home. I was attacked three times on the street, and I was afraid the fourth time would kill me."

"I know you had it hard out there, Marlise. Even though Red Rye wasn't what they promised, you still felt safer?"

"I did at first," she said, "but then the men started coming to the house."

"You mean men came to the house before I got there?"

"In the beginning, yes. Supposedly, the men came so we could practice going on dates. However, more than innocent dating occurred, and I think the police found out."

"Why do you think that?"

"Well, the men stopped coming after The Miss had a cop knock on the door one day. I was standing there and heard her tell them the men were from the city, and they were just inspecting the house. She told the cop to talk to city hall about it. After that, we never saw another man in the house. Instead, we started going away on the weekends to practice our dates at hotels. No one asked questions there."

"I see," Mina said, trying to take in all the information and sort out what was important. Her mention of city hall had her brain spinning, but she didn't want to plant any ideas in Marlise's head before she showed her the picture. "If I show you a photo, can you tell me if you've ever seen the people in it before?"

"I can try," she said on a shrug.

"Don't worry about it if you don't recognize them, okay?" Mina smiled encouragingly while she pulled out her phone. She hoped the somewhat grainy image was enough to trigger recognition for Marlise. She held up the phone and was shocked when her friend's eyes closed, and she pushed the phone away.

"I'm not supposed to talk about them," she whispered. She trembled when she spoke, and Mina had to lean in to hear her.

"It's okay to talk to me, Marlise. If these people were involved with the Red Rye house, they might help me find The Madame. Isn't that what you want?"

"Yes," she whispered.

Before Mina could say anything more, Cal materialized in the room. "I said she wasn't to be disturbed."

Mina fought hard against the threatening eye roll. She wouldn't disrespect what he was doing here, even if it made it hard for her to get the information she needed.

"Cal, I know you've saved my bacon more times than I can count the last few days, and I am not trying to be ungrateful, but I have a lead. If I wanted to continue living my life and free Marlise to do the same, I needed to ask her a question."

"It couldn't keep until a saner time of the day?"

"No," she whispered, "because every hour that passes is another hour closer to The Madame finding us."

"I wasn't sleeping anyway," Marlise said, her shoulders stiff. "My arm was bothering me. Mina is okay here."

Cal softened after the woman spoke. "Fine, but you need to rest, so wrap this up."

He stepped out into the hall, and Mina fought a smile as Marlise chuckled. "He's like a combination of a jailer and a bodyguard all wrapped up in one."

Mina was relieved to hear her friend laugh, so she joined in. "I would say he's used to people doing what he says without any pushback."

"I guess he isn't used to strong women then, is he?" Marlise asked, squaring her shoulders. "I'm going to tell you what I know about those men because I trust you. If anyone can get us out of this mess, it's you."

"And if I can't, I'm going to go down trying." Her promise was made with a squeeze of Marlise's hand.

Marlise picked up the phone again and pointed to the picture. "They both used to come around the house when we first got to Red Rye. We practiced our dates with them." Her words stuttered, and she cleared her throat before going on. "This one," she pointed to the man on the left, "he would go upstairs with some of the other girls. They said he was just helping them with private tutoring. I might not have gone to high school, but I'm not an idiot. I knew what was going on up there. I was just glad I didn't have to be part of it."

"This guy didn't do the same personal tutoring?" Mina asked, pointing to the man on the right.

"He only came to the house twice before he stopped

coming with the other guy. I never saw him again once The Miss started taking us to hotels for the practice dates."

"Do you know their names?" Mina asked, tucking the phone back in her pocket.

"No, but I'm sure they aren't Tom and Jerry like they told us they were."

A heavy sigh escaped Mina's lips. No, they weren't Tom and Jerry. She knew who they were, but that didn't matter to Marlise tonight. "That's okay. Thanks for being honest with me about knowing them. I know who they are, and now I can tie them into finding The Miss and then The Madame. I'm going to go back to the house so you can get some rest. I'll have Cal send Selina in with some medication?"

"That would be great," she said, her head falling back to the pillow and exhaustion falling across her face like a blanket. "I would love to get some sleep."

Mina patted her shoulder. "I'll see you later."

She turned, but Marlise grabbed her sleeve. "Can you find her now?"

Mina's smile was forced, but she hoped the girl wouldn't notice. "Now that I know these two men were involved, I have a trail to follow. That's only because you were brave enough to tell me the truth. I need to work for a few hours, but I'll have Mack and Cal keep you informed when you wake up. I want you to rest."

"Okay. Good luck," she whispered, her eyes going closed. "I'll see you tomorrow."

Mina walked out, stopping next to Cal when she found him in the living room. "She's requesting some medication for her arm. It's keeping her awake. Do we need to take her back to a hospital?"

Cal stood to his formidable size and shook his head. "No. Selina said the first few days after a break like that would be rough. I'll take care of her. Did you get what you need?"

"Yes," she sighed. "I wish I hadn't had to wake her, but it was the fastest route to the answers I needed. I'm going back to the lodge. There's work to be done."

"Mack is waiting to escort you. Fair warning, Jacobs is madder than a wet hen that you didn't wake him. Be ready for a tongue lashing when you get back."

Her laughter filled the cabin as she walked to the door. "This is not my first rodeo with Roman Jacobs. I can handle him with one hand tied behind my back."

Cal grinned and tipped his head to the left. "Since you showed up, my bet has been on you all along."

Cal gave her a finger gun and then walked into the other room, leaving Mina to wonder what he meant by that. She shook it off and headed down the porch with Mack, the sky still eerily black as it neared four in the morning. Storm clouds had rolled in overnight, and her foot told her the storm was going to be a doozy.

"We're one step closer, Mack," she said to the man walking next to her, his hand grasping her elbow.

"I sure hope so because Roman is on his way over here now. He's spitting mad that none of us stopped you from leaving the room. We should probably double-time it back before he meets us halfway. You should not mess with a man in love."

"A man in love?" she asked, a brow raised in the air, even if it was too dark to see.

"Calling it as I see it," Mack said with a shoulder shrug. "When you two are together, it's pathetically easy to see you're in love. The way you make googly eyes at each other is enough to—"

"I get it, Mack," Mina said, forcing a chuckle, though it sounded as fake as it was. "We need to slow down. My foot can't handle the terrain this quickly."

They slowed, and suddenly, Mina was yanked backward with a hand over her mouth. Her arms were pulled behind her, and her feet left the ground. A hulking man dressed in all black was in hand-to-hand combat with Mack, but Mack wasn't winning. She had to help him! Mina kicked upward with her cast boot, trying to catch her assailant with the rubber sole. Before she could twist to fight back, a fist came at her. The last thing she saw was Mack dropping to the ground before the blackness closed in around her.

HIS GUT DIDN'T LIE, and right now, his gut said to find her. Roman jogged down the hallway to the back door and scanned his thumbprint, waiting impatiently for the system to recognize him and open the door. When it finally clicked, he squeezed through the slit before it had a chance to open all the way. He headed across the lawn for the cottage where Cal had moved Marlise earlier today. If Roman didn't know better, he'd think Cal had a crush on the woman. Roman knew better. His brother never dated. Cal preferred no-strings-attached kinds of relationships. Considering what they'd both seen of human nature over the years, Roman understood it. He wasn't much of a dater himself before seven years ago, when he met Mina August for the first time. Dating hadn't happened at all since then. Roman always blamed it on the job, but he knew that wasn't fair to the job.

The truth was, he knew it wasn't fair to compare every woman he took out to Mina, and that was precisely what he'd do. He regretted not telling her that he loved her a year ago. When he woke up alone and found her note, those same regrets hit him. He was desperate to tell her now before he couldn't.

His nerves were jumpy, which was never a good sign. That meant trouble was coming or was already here. He hadn't stayed alive all these years as an agent by not trusting his gut. Roman pushed the thoughts of Mina's damaged foot out of his mind. She could take care of herself even with one foot. A little part of him was glad she'd never be in the field again to get hurt or worse—killed. Maybe he shouldn't feel that way, but losing her again was not an option.

Before he could form another thought, he was on the ground and then rolling right back up onto his feet, his body in a fighting stance. Something had knocked him down, and he was ready for the fight. It wasn't until he glanced down that he realized he hadn't been pushed, but rather tripped.

Roman dropped to his knee and rolled the man over, shocked to see Mack out cold on the ground. "Mack," he said, slapping his face a couple of times. When the man didn't come around, he grabbed his radio from his pocket and hit the button. "This is Jacobs. Mack is down."

"What do you mean, Mack is down?" Cal asked when Roman released the button.

"I was running to the cabin when I tripped over his body. He's down. Out cold. I need a med team."

"Why didn't Mina radio for help? They left twenty minutes ago."

"Mina?" Roman asked with his teeth clenched. "She isn't with Mack." Roman released the radio button. That tendril of fear ran up his spine as he glanced around the area. There was no place for her to hide unless she escaped and ran into an empty cabin. He put his hands together and clapped out the rhythm she'd recognize, waiting for a response. When he got none, his heart banged against his ribs. He pulled a flashlight off Mack's belt and shone it around the area. That was when he noticed the grass flattened in one area as it disappeared into the woods. He hit the radio again. "Send help for Mack. Mina is rogue."

There was shouting before light flooded the area. Guys came running out of the lodge while Cal ran full out from the back cabin. He reached Roman in seconds, grabbed his arm and held him in place. "Marlise answered Mina's question, and when they left, I told Mack to get her back to you since I knew you were hot about her leaving. There's no way you missed her on the way out?"

Roman motioned at Mack. "As if she'd just leave him lying here." He pointed at the grass to his right. "Drag marks."

A medical team swarmed Mack, so the two men stepped back. Mack groaned and tried to sit up, but Selina held him down. "Got jumped," he said, his words tight. "Two, maybe three guys. They took Mina."

Roman was running before Mack finished his sentence. They ran into the guest suite, but Mina wasn't waiting for them. The hatch to the bunker was still up, and Cal put his finger to his lips before he pulled his gun. "Hatch was up when I left," Roman whispered. Cal nodded but silently walked to the metal railing protecting the hatch. He swung the gun down the hole several times before he motioned Roman over.

"Mina said she had to talk to Marlise tonight because of something she found. Maybe she left a note."

Cal and Roman climbed down the ladder and stood in the small computer room. "Everything looks like it did last night," Roman said, more fear spiraling in his gut. "If The Madame has her, we're losing precious time here, Cal!"

Cal jiggled the mouse on the desk, and the screen came to life. A search was open with the picture of two men standing next to each other at a charity event of some sort.

"This mean anything to you?" Cal asked Roman, who jogged over and read the caption.

"Son of a—" Roman ran his hand through his hair to keep from kicking something. "Liam Albrecht and Benjamin Bartos. Liam is the city manager of Red Rye, the office we know stopped her SOS message from going through. Benjamin Bartos is the mayor of a town called Santa Macko in Arizona. Do you think this is what Mina wanted to ask Marlise about?"

Cal grabbed his radio. "One way to find out." He radioed over to the house and asked Selina to find out what Mina needed to know when she was there. While they waited, Roman paced the floor, his mind turning over what little information they had. "What was she thinking leaving without me?" He kicked the chair, sending it spinning across the floor.

"What was I thinking not sending more than one guy with her?" Cal asked, rubbing his forehead. "I was distracted trying to get the nurse to help Marlise."

Roman noticed the fatigue lacing his brother's words

and the worry lines creasing his forehead. "Cal, this isn't your fault. Min knows the risks. She doesn't think she deserves to call herself an agent anymore. That's why she's willing to put her neck on the line to expose The Madame."

"She blames herself for an undercover sting going sideways? That happens all the time, Roman."

"She knows that, too, but this is personal. She feels like she let all those girls down who are trapped by The Madame. Girls like—"

"Marlise." Cal said the name in a tone Roman had never heard come from him before. It was indescribable the pain it held but also the pride.

"She would die to make sure that woman had a chance at life," Roman ground out, his finger pointing toward the cabin beyond the tunnel. "Now I have to be the one to save them both. I cannot lose her again."

Cal squeezed Roman's shoulder. "Does she know you love her?"

The slight shake of his head was enough for Cal to understand. "Then we need to make sure she's around for your lug head to tell her. Tell me what you know about these two guys."

Chapter Seventeen

Where was she? Mina's eyes came open slowly, but she remained still. The air was thick with danger, and it was hard to breathe around the gag in her mouth. She fought the pounding in her head while she gauged the situation. Her body rocked back and forth uncontrollably in the darkness, and she recognized the sensation. She was in a vehicle. It was too dark to see anything, which meant one thing, she was in a trunk or a cargo bay. Her hands were tied behind her back, and her feet were lashed together. Her boot was gone, which would be a real problem if they made her walk anywhere, but thankfully, her feet weren't tied to her hands. She moved her feet forward and back, touching the sides of her cell until she was satisfied that she was indeed in a trunk.

Where were they taking her? The Madame sent her men, but they didn't kill her, which meant maybe they had instructions to bring Mina in alive. She could only hope that was true. It was time to end this game once and for all. She might go down swinging, but at least the other girls would be safe. How, though? How was she going to bring down The Madame by herself with a busted-up foot, no weapon and no way to call for backup?

Mina lowered her head back to the floor and closed her eyes, willing the cobwebs away so she could think clearly. Try to escape. The thought came and went quickly. Even if they hadn't reinforced the trunk latch and taillights, dropping out of a vehicle while tied up was a death sentence. She estimated they were doing at least sixty miles an hour, and there was no way she could outrun them if she did get out. Besides, if they were taking her to The Madame, she wanted a chance to confront the woman.

Fat lot of good that'll do you when you're dead, she thought to herself.

She shifted to get more comfortable when something dug into her knee. She nearly yelped but bit it back in time. Her hands were behind her back, and it took some contorting, but she managed to feel around the pocket of her cargo pants.

Her heart pounded with excitement when she realized she still had Cal's tracking phone! They didn't check her for a phone! That would be their first mistake. If she had anything to say about it, it would also be her last.

Holding herself at a funny angle, she managed to get the phone out and check the display when it lit up. It was almost five o'clock, which meant she'd been out for an hour already. She threw up a prayer of desperation and clicked the star button twice. Then she put the phone on sleep. Ready to slip the phone back in her pocket so they wouldn't find it when they stopped, she hesitated. This might be her only chance to tell Roman how she felt about him.

She painstakingly typed out a message with one hand and sent it, then slid the phone back in her pocket. She had to conserve the battery. If they didn't find her before it went dead, she would be, too.

SHE HAD BEEN gone for an hour already, and they were no closer to finding her. Cal had monitored all outgoing flights from the local airstrips, and there weren't any suspicious ones without a flight plan. She had to be in a car headed to meet The Madame. They had no idea what kind of car or where they were taking her, which only served to fill Roman's gut to overflowing. He had to find her.

Stop. Think.

"Cal!" Roman yelled from where he was strapping on tactical gear and preparing to head out with the rest of the team. "We need to talk to Marlise again!"

Roman heard the squeak of Cal's boots on the ladder, and then he was jogging toward him. "Why?"

"She mentioned that after the cops caught on to their operation, they moved the practice dates to hotels. We need to find out what hotels. One of them may be where The Madame always stays when she's in town."

"I doubt they'd take her back to Red Rye. Too risky, Roman."

"Marlise never said the hotels were in Red Rye," he pointed out and then waited for Cal to catch up with him.

"Good poin—"

"What is that sound?" Roman asked with his head tipped to the left.

Cal's eyes widened when he grabbed the front of Roman's shirt. "Where's the phone I gave you before the trip to St. Paul? The tracker has been activated."

Roman wrenched himself out of Cal's hands and

practically skipped the ladder altogether to get to the computer room. He pushed papers aside, cussing up a blue streak until the black device came into view.

"I got it!" he yelled as Cal landed on the concrete surefooted. "It has to be her, right?"

Cal grabbed the phone and slid the bar open to reveal a message. "Oh, it's our Mina," he said, turning the phone back to Roman to read the text. "Meet me at the front of the lodge in three minutes. I need to grab the portable tablet to keep tracking her, and then we're moving."

Roman should have said something in response, but he couldn't. All the air had been knocked from him when his eyes rested on the message she'd sent.

Roman, I'm sorry. I didn't want it to end this way. In a car trunk on the highway. The battery has half life. Find me before it dies, or I do too. Just in case, I love you, Jacobs. Wish I had said it sooner. Maybe we wouldn't be here. Find me.

Roman poised his fingers over the keyboard but hesitated. He couldn't risk sending a message and alerting the people who had her about the phone. It was their only link to her. He'd tell her when he found her. He holstered his gun and took a deep breath. He was ready to fight for the woman he loved.

THE CAR HAD slowed and was driving erratically now. Mina suspected they had reached a city, and she had checked the phone a few miles ago to see they'd been on the road almost ninety minutes since she'd sent the text to Roman. It showed that it had been read, but there was no response. She convinced herself he was afraid to send a message and have it buzz in her pocket. As an FBI agent, she knew he'd made the right choice, but as a woman terrified her life was about to end, she was hoping for an *I love you* back.

She snapped her head around when she heard the siren. It was coming at them, and the car slowed, moving to the right. She could not get this lucky, could she? If a cop pulled them over, she'd make a racket in hopes of getting the officer's attention. Best-case scenario, they get the plate if the driver takes off. She hated that her mind went to the worst-case scenario, and that was the cop getting shot.

She blew out a breath when the siren whizzed past them on its way to a different emergency. Mina estimated it was ten minutes later when the car slowed to a crawl and then came to a stop altogether. She shifted, knowing the time was coming for them to open the trunk. She didn't want them to see the phone, so she rolled onto her side to keep it hidden. Mina could make out the sounds of men's voices just before the trunk popped, blinding her with a bright light. She squinted and blinked until someone leaned in and dimmed the light in her eyes.

"Well, it looks like the special agent is awake. I bet you'd like to stretch your legs for a bit, eh?"

Mina let them manhandle her out of the trunk and set her on her feet. "I can't walk like this. My foot barely works." She had to mutter it around the gag and hoped they understood.

"If you think I'm untying you, you're crazy. Neptune, give me a hand."

She had to work hard not to roll her eyes at their

"code" names. Who were these idiots? They wore all black, including black face masks. They looked like a bunch of penny-ante bank robbers, but she wasn't going to egg them on to a beating. They lifted her by her arms, making her shoulders scream in pain, but she kept her face neutral rather than give them the satisfaction of knowing they'd hurt her. They dragged her up a set of stairs in an abandoned warehouse and dumped her onto an old sofa that had been new in the eighties. Neptune yanked her gag down.

"You guys aren't great hosts," she said, shifting to a sitting position, wishing her hands weren't behind her back. "Not even a cocktail?"

The punch to her jaw was quick and unexpected. It knocked her sideways onto the couch. When the stars disappeared from her vision, she sat up again and moved her jaw around a couple of times.

"Is that all you've got?"

Ninja one cocked his fist again, but Neptune caught his arm and held it. "Knock it off, Mercury. They want her alive when they get here. If you don't want to listen to her smart mouth, put the gag back in."

Mina didn't want to be silenced again on the off chance Roman found her before she was dead. "I'll be good," she promised quickly. "Just don't gag me again. I might throw up, and with a gag in my mouth, I could aspirate."

Mercury shrugged his shoulder, ripped the gag up and stuffed it back in her mouth. "You're going to die anyway."

He walked away, and Mina swallowed around the dryness in her throat. She was running out of time and options if Roman didn't get here sooner rather than later. The gag was loose, and she pushed against it with her tongue. She could lower it quickly if she needed to scream, but for now, she'd leave it in place. Better to let them think they'd won. Maybe they had, but she wasn't going down without participating in the fight.

ROMAN HELD THE tablet on his lap. He'd been giving directions over the headset as Cal piloted the helicopter along 35E. It didn't take long for Roman to figure out they were headed for St. Paul. The red dot on the screen stopped, and he held his breath. They were somewhere downtown, but he didn't want to flip into street view yet. It took the tablet too long to switch back if they started moving again.

"They've stopped," Roman said to Cal over the headset. "How far out are we?"

"I've been hanging back, so they don't hear the chopper," he answered. "About ten minutes out from the last coordinates you gave me."

Roman read off the new coordinates. "Get us there, now," he hissed, counting the seconds since the car had moved. "They've been stopped for four minutes."

"Is the tracker moving?"

"Yes, but barely." It was time to hit street view, which he did. When it loaded, his heart sank. "It's a warehouse. I think they're moving her somewhere inside it."

"Give me the address."

Roman rattled it off, his focus never leaving the blinking red dot in the center of the screen. Cal flipped buttons and then motioned above his head for the guys in the back to get ready.

"I'm landing this at the airport. Any closer, and they're going to hear the blades."

"How far out will we be?"

"About a mile the way the crow flies. We'll cover it on foot. There's no other way."

"We may need more firepower."

"We'll call it in."

"Not the FBI," Roman said. "Local guys only. I don't know who we can trust on the team anymore."

"I've got a friend on the force. I've already reached out. When we land, I'll send him the address, and he'll await our assessment."

Roman nodded once as Cal gripped his shoulder for a hot second before the airport came into view. "She's stopped moving."

"Let's hope she's awaiting a meeting with the woman herself. We can scoop up Mina and The Madame and be home by lunchtime."

Roman snorted half a laugh. "It's never that easy with The Madame. But I'm willing to hope you're right."

After Cal set them down, they piled out of the chopper, their tactical gear and automatic rifles at the ready for a fight they hoped didn't materialize. Bullets and dead bodies made for messy final reports when the day was done. It was even harder to explain to the authorities. Cal called his friend and then lined his guys up, Roman directly in front with the tablet.

"We move quickly and quietly. Roman, you're on lead. Anything changes on the tracker, divert, and we'll follow. When we reach the building, we pause and assess."

Everyone nodded, and then Roman led them off to the right, their boots silent in the tall grass, but Roman's heart was pounding so hard he was sure Mina could hear it. He prayed she could because it was the only way he could tell her to hang on.

He pushed the men to move faster, sliding up along the building and holding up his fist, signaling the men behind him to hold. He lifted the infrared scanner to assess the building. It was better than any he'd used in the field. That shouldn't surprise him, considering Cal's ability to get products not even on the market yet. Roman's heart paused in his chest when the scanner picked out a figure in an upstairs room. It had to be her. He called out to her in his head, begging her to hold on. There was another figure in the room, and Roman assessed the first floor before he hustled back to the men awaiting instruction.

"There are three on the main floor inside. A guard at each door makes five. Top floor has two in one room. I know the one figure is Mina. I would guess the other one is The Madame. There are two more outside that room standing guard." The men nodded understanding, but Roman had more information they weren't going to like. "There are two more on the ground, both losing body heat." Everyone knew what that meant. "Watch your six. There will be guns."

Cal was the one to speak next. "We must disarm the guards in silence—no guns or hand-to-hand. Get them from behind and drop them. Roman and I will take out the two guards at the doors simultaneously, leaving the other three guards on the first floor for you four. Whoever is closest takes them down." Everyone nodded, so Cal continued. "Then we'll regroup and rescan the second floor."

Roman used the infrared to scan one more time and gave a thumbs up that nothing had changed. He and Cal set off for the two guarded entry doors while the other men waited to enter the building when those guards were out of commission. Roman wanted to throw the doors open and pound his way through, shooting anyone in his way to Mina, but that wasn't an option. He had to do it right. It was the only way to ensure that she was still alive when they got to her. He swallowed down his terror and crept closer to the guard who had his back to him. How many times had he done this same kind of mission with Min by his side? Countless.

This time, it was on him to save her from certain death. The thought sent a shiver up his spine. It was now or never to be the hero, Roman. Three quick steps had the guard in a headlock and on the ground unconscious. Roman zip-tied him with precision and stuffed a gag in his mouth before he stepped over his flaccid body to the door. The other four men fell in line behind him and Cal, and on three, Roman pulled it open and stepped inside.

Chapter Eighteen

When the door opened, Mina thought she would meet Liam, Benjamin and The Madame, who wouldn't be a woman at all but a sitting senator from Maine. She gave herself a mental shake out and steadied her breathing. She had remained as still as possible for the last half an hour, praying it was enough of a signal to Roman that they'd stopped moving.

It would be. Mina believed he was looking for her because believing anything else meant she would die at the hands of The Madame this time. Her nerves were shot, and her foot ached in a way it never had before. If she got out of this alive, she had a lot of unpleasant situations to face, but she had to hope Roman would be there holding her hand through them all. She believed Mack when he said Roman loved her. If she didn't, she wasn't going to find the will to survive this. She might be an FBI agent, but right now, she was tied up and trapped, which meant the only emotions coursing through her were those of a terrified woman who could barely walk, much less run. Her mind analyzed as much as it could take in, but it kept coming back with the same answer. She was screwed. Sometimes you had to know when to fold them.

The door opened, and three men walked in, but it was the last one who had her sagging against the couch in relief. "SAC Moore," she said, her voice a mess of relief and respect. "Thank God." Her gaze dashed to the other two men standing next to him. "You got Albrecht and Bartos, good. Did you round up The Madame, too?"

The SAC grabbed a chair and spun it around, straddling it to face her. "I did. I shouldn't be surprised that you recognize these two guys."

"From what Marlise tells me, Liam enjoyed his dates at the Red Rye house a little bit too much." She spat the sentence like filth on her tongue.

"A perk of The Madame," the SAC said. "If he did her bidding, her ladies would do his. It was a win-win."

Mina's gaze tracked the three men, landing on the man who had been her SAC for six years. It wasn't lost on her that he hadn't untied her yet. Also, why was Moore here? If he were here to bust the guys who took her from Cal's, this place would be swarming with the FBI. The rest of the building was silent. The truth slammed into her, and the picture became clear. Disbelieving, she knew there was only one way to find out. She lifted her legs. "How about you untie me, and I'll help you arrest these guys."

"I don't think so."

"You're The Madame," she said, not as a question but as a statement.

The SAC made a so-so hand. "Technically, my wife is The Madame, but you could say we run the business together. You know what they say, if the wife ain't happy, ain't nobody happy."

"So, you run an illegal drug-trafficking business,

money-laundering scheme and sex-slave enterprise to keep your wife happy?"

"Well, well, Agent August is well-informed. When this is over, I'll have to find Marlise and have a word with her," he said, practically spitting venom. "I did instruct my men to bring her, too, but once again, their ineptness is astounding. That's what happens when you can't use real agents to get the job done. No matter. I've got you, and you're all I need. Marlise is easy enough to dispatch, and then no one else knows what went on in Red Rye."

"That's not true. Roman knows." Mina was fibbing, but she had to buy herself time before one of the guys with guns came in and dispatched her.

A realization struck Mina. Greg Weiss had been nothing more than a red herring in Red Rye. Mina hated herself for not seeing that and for dedicating so much time to finding a connection between the other two men. Logically there was no way she could have known, but when the trail didn't add up, she should have known it was a ploy.

The SAC motioned the other two men to the door with his head. They left, and it wasn't three seconds after they closed the door that gunshots rang out. She grimaced, but all Moore did was laugh.

"I was done with those two yes men. Let me tell you what, Liam had some serious kinks. The Miss even had a little cleanup with a couple of those girls after he got done with them. At least they were at a hotel, and it couldn't be tied back to Red Rye. Now then, where were we? Oh, yes, Roman Jacobs." The SAC shook his head. "What a lovesick puppy dog he was the past year. Pathetic."

"What does that mean?" she asked, her heart pounding in her chest. They shot the other two men in cold blood, and they'd do the same to her as soon as the SAC tired of their discussion. She had to keep him talking long enough for Roman to find her.

He leaned back, grasping the front of the chair with his hands so he didn't fall. "I was already planning your funeral when he called to tell me you were alive and barely hanging on in the hospital. Of course, by the time I found out what hospital you were at and got a team there, you were gone. I must give you props for that, August. I wasn't expecting you to run in your condition. That took guts."

"Your compliments fall flat when you have assassins at your beck and call."

He shrugged as though her words didn't bite. "Probably true, but don't worry, you won't be facing a firing squad. I'll be the one to dispatch you this time, just to make sure the job gets done right. The last year has been..." he paused and motioned around with his hand. "Trying. I had to listen to my wife complain about you being on the run at home while I listened to Roman whine about you being on the run at work. It was exhausting." He rubbed his temples with his fingers. "Agent Jacobs's desperate desire to find his little woman did offer me an unexpected hand, though."

"His little woman?" she asked with a brow in the air. "I'm his partner. Nothing more."

He waved his hand at her face. "Nice try. As if we're all blind and couldn't see the way you two looked at each other."

"Nothing happened between us," she insisted. It

didn't matter to her what he thought, but if it kept him talking, she'd play the game.

"I couldn't care less if it did," he said, his head shaking.

"Partners can't also be lovers. We both knew that."

Her boss shrugged nonchalantly as though they were having a friendly chat rather than working toward her death. "Wouldn't matter to me if you had been. Who am I to judge? Look at me. I'm helping my wife run a criminal enterprise and using my connections at the bureau to do it. What's a little impropriety between friends?"

Apparently, nothing, which Mina never expected from SAC Moore. He was always a by-the-book kind of SAC, at least to their faces.

"That's how the girls' histories and any evidence they ever existed was wiped away. You used your connections with the bureau."

She could see the gleefulness in his eyes when he leaned toward her. "It's quite easy when you have the right tools."

"Forgive my confusion then, SAC, but if things were going along swimmingly, why did you need to put me undercover in Red Rye?"

He stood and started pacing the length of the room. "I'm so glad you asked, Agent August. We needed someone who could produce an app for us, but first, we needed them to understand the business."

"But I didn't understand the business. I had no idea drugs were involved, though I suspected that money laundering was happening."

He tipped his head back and forth a couple of times. "Okay, that's fair, but you didn't need all the particulars to create the app, only the stuff on the surface that was legal."

"And I handed it to you on a silver platter." She paused and then groaned, her head falling back on the couch.

"It just hit you, right?" he asked, and she glanced up to see him rubbing his hands together.

"The fire happened as soon as I had the app perfected and running smoothly."

"Bingo," he gave her the finger guns. "Thanks for that, by the way. It's a brilliant piece of technology."

"You always intended to kill me once you had the app, right?" The slight tip of his head answered her question. "How did you plan to get into the backdoor of the app where I stored all the evidence if I were dead?"

"That part didn't matter, did it, Agent August? I had no interest in what evidence you gathered or if I could ever access it. We both know none of it was usable in a court of law, no matter the lies I told you to convince you otherwise. That evidence would sit untouched for decades while we ran the operation."

"Which means you didn't keep the app open in case I tried to access it. You kept the app open because you were still using it."

"Both, if that makes you feel better. I prayed you'd try to access it. If you did, Roman would find you, and since we were tagging him, he'd lead us right to you."

"Looks like it worked."

He sat again and leaned forward on the back of the chair. He smiled at Mina with malice she had never seen before. Not even from some of the worst criminals she'd dealt with in the past. This guy was high on power, and he wasn't coming down anytime soon. "Not the exact way I'd hoped, but at the end, when Roman needed some 'mental health' time, I gave it to him." He was throwing air quotes around like a middle-aged woman speaking to a manager. "Then I tagged him and waited. It was only a matter of time. As soon as someone started poking around Marlise, I used her, too. Shame I had to beat up that cute little thing, but I did manage to get you guys to tag her. Always so valiant when it comes to protecting the innocent, aren't you, Agent August?"

"You know you're not going to get away with this, right?" she asked, unable to play nice, knowing the man she had put her trust in was the one to ruin her life.

"Oh, but I am. No one is going to find you. Hard to find someone weighed down with bricks in the Mississippi. I'll go back to work and sit at my desk while Roman searches for you frantically. I'll offer all the resources I can, but eventually, I'll have to have a heart-to-heart with him and tell him it's over. You're lost forever, and he must move on with his life. I have it all planned. It'll be touching."

Mina was about to say something when they heard a noise, and the SAC turned his attention toward the door. She seized the opening she'd been given, and with his back turned to her, she threw herself at him. It didn't matter that she was still tied up. She just wanted the upper hand by dropping his head to the concrete.

They both went down rolling, and Mina fought to get her tied feet to kick out, striking him wherever she could in hopes of keeping him down. His left fist swung out and caught her on the cheek, spinning her head so hard she saw stars, but she couldn't, no, she wouldn't, give him the satisfaction of backing down. He pummeled her head, his mouth spewing obscenities and spit until Mina was nearly unconscious. Her strength almost gone, she struck out one more time—her foot connected with the SAC's jaw and slammed his head to the ground. Mina couldn't celebrate her victory because the impact shattered her glass-like foot.

Her piercing scream of pain filled her ears, and when the door opened, she swore she saw Roman. The darkness tried to take her, but she wouldn't let it. If she did, Roman might let the SAC go thinking he was there to help.

"Mina!" Roman yelled, running through the door and stopping short when he came face-to-face with the SAC, this time with a gun. He'd been hiding it, she knew, because there was no way he was going to leave another attempt at her murder to the men who couldn't get the job done before. He'd been waiting for the perfect time, but now, he was going to get a twofer if Roman didn't have any backup.

"What is going on?" Roman asked, his hands to his sides to show that he had no weapons.

The SAC pushed himself to his feet with a grunt. He swayed visibly from the kick to his head but still managed to hold the gun steady on them. "I should have known the gallant agent would rush in to save his woman at the last minute. Props. I figured I'd tied your hands enough that you wouldn't have a trace on her before it was too late."

Roman took a step to the side, trying to put himself between the SAC and her. "I wouldn't have, but Special Agent August was smart enough to activate the tracker on her phone."

The gun wavered in his hand, and his face lost what little bit of color was left in it.

Roman smiled a smile he saved for their most sought-after criminals. "I guess your guys forgot to check her for a phone. Classic rookie mistake."

"Don't push me, Jacobs!" the SAC bellowed, flinging the gun around in the air. "There are enough bullets in this gun to dispatch you both multiple times, which is exactly what's going to happen now. I'd planned to let you live. I was looking forward to the months of torture you'd endure looking for your precious Mina, only to find her dead along a riverbank in the spring. Looks like I'll lose out on that funfest this winter. Oh well. I'll have enough to keep me busy trying to clean up the mess August made of Red Rye. If she had just died that night I started the fire, then we wouldn't be here right now. Shame you're going to have to die, too."

"You started the fire?" Roman asked.

Mina saw the exact moment the whole scene came into focus for him.

"You're The Madame?"

Her boss's annoying cackle sent a shiver down her spine. She always hated his laugh. Now she knew why.

"No, but I'm The Madame's better half. It's the little things that matter to the women in our lives, Jacobs. Imagine if I wasn't here to support my wife's entrepreneurial adventures."

"It's hard to fathom, honestly," Roman said, but she noticed his gaze flick to the door.

Unfortunately, the SAC saw it, too. He got off a shot before a body landed on her, stealing her breath. The weight of him shot a new wave of pain through her.

"Stay down," Roman whispered into her ear.

There was shouting, shooting and chaos for seconds before silence prevailed again.

"Roll call!" Cal yelled out, and all the men responded, including the voice of the man she loved.

"Anyone hit?" Cal asked, but she wasn't paying attention to him. She was staring into the pair of eyes she had seen so many times in her dreams.

"You found me," she whispered, tears in her eyes.

"I'll always find you, Min. Are you hit?"

"I don't think so, but my foot… It's bad, Roman," she said, her voice cracking. "It's bad, isn't it?" She tried to sit up, but he kept her down on the ground, her head cradled by his hand.

"Don't look at it, okay? Police and EMS are on their way. We're going to get you to the hospital."

"The SAC planned this all along," she said, her voice weak from the pain and the terror.

His finger came down on her lips, and he hushed her. "Not another word. You'll need to be debriefed, but you know he's not going to confess."

"He's not going to be breathing if EMS doesn't get here soon," Cal called over his shoulder from where he knelt next to the man she'd trusted with her life, only to learn he couldn't care less about hers. He was holding pressure on a wound near the SAC's arm while the man was unconscious.

Roman had freed her hands and was rubbing her wrists to get feeling back in them. "I'm going to leave your ankles tied. I don't want to jar that foot, and the other one is keeping it stable. Just concentrate on me, okay, baby?"

"It's bad, Roman. I can't feel my foot."

"It is bad, but I'm here now. We'll get through this together. We'll get you back on your feet and put Moore and his wife behind bars. Together."

"He doesn't need to confess," she said, reaching into the pocket of her pants and pulling out the phone. "It's been recording since I tagged the tracker. I wasn't sure how long the battery would last, but if I had the chance to capture the voice of The Madame, I had to try."

Roman wrapped his hand around her hand, still holding the phone. "That's my girl. An agent until the very end."

"I'm done being an agent now," she whispered, her head falling back into his hand.

He kissed her until she was silent. "I don't care if you ever wear the badge again, Wilhelmina August. You don't have to prove yourself to anyone. We'll get through this together. I hope, when all is said and done, you walk away from the bureau. Hell, I'll follow you."

"Why?" she asked, her hand tucked inside his vest to rest against his chest.

"Department protocol states couples can't be partners. I don't want to work with anyone else."

"Couples? We're not a couple."

"Yet," he whispered, smiling down at her as commotion filled the room. "But I love you, Mina August. I flew all the way here in a helicopter just to tell you that because I refused to tell you by text. You aren't an I-love-you-by-text kind of woman. You're a fancy dinner, roses and the finest champagne kind of I love you. I'll have to give you an IOU on those, but in the meantime, hold on to my love. It will help you get through this."

"You love me?"

"I could say I love you until I'm blue in the face, but sometimes showing is better than telling," he whispered before he captured her lips again.

For the first time since Mina went on the run, she

was finally safe from The Madame. She knew from this day forward, the man holding her would be her partner and protector.

Epilogue

"Where are we going?" Mina asked, her laughter filling the late afternoon sky. It was early May, and the weather was warming in Minnesota. It had been a long winter, but she was finally back on her feet and finding joy in life again.

"To my office," Roman said, his arm around her waist and his lips nuzzling her ear. "We have the terms of your employment to discuss."

"My terms of employment? I don't work for you. I work for Secure One."

Right after the New Year, the SAC and his wife were formally indicted for their crimes. They'd stand trial, but with the depth and breadth of the investigation, they were remanded to federal prison until that time. His confession on the audio recording might not be admissible in a court case, and he knew it, but he also knew there was no getting out of the charges of kidnapping and murder.

Mina spent the next two months working with the sex-trafficking team of the FBI. Together, they took statements from the girls in the twelve houses run by The Madame, and helped them find therapy, housing and jobs. She refused to rest until all the girls who wanted help had gotten it.

It helped her work through what she needed to process, too. It reminded her that even though the doctors had to amputate her foot, she could still make a difference in the world. Focusing on the girls made her rehab easier to face and fortified her belief that she could get stronger again. If those women who had gone through hell could find normalcy in life again, so could she.

Though she had a state-of-the-art prosthesis and was active and happy, she didn't have the heart to work for the FBI again. That was probably because the man walking beside her had stolen her heart. When Roman retired from the FBI, she followed suit, and they were hired by Secure One in April. They were still partners, just in a less dangerous way. Mina focused on helping the Secure One team with internet crimes, while Roman taught the team advanced combat techniques and training exercises.

Above all, living and working together made them happy. Mina supposed she could only speak for herself, but she never heard Roman complain about their new arrangement. He woke up every morning kissing her and fell asleep the same way.

From the moment she woke up from surgery after her rescue, she knew he would always be by her side. He was holding her hand, and a tear slipped down his cheek when he had to be the one to tell her the doctors couldn't save her foot. He'd been the one to give them the go-ahead for the amputation, and he begged her not to hate him for that decision.

The truth was, Mina already knew her foot was beyond repair, and the kick to the SAC's face, while satisfying, was the final nail in the coffin for her poor bones. She had slid her hand along his face and wiped his tears, promising that she didn't hate him. He hadn't left her side since. He kept her comfortable and nourished in the early days and motivated her to get up and walk on the hard ones. Now, he kept her up making love half the night, but she wasn't averse to spending every night with him for the rest of her life, so she certainly wasn't complaining.

"I guess we can't discuss your employment then," he said, somewhat downtrodden.

When they reached the lake, most of the Secure One team were walking around sipping on beer bottles and jamming burgers in their mouths.

"We're having a picnic?" she asked, clapping excitedly. "This is great!"

"More like a party, maybe," he said, taking her hand as they approached the group of people milling around.

A woman stepped out of the crowd and ran toward them, grabbing Mina in a hug so tightly that Roman had to grab them to keep them from falling.

"Marlise!" Mina cried with her arms wrapped around the woman. "No one told me you were here!"

"I just got here," she promised, stepping out of the hug to smile at her friend. "I couldn't miss the party, so Cal picked me up in the chopper. I guess I'm staying for the summer," she said on a shrug.

"That's great, Marlise," Mina said, squeezing her friend's hand.

After The Madame was caught, Marlise was moved to a rehab facility that concentrated on physical and emotional healing. She had needed both, but Mina had visited her as often as she could, always with an invitation to return to Secure One when she was ready. Mina had it on good authority that Cal spent a lot of time visiting Marlise, even if he'd claimed he was simply providing protection while she was in the facility. When they raided the other houses around the country, more than one "Miss" had escaped capture, including the one from Red Rye. Until they were all tracked down and brought into custody, any one of them could decide Marlise was a dangerous string to let dangle. The only other strings still dangling from the investigation were the girls in the river. The FBI was trying to tie them to The Madame, but so far, they hadn't offered a big enough carrot to make her talk.

"I'm going to take over the kitchen here at Secure One. I think, anyway. Maybe."

"I hope you do," Mina said with a smile. "Mack is a terrible cook. I told Cal he should offer you the deed to the whole place to get you out here. It looks like he did."

Marlise shook her head shyly. "No, I agreed to try it for a few months to see if I was the right fit for Secure One."

Mina winked at Roman before she turned back to the woman. "I already know you are."

And she didn't just mean in Cal's kitchen.

"I feel safer having you here. Until we find The Miss, you're in danger, Marlise."

"Cal said the same thing, and don't worry. I lived through enough danger to know I don't want to fall into their hands again."

The woman was shaking, so Mina took her hands and squeezed them. "The Secure One team will take care of you until we find her. Then you'll be free to live your life your way."

"I hope so. I also hope I'll figure out what I want to do with my life in the meantime."

"You will, and by the smell of that food, you've already found your calling. Let's eat!"

"Not yet, Agent August," Roman said, pulling her into him and planting a kiss on the top of her head.

"Why not? If Cal's throwing a party, then I'm taking advantage of it."

She noticed his laughter was nervous, and she felt a tremble go through him before he spoke. "Cal's not throwing the party. I am."

"You are?" Mina asked with confusion.

"Right now, it's a picnic. It can't be a party until you answer a question for me."

"Answer a question? What kind of party requires a question to convert it?"

Roman lowered himself to one knee and held up a box. "An engagement party," he said, his voice wavering enough he had to clear his throat.

Mina's hands shook as she brought them to her lips, her gaze drifting to the box when he cracked it open. Shining back at her was a diamond ring in the shape of a star.

"This is the first ring I saw at the jewelers," he whispered, holding up the box in earnest. "I never looked at another ring. This one signified who you are to me. You are my star. You have been since I met you eight years ago today."

Her gasp echoed across the lake now that the picnic had gone silent. "I'd forgotten, but today is the sixth."

"It is, and that's why I waited to ask you this question today. Eight years ago, you agreed to be my partner on the job. I'm hoping today you'll agree to be my life partner. Mina, will you marry me?"

He stood, and she took his face in her hands, planting a kiss on his lips that lasted longer than appropriate when the man was waiting for an answer.

"Was that a yes?"

"Of course, it was a yes. You're my universe, Roman Jacobs. Now put that ring on my finger!"

The team clapped and whistled as Roman slid the ring on her finger and then pulled her close. "And you're my North Star in the night sky, Wilhelmina August. I'll follow you anywhere."

Roman's lips captured hers again, and Mina sighed with contentment. This was the first day of the rest of their lives, and together, they were unstoppable.

* * * * *

CAVANAUGH JUSTICE: DETECTING A KILLER

MARIE FERRARELLA

To
Autumn Marceline Ferrarella
Welcome to the world, Little One
Love,
G-Mama

Prologue

Andrew Cavanaugh, the former police chief of Aurora, California, was finally about to sit down at the dining room table opposite his wife, Rose. He had just finished preparing a late supper for them, and for once, they were alone. It was a rare occurrence, given the numerous members in their family.

And just when he was about to pull out his chair, the doorbell rang.

Rose looked at her husband quizzically. He had already told her that they were going to be alone for a change. "Are you expecting anyone, Andy?"

It was meant as a tongue-in-cheek question, seeing as how there was hardly ever a time when they—especially Andrew—weren't expecting *someone* to drop by. The standing joke was that their home saw so much foot traffic, it could have easily doubled as Grand Central Station.

"I thought we were supposed to be alone tonight,"

Andrew replied. Resigned, the former chief of police made his way toward the front door.

He moved like a much younger man, Rose caught herself thinking with no small amount of pride and not for the first time. Even after so many years together, she considered herself blessed. They'd been in lockstep from the beginning, finishing each other's sentences and acting on the same thought. If he went in another room, eventually she'd find him. Always together and happy in the other's company. Well, except for one long period when she'd lost her way and forgotten how to get home. But Andrew never let go, thank God.

Leaving her napkin on her plate, she followed directly behind her husband, curious. One of their younger relatives must be paying a surprise visit or, more likely, was in search of a home-cooked meal.

When she reached him, Andrew had already looked through the peephole and was in the process of unlocking the front door.

His father, Seamus Cavanaugh, the former chief of the Aurora Police Department and official family patriarch, was standing on the other side of the door. Seamus's usual deep, warm smile was conspicuously missing. In its place was a look of deep concern.

"C'mon in, Pop," Andrew said, closing the front door behind the gray-haired man. When he turned to regard the older man, he felt he had a cause for concern. "I know that look, Pop. What's up?"

To his surprise—because his father loved to talk about everything and anything at the drop of a hat— Seamus Cavanaugh did not immediately answer the question.

"We were just about to sit down to dinner, Pop," Rose told her father-in-law, gesturing toward the table. "Join us," she said, inviting him in.

His father looked like a man who had just been caught in the middle of sleepwalking, Andrew couldn't help thinking. The man hadn't brushed his hair and looked as if he'd woken from a nightmare. Something was off and that worried him. Due to his advancing age, Seamus Cavanaugh had lost a little of his vim and vigor, but the light in his eyes had never lessened.

Until now.

This wasn't right.

At the very least, his father appeared troubled.

Andrew waited until his father had helped himself to several slices of pot roast and a healthy serving of mashed potatoes before attempting to engage him in conversation.

Seamus bathed the roast beef and mashed potatoes in gravy while totally ignoring the bowl of mixed vegetables awaiting his attention. Vegetables had never been the older man's favorite. The man groused often about how "leafy greens" were overhyped.

Andrew waited patiently until his father was

finished putting his dinner together, then asked his question again.

"Okay, out with it. What has you looking as if you've just taken a large bite out of a particularly bitter lemon?" Andrew asked.

"Andrew, let your father eat," Rose chided, gesturing at her father-in-law's plate.

"I'm not telling him not to eat," Andrew said. "I'm just urging him to indulge in his second favorite hobby—talking. If he doesn't do that, he just might wind up hurting himself." When Rose raised her eyebrows, Andrew elaborated. "Keeping all that in."

He half expected his father to snarl at the remark. It was part of their usual give and take.

But this time, there was no snarling on the older man's part. There wasn't so much as a hint as to what had caused him to come over so suddenly.

The silence hanging between them seemed to go a great deal deeper than any situation warranted. Either his father wanted to concentrate on eating, or something was terribly wrong.

Andrew shifted in his chair, his carefully prepared dinner completely forgotten. "Okay, Pop, now you've really got me concerned. What's going on?" the former chief of police asked.

In response, Seamus sighed. Andrew was well acquainted with that sound. He braced himself for a long, involved story, one that would likely rob him of sleep.

Seamus rested his fork on his plate, then looked from one member of the couple to the other. "Did I ever mention Nathan Cavanaugh to either of you?"

Rose shook her head.

"Not that I recall," Andrew told his father. It was not just a throwaway statement. The former chief of police prided himself on his memory. Had his father mentioned the name to him, even once, Andrew was certain that he would have remembered.

"I didn't think so," Seamus murmured, more to himself than to either person sitting at the table with him. "Nathan is the Cavanaugh nephew no one ever talked about. I hear that he was a rebel who always seemed to march to his own drummer." Seamus smiled sadly. "Making the family proud never seemed to be on his agenda. Instead of getting involved with law enforcement the way the rest of the family eventually did, or any sort of service-related way of life for that matter, Nathan just focused on having a good time."

Seamus looked as if every word he uttered pained him. "His father, Ethan, *was* in law enforcement, but he died in a traffic accident when Nathan was still a kid.

"As it turned out," Seamus said, continuing, "Nathan's mother, Barbara, never seemed to be all that up to the job of single-handedly raising a child. And she deeply resented Ethan's family—meaning us," he clarified, looking squarely into Andrew's eyes, "meddling in her life and her son's life. So, not long after Ethan was killed, Barbara took off with her son. Nathan was eleven at the time and was already getting into trouble."

"You couldn't find a way to stop her?" Rose asked, surprised. As far as she was concerned, the Cavanaughs had always been a force to be reckoned with. In addition to being a close-knit family, each member kept tabs on the other. If one was in dire straits, the Cavanaughs rallied around until the matter was resolved. Usually, it all ended in a massive family party. But maybe not this time.

"So, when Barbara and Nathan left, I thought it was better for everyone all around just to step out of the way," Seamus confessed. "I know that Brian," he said, mentioning one of Andrew's brothers and the current chief of detectives, "attempted to keep tabs on Barbara and the boy, but then they moved to New York City. Shortly after that, they proceeded to disappear off the face of the earth. That was approximately fifteen years ago."

"Not that I don't find all this fascinating," Andrew told his father, "but where is this going, Pop?"

The expression on Seamus's face turned grim right before Andrew's eyes. "Nathan's remains were just discovered, along with the remains of several other people, in a mass grave unearthed by a construction crew. The company was in the process of clearing a very large site of land. The idea was to build on it. That poor kid," Seamus lamented. "He never had a chance. We could have done something to stop this."

Andrew exchanged looks with his wife. Nothing was ever simple when it came to the family, he couldn't help thinking. His father's guilt alone warranted a few extra hours of consoling. But with this discovery about Nathan, Andrew understood that the Cavanaughs had to rally around one of their own, even if only to find out the real story behind his death.

"This just got a lot more interesting rather quickly," Andrew commented.

"Tell me about it," Seamus said, reaching for the bottle of wine next to him.

Chapter One

"Are you sure the remains belong to a Cavanaugh?" Brian Cavanaugh asked his father the moment he walked in through the front door that evening.

Andrew had called him with the news. This was the first Brian had heard of Nathan Cavanaugh, resurfacing after all this time, but the chief of detectives supposed that anything was possible.

Andrew had called in both of his younger brothers to the house. Since their brother rarely invited anyone over without mentioning the words "impromptu party," Brian and Sean knew this had to be something serious.

They had lost no time in arrived at the former chief of police's house. Living close to one another, Brian and Sean arrived quickly, practically within two minutes of one another.

Seamus frowned at his sons. "Do the letters D-N-A mean anything to any of you boys?" he asked after giving each of his sons, including Andrew, a steely look that felt as if it had gone clear down to the bone. "With our collective experience in law enforcement, you'd think some of the brains would have rubbed off on you three."

Andrew sighed, digging deep for his patience. "Yes, Pop, we're all aware of DNA and the advancements made in the field of forensics since you were in your heyday."

Seamus shot his oldest a warning look. "Watch your tongue, boy."

"That goes both ways, Pop," Andrew said patiently.

"Okay, boys, back to your corners, or I'm sending all of you to bed without any dessert," Rose warned the men who were sitting around her table.

Seamus pretended to huff as he gave his oldest son a glare. "She's certainly become cheekier since she got back."

"She certainly has," Andrew confirmed with a laugh, giving Rose a one-arm hug.

Everyone at the table knew that the elder Cavanaugh was referring to the period of time that happened years ago. Andrew's wife had left the house to clear her head after they had had a rare argument, and due to a sudden, unexpected rainstorm, she had wound up driving her car into the river.

Swept away, she came very close to drowning. The whole incident had given her amnesia. Because of that, she went missing for a number of years until fortuitous events had her crossing paths with her youngest child, Rayn, in the upstate diner where she had wound up working. Rayn immediately told her father, and Andrew quickly drove up to see for himself if this was the woman he had never given up hope of finding. It was.

Elated, he proceeded to work with Rose, and eventually, her memory did return.

"Never mind me," Rose instructed, knowing full well how very lucky she wound up being. "Just how sure are you that these bones that were uncovered actually belonged a Cavanaugh?"

"Very sure," Seamus assured his daughter-in-law. "The ME working the case is the grandson of an old friend of mine—and he has excellent credentials."

Andrew laughed softly under his breath. "'Of all the gin joints in all the towns in all the world, he walked into mine…'" the former chief of police murmured, allowing his voice to trail off.

"First of all, it's 'she,' not 'he.' And that's 'walks,' not walked," Brian told his older brother. "'She walks into mine,'" he quoted the movie line.

Andrew shot Brian an impatient look.

"Well, if you're going to quote it, quote it right," the chief of detectives told his older brother. "As for the sentiment, that still holds," Brian said. "Even across the country, there's no escaping the Cavanaugh penchant for getting involved in things."

It was Sean's turn to laugh. "That goes along with

the fact that no matter which way you slice it, there are a lot of us."

"Apparently," Brian willingly agreed. "So, what's next? You want some of us to go and check out the validity of this story?" he asked. "That these bones actually belong to a distant member of the family?"

"My friend's granddaughter is no dummy," Seamus stated. He sensed that his sons were skeptical, but that didn't mean disrespecting the professionals. Just because it wasn't reviewed by a Cavanaugh didn't mean it wasn't legit. These remains were their blood.

"No one said she was incompetent, Dad. This is one of those 'trust but verify' cases," Sean told the others. "So, when do we go and collect these 'bones' and bring them back to bury in the family plot, where they belong?"

"I'm thinking that it's too soon for that," Andrew said to the others. "I'd hazard a guess that they're still trying to put the pieces together so they can figure out who killed these people and why."

"It's not just Nathan," Seamus told the gathering. "My guess is that they're trying to figure out who killed and dismembered the other people who were buried in that mass grave as well." His sons turned to look at him, which encouraged Seamus to continue. "I know I'm just an old man to you boys," he began, only to have Brian interrupt him.

"No one was saying that, Dad," Brian said.

"You didn't have to, boy," Seamus snapped. "It's written all over your faces." When Andrew began to protest, Seamus held up his hand to silence his oldest, not wanting to get embroiled in a pointless argument. "But if you ask me, I would say that the collections of bones points to the fact that this could very well be the work of a serial killer. A very specific kind of serial killer."

It sounded like a viable theory, but Sean knew the danger of jumping to that conclusion too soon. They'd seen enough cases go south due to assumptions made on little to no evidence.

"What makes you say that?" Sean asked. His interest was thoroughly piqued, as always. He considered himself invested. Not only was Nathan Cavanaugh likely family, but a serial killer at large meant more victims.

"The number of dismembered bones that were discovered says it all," Seamus said.

"The entire area could have once been a cemetery," Andrew said, for once going with the simplest explanation, even though in his heart, he knew he was reaching.

"It could have been," Seamus magnanimously agreed. And then his green eyes narrowed. "But it wasn't."

"And how would you come to that conclusion?" Sean asked.

"That was the first theory that was considered

and then discarded by my friend's granddaughter," Seamus answered.

"Your friend's granddaughter," Brian repeated. "Is she the one who came up with the serial killer theory?"

"It's not exactly a far-fetched theory," Sean interjected before their father could answer. His work in crime scene investigations had involved some rather heavy-duty crimes. It had shown him that there were more serial killers than he or anyone on his team was comfortable with. "Bear in mind that New York isn't some quiet, peaceful small town. At any given time, there are eight million people living in a rather small, crowded area. I assure you that they're not all going to be getting along," Sean said. "As a matter of fact, I'm rather surprised that New York City doesn't have *more* serial killers populating the area."

Seamus nodded his head. "That's putting it mildly."

There was something in his father's voice that caught Andrew's attention. "Do you know something, Pop?" he asked. "What's your angle on all of this?"

"Only that I've brought this rather troubling puzzle and placed it in the laps of possibly the best law enforcement officers the area has ever had the good fortune of possessing," Seamus told his three sons.

Andrew exchanged looks with his brothers. That had to be the most flattering thing any of them had

ever heard coming out of their father's mouth—
which instantly made Andrew suspicious. "The man
is definitely after something," he declared knowingly.

All three turned toward their father and eyed him
while they waited. Seamus appeared the soul of innocence, his eyes darting back and forth, as if about
to deliver the mother of all assignments to them.

"Out with it, Pop. What are you looking for?"
Andrew asked.

"That's simple enough. Closure." Seamus answered the questions so simply, he momentarily succeeded in shaming his sons for thinking there was
something more sinister behind his motivation. "If
this collection of bones does turn out to be a Cavanaugh, we owe it to the boy—and the family—to
make the identification in person."

"And if he isn't a Cavanaugh?" Andrew asked,
picking up on the way his father had phrased his
statement.

Seamus considered the question for a moment,
wanting to word his answer just right in order to mo-
tivate his sons. They had to join him on this quest.
The idea that one of their own would lie in an un-
marked grave turned his insides cold. Nathan Cavanaugh deserved to come home.

"We've all made our livings by pursuing justice,
trying to bring it to the victims whose paths we've
crossed as well as all the people we've come in con-

tact with along the way. This isn't really any different than that. It just might wind up proving to be more personal," the senior Cavanaugh said.

"And if not, this is still part—I'm proud to say— of the service that we provide to the general public." Seamus paused to catch his breath as he surveyed his sons, waiting for their confirmation. "Am I right?"

Andrew felt as if he spoke for all of them as he nodded his head. "You're right, Pop. So, what do you propose we do next?" he asked, aware that his father loved being consulted about procedure.

Seamus never hesitated. "I'd suggest sending a few of our people to offer their services to the NYPD to try to solve this case. I'm sure that, given the situation, they wouldn't turn down the help. We all have to help each other whenever we can. At any given time, they probably have more than enough to keep them busy without taking on a cold case—or several cold cases, as it looks like it's going to turn out," Seamus amended knowingly.

Andrew nodded, glancing toward his brothers. "Sounds like a good suggestion to me."

"You're already in the will, Andy. No need to kiss up to me," his father told him.

Andrew laughed, shaking his head. "There really is no getting along with you, is there, Pop?"

The remark was met with pseudo surprise on Seamus's part. "That *was* getting along with me," his father informed him. "And of course, now I'm hungry again. Go figure."

The four men chuckled, which was the moment when Rose chose to walk back into the dining room. She came in carrying a tray covered with five plates of coconut cream pie that she had prepared earlier. Years of being married to Andrew had taught her to always be prepared to feed any number of her husband's relatives at any given moment. She felt she couldn't go wrong with this dessert.

She looked from one man to another, her gaze stopping with her husband. "Is it safe to come in?" Rose asked.

"It was always safe to come in," Brian told his sister-in-law. "Especially for you."

"Let me rephrase that. Are you finished making negotiations?" she asked.

Seamus smiled. "They're all but set in stone, my dear," he assured his daughter-in-law.

"So, they agreed with you?" Rose asked, setting the tray down in the middle of the dining room table. It was a far smaller version of the one that Andrew often used when he held the family gatherings. Just a cozy, well-used cherrywood table for six. There had been decades spent sitting in this space and hammering out the problems of the world—and celebrating the joys of family.

"The boys' mama didn't raise any fools," Seamus

assured his oldest son's wife with a broad, knowing smile.

"I'm sure you had a lot to do with their upbringing," Andrew's wife said with a wink. She had heard
enough stories from her husband to know that her
take on his and his brothers' upbringing was correct.

Seamus smiled broadly for the first time since he
had crossed his oldest son's threshold this evening to
deliver this unsettling piece of information.

"Andrew did very well hooking his star up to
yours," Seamus told Rose, displaying very obvious
approval.

"I'd say that we were both lucky," Andrew told
his father, his eyes meeting his wife's.

Brian laughed, shaking his head. "Get a room,
you two," he told the couple, pleased that the duo
was still very much together.

It was Andrew's wife who answered him instead
of Andrew. "We fully intend to just as soon as the
three of you all leave," she informed her father-in-
law and Andrew's brothers.

Seamus chuckled sadly. Lord, but he did miss his
wife, he thought.

Months would go by without that old familiar
feeling seeping into his bones and nibbling away at
his gut. Even so, he never doubted that it was there,
lurking in the shadows, waiting for him to let his
guard down before it would finally pounce and take
a chunk out of him.

It was the price a man paid for being fortunate enough to experience one great love in his life, Seamus thought philosophically.

Belatedly, Rose began to distribute the desserts, placing one plate before each of the men at the table and finishing putting one in front of her own space. She looked around at the men seated at the table.

"Can I get you boys something to drink? Coffee? Tea? Liquor?" Rose asked, going through what she had learned were the logical choices first.

"Sit," Andrew urged, rising to his feet as he said it. He nodded toward the men seated around them. "I'll water these heathens."

"You did the cooking—again," Rose emphasized. "The least I can do is distribute the dessert and get them something to drink so that you can go back to talking about this family member no one can remember ever meeting." She looked at Sean and Brian, "Although, one would think that you wouldn't have to go looking for something to occupy yourselves with, given that there is really enough for the police department to do right here in Aurora."

"This is family," Andrew told his wife in all seriousness. "And we never give up on family, no matter how much time might have gone by since he or she sat at this table," he said. For the time being, he was speaking hypothetically. "We will be there for them no matter what, when it really counts."

Rose nodded. There was no missing the message that her husband was leaving her.

She pressed her lips together. "I know," she answered.

And no matter what else happened, she would absolutely and endlessly always be grateful for that. Because if Andrew hadn't subscribed to that way of thinking, she might still be up north working in that sad little diner at the end of the road, feeling like there was a huge part of her life that was still missing—without having so much as a clue as to what it was and how to find it.

Rose found herself looking at Andrew and, for the umpteenth time that month, thought about how very lucky she was to have married Andrew Cavanaugh.

Chapter Two

It was a known fact that there were no real secrets within the Aurora Police Department. That fact was doubly true when it came to the Cavanaugh contingent that existed within the various sections of that police department.

The rumor went that something only needed to be *thought* about before it was conveyed from family member to family member at lightning speed.

That was, according to Brian Cavanaugh, only a standing joke of course, but there were times when the chief of detectives had his doubts as to just how much of a joke it actually was. So, when he called in a few members of his clan, his eyes swept over them, wondering if any of them knew why he had called them in, or if they were going to get ahead of themselves and *tell* him why they thought they were being summoned into his office.

Travis and Murdoch, the two young men, and Cassandra as well as Jacqui, the two young women, all part of the police force, looked amazingly similar to one another. There was no mistaking the fact that they were all related by blood.

The amazing thing was that they were all the product of two people who did not get along. In an era when few married people ever got a divorce, the couple did divorce when their sons were still young boys.

The boys' mother took the younger son, Murdoch, and went her own way while their father remained where he was, keeping the older son, Seamus. The boys grew up without ever interfacing with one another. It was a tragic reality of divorce, though both boys had grown into fine members of the Cavanaugh brood.

Two extra chairs were brought into the chief of detectives' office so that everyone was able to sit down for this meeting. Consequently, since there were four chairs in total facing the chief of detectives' desk, it was a little more crowded than usual. He went over to close the door and pull down the shades in case fellow detectives got too curious.

Brian then took his place behind his desk and smiled at the detectives facing him. The chief proceeded rather slowly, feeling the young people out.

"Do you have any idea why I've called the four of you in here?" he asked them, looking from one to the other.

He waited for someone to speak up, wondering if

he would be interrupted immediately or if the young family members would be polite and wait for him to speak first.

Cassandra was the youngest of the late Angus Cavanaugh's offspring. She was also one of the quieter ones. But after working steadily six days a week without a break for close to nine months on what had initially seemed like a simple homicide case but wasn't, she and her partner had finally wrapped up the case.

Cassandra was more than ready for a break. She was planning on looking into taking a vacation the moment today was officially over. Heaven knew, she had the time coming to her. Her mind started to wander toward visions of a beach vacation and nothing but a thick book and a fruity cocktail with an umbrella. No, that wasn't really her style, was it? She'd be bored after twenty minutes.

And right now, she wanted to know why she was sitting here with her cousins. No one was talking, which put her nerves on edge. She had to say something. Now.

"Word has it you called us here because of what Grandfather Seamus discovered on his trip to New York City." Cassandra was only putting into words what the rest of her cousins had already been speculating about the moment they received the summons to come to the chief of detectives' office.

Secrets were extremely hard to come by, especially in her family, Cassandra couldn't help thinking.

"And what was it that he discovered?" Brian asked innocently, baiting the newly promoted detective who had more than performed admirably in the department. It was why she had initially secured that position in the first place.

Cassandra was aware that everyone in the room knew the answer to the question that the chief had just asked, but because Brian had never been anything but extremely fair without being unduly partial, Cassandra willingly played along and answered his question.

She dutifully recited what she herself had just recently discovered. "That Granddad Seamus discovered that there was a Cavanaugh that the rest of us were not really aware of and that his body had been discovered buried in what turned out to be a mass grave."

That was rather a vague explanation, but Brian was satisfied with it. "Word really does get around the ranks rather quickly, doesn't it?"

"We're detectives, sir," Travis Cavanaugh, one of the detectives attached to the fraud division, said, speaking up. "We detect."

"After all, it's in our blood," Jacqui, Cassandra's older sister, added to her cousin's assessment. "Not doing so would probably wind up driving us crazy, not to mention going against the laws of nature."

Brian nodded. He had expected nothing less from the young people sitting in his office. At this age, they were still all eager to solve crimes and every single mystery they came across. Time would teach them to savor those rare down moments when they did come around.

"I'm thinking of sending one or two of you to New York to find out what happened to this unknown, estranged Cavanaugh member—and why," Brian stressed.

"And what do you want us to do with the rest of the day?" Cassandra murmured under her breath, purely tongue-in-cheek. Accustomed to talking to herself, she didn't realize that her voice had carried.

But it did.

Brian's mouth curved. "Well, that will be entirely up to you, Detective," he answered, his eyes lighting up.

Startled, Cassandra looked up at the chief of detectives, the gist of his words sinking in. "Are you saying that you want me to go to New York to investigate?" she asked, stunned. She hadn't been expecting that. *Well, there goes that boring beach vacation—thank goodness.*

"Is there any reason that you wouldn't be able to go?" Brian asked. He glanced at the pages on the side of his desk, but there was no reason to review them. He already knew what was there, thanks to his ability for total recall. "I see that you have a lot of vacation time on the books, time you need to take before you lose it."

Cassandra shook her head. "No, no reason, Chief. But going to New York would be kind of expensive. Prohibitively so," she added.

As a rule, Cassandra had always been careful with her money. It was one of the first things she could remember her father teaching her. He was very big on saving money, teaching his seven children to always weigh whether or not they could do without something rather than just spending money on it willy-nilly. And coupons. What wasn't to love about coupons? Cassandra kept a stack of them, feeling great satisfaction when she could present them at the grocery store.

Yeah, New York would likely drain her bank account.

"Cassandra, if you go, you would be going there as a police detective. The trip and everything associated with it would be covered and on the Aurora Police Department's dime—as long as you don't suddenly decide to go crazy spending," he added with a laugh. "And, from what I am told, going crazy isn't exactly your style.

"When all is said and done, you would be going to bring back Nathan Cavanaugh's body—or what there is left of it—so that it can to be buried in the family plot.

"Hopefully, along the way, you would be able to

find out what happened to him. At the time Nathan went missing, I gather that his friends just assumed he disappeared of his own volition and not because something had happened to him."

Cassandra stared, amazed. "Does this mean I can order room service for every meal?"

Her cousins chuckled.

"Don't push it. But you should rest up and take care of yourself. This will be a tough assignment," Brian said. "And it's a sad story, no doubt about it."

Brian continued with a sigh, "Barbara, his mother had run off with the guy she had taken up with at the time." An unreadable expression passed over his face. "I hear she passed away not too long after that."

He didn't mention that it took a lot of detective work on his part to find that out, but the long-distance detective work he had put in did not yield what happened to Nathan at the time. Cassandra would likely dig up more information when she got to the city.

"Apparently," Brian said, continuing, "there turned out to be more to his disappearance than just that, since fifteen years later, Nathan has managed to turn up in small pieces in a mass grave along with the bones of what I was informed were several other people."

Brian's eyes met those of his daughter, Janelle. The only lawyer in the family, she had been called in for the meeting as well. He wanted to get her take on the matter.

"Did I get that right?" the chief asked his daughter innocently.

Janelle flashed a smile at her father.

"Yes," she confirmed. "As always, Chief." They both knew that she was not there to rubber-stamp her father's actions but to make sure that he recounted them accurately and that the others in the room had no questions about what was happening. The last thing she wanted was to have her father sound as if he were making a mistake. Things like that, even in Aurora, had a way of blowing up.

Brian turned his attention back to Cassandra. "If I do wind up sending you to New York," he said, picking up where he left off, "do you think you can handle this assignment, Detective?"

So, he was being serious, Cassandra thought. She unconsciously straightened her shoulders as she answered, "Yes, sir. Absolutely."

I like her confidence, Brian thought as he nodded his head. "Good to know, Detective. Let me review a few more things, and I'll get back to you before the end of the day." He glanced around at the other faces surrounding his desk. "How about the rest of you? Any volunteers—or conversely, any objections to the idea of being sent to New York City? I grant you, it's not like Aurora. The weather's definitely a lot colder there these days."

"Might be nice to experience something resembling the seasons that the rest of the country faces," Murdoch commented.

"Said the man who never had to stand on the corner waiting for the bus in twenty-degree weather where the chill factor was down to five degrees," Brian said with a laugh as he looked at his nephew.

Janelle turned in her seat to look at her father. "And when did you have to face twenty-degree weather in New York?" she asked, curious.

"Not New York," he corrected. "But I was loaned out to the police department in Montana." He thought back, vividly recalling that time. "It was almost thirty years ago. At the time, they said it was the coldest winter on record." He laughed under his breath. "Anything you think is cold doesn't come anywhere near to the freezing weather in Montana. Not even close. I still shiver when I think about it," Brian admitted to the younger people in the room, all of whom had never experienced anything but the warm California sun.

"You're not exactly selling this assignment, Chief," Cassandra commented to the man. Maybe the beach vacation would be in order after New York City.

"Oh, where's your sense of adventure?" Brian asked good-naturedly.

She looked at her superior ruefully. "Solving that last crime wave was more than enough of an adventure for me, sir," Cassandra said to the Chief. Not to mention, New York was a city of eight million people, which meant it was crowded at all times. Cold and crowded didn't sound like a picnic.

Brian looked at the young woman, quietly studying her. Because of the number of his relatives that abounded in all capacities on the police force, he admittedly was more acquainted with Cassandra on paper than he actually was in real life.

In his opinion, she was being refreshingly honest right now. He had to admit that he would have thought that she would be chomping at the bit to be sent to the big city for free under the guise of taking care of business. That she appeared to be indifferent to the idea of experiencing all that without any actual cost to her surprised the chief, causing him to take an even closer look at her.

He had all but made up his mind to send her—but in his opinion, there was nothing to be gained sending her against her will if that turned out to actually be the case. There were enough capable people for him to choose from.

"Would you rather not go?" Brian asked Cassandra.

"It's not up to me," she told him in all innocence. "I will do whatever you and the job requires of me," Cassandra replied. *Even if it kills me.* She was a Cavanaugh, after all.

Brian sat back in his chair, quietly studying the

young woman on his left. In his opinion, Cassandra had just managed to tilt the balance in her favor. That made her the right person for the job.

But this was not just some simple walk down the street or around the block.

This required a good deal more than that, and he did not want to have to be responsible for having to twist the young detective's arm in any way. He put his question to her as openly as possible.

"Do you have any objections to going to New York?" he asked.

Cassandra thought for a moment. "I've never been," she answered.

"I already know that," Brian told her. "But that doesn't answer my question. Would going to New York City present any problems for you?" he asked point-blank.

"I'll go if she doesn't want to or can't for some reason," Jacqui said, speaking up, all but waving her hand in the air in order to take her sister's place.

Brian's smile rose all the way to his eyes. "I think we all realize that, but your sister is the one with an abundance of vacation days that are all but crushing each other. It's the opinion of the personnel department that she needs to take the time before she winds up losing it. Vacation time does not accumulate indefinitely," the chief reminded all of the detectives seated before him.

His eyes turned toward Cassandra. "Now, unless

you have some objection about going to New York on this assignment..." His voice trailed off as he waited for her to give him an answer one way or another.

She could just visualize her brother Morgan shaking his head and saying to her, "Where's your sense of adventure, Cass?" He'd be the first in line to try to prod her into going.

Though her job provided enough adventure for several lifetimes, Cassandra had never been any farther away from home than San Francisco. As many times as she thought about vacations, something always prevented her from seeing what else was out there. Maybe she was the one preventing herself from exploring outside of her comfort zone, which was the world of crime. Of course she needed to take part in this exciting adventure, especially if it would help the family.

She pressed her lips together. She didn't want the others, especially not the chief of D's, thinking that she was some sort of stick-in-the-mud who was willing to turn down a chance for a free trip to New York City. It was just that she was experiencing a little burnout.

But that would go away, she assured herself.

"Well, Detective?" Brian asked, waiting for his niece to give him an answer. He had the impression that he already had his answer, but he might just be jumping to conclusions.

Either that, or maybe Cassandra was afraid to

grab at the chance he was offering her, and she really did want to go, but for some reason, she wasn't admitting that to him. Or for that matter, to herself.

Cassandra spoke slowly, quietly reviewing this opportunity she was being offered from all possible sides.

The more she thought about it, the more excuses began to melt away until they completely eluded her. It occurred to her that she had nothing concrete to offer the man she thought of more as the extremely capable chief of detectives than her uncle.

"No, sir," Cassandra informed him quietly. "I have nothing stopping me from going to New York City," she admitted. "As a matter of fact," she added, her voice growing stronger and more positive with each word she spoke, "I think that my going there to retrieve the long-lost member of our family is a wonderful idea."

"Terrific," Brian concluded with a wide smile as his eyes met hers. "So do I."

Chapter Three

Cassandra had just gotten off the elevator when she all but collided with Travis. Catching hold of her shoulders, her dark-haired cousin kept the slender young blonde from falling as he grinned at her.

"Just the person I was hoping to run into," Travis said. He had just left the chief of D's office and was holding a manila envelope in his hand. "I've picked up the plane tickets and all the other necessary information from the chief for that trip to New York City. I was just about to go looking for you."

"Well, you found me," she said, amazed that he was back at the precinct, much less that he had accomplished so much in what amounted to such a very short amount of time.

"I can see that," he answered, pushing onward. "I thought that maybe we could catch a ride to LAX together."

She looked at him in surprise. Travis made it sound as if the details had been prearranged. "Did we talk about this?" she asked. If they had, it must have slipped her mind, she thought, annoyed with herself. But then, what with closing the old case she had been working and now thinking about the new one, she supposed that it was a little difficult keeping all her facts straight in her head at the moment.

"No," Travis said, "We didn't. But it only seemed like the logical way to go." He held up the envelope in his hand. "These are the plane tickets as well as the information about the hotel we'll be staying in and who to talk to at the Manhattan precinct about this case once we get there."

Cassandra suddenly felt as if she had somehow missed a step. She was used to being the one handling all the details, large and small. "Looks like you took care of everything that needed doing," she commented.

He had no intention of rubbing her nose in it. As far as he was concerned, this was her show. He was there just to help out—and to guard her, although he wasn't about to mention that part.

"I just got back before you did, that's all," Travis told her, then very quickly changed the subject. "Cullen's taking us to the airport. Unless you've already made other arrangements for us."

Cassandra shook her head. "No, not yet." She looked at her cousin. "Apparently, you've taken care of everything." Cullen was one of Travis's older brothers and worked cases that came up in the Fraud

Division. "I never realized that you were such an eager beaver."

Travis shrugged. "You've got to admit that this whole thing is out of the ordinary, and I guess that I'm just anxious to do the very best job I can. Who knows, this might even wind up leading to other things."

She took that to mean that he was looking into changing his career choice. She looked at him in surprise. "You're not happy in the division that you're in?"

"Oh, it's not that," he said, quick to deny her assumption. "I'm happy, but it never hurts to explore other possibilities." They were outside the building and heading toward the back parking lot. Changing subjects again, Travis told her, "I left my go-bag in my car."

"I did too—I left my go-bag in my car," she clarified, in case he thought that she had somehow gotten into his vehicle when she arrived. She glanced at her watch just as she saw Cullen's large beige car pulling up into the rear parking lot.

It was just a little after twelve o'clock. Traffic into Los Angeles was going to be absolutely awful, she thought, somewhat daunted. Most likely, it would be all stop and go.

"Are you sure that Cullen isn't going to mind driving us?" she asked. "Traffic is going to be in full swing."

"Cullen is usually up for absolutely anything," Travis assured her. "Why don't we collect your go-bag first, then we'll go get mine so we don't have to waste any of his time and get going?"

"Sounds good," Cassandra agreed. She was already heading to where she had parked her car. She expected to be making her way there alone, but she found that Travis was coming with her, shadowing her every step.

Cassandra couldn't help wondering if this was a sign of things to come, regarding their working together in New York. She honestly didn't know how she felt about that.

She had left her go-bag on the passenger seat next to the driver's side. She unlocked the door and opened it, which was when Travis leaned in and retrieved the bag for her. Looking at him in surprise, she found him grinning at her.

"I've got longer arms," he told her, handing it to Cassandra.

This was more than she was expecting. "I can carry my own go-bag," she informed her cousin rather crisply.

"No one's disputing that," he answered. "I just thought you looked a little tired and might want some help." He made no move to surrender the bag to her.

Shrugging, Cassandra decided there was nothing to be gained making a big deal out of what was, at bottom, courteous behavior. She knew for a fact that they had all been raised that way.

Locking up her vehicle, she pocketed her key. "Let's go get yours," she said.

At that moment, Cullen pulled his car up next to his brother and their cousin. He rolled down the window on his side.

"Your chariot awaits," he declared. Pulling up the handbrake, he got out of his car. "I can put that in the trunk for you, Cass," Cullen offered, taking Cassandra's go-bag from his brother.

"How do you know that's not mine?" Travis asked.

Cullen dropped the go-bag into his open trunk. "Because this go-bag doesn't look as if it's been through a war." He winked at Cassandra. "I know for a fact that Cass is a lot neater than you are, little brother," he said to Travis.

Turning on his heel, Travis retrieved his go-bag out of his trunk. The packed bag appeared dusty and badly in need of a cleaning. Packed tight, it was also straining at the seams.

"See what I mean?" Cullen asked Cassandra, pointing to his brother's bag.

Travis pretended to take offense at his brother's inference. "Very funny, wise guy."

"Just being observant," Cullen told Travis. Holding the passenger side door opened for Cassandra, he waited until she took her seat, then turned toward his brother who people had commented looked almost like his twin, except for being a little taller. "You get to ride in the back." When his brother frowned slightly, Cullen quipped, "Hey, it's either in the back or on the roof."

Sparing a glance at his passengers, Cullen paused before getting in on the driver's side. "You two all set?" he asked casually. "Nobody forget anything?"

"I think we're all ready to go," Cassandra told her cousin, then added with a warm smile, "You know you're going to make a great father someday, Cullen."

Travis rolled his eyes. "Don't encourage him, Cassandra. His ego's already the size of an ocean liner."

Cullen waved away his younger brother's comment. "Don't listen to him, Cass. You can say anything you want to me." He gave his brother what passed as a censoring look. "Travis already thinks he walks on water."

"Compared to you," Travis interjected pointedly, "I do."

Listening to the banter between her cousins, Cassandra realized how much she missed that sort of thing these days. Her five brothers were all married now, and between work and the separate lives they had established, she only got to see them occasionally.

Because she'd been so busy, she hadn't reached out to her brothers or their spouses enough. It was almost as if they lived on different continents instead of the same part of California. Part of her wished they would be in better touch with her, but they had their own lives. This happened when one partnered up; she understood that. How she wanted sometimes to belong to someone, to have one special person to talk to. But then, people like her were born to be 100 percent about their jobs. No time for other things. Right?

Cullen noticed the expression on Cassandra's face. "Everything okay?" he asked, sounding a lot more serious than he had when he had first arrived.

"Everything's fine," she assured Cullen. "Listening to the two of you just now, I remember how much I've missed my own brothers going at it like that."

Travis pretended to frown at her comment. "Don't encourage him, Cassandra, or he'll never shut up."

Cullen made a noise registering his displeasure over Travis's response. "Ah, you should talk," he told his brother.

"Well, yeah, I should," Travis agreed with no hesitation. "It's definitely preferable to listening to you doing all the talking."

Cullen glanced at Cassandra as he started up his vehicle again. "See what I have to put up with?" he complained, nodding at his younger brother.

She smiled at him. More accurately, at both of her cousins. "Yes, I do," she told Cullen. "And I have to admit that I'm a little jealous of that easy relationship the two of you have going for you."

"Speaking of being jealous," Cullen said, switching subjects easily. "I am."

"You want to back up a little there, big brother?" Travis requested. "What are *you* jealous about?"

Cullen glanced in his direction for half a second, "You're kidding, right?" he asked Travis, squeaking through the light as it went from green to yellow.

"Not that I know of," Travis answered, finding himself in the dark about his brother's comment.

Cassandra, however, knew exactly what her cousin was referring to. "I think he's talking about our trip to New York City," she said to Travis.

Travis leaned forward in his seat as he looked at his brother in surprise. "You never mentioned that you wanted to go to New York."

"What, you think I tell you everything?" he asked, feigning surprise.

Travis had another take on the subject. "You've never been quiet about anything," he said to his brother.

"You're getting me confused with yourself," Cullen told Travis matter-of-factly.

In response, Cassandra began to laugh. When Cullen came to a stop at the light, glancing in her direction for an explanation, she told both of her cousins, "You most definitely remind me of the way my brothers would go at it, dragging me into it when I least expected." Her expression grew wistful. "I had forgotten how much I really miss that time."

"Well, I just want you to know that you're welcome to hang around and listen to Cullen run his mouth off like that any time you like," Travis told her.

"Me?" Cullen questioned in surprise. "You should talk."

"I thought I was," Travis said to his older brother.

Cassandra crossed her arms before her as she sat back in the passenger seat and enjoyed what she thought of as "the show."

Without being conscious of it, the tension she had been experiencing for the last few weeks because of the case she had been working began to drain from her slowly and completely.

THE TRAFFIC FROM Aurora to LAX was even heavier than it usually was.

Normally, she would have been worried that they'd arrive late to the airport and wind up missing their flight. But in this new, relaxed state, Cassandra just leaned back and let life unfold.

"I've forgotten just how overwhelming the traffic to LAX can be," Travis said, sitting on the edge of his seat and watching the way the cars and trucks crawled by, seemingly making their way by inches.

"Don't worry, I'll get you there," Cullen promised confidently. "We've still got time. The trick is to give yourself plenty of time to reach your destination without breaking a sweat."

"I wasn't aware that you could sweat, big brother," Travis said.

"I just made a point of the fact that I couldn't sweat. Weren't you listening, Travis?" he asked pointedly.

Cassandra could see the outline of LAX coming into view, and she had to admit that she felt a sense of disappointment. Despite the fact that she knew they were supposed to reach the airport in time to be able to catch their flight to New York, getting to the airport meant that the show her cousins were putting on for her benefit—ragging on one another and bringing up memories of the way her brothers had been with each other around her—was sadly coming to an end.

Cassandra forced a smile to her lips, doing her best to seem carefree.

"Give me a call when you know when you're coming back to LAX," Cullen told her as he drove into the general lot. "I'll pick you up."

Travis spoke up, his voice breaking into his Cullen's thoughts. "I'm touched, big brother," he said.

"Yeah, I guess I'll pick you up too," Cullen said to him, sounding resigned. "But to be honest, I was thinking about just picking up Cassandra," he admitted.

Cassandra grinned. "You don't mean that."

"Oh yes, I do," Cullen assured her. He was approaching the terminal where their airline was housed. There wasn't a single parking space available anywhere near the terminal.

"Would you mind if I just let you off at the terminal?" he asked Cassandra. "It looks like it's going to be extremely crowded and impossible to park my car. I can either swing by and let you off at the entrance or park my car like several miles away so I can walk you two to the terminal."

"You'll do anything to get out of getting some exercise, won't you?" Travis cracked with a chuckle.

"Funny, I was thinking the same thing about you," Cullen told his younger brother.

Cassandra decided that she needed to call an end to this so-called dispute just in case it actually did get out of hand.

"Well, I for one think that dropping us off at the terminal is the right way to go. I have no desire to arrive in New York City exhausted and drained."

Cullen nodded. "Your wish is my command," he told his cousin.

The truth of it was that neither he nor his brother had any intensions of walking the long distance to reach their terminal. Pulling up at the terminal entrance, Cullen stopped his vehicle, allowing it to idle for several moments.

"Last stop," he announced. Remaining in the car, he popped his trunk so that they could retrieve their go-bags.

Travis lifted both his and Cassandra's go-bags

out of his brother's trunk. Once he had them, holding them in one hand, he slammed the trunk shut.

Leaning his head out of the window, Cullen told both his younger brother and his cousin, "Have a safe flight."

It was Cassandra who flashed a smile at her cousin as she said, "We'll definitely try our best, Cullen."

It was a promise that she intended to keep as she hurried toward the airport's electronic doors half a step behind Travis.

Chapter Four

"You're kidding."

Detective Danny Doyle of the Cold Case Division in a midtown Manhattan police department moaned in response to what Simon Lee, the man he had been partnered with on more than one occasion, had just said to him.

He looked at the detective whose desk was half a breath away from his, hoping to catch Lee grinning at him. That would mean that he was kidding.

But he wasn't.

On the contrary, Simon Lee had a very serious expression on his face. When a new case came in, Simon went from the jovial jokester to a serious and dangerous detective. Even though a few inches shorter and leaner than Danny, Simon could take down a fleet. And his partner knew how to lead him gently into bad news.

"Why would I kid about something like this?" Lee finally asked.

Doyle glared at the other man impatiently. "Because you have a sick sense of humor, and I'm up to my eyeballs in paperwork." If Lee was on the level, this was really going to impede his working on the case, not to mention everything else. "Whose idea was this, anyway?" Danny asked. He blew out a breath as his frown deepened. "This isn't funny, you know."

Danny took a deep gulp of his lukewarm coffee in the hopes that it would revive him.

"Nobody's laughing," Lee countered. "And from what I hear, the captain said to pass the word to the team that was identifying all those old bones that had been dug up at the construction site last week. That would be you—and me, as well as Davidson— but mainly you, because you caught this assignment first."

Danny blew out a breath. "Thanks for reminding me. It's yours if you want it," Danny told the other detective, raising his hands up as if to surrender all claim to the case. And then he looked at Lee more closely. "You're sure about your information? Because maybe you got it wrong," he suggested hopefully. "Maybe those California detectives were just calling here to get some information."

"No, they weren't calling for information," Lee told the other detective. "From what I hear, there are two full-grown detectives descending on us. They're cousins, I'm told."

"Cousins?" Doyle repeated, shaking his head. "Great. So this is supposedly a family affair?"

"More than you think," Lee told him. "The detectives who are descending on us are not only related to each other; they're also related to one of the dead men whose bones were unearthed at that construction site."

Doyle rolled his eyes, and for a moment, he just closed them, gathering strength. "Oh, this is just getting better and better by the moment," he told his sometimes partner.

When a group of people descended on one small case, that didn't always bode well. There were turf wars, especially if you weren't familiar with the other detectives. But family intervening on a case? Not a good idea, even if the case was ice cold.

Danny didn't enjoy the idea of California detectives shadowing him, probably making annoying suggestions.

But then he thought for another moment. As a good detective, he had to examine the case from every angle. "Well, maybe we'll wind up getting lucky."

"How so?" Lee asked gamely, not sure where Doyle was going with this.

"Maybe they'll get lost between leaving JFK

and getting here," Doyle suggested, then smiled as he thought the idea over. "At least, one can always hope." Of course they wouldn't get lost. All it took was a tap on a phone before a car magically appeared to deliver parties to their destinations. No, these detectives would arrive safely and ready to go.

Technology had changed their profession by leaps and bounds over the last twenty years. Sometimes he complained about it, but most of the time, he was grateful, especially when solving cold cases. Still, he was irritated by the impending arrival of the California detectives.

"It's hard enough playing musical bones as it is without having to answer inane questions from people who are more interested in working on their tans than in finding out who's responsible for killing victims from over fifteen years ago—and why," Danny complained.

Not only did his quip amuse him, but he was also quite proud of the fact that he had done most of the legwork. He'd been able to date the bones that had been brought to his attention. It had definitely not been easy, but then he had never taken the easy way out.

Before he had ever gotten into the field of forensics, he would have never guessed that the human body had so many bones. The fact that he had wound up working with six bodies from over a decade and a half ago felt as if he were immersed in playing a mind-numbing game of fifty-two pickup, except that there were a lot more body parts involved than just that small number.

"Maybe you're being a little too hard on these California detectives," Lee said.

"They're coming in from California when they could have just as easily called in with their questions instead of disrupting my concentration." Danny shrugged. "Maybe I am being too easy on them."

He didn't take kindly to having his work interrupted.

"Sounds to me like you woke up on the wrong side of the bed. Did you?" Lee asked, curious, a wistful expression on his face.

Danny frowned. "If that's your subtle way of asking if I got any sleep last night, the answer is that I really didn't. This case has been eating away at me ever since those body parts turned up and landed in my lap," Doyle complained with feeling. "This case is definitely enough to cross my eyes."

At this point, Doyle was having trouble keeping his eyes open. The detective blinked twice, then dragged his hand through his hair. Things were beginning to look fuzzy to him. He was doing his best to focus. After all the time he had put in working this case, it was getting more and more difficult for him to be able to concentrate to do that.

Lee saw the tired look in the other detective's eyes and face. He wasn't used to seeing Doyle like this.

"Why don't you call it a day and go home, Doyle?" the other detective suggested. "You can come in and start fresh in the morning. Besides, something tells me that you're going to need all your strength and patience to deal with those body parts. I've got a hunch that we haven't seen the last of them. I think that stray bones are going to continue to keep turning up for a while longer," Lee said.

Danny was looking at this from an entirely different angle. "Those bones are probably going to be easier to deal with than those California dreamers who are on their way here," the detective reasoned. "Just why are they coming to New York, anyway?"

"From what I gather," Lee told his friend, "they're under the impression that one of the people we've dug up is a long lost relative of theirs. The guy went missing years ago, and his location was entirely unknown—that is until last week," Doyle said.

"You know," Danny continued, "I can understand wanting to identify a family member, but I can't see why we can't do it here for them. And once we pin down who might have killed the newly discovered family member, we can send them the body."

Lee looked at the younger detective knowingly. They had worked together enough times for Lee to be able to guess what was going through Doyle's mind.

"You just don't want them getting underfoot," Lee guessed.

"Yeah, there's that too," Doyle agreed matter-of-factly. "The way I see it, we've got enough people here in New York City. We don't need to bring in a couple more bodies to join in," he said, rationalizing.

"Maybe they'll turn out to be helpful," Lee suggested.

"Yeah, right." The look on Doyle's face said exactly what he thought of that speculation. Not much.

Lee laughed. "And maybe having the others spend a few hours in your company will cause you to drive these 'California dreamers' back to where they came from," the detective told his partner with a grin.

Danny shook his head, looking far from friendly. "One can only hope. Okay," he announced, turning off his computer. When the light went off on his monitor, he locked up his desk, "You've convinced me. I'm going to call it a day and go home."

"Calling it a night would be more accurate," Lee told the other detective. He had already turned off his own computer earlier and was now locking up his desk. "All right, I'll see you in the morning," he promised Danny. "Try not to come in with the roosters this time," he added.

Danny pretended to sigh, feigning disappointment. "Well, I guess there go my plans for the morning," the younger detective said.

"Very funny," Lee said, then pointedly told Doyle, "See you in the morning."

THE FACT THAT there might be more unaccounted for body parts out there kept Danny Doyle up for most of the night.

You would think, the detective reasoned to himself, *that after going through the dismembered limbs for more than a week, I would have gotten used to sifting through them by now.*

But that just wasn't the case. At least not yet. All those unaccounted for limbs still comprised a mystery to him.

Well, at least one dismembered individual would be going home soon, Danny told himself. He supposed he could call that a win. A couple of other body parts had finally been identified as well, but not all of them. The only thing that had been identified was the manner of death. Obviously, to him that manner was homicide. The way the individuals had been killed and dismembered led Danny to believe that this was the work of the same serial killer, one that might still be active.

At least that knowledge was something, Danny thought, comforting himself. Now all he needed to do was find out who was responsible for these deaths, which was not nearly as easy as it sounded. Killers could come and go on a whim, though with updated technology, they had more ways to find them. There were fewer places to hide, especially in a city with top notch security.

Yeah, he could solve this case, provided that he didn't make a mistake.

DANNY STOPPED AT the café in the lobby and picked up his morning coffee. Something told him that he would need to treat himself to an extra large cup of the strong brew before facing these so-called detectives from California.

He just hoped he could hold on to his temper. He didn't like being told what to do. Over the years, he'd learned to swallow the resentment if someone went too far trying to step on his work. He wanted to move ahead and get the job done. This case might take extra restraint on his part.

Rather than the elevator, he decided to take the stairs to the fourth floor. He was a firm believer in getting his exercise in whenever possible.

Danny glanced at his watch when he reached the third floor. Despite all his efforts to catch a few extra minutes of sleep, he had still managed to get into the office early. There was something about the bodies that had been retrieved that still bothered him. He felt as if he had somehow failed to address something right out there in plain sight, but for some reason, he kept missing it.

But what?

It did not exactly put him in a good mood.

He supposed it was probably all just his imagination. There were times when he almost felt that there were serial killers hiding within every nook and cranny. Other times, he felt as if he were just letting his imagination get carried away. The one thing he wouldn't have ever believed until he became part of the police force was that there were so many of these killers out there, people who thought nothing of snuffing out a life.

That was because New York was a big city, he told himself as he walked into the Cold Case Squad Room. At this time of the morning, Danny expected to find the area fairly empty. And it was.

Except for the gorgeous blonde sitting one desk over from his. She wore a sleek gray suit, and her thick hair fell about her shoulders. Obviously, she was a supermodel or a test to see if he could be distracted. Just his dumb luck.

Assuming this was the woman who had come in from Southern California, he looked around for her companion. But the very stunning woman appeared to be quite alone…and waiting just for him. This had to be a dream come true or the universe's idea of a cruel joke.

Walking in toward his desk, he set down his sealed coffee container in the middle of the desk, took off his jacket, then draped the jacket over the back of his chair.

"Can I help you with anything or find someone for you?" he finally asked the woman after briefly making eye contact with her. Her large green eyes slayed him.

"That all depends," she replied.

"On?"

"On whether or not you can point me toward Detective Danny Doyle."

For a second, he thought she was kidding, then he realized that she was being serious. Not once did she look away from him, which was unnerving, to say the least. Obviously, this was how she got criminals to confess their bad deeds.

He glanced around to see if Simon Lee was somewhere hovering in the shadows, maybe to save him from his inevitable downfall. When he didn't appear to be, Danny still made no reply, but what he did do was raise his hand and silently point it to himself.

"You're Detective Danny Doyle?" she asked him, surprised.

"I am."

"Wow, what are the odds?" she marveled. He found the smile that rose to her lips absolutely mesmerizing.

Did she have any idea how lethal she was to him right now? He felt an urge to sit down but resisted it. Talk. That's what he had to do. Put words together and say them.

"I always thought they were pretty good, seeing as how that was the name on my birth certificate. I take it that you're the detective from Southern California who's come here to claim the body of your relative."

Cassandra nodded, putting out her hand toward

him. "I am. Detective Cassandra Cavanaugh, at your service," she said.

He shook her hand, hoping his grip wasn't too clammy, given how she started to make him sweat.

"Wasn't there supposed to be one more of you?" he asked, looking around.

He wasn't prepared to hear her laugh in response. "Did I say something funny?" he asked.

"There are actually a great many of us," she told him. "There are times that I feel like we comprise half of the Aurora Police Department."

Her lighthearted tone charmed him. Danny felt less on edge and more curious, which could be her way of trapping him into liking her. It was working. "Your whole family isn't here, right?"

"No." Cassandra got a kick out of the expression on his face. "They're back in Aurora, minding the store."

"So, you came alone?" he asked. Maybe saying that there were two of them coming had been a mistake.

"No, not alone. The chief of police insisted that my cousin come along with me, so there're two of us here."

Danny scanned the squad room for a second time, thinking he might have missed seeing the other detective.

But he still came up empty. "So, where is he?" Doyle asked, suddenly fidgeting with his hands.

"He's presently down in your cafeteria. Detective Cavanaugh wanted to stop for breakfast. He should be up here in a few minutes," she promised, saying, "Travis eats fast."

"Travis?" he repeated, wondering if he had heard her correctly. The heat had just turned on in the precinct, and the cycling noise temporarily blocked her out. He instantly felt the room getting warmer.

"My cousin," Cassandra clarified, raising her voice. "When we came to the precinct and explained what we were doing here, one of your officers escorted us into the building. An Officer Saunders," she recalled. "He asked us if we wanted to get something to eat or drink, and my cousin Travis is a walking bottomless pit, so naturally, he said yes."

Cassandra gestured around the area she was sitting in. "I wanted to come up here and get acquainted with whoever is dealing with the bodies that had been dug up." Her mouth quickened. "In other words, you," she told Doyle. "My cousin will be here soon," she said. "Travis hardly chews his food. He just swallows."

"Doesn't exactly sound like a pleasant experience," the detective commented.

Cassandra shrugged. "I wouldn't think so either," she agreed, "but from what I've been able to ascertain, eating that way seems to make Travis happy."

Danny frowned, more to himself than at the woman

he felt he was being saddled with. He raised and lowered his shoulders in an utterly careless gesture.

"Whatever makes the man happy," the detective commented.

"Trust me, you wouldn't want to have to deal with Travis when he's hungry. It's not exactly the most pleasant experience," she said, then grinned. "Picture trying to carry on a discussion with a hungry bear. A very grouchy hungry bear."

Danny gave her a look, wondering if she was kidding or just telling tales out of school for some unknown reason. Whatever happened to presenting a united front? Or hadn't these Californians heard of that?

Probably not, he caught himself thinking. He doubted that they were even capable of thinking. The part that irked him most was how she felt so comfortable sitting next to his desk first thing in the morning, as if she'd been here before and owned his turf.

Even though this person was alluring as hell, he couldn't deny his resentment. This was *his* case, and no amount of easy charm could sway him from that fact.

Chapter Five

Cassandra could see by the detective's expression that he was more than a little skeptical. "You don't believe me, do you?" she asked him good-naturedly.

It was difficult for her to breathe, but she forced herself. The man she'd be working with couldn't have been more handsome if she'd dreamt him herself. With his short brown hair, blue eyes and rugged stance, he looked like he'd walked out of an action-adventure movie. And yet, something about him seemed tired. New York tired. She didn't know him, but obviously, he'd been working hard and not getting enough sleep. In such a busy city, she could see getting lost in the whir of activity, especially when dealing with murder. And the detective certainly didn't want to mince words with her.

His expression grew dour. "It's not a matter of not believing you."

"Then what is it?" Cassandra asked, curious. Her blunt question managed to throw Doyle completely off guard.

The suspicious look in his eyes intensified. "Just why are you telling me any of these mundane things?" he said. "We need to focus on the case, like now."

"I'm just painting a broader picture for you," she told him, then added, "or filling in the blanks so you can get to know a little more about the dead man. Take your pick," Cassandra said, flashing a thousand-watt smile at him. She was determined to break through the glass wall he seemed to have erected around himself in order to keep her out.

Two things she'd learned from her work: (1) Cheerfulness went a long way. She'd managed to warm up the iciest of colleagues with a kind word. (2) Always be the last one standing. She could wait out even the most stubborn person, and she sensed that this guy wanted to play only by his rules. That did not make for a good team.

Could this detective be too stubborn even for her? The next few seconds would tell.

And then Danny blew out a breath, showing her once again the virtue of patience. "What I'd like to find out is what there was about your relative that would single him out to a serial killer, making his death more appealing over someone else's for some reason."

"And you're sure that this is the work of a serial killer?" Cassandra asked him.

It sounded like a challenge to him—and not one

without merit, he'd give her that—even though he didn't really want to. "Right now, I'm not sure of anything, but it's beginning to look that way," Danny said.

And then he sighed. It occurred to him that he wasn't being fair about this. That was what happened when he didn't get his required twelve and a half minutes sleep a night, he thought impatiently. People in his line of work took sleep for granted, never realizing how crucial it was for brain function.

"Sorry, I didn't mean to jump all over you like that," Doyle said.

Since he apologized, she waved the offense away. "Don't worry about it. I have five brothers," she told him. "It would take more than a misplaced curt word or two to hurt my feelings." Cassandra smiled. "We Cavanaughs are a lot tougher than we look."

"I'll remember that. Provided we work together long enough for that to matter," he added as a post-script.

She interpreted his words in her own way. "So, I take it that you're on the verge of wrapping this up quickly?"

Danny laughed under his breath. She was a sharp one. In his own fashion, he could admire that. "One can always hope."

"Funny," Cassandra couldn't help commenting, "you didn't strike me as someone who would be acquainted with something as nebulous as hope."

"Why?" he asked, pinning the California invader with a penetrating stare. "You don't know a thing about me."

A lopsided smile had slipped over her face, curving her lips. One skeptical eyebrow rose. "Are you sure about that?"

Just one question, and she leveled him. This case would be a challenge, for sure. But this intriguing new element might devastate him. Just yesterday, he hadn't known that Cassandra Cavanaugh even existed. He hadn't known that this woman and her cousin were descending on the precinct until just late yesterday. Danny assumed that when it came to that, it was a two-way street, which meant that she hadn't known anything about the people she was descending on either.

"Yes, I'm sure," Doyle told her after a beat.

Just before she and Travis had left, the chief had told her what and who to expect as part of her welcoming committee. In addition, she was also blessed with the kind of memory that never allowed anything to slip away into the recesses of her mind once she became aware of it. Especially when it had something to do with her family—and the idea of a serial killer being involved in this somehow only made it doubly so.

The moment she had learned the name of the detective in charge of this case, she immediately educated herself regarding Detective Danny Doyle.

The internet was a wonderful place for that. She had found all sorts of interesting things about him.

Cassandra's smile widened even more. She took a breath and launched into her recitation. "Okay, here goes. You put yourself through school by holding down two jobs. You took on a third part-time job to help support your mother when she had to stop working because she had leukemia. Any extra money you made went to pay her bills—until the day she passed away.

"Your biggest regret," Cassandra continued as he looked at her, stunned, "was that she didn't live long enough to see you graduate from the police academy—but she knew," she told him with certainty. "Trust me, she knew."

That was much closer to home than he was comfortable with. Doyle frowned. "You pretending to be some kind of clairvoyant?" the detective demanded.

"No, just a believer," she informed him with a soft smile. "You also have a tendency to keep your distance from people. That's an obvious effort to keep from getting hurt."

He was surprised at how dead-on accurate this detective from California was. Someone must have fed her the information. But who? And why?

"Not bad," Doyle told her coldly, inclining his head. "And just what am I thinking right now?" he challenged, his eyes meeting hers.

Cassandra laughed, her expression turned just a

touch somber as she shook her head. "Oh no, I don't use that kind of language," she told him seriously.

Doyle's eyes widened for a moment, and then he began to laugh, as if the revelation she had just made was dead-on and wound up utterly tickling him.

It was Cassandra's turn to be surprised. "You *can* laugh," she noted. "I didn't think that was something you were up to."

The laugh had just slipped out. Doyle backtracked. "Don't get used to it." he warned.

"I'll try hard not to," Cassandra answered, doing her best to sound solemn. Then she blew that all to hell when she added, "But you should know that you really do have a great smile. And that it interferes with your big bad wolf image."

"I'm not moved by empty words."

"That's good," Cassandra responded, "because I don't believe in using them."

A movement at the far end of the room caught her eye and she turned toward it. She discovered that Travis had picked that moment to walk into the squad room.

"Thank you," he said to the officer who had escorted him to the area. The moment he saw Cassandra, Travis's face lit up. "You *are* here," he declared as if finding her represented his journey's end.

"Certainly looks like it, doesn't it?" Her eyes dipped lower to his waist. "You get enough to eat?" Cassandra asked her cousin.

Travis smiled broadly and nodded. "They've got a great cafeteria, Cass. Doesn't hold a candle to Uncle Andrew's kitchen, of course, but then, nothing really does," he acknowledged. "Still, I can't complain."

"Detective Doyle," Cassandra said, assuming a formal tone as she turned toward the man she had been talking to, "I'd like you to meet my cousin, Travis Cavanaugh. Travis, this is Detective Danny Doyle. Looks like we're going to be working with him."

Danny felt as if he were listening to his own death sentence being recited. Now there were two Cavanaughs in his squad room. That couldn't be good.

Travis put his hand out toward the detective. "You don't look overly happy about working with my cousin," he noted with an understanding grin. "Don't worry, she'll grow on you."

"Like fungus?" Danny couldn't help asking. The words seemed to find their way to his lips automatically.

Rather than take offense for his cousin, Travis exchanged looks with Cassandra as he laughed. "How long were you up here with him?"

"Not that long," Cassandra answered innocently.

"Man must be a quick study," Travis said.

And then Cassandra got down to business. "He thinks that Nathan might have run afoul of a serial killer," she told her cousin.

"What I said," Danny interjected pointedly, "was that it was one possibility."

"Well, for lack of anything more concrete to send us in another direction, I'd say that this is as good a direction as any to start out with until something better turns up," Cassandra said.

"Around here, we don't just jump at the very first thing that comes along," Danny told the visitors.

Cassandra flashed a patient smile at the detective. "Good thing that we came along when we did; otherwise, these body parts might have gone back into the ground again, rotting for another twenty years, if not more."

Irritation creased Doyle's brow. "We don't rebury evidence."

"Good, then let's go on trying to identify who these body parts belong to and just what their last movements were before they became *disjoined* body parts," Cassandra said.

Exasperation creased Danny's brow. Why did every word out of this woman's mouth irritate him this way—because there was no denying the fact that it did.

"Is she always this annoying?" Danny asked her cousin.

Travis congratulated himself for not laughing out loud. "Hell, no. This is one of her better days," he told the other man. "You should see what she's like when she's going full steam ahead."

Cassandra shot her cousin an irritated look. "I can speak for myself, Travis."

Travis gestured with a flourish, encouraging her to continue. "Then go right ahead, Cass."

Cassandra turned to the detective who was supposedly hosting them, knowing full well that if it was up to him, they'd be boarding a plane, bound for Aurora, California, right at this instant. The more he warned them off, the more she wanted to dig in her heels. Not only for professional reasons, but also it struck a personal chord for her entire family.

"Have you managed to identify who the other bones belonged to, other than our long-lost cousin?" she asked.

"Our forensic pathologist is running tests, doing her best to put a name to the pile of bones we retrieved. At the moment, she's managed to place them into six separate piles, and so far, we might have names for four of the piles. One for certain—your long-lost cousin," he said. "The other three piles have temporarily been identified. That leaves us with two unidentified piles of bones still in need of names. But it's just going to be a matter of time."

"That sounds promising. Why don't we divide up what we have at the moment?" she suggested. She realized that she was usurping Detective Doyle's position, but when she got excited, she just couldn't help herself. "If these people have any relatives around, we can start asking questions, eliminating possibilities." She could see the reluctance in the detective's eyes. "It beats sitting around, watching our nails grow."

"I thought we were the ones with the reputation of jumping in with both feet?" Danny said, referring to the fact that supposedly, outsiders felt that New Yorkers got ahead of themselves.

Cassandra laughed. "We just let you think that. That's mostly for camouflage," she confided. "Mostly, we observe and make mental notes—and then we lay traps. Real ones."

Danny sighed, taking a folder out of his drawer. "It's times like this that I regret not following my first dream," he murmured, mostly to himself.

He should have known better. By the look on Cassandra's face, he had managed to pique her curiosity. "Which was?" she asked the detective when he didn't elaborate.

It was obviously too late to take back what he had just said. "Becoming a fireman."

"A fireman?" Cassandra echoed seeming mildly intrigued.

"Yes," Danny bit off.

"How old were you?" she asked, trying to put this in the proper perspective.

"Doesn't matter," Danny told her, dismissing her question.

"It does if you were five years old at the time," Cassandra countered.

Doyle looked at her, surprise registering on his face.

"Not bad," he said. He knew that piece of information hadn't made it into any file. That had to be pure intuition on her part. "Is that your gut talking?"

She placed a spread-out hand over her stomach as if to press back any possible rumbling sound that might have risen to the surface. "I certainly hope not," Cassandra quipped.

"Do you charge extra for the comedy act?" Danny asked cryptically.

"Nope," she informed him with a grin and then winked at him. "That's on the house."

It was an odd time for him to notice that her eyes, which were an incredible shade of green, were sparkling as she looked at him, but nonetheless, he did. It caused the cryptic words that had risen to his lips in response to temporarily fade away.

"If you don't mind," he heard himself saying, "I'd rather that drinks were on the house, not your comments."

"Tell you what, we identify all six sets of bones and bring this case to a satisfactory end, and I'll definitely spot you those drinks," she promised.

Danny's eyes met hers. "All right," the detective told her, then he shifted to look at the man who had come with this annoying woman.

As if on cue, Travis turned to him. "Don't worry, Cassandra has always been as good as her word."

Danny wasn't at all convinced. Still, he couldn't

exactly come out and contradict the detectives that had descended on his precinct—and him as well. It didn't make for a good working relationship—however long that was going to last.

And he hoped not long. With luck, by the end of the week, this irritating woman and her partner would stop disrupting his life and be on their way back to where they came from.

He just had to last that long, he thought. That meant hanging on to his temper. That was not as easy as it might seem, Doyle couldn't help thinking.

Gritting his teeth, he managed to squeeze out the words, "I certainly hope so."

Travis felt that the response merited one from him.

"There's no reason to doubt that," he told the New York detective, coming to his cousin's defense. "Trust me, there's no reason at all."

Chapter Six

The newscaster's voice echoed ominously in the dark, all but empty apartment, eerily recounting a story about the number of skeletal bones that had just recently been unearthed, thanks to a construction crew clearing through an old, long-neglected site.

"The site has incurred a temporary work stoppage until the bones that were found—overwhelming in number—can be identified." Pausing, the young woman took in a deep breath. "Progress unfortunately is very slow due to the weather conditions," the pert newscaster added.

The man who was bent over the coffee table, intent on consuming the omelet he had made, stopped eating. He raised his fork from the plate and used it to give the reporter a mock salute.

"Yeah, well, good luck with that," he said, laughing under his breath.

He was more than well acquainted with all the bones that had been found at the site. Was responsible for not only all of them but the manner in which they had been laid out. He had documented them all in his head—doing it on paper was far too dangerous and incriminating. But no matter, he was the only person who mattered here.

After all, he had been the one to have laid these men to rest in the first place.

These men as well as so many others.

He hadn't expected for the bodies to have been discovered for a very long time. That they had been after all his precautions was a real surprise. But that was neither here nor there. After all, he hadn't done it for the notoriety in the first place. At least, not at the time. He had done it because each and every one of those pretty boys that he had skinned and buried had had it coming to them.

As he thought about it—lost in a world of his own making—he paused as he savored the last of the omelet he had made—just the way he had been taught to do all those years ago.

The taste of the omelet reminded him of the child he had been—and the way his mother had always made him clean his plate.

Insisted on it, really. Otherwise, he was not allowed to get up from the table. Instead, he would be forced to sit there no matter how long it took to finish his meal. Sometimes that meant hours on end. A few times, he'd spend the night sitting at the table and staring at his uneaten food. Then, his mother would find him in the morning and yell at him to clean up and go to school. Those memories haunted him. Maybe not haunted, he amended, but inspired him to lead life the correct way.

He could still hear his mother's voice in his head. *Don't you want to make your mama happy?* she had demanded. *Well, don't you?* she had asked, her voice growing more and more shrill when fear of his mother had stolen the words from his lips.

He had been small for his age and was very easily intimidated.

Until the day that he wasn't, he recalled with a tight, satisfied smile.

He spent a few moments reliving the memory of that day in the dark recesses of his mind before he rose to clear away his empty plate.

He would have rather just left the plate where it was for now, but again, he could hear his mother's voice in his head, reminding him, *Messes don't take care of themselves, you know—and I'm not your maid, Pretty Boy. If you think that, well, you just have another think coming.*

A shiver went down his spine as he did his best to banish all thoughts of his mother from his mind. Instead, he kept his eyes on the screen, absorbing every single nuance of the news as he washed his plate, utensils and frying pan in the sink.

If anyone could see him now, they wouldn't notice a thing out of place—just a guy rotting in a small room with its peeling wallpaper and fetid air. The whole city was a decomposing body; so much so, it was easy to go forgotten. Just one wrong turn and his past showed up on the news. But then, no one would be able to find him, and he didn't need a lot of space to continue his work.

A sense of satisfaction slowly marched through him.

"How's THE MEDICAL examiner coming along with making the IDs on the bones that had been unearthed?" Cassandra asked as she walked beside Travis, following Detective Doyle to where the young ME was faced with trying to make sense of what amounted to a bone jigsaw puzzle.

Walking into the room, she had taken note of the fact that there were collections of bones laid out on the various tables. At first, there seemed to be no rhyme or reason to it. But then, as she studied the various tables, she saw that four of them held what appeared to be approximately the same number of bones, more or less neatly arranged in some semblance of order, while the other two tables were not nearly as filled yet.

The jigsaw puzzles on those tables appeared to be in the middle of being sorted. None of those puzzles seemed close to complete, certainly not nearly ready to be identified, the way the bodies arranged on the first four tables were.

"Works in progress," Cassandra murmured to herself, doing her best to focus on the final outcome. Just discovering the fact that the compilation of bones appeared to be the work of a serial killer was a big deal. Whatever came after that could be viewed as a bonus.

Like nailing the killer who was responsible for these deaths.

"Baby steps," Cassandra said in an effort to comfort herself. She hadn't meant for the words to slip out, but they obviously had.

Danny looked at her over his shoulder. "Did you say something?"

Oh, no, she wasn't about to admit to that. Cassandra could just anticipate this sexy detective's critical comments. She was not about to give him the chance to laugh at her.

"Nothing that bears repeating," she told Danny lightly, silently adding, *At least, not for the time being.* She intended to forgo that conversation until much later.

But apparently, the New York detective was not ready to drop the conversation just yet.

"Oh, I'm pretty sure that you did say something," Danny told her, humor curving a mouth that, at rest, could be described as being more than generous. The look in his eyes silently told her that he was waiting for her to own up to what he was saying.

"Sorry," she told him. "I'm afraid that it just

slipped my mind." She switched her focus slightly. "I'm really anxious to find out what we have on these people and how we can tie them to this being the work of a serial killer." She took a deep breath. "Where can we begin?"

The detective glanced at Cassandra's cousin and then at her. He had to admit that he had not been in the presence of this sort of blatant enthusiasm since—well, he really couldn't accurately pinpoint exactly when he had been confronted with this sort of eagerness to arrive at such needed answers.

Possibly never.

In New York, it was easy to burn out after a few brutal cases. After years, he'd seen the light go out of several colleagues' eyes. He just hoped he could muster the same workaholic tendencies and keep going until he felt his work was done. Maybe being around these two detectives was a good thing, though he couldn't admit this out loud.

"Look, I *know* you have to have serial killers back in Southern California," he told the cousins. "They're not just exclusive to New York City."

"I know that. They most definitely exist in California," Cassandra answered before Travis could say a word.

Danny blew out a breath as he shook his head. "Then I don't get it. Why are you so excited about this case?"

Cassandra never hesitated. "Number one, it answers questions about what happened to our long-lost cousin, and number two, there are endless possibilities regarding the other murders as to who the victims are and why they were killed." She looked at the detective. "If we find out who these victims are, maybe we can find out what it was that they had in common that might have led to their demise."

"In other words, we resort to the usual," Danny told the visiting detectives.

"The usual?" Cassandra questioned.

"Yes. Working hard, putting in long hours and juggling a ton of unanswered questions," Danny said.

Cassandra shook her head. There was almost a depressing, hopeless note to Doyle's voice. "Oh, Detective, you have to be more positive than that."

"This *is* me being positive," he answered.

She stared at him in silence for a moment and then surprised him as she began to laugh in response to his comment. Obviously, Danny Doyle wasn't used to uplifting banter in any way. He was a pessimistic, just-the-facts kind of man. She usually didn't find this at all charming, but this one man tickled her. Yes, he made her laugh, maybe without trying.

"I believe you," Cassandra said. Taking a deep breath to attempt to regain her composure, she got down to business. "Do you have any reports or paperwork attached to any of these people?" she asked, waving her hand at the tables with their various collections of arranged bones.

Danny laughed to himself in response to her question.

"Something funny, Detective Doyle?" Travis asked. He was attempting to field the question for his cousin. He wasn't sure if this New York detective was just being callous or if there was something more at play here, but whatever it was, if it did turn out to be callous, he had been sent by the chief of detectives to protect her, and protect her he fully intended to do.

"I think that your cousin is the only detective I've ever heard referring to a collection of bleached bones as 'people,'" Danny admitted.

Cassandra examined the bones that had been laid out on the closest table and then looked at him in mild surprise.

"Well, they were people—once. The body parts on these tables represent someone's husband, lover, significant other, son, father… You name it, the possibilities are endless," Cassandra said, the look on her face challenging him to say otherwise.

Danny inclined his head, looking at the various bones spread out on six tables. "You are assuming that they were all males," he said. Other than the identification of her cousin, no one had said anything one way or another about these victims being men. "Why?"

Cassandra shrugged. "Call it a gut feeling," she replied guilelessly.

Travis glanced at the other detective, a touch of pity entering his eyes. He had just watched the New York detective slip unknowingly over toward his cousin's side, even if he didn't realize it. The man was a goner.

Cassandra's cousin glanced toward the medical examiner. The woman appeared to be totally enjoying the show from the sidelines.

Danny looked at the ME. The woman had been silent and appeared to be all but bursting to say something. "Do you have anything to add, Dr. Wade?" he asked, encouraging the woman to add in her two cents.

"Well, personally, I think this killer left more bodies in his wake," the ME said.

It wasn't what any of them had expected—or hoped to hear. "What makes you say that?" Cassandra asked, curious. Personally, she agreed with the woman.

"The bodies all appear to have been killed during approximately the same time period," Dr. Wade answered. "No one kills this many people and then stops cold."

"He might have been arrested for another crime and imprisoned—or even killed," Cassandra suggested.

"Maybe," Danny agreed, getting into the discussion. "Or maybe he just stashed his kills elsewhere."

"Which means they could still turn up at any time," Cassandra theorized.

Danny nodded grimly. "You're probably right. They could." The New York detective was far from happy over the thought.

Neither was Travis, who shook his head as he murmured darkly to himself, "Something to look forward to."

"Hey," Cassandra said to the others, sounding cheerful, "everyone needs a reason to get out of bed in the morning."

"How about just looking forward to a good breakfast?" Travis countered.

Cassandra laughed. Travis *would* focus on food, she thought. "Leave it to you," she told her cousin, laughing.

And then she turned toward Danny. She was surprised to see that his partner, Det. Lee, had come in to join them.

She had almost forgotten about the man, she realized. The man was being exceptionally quiet. He seemed like one of those people who kept to himself and remained quiet unless he had something worthwhile to say.

Well, she had no intention of just remaining here, aging without saying a word. Cassandra was all about jumping in and getting things moving. New York might be an incredibly interesting city with a lot to offer, but at the moment, all she was interested in was being able to close the case involving her cousin and taking him home.

And right now, all she had were questions, but no answers. She needed to know just how Nathan Cavanaugh went from turning his back on his family in California to being a pile of bones that had been dug up in New York City fifteen years later.

"Do we have any kind of a last known address for Nathan or his mother?" she asked Danny. "I realize that in all probability, it can't possibly be current since they're both dead, but at least it might give us a place to start. This way, we might have a fighting chance of piecing together what Nathan did, who he did it with—and maybe, just maybe, who terminated him."

"I take it that you also buy into the story about 'Goldilocks and the Three Bears,'" Danny told her, eying her rather skeptically.

She frowned at him. She didn't appreciate being ridiculed and took offense at Danny's words. She raised her chin in defiance.

"I don't believe in fairy tales," she informed him coldly. "I do, however, believe in ruling things out, and that's what I'm attempting to do at the moment. Do you have a problem with that?"

He opened his mouth, about to answer her, then

realized that maybe he was allowing the chip on his shoulder to get in the way of his thought process.

"Sorry," he finally said.

A host of different thoughts seemed to pass through her mind. They all registered on her face as well. And then, ever so slowly, she sighed and released the breath that she had obviously been holding.

"Apology accepted. Why don't we each go back to our respective corners and start fresh?" she suggested to the New York detective.

She could see that he was considering the idea, not jumping at it one way or the other, and then finally, he nodded. "I can go along with that," he told her, agreeing.

"Do you have anywhere that we can set up and get to work, or do we have to share space with these bleached bones?" Travis asked, nodding at one of the tables.

"We were told we could use the conference room for the time being," Danny told the duo.

"Sounds good to me," Cassandra told the other man. She gestured toward the door. "Lead the way."

Danny picked up all the folders that had been put together regarding the bodies. "See you later, Doc," he said to the medical examiner.

The latter nodded, her attention already back on her work. "I'm sure it won't be long before you're here again, unfortunately," she told the gathering. "But you know where to find me if you have any questions."

With this ominous goodbye hanging over them, the detectives left.

Chapter Seven

Chapter Seven

After ushering the visiting detectives into the conference room, Danny proceeded to come up with
reasons to remain away from there for several hours.

It wasn't as if he didn't have anything else to do—
he did. As a detective juggling cold case files, there
was always more than enough for him to do.

He went to the makeshift kitchen—or corner with
a small refrigerator—and pulled out small bottles
of water for them. On the counter, he noticed a few
packages of cookies. Maybe he should bring them
too in case they needed a little pick-me-up.

Absolutely not, he told himself. What was wrong
with him? Usually, he didn't think of these details,
but part of him didn't want to face what was in the
conference room. The idea of spending hours upon
days with Cassandra Cavanaugh made him hesitate.
This wasn't just a case between the two of them.

She affected him. The more time she spent with

him, the more obvious it would become. Like, inevitable that their lives might wind up intertwined.

No. Just no.

Eventually, he found himself being drawn back to the conference room with its posters and notes mounted on a bulletin board, as well as the people who were apparently painstakingly going over the evidence spread out before them.

Going into the conference room was almost against his will. The detective reminded himself he was only looking in on the visiting Californians—as well as on his partner—to check if there had been any sort of progress made—or even if there was a hint of some sort of progress.

When he walked in, he had to admit that he highly doubted it. After all, not nearly enough time had gone by to even unpack the files that had been found, much less make any headway in them.

But he had to admit—albeit silently and just to himself—that he was open to any sort of pleasant surprises. There was a chance—even a slim one—that he was wrong about them. Maybe they could make the difference in solving this case.

Danny walked into the conference room, not really sure what he would find. The logical thing to expect was that the detectives were ready to call it quits for the day—if not for more than that—and maybe even go back to where they came from, because the search was leading to nothing but depressing dead ends. California detectives maybe didn't have the same work ethic that New York detectives did. An absurd notion, but of course, he had to take any potshot at them in case they screwed up everything he'd done so far with this case.

He was surprised to find that Cassandra and her cousin were all but buried in a mountain of paperwork that they were reviewing. They had painstakingly—and quickly—gone through the various notes and folders that had been compiled on the victims.

Cassandra certainly wasn't going through the same existential crisis he was. She didn't show any competitiveness toward him or his team. On the contrary, she seemed unaware of anything except the case. Maybe that was her plan.

At the moment, they were in the process of making the notes to go with them.

Danny looked at the piles of papers scattered about the table. "Did you actually find something to follow up on?" he asked incredulously, looking at Cassandra, who was seated closest to him.

"Possibly" was her vague, drawn-out response as she continued studying the notes she was reading. "The DNA identifying our cousin gives us some information to work with. The other three bodies that had been unearthed around the same time broadened the base of our scope. Based on that and the information gathered about these victims, I would say that it looks as if all four were good-looking men."

"Okay," Danny agreed expansively. "But just why would that matter one way or another?"

"Maybe it doesn't," Cassandra allowed, since she couldn't really say anything definitively—yet. "But maybe our serial killer had a vendetta against good-looking men for one reason or another, and that was why they wound up dead."

"And what would that mean?" Detective Simon Lee asked, curious as to what the California detective was thinking.

She turned toward the man, her expression appearing to be utterly guileless and an open book. "Maybe something, maybe nothing," she said expansively. "That's what we're going to have to find out."

Danny looked somewhat impressed despite himself. "And here I thought all you California types like to do is surf and work on your suntans."

"Only when there are no bodies lying around," she told him, doing her best to deadpan. She was betrayed by the appearance of what looked like a spasmodic smile that was curving the corners of her mouth.

Danny nodded, quietly kicking himself for bringing up the cliché yet again. And he didn't like that he was so self-conscious around her. She and her cousin were 100 percent focused on the case. Whatever answers they had managed to come up with, they were obviously working hard. He supposed it was time to reward that effort.

"Well, I think you guys have earned dinner. What do you think?" Danny asked, looking around the room at the detectives, including his partner seated there.

Cassandra exchanged glances with her cousin, then nodded. "I think I can be bribed," she told the lead detective agreeably.

"This is fuel for energy," Danny said. "Not a bribe."

This time, Cassandra's eyes lit up as she grinned. She was not about to argue semantics with the other detective. It certainly wasn't worth it. She would have to fight for every teasing word she said.

"Potato, po-ta-to," she replied, then told him, "Okay, we'll do it your way. However you choose to look at it, I suddenly realize that I am pretty hungry."

Danny was surprised by her admission. "I would have thought I would have had to drag that information out of you."

Her smiled only widened. "It's you New Yorkers that have to have things dragged out of them," she told him. "Not us." Cassandra spread her hands wide in an exaggerated gesture of innocence. "Our lives, in case you haven't guessed this yet, are open books." Making the declaration, she grinned and nodded toward Travis in order to include him in this dynamic as well. "There's really no point in hiding who you are, and that goes double for when you're hungry. Say it and get thee to a restaurant, fast."

Not for the first time, Danny found himself intrigued by the woman's smile. The more he looked at it, the more it seemed to draw him in with absolutely no effort exerted whatsoever.

When the thought hit him, Danny frowned. He couldn't afford to be distracted by her sea-green eyes, which looked as if they had literally been lifted straight out of tropical waters.

"Detective?" Cassandra noticed the momentary distracted look on Doyle's face. "Did I just lose you? Or do you not like hungry women?"

"Hmmm?" Her question had managed to snap him out of his mental revelry. He cleared his throat, attempting to cover up his momentary wanderings. "No, I was just temporarily distracted," he said, deliberately avoiding her eyes.

Cassandra's smile grew wider as she said, "Well, nice to know that you're human."

His expression never changed as he told her, "Hey, it's the number one requirement for joining the NYPD. Although, don't tell this to Simon Lee." He laughed out loud before realizing that they didn't really know Simon well enough to get the joke. "Some of my colleagues act like robots. That's what I meant."

Several sarcastic remarks rose to Cassandra's lips, but in the interest of the dinner that lay ahead of her, even if it turned out to be at a quickie take-out place, she decided to swallow the remarks and keep them to herself. No point in antagonizing the New York detective needlessly. She was determined to maintain a friendly front and possibly, just possibly, build some sort of a positive working relationship with the man, however temporary it might turn out to be.

Besides, she liked watching him navigate this uncomfortable relationship between them. He was doing his best, and that warmed her heart.

"I find that encouraging," she told Danny cheerfully. "So, what sort of restaurant did you have in mind?" she asked. "Takeout? Pizza? Or...?" she looked at him, her eyes widening in a silent query.

"Well, I thought pizza," he answered. "But if you'd rather have something else, maybe something fancier..." His voice trailed off, allowing her to fill the space in with a more exotic choice for dinner.

"Oh, no, no." Cassandra was quick to turn down the idea of going to some sort of a fancy restaurant. "I have heard nothing but positive things about New York pizza," she told the detective. "There's no way I'll be able to go back home once this is all wrapped up without having checked out exactly what a New York pizza has to offer that makes it supposedly superior to the kind of pizzas that we serve up within our own humble pizzerias."

Danny eyed her somewhat skeptically, wondering if she was pulling his leg or if she was actually being serious.

For now, he decided to give her the benefit of the doubt.

"Okay, get your coat, Cavanaugh. You are about to be educated," Danny said. Then, backtracking, the detective actually did the honors for her, fetching her coat and helping her with it as he stood behind her.

Cassandra's mouth all but dropped open, as she found herself completely caught off guard by the detective's manners. She hadn't pegged Detective Doyle for being such a gentlemen. Reasonably polite, yes, but definitely not an out and out gentlemen.

She had to admit that it was rather a nice discovery—and she felt a delicious shiver go down her spine. The way he could be nice to her, it seemed a bit…intimate.

Cassandra turned her head in order to look behind her, not bothering to hide her look of unabashed surprise.

As he slipped the coat onto her shoulders, he caught the expression on her face.

"What?" he asked, somewhat confused.

She didn't want to be blunt about her reaction. Clearing her throat slightly, Cassandra murmured, "Nothing, just didn't expect you to be so…helpful," she finally said, for lack of a better word.

"I take it you buy into the brash New Yorker stereotype," Danny said, guessing.

"No," Cassandra quickly denied, then retracted

that assessment with a rueful expression. "Well, maybe just a little bit."

He watched her for a long moment. "Suffice to say that nobody we're dealing with is actually a one-dimensional character," the detective told her. "There are *always* extenuating circumstances."

"I'm beginning to see that." She looked around at the other detectives in the room. "So, are we all going out for pizza?" she asked, raising her voice to be heard above the noise.

Danny's partner, Simon, laughed. "Tempting though that really sounds, if I don't get home to Alice at a decent hour at least once this week, she is going to cut off my head and hand it to me, at which point, I won't be any good to anyone tomorrow—or possibly for the rest of my life," he said whimsically.

Cassandra smiled at the information the detective had just voiced. "Sounds reasonable to me," she said. "Travis?" She turned toward her cousin. "Are you going to be coming with us?" She fully expected him to say he was.

But her cousin answered by flashing a lopsided smile at her. "Well, ordinarily, I would, except that Joyce made me a really good offer that I just couldn't refuse."

"Joyce?" Cassandra repeated quizzically as she raised one bewildered eyebrow in a silent question.

Travis was more than happy to fill in the details for his cousin. "That really cute police officer who came in earlier. You know, the redhead who supplied us with all the files we currently have spread out all over the conference table. Anyway, we got to talking…" he began to confess, his voice trailing off.

"Of course you did," Cassandra said with a laugh, shaking her head. "Can't take you anywhere, can I?"

Her cousin ignored her remark and just continued with his explanation. "She told me that she knew of this really great out-of-the-way place that most people don't even frequent. They just drive right past it," Travis said. "To quote Joyce, 'The food is to die for,'" her cousin added with a wide grin.

Cassandra regarded him with a slight show of concern. She wasn't thrilled with his choice of words, not after what they had discovered happened to Nathan all those years ago.

"Just make sure that you don't," Cassandra cautioned.

"Hey, Cass," Travis answered, amused. "I'm touched." He dramatically placed his hand over his heart. "But I can take care of myself. Trust me," he said with a wink.

This case was getting to her. This was the first time that the family had lost someone to murder, and she had to admit that that did make her feel more than just a little bit vulnerable.

"I know you can," she told him, "but just in case, don't forget to be aware of your surroundings."

"Yes, ma'am," Travis replied solemnly, giving her a smart military salute.

At that moment, a rather pretty young officer looked into the conference room. Her eyes instantly met Travis's.

"Ready?" the redhead asked brightly, obviously eager to leave the conference room and get rolling.

"Absolutely," Cassandra's cousin replied. "See you in the morning, Cass." He nodded at her, then turned his attention toward Doyle. "Detective," he said, nodding at the man.

With that, Cassandra's cousin walked out of the room, allowing the attractive officer to lead the way.

The conference room had emptied rather quickly, Cassandra noted.

Danny had turned toward Cassandra. "Guess that just leaves us," he said. "Unless you'd just rather go straight to your hotel room and go to bed," he suggested.

Cassandra blinked. "Excuse me?" she asked, looking at the detective as if the latter had just slipped into some sort of a foreign language.

Danny suddenly realized what the woman from California thought he was saying to her. His skin went hot from the mere suggestion. He definitely wasn't thinking straight. "I meant to get some sleep, not anything else."

Indignant, Cassandra tossed her head slightly,

sending her straight blond hair flying over her shoulder. "I know that," she informed him crisply.

"Good," Danny replied. "Because if I was tempted to say anything else to you," the detective told her, "I guarantee that you would definitely know it. Now then, are you ready?"

"Absolutely," she announced.

Danny shut off the light in the conference room. Following him, Cassandra raised the back of her collar as they went toward the elevator.

BECAUSE IT WAS dark and growing colder by the moment, once they were outside, Danny decided that although the restaurant he had in mind wasn't all that far away, they would be better served if he drove there rather than just walk.

"Walking there would probably be faster," Danny told her. "But definitely not warmer, so we're taking my car," he told her, bringing her over to the parked vehicle.

Cassandra obligingly slid into the passenger seat, doing her best to try to warm up.

"I'd turn up the heat," Danny offered once she was in the car. "But by the time it finally kicked in and did its job, we'll be at the restaurant," he told her. "But finding parking might take a little longer."

She was doing her best to huddle into herself and attempt to keep warm. Complaining about how she felt was not her style. But she had to admit that this

New York weather certainly made her miss Southern California.

Cassandra had no intentions of commenting on how cold she felt. "You know best," she told him agreeably, doing her best to be positive.

One would have thought that skyscrapers would keep out the cold, but instead, the wind whipped against the buildings and onto unsuspecting humans trying to navigate this efficient city. One gust had almost knocked her over just before she'd gotten into his car.

"It's nice the department has such convenient parking," she commented. Her teeth were still chattering.

"One of the few perks, making sure the car is ready to go."

Danny took a corner, coasting to a stop as the light changed. He turned and smiled at her. "You're nicer when we're not reviewing information that has to do with the work of a serial killer and the guy's victims," he commented.

"Hey, cracking wise helps to keep me sane," she told the detective. Her hands started to warm up.

Danny nodded. "I can definitely see the need for that," he told her agreeably.

There was a great deal of traffic in the streets, he noted. So, what else was new? One had to learn to maintain serenity in Manhattan traffic and pad at least thirty minutes into travel time. Danny weaved his way toward the restaurant he had selected, the one he tended to frequent whenever he wanted to sample a really excellent slice of pizza.

The great part about living in the city was finding these gems hidden in neighborhoods far away from work. About twenty blocks from the squad room was his favorite haven, where he'd spent many a frustrating evening poring over case details and enjoying pizza and a cannoli or two.

Within moments, Danny pulled his vehicle up in front of the very small space directly in front of the compact pizza restaurant. As he stepped out of the car, he realized that this might have been the only time he'd brought someone to his special place. For the first time, the cold hit him hard.

Chapter Eight

The aroma, once they walked into the restaurant, was absolute heaven. The moment Cassandra took a deep breath, her stomach instantly responded.

She hadn't realized that she was *this* hungry until now.

If the pizza tasted half as good as it smelled, she was very glad that the detective had offered to bring her here. She could get good food in Aurora, but she had the feeling New York pizza would be an extra special experience, especially with Detective Doyle.

The restaurant's finished mahogany interior was modest with maps and prints supporting all things Italian, especially food. Cassandra admired drawings of celebrities who had visited the establishment. There was nothing glitzy about this place, but it seemed well loved.

"Uncle Andrew would just love this place," she commented to the detective as the aroma seemed to continue to swirl around her, teasing her appetite.

The moment they were shown to their table and took their seats, Danny pushed the menu toward her. He knew the selection by heart and already knew what he was going to order.

"Uncle Andrew?" the detective questioned.

"Sorry," Cassandra apologized. She realized that the detective undoubtedly didn't have a clue who she was talking about. "I have a tendency to think that people know who I'm talking about when I'm making references to members of my family," she said to the detective. Taking a breath, she proceeded to launch into an explanation and to enlighten the man. "Aside from being the family patriarch, Andrew Cavanaugh was once the chief of the Aurora Police Department."

"What happened?" Danny asked her. "Did he get voted out?" He would have assumed that had to be the logical answer. Just then, he saw the waitress pass by and raised his hand to catch her attention. Seeing him, the woman held her hand up, indicating that she would be there shortly.

"No." Cassandra shot down the detective's logical conclusion to fill him in on what actually happened. "Uncle Andrew's wife disappeared one evening after they had had a rare argument. When she didn't come home, he went looking for her. That was when he discovered that it appeared her car had gone over the side of the road and right into the river, washing downstream.

"When all attempts at finding Rose wound up failing, Uncle Andrew was forced to resign and take an early retirement. He had five kids to take care of, not all of whom were grown yet. Eventually, he fell back on the occupation that had seen him through his college days."

"Which was?" Danny asked as the waitress finally approached their tiny table.

"Cooking," Cassandra told the detective brightly.

The dark-haired young woman stopped at their table and flashed a warm smile at them. "What can I get for you folks?"

Cassandra gestured toward the detective. "I think you have a better idea of the kind of things that they serve here that really taste excellent," she told the detective as she put down her menu. "I'll let you make the selection for me."

Danny didn't seem all that sure about the matter. A lot of people could be very fussy about what they ate. "Are you sure about this?"

Cassandra never hesitated. "Absolutely. And remember, serial killers make me hungry, so no need to get me just a big salad."

Danny caught himself laughing at her declaration. "Wow, serial killers make you hungry. First time I ever heard of that being used as an excuse," he told the visiting detective. "For me, killers tend to kill my appetite. Don't know why I'm hungry now."

Her eyes sparkled as she grinned up at the detective. "Guess there's a first time for everything," Cassandra told him.

Danny placed their dinner order, then handed the menus back to the waitress. "Guess so."

She waited until the waitress retreated, then turned toward the detective. "I'm kind of curious," Cassandra began.

Danny blew out a breath. "Now there's a surprise," he commented, hints of amusement in his eyes.

"I'll ignore that," she told him, then continued, saying, "I know why I'm in this insane business. This is all that I've ever wanted to be since I was a little girl, but why did you get mixed up in it? Did you feel it was a calling, or was this the only thing open that you felt you could sign up for at the time?" Cassandra cocked her head, waiting for his answer.

Danny frowned at her. He felt as if he had been put on the spot. "You're awfully nosy, you know that?"

She lifted her shoulders in a careless gesture, then let them drop. "I guess you could say that being nosy is all part of the family business," Cassandra said. "But that still really doesn't get you out of answering my question."

He didn't understand why the woman was asking these questions. "I thought you said that you knew all about me," he reminded her, referring to their earlier conversation.

"I'm not talking about the intimate, important stuff," she admitted. "I mean, why do you do what you do? And don't tell me it's for the pay, because I know better," she told him. "You could earn a lot more in another line of work."

Danny frowned at the woman sitting across from him. He hated baring his soul, it just wasn't his way. But then, maybe he owed it to his aunt to have this story finally come out and see the light of day.

He was about to begin talking, but at that moment, their perky waitress returned with their extra large pepperoni pizza. She placed the tray on the table between the two of them, then moved back.

"Will there be anything else, sir?" the young woman asked.

"Not right now," he told her. "I'll let you know if there is."

The waitress nodded. Danny waited until she withdrew before he finally continued answering Cassandra's question.

For a long moment, he stared at his serving, looking for the right words. Remembering this part of his life was not easy for him.

Finally he told her, "My Aunt Gina was killed by a serial killer."

Her eyes widened. She hadn't been expecting that. For a second, the detective had managed to steal her breath from her.

Cassandra reached across the table, surprising

the detective by covering his hand with her own. "Oh, Doyle, I'm so very sorry to hear that. Did you ever catch the guy?" Because she had such faith in him, she fully expected the detective to tell her that he had. So, when he shook his head, admitting that he hadn't, she found herself doubly stunned. "That must have been so hard for you. I'm *really* sorry," she told him in all sincerity.

The pizza, as gorgeous as it was, sat between them untouched. At least for now. Instinctively, Danny wanted to change the subject, but that would have been too awkward. Plus, something about Cassandra made him want to confide in her.

But the failure in Aunt Gina's case still gnawed at him. He tried to shrug off his inability to find his aunt's killer. "Hey, this isn't like the movies," he told her. "This is to remind me that despite all the work that's put in, sometimes things just don't have a way of working themselves out. What this did," he told the California detective, "was make me even more determined to capture killers and bring them to justice whenever possible."

She nodded. "I totally understand," Cassandra said. "Just don't forget to take two breaths in quick succession."

He looked at her, rather astonished. "You're giving me tips?"

"Just trying to be helpful." She paused. She just had to ask. "Were you and your aunt close?"

He stared off into the distance. "She was family." He pressed his lips together, remembering things he was not about to say out loud. "One day she was there, the next, she wasn't." He looked rather saddened by the recollection. "She was a nice lady. Kind of close to my age," he recalled. "The day that it happened, it hit my mother really hard. She had practically raised Aunt Gina, who was a lot younger than she was." He sighed to himself, unaware that the sound carried over to Cassandra. "One day she just never came home from school."

Cassandra nodded, taking it all in. And then she asked, "Are you still keeping notes on her disappearance?"

He stared at the woman sitting across from him, surprised that she would ask something so intuitive. "How did you know?"

Cassandra's smile widened. "We're not all that different, you and I," she told him. Finally turning her attention to the pizza, she took a bite and the moment she did, her eyes all but lit up as she smiled broadly.

Cassandra nodded at her plate. "This tastes really fantastic."

Danny was pleased by her response. "Did you think I was making it up?" he asked her incredulously.

"No," she denied, then went on to say, "but, well, I thought that maybe you were exaggerating just a little." Cassandra held up her thumb and forefinger to create a tiny space.

"I never exaggerate," he told her. "The consequences for that sort of thing are just way too great. You get caught in an exaggeration, and when that comes to light, nobody ever believes you again."

"Can't argue with that," she agreed.

"Oh sure you can," he told her. He had the impression that the woman could argue the fur off a cat.

BETWEEN THE TWO of them, the pizza disappeared quickly. Before she knew it, the slices were gone, and she found herself staring at an empty pizza dish.

Danny saw the way she was eying the tray. "Would you like me to order more?"

"Yes," she answered with feeling. "But I'll have to pass on that. Otherwise, I'm really going to explode."

"No, you wouldn't," he contradicted.

She laughed. "If I were you, I wouldn't bet the family farm on that. Or stand too close," she warned.

He knew she wasn't about to explode, but he decided to keep that to himself. There was no point in getting into any sort of a dispute with her. He was just grateful that she'd gotten off the subject of his aunt's killer. Discussing personal matters took him out of his comfort zone. Everything about Cassandra took him out of his comfort zone. If they focused on pizza and the case, everything would be okay.

Looking at her empty plate, he did ask, "Can I get you anything else?"

But Cassandra shook her head. "Oh, no, I really am *more* than full," she told him. Her eyes crinkled as she smiled at the detective. "That had to be the best pizza I've ever had, bar none."

"Glad you feel that way." It was time to call it a night, he thought. "Can I take you to the hotel?"

"You don't have to go out of your way and do that," she told him. "I can definitely walk to the hotel. It's not all that far away."

To Cassandra's surprise, the detective shook his head. "Sorry, but you're much too attractive to walk that distance in the dark. Things have changed around here lately, and as long as I'm responsible for you, I'm not about to take any chances."

She actually was safe to walk around at night by herself, but he still wanted to keep an eye on her. Part of his job was to protect others, and he took that seriously. Plus, she wasn't a New Yorker. How ungentlemanly he'd be if he just let her go to the hotel by herself.

Still seated at the small table for two, she looked up at the detective. "When did you become responsible for me?"

"Since you and your cousin walked into my department to help work on my cold cases," he told her. Taking out his wallet, he peeled off a couple of twenties and left them on the table to pay for the meal and leave a healthy tip for the waitress.

"Ready to go?" he asked her as he rose to his feet.

For a moment, she felt like arguing with him over his intention to drive her to her hotel, but what was the point? It would only ruin what had been, up until now, a very enjoyable evening. So she agreed to what he had said.

"Sure," she told him. "Let's go."

Danny paused to help Cassandra with her coat. She twisted around to look at him. Once again, surprise registered on her face.

"Why do you look so surprised?" he asked. After all, he had helped her on with her coat once already.

"I thought maybe you grew tired of being the gentleman," she told him, nodding at the coat on her shoulders.

"You don't think all that much of me, do you?" he asked.

"No, it's not that," she said as they walked out of the restaurant and over to where he parked his vehicle. "I've just learned that despite everything, I just should never take anything for granted—no matter how much I might be tempted to do just that."

Reaching his car, she paused as he opened the door for her. A really cold breeze had picked up, sending an even colder chill up and down her body.

She did her best not to shiver.

Closing the door behind her, Danny got in on the

other side of the vehicle. He noted the look on her face. The cold made her really uncomfortable. He could tell by her apparent stiffness. Her features seemed closed off, focusing on the sudden drop in temperature. Sometimes, it even took his breath away.

"I bet you can't wait to get back to sunny California," Danny commented.

"We have our cold days," she told him. "Not like this, of course." She had to agree. "But it can get pretty cold in Southern California."

The detective truly doubted it, but for now, he just went along with what she said for the sake of not getting into an argument.

"If you say so," Danny told her. He started up his vehicle, then looked in her direction. "What hotel are you staying in?"

She rattled off the name of the hotel, then started to give him directions. She stopped when he began to laugh.

Cassandra looked at him quizzically.

"I've lived here all my life," he told her. "I know where the hotel is. I know every subway station, street, rodent, bodega, park…"

"You did not just say rodent, did you?"

Danny chuckled. "I sure did. Before you leave, we're going to take the subway. You'll see the finer things in this great city."

"You're trying to scare me," Cassandra said.

"Is that even possible?"

Cassandra folded her arms. He was really trying to get to her, and no way could he uncover her very minor fear of small living things…like rats. "No, we have our own special creatures in California."

"Well, there's nothing like a New York subway rat looking for its dinner."

"You can stop talking about rats now, Detective Doyle."

They both laughed and then paused as Danny drove the few blocks to Cassandra's hotel. He pulled up to the front and parked the vehicle in front of the revolving door. "Here you go, door to door service," he announced. "I'll be by tomorrow morning to pick you and your cousin up. Eight o'clock all right with you?"

She thought about her cousin. Travis would be all right with it, she decided. "Eight o'clock will be fine."

And then Cassandra proceeded to completely surprise Danny by leaning in and brushing a kiss against his lips. She didn't know what had gotten into her, but it seemed a natural way to end the night. Plus, the urge had overpowered her. The second her lips touched his, she felt a giddiness that had been building all day long. She'd needed this kiss, wanted it for herself and for him. It didn't seem likely that he'd had enough California sunshine in his life.

"Thank you for the pizza," she said, drawing her

head back, and then, with that, she got out of the car and closed the door behind her.

She left him utterly stunned, staring after her as she quickly hurried up to the hotel and then made her way to the revolving door.

Pushing against it, she proceeded to disappear into the interior of the hotel.

The detective continued staring at the hotel's interior, doing his best to attempt to recover. What the hell had just happened?

Yesterday, all he'd seen were the details of this case, and now, this detective from the other coast had kissed him. A lot could change in a day.

Not to mention, he could feel her lips on his long after the moment had faded.

The word *Wow* continued to echo in his head even after she had disappeared into the hotel.

Part of him couldn't wait for tomorrow to come. The other part was deeply afraid. Afraid he couldn't control this new element in his life.

Chapter Nine

Rather than go to bed and get some much-needed sleep, Cassandra decided to try to piece together the last few days of her late cousin's life. Was Nathan killed by someone he just happen to stumble across, and it was just a murder of convenience? Or did the killer target Nathan on purpose?

Maybe, for lack of a better motive, it had been someone who was jealous of Nathan and had decided to kill him for some reason known only to the killer.

It was definitely a puzzle, Cassandra thought, frustrated.

She decided to make a list to send to Valri. Her cousin was an ace when it came to anything related to technology. Her searches were famous, and Cassandra felt confident that Valri could make heads or tails out of the situation. Because of the hour—and in deference to the fact that Valri did have a home life, rather than call her computer wizard of a cousin, she decided to text.

Cassandra included a homey greeting along with her question.

New York is every bit as busy as its reputation makes it out to be, and Nathan's life remains as big a mystery as you might think. If it's not too much trouble, could you possibly trace his last steps before he met his untimely end? Nobody here in the city is as great as you are at unearthing hidden facts.

By the way, Travis says hi!

Travis, of course, had no idea she was texting Valri, but she thought it was a nice touch to include him in the missive. It made for a united front.

Crossing her fingers, Cassandra sent the text.

After placing her cell phone next to her bed, she switched off the light and finally lay down. She stifled a yawn, waiting to fall asleep. For some reason, her body wouldn't relax. Perhaps it was the city's energy surging through her. They didn't call it the city that never sleeps for nothing. Maybe it was the case or even a touch of jet lag. There was a three-hour difference, which actually did make a difference.

Sadly, sleep came in small snatches and whenever she would wake up, it was as if she hadn't closed her eyes at all.

This case was getting to her, she thought. There was no other explanation for the restlessness that had taken over her body.

EXHAUSTED AND SLEEPY because of her highly ingrained sense of duty, Cassandra was still up, so she showered and dressed before dawn. She took a quick peek out her window, then shut the shades again. It still looked pretty cold outside, with thick gray clouds covering the city.

She fully intended to make her way downstairs, grab a cup of coffee in the hotel café and get to the precinct before Danny had a chance to come by and pick her up.

It was against her better nature to be indebted to anyone, even to someone who was as good-looking as Detective Danny Doyle. She hadn't been raised that way, she thought as she collected her cell phone and her laptop. Putting both items into her backpack, she zipped it up, then grabbed her winter coat.

She had just slipped it on and was about to leave her hotel room when she heard a knock on her door.

Habit had her placing her hand on the weapon in her pocket before she went to the door. She kept the chain in place as she cautiously asked, "Who is it?"

"Rudolph. Santa's reindeer," the voice on the other side of the door answered. "I got lost."

Instantly recognizing the voice, Cassandra glanced at her watch. Danny. Didn't this guy ever sleep? He was worse than she was.

"Danny?" Cassandra asked just to be certain her imagination wasn't playing tricks on her.

"Very good," he commended her. "What gave me away?"

She laughed. "Nobody I met here so far sounds as grumpy as you do," she told him.

"You're turning my head with your flattery," he told her sarcastically. "C'mon, Cassandra, open the door before someone phones the front desk and complains about being disturbed by the sound of raised voices."

In response to his instruction, he heard the locks being clicked open. Within less than a minute, he found himself gazing at the startlingly awake California detective.

"Why are you here?" she asked.

He made a guess as to what had prompted her to ask that since they had agreed to his coming by to pick her and her cousin up last night. "Is it too early for you?"

In response, Cassandra spread out her hands to indicate that not only was she up, but she was dressed and about to leave the room.

"No," she said. "But I would have thought you wouldn't want to miss out on getting a little extra sleep yourself."

"Oh, but I did," Danny told her innocently.

Her brow furrowed. Right, like she believed that.

"Do you New Yorkers measure sleep by the thimbleful?" she asked him. "Because I figure that you didn't get any kind of decent sleep at all."

"It's not how much sleep you get, it's the kind of sleep you manage to log in," Danny said.

He actually sounded as if he believed that, she thought. Cassandra looked at him skeptically. "Meaning?"

"Meaning I'm ready to get back to work if you are—or I can just leave you here and come back later," he told her.

Oh, no, he wasn't about to treat her as if she were some sort of frail princess. She was here for a reason, and she intended to fulfill that reason, she thought.

"Now will be fine," Cassandra assured him. "You know," she told him, "I'm not used to having someone hovering over me, acting like he's waiting for me to cave in on myself."

"I am not hovering," he said. "I'm *watching over* you. There is a difference," he assured her. "Do you have any way of knowing if your cousin is ready yet? I can take him to the precinct as well."

"I'm sure he would appreciate it, although I don't know if he's awake yet. It's three hours earlier in California. Working this case—all of it—is rather exhausting, and I have no idea what time he turned in last night." A smile played on her lips. "Or if he even turned in. The last I heard, he was having a late dinner with that policewoman who picked him up."

Travis was a charmer, for sure. It wouldn't be out of character for him to be still on his date. But she also knew that it wasn't a good idea to wake him out of a sound sleep. Her cousin could catch up to them later.

"Why don't you call his room? If he doesn't pick up, just leave him a message," the detective suggested. "As you pointed out, your cousin can take care of himself."

"What I pointed out is that my cousin and *I* can take care of ourselves. I was the primary person in that sentence," Cassandra said quickly.

Danny pretended not to hear that part of it. "Why don't you give your cousin a call and ask him if he wants a ride?"

Frowning at him, she proceeded to dial Travis's cell phone. Mentally, she counted off the number of rings she heard on the other end and was about to hang up after she got to six, but she suddenly heard the line pick up.

Travis's incredibly sleepy voice barked a barely audible "Hello?" in Cassandra's ear.

"So, you are alive," she said, feigning surprise.

Her cousin sighed deeply into her ear. "And so, apparently, are you. You're a terrible person to call me this early." He yawned, trying to pull himself together. "Didn't Uncle Angus teach you anything about knowing how important it is to get a decent night's sleep?"

She turned away so that Danny couldn't overhear her. "No, he was too busy stressing doing a decent job. His favorite saying was always, 'It ain't over until it's over,' and these bodies that were discovered tell us that this is definitely *not* over.

"I called Valri and gave her all the information we had. Hopefully, we can recreate Nathan's last known movements. Maybe that'll help us find out who the other people were who were buried with him—and how they all wound up getting there."

Travis yawned in her ear again. She knew that meant he was getting up and coming to. "Has she gotten back to you yet?" her cousin asked.

She could only laugh in response. She was very aware that Danny gave her a curious look. "Valri's fast, but she's not superhuman, Travis. Besides, I just left her that message late last night. We'll hear from her," she told her cousin confidently. "Now get dressed. Detective Doyle has graciously volunteered to bring us back to the police station."

She couldn't read the detective's expression at the moment, but she could guess that it probably had something to do with the last thing that had gone down last night.

She had kissed Danny last night. It was an impulse, and the last thing she wanted was for him to think that was an open invitation on her part. When it came to the detective, she definitely liked what she saw, but she didn't want him believing that she was throwing herself at him.

At least, not until she knew how he felt about her. This wasn't about insecurity. . But…he moved her.

More than that. He'd shaken her in a way she hadn't felt. She saw deep into him, the way he carried himself and went about his case, his life.

He needed someone like her. Not only did she share his passion for the job, but she also liked how being with him stopped time—in the best possible way.

"So?" Danny asked Cassandra the second she terminated the call and closed her phone.

"He'll be here in ten minutes," she told the detective, knowing how her cousin operated.

Danny looked unconvinced. "We'll see."

Suddenly, they were truly alone together with what happened the night before. What could possibly go wrong?

As IT TURNED OUT, Travis was not ready in ten minutes. He was ready in eleven.

Danny glanced at the detective from Southern California. "You people are freakishly on time," he couldn't help commenting. "It's very strange. I was thinking maybe an hour, two tops before he'd be ready."

She grinned at him. "Told you." As Travis walked into the hotel room, she pushed a container of coffee into his hand. "I took the liberty of getting your coffee for you. Drink up and let's go." With that, she turned on her heel and led the way out.

Danny looked at the woman's cousin. "Has she

always been this bossy?" he asked as he followed Travis out.

Travis laughed. "From the first moment she opened her eyes—not in the morning but *ever*," he emphasized. "My theory is that Cass hears music from an entirely different drummer and just marches to it."

Getting on the elevator, she turned toward the two men who got on behind her. Danny pressed the down button. "You do realize that I'm right here and can hear every word you're saying, right?" she asked as she looked at the two men.

"Never doubted it for a moment," Danny told her.

Reaching the ground floor, they stepped off the elevator. The moment they did, Cassandra's phone began to ring. Mentally crossing her fingers for good news, she took her cell out and held it to her ear.

"This is Detective Cavanaugh."

"Apparently, I don't even get a break when you go away, do I?"

The second Cassandra heard Valri's voice, she immediately drew her shoulders back a little.

"I'm afraid that's what you get for being the best, Valri. Your reputation has spread far and wide."

"Yeah, yeah. I also know what else is being spread," Valri told her cousin. She could just see Cassandra rolling her eyes. Time to get down to business. "I don't have anything for you yet, but I'll get back to you the second that I do," Valri promised her.

"I'm going to hold you to that," Cassandra promised. "Talk to you later," she said, concluding the conversation. Cassandra tucked her phone away into her coat pocket, leaving it within accessible reach. "Valri said she'd get back to us," she told both men.

It was Danny who nodded. "I heard. How good is this Valri person at keeping her word? I mean, all she did was call you to say she's going to call you later. Isn't that like having a meeting about meetings?"

Travis smothered a laugh.

"Well, aren't you a funny guy with your New York sense of humor? It's called communication, fella. And Valri is better than anyone you've ever met," Cassandra told him with conviction. "Besides, Valri knows that I'll haunt her until I get an answer," she said with a grin. "Let's call it a preemptive strike."

Danny laughed. "I can totally believe that." Walking out of the hotel, the detective led the way to where he had parked his vehicle. He had actually found a space and congratulated himself about it.

He waited until Cassandra got into the passenger seat and Travis climbed into the back seat behind him.

The detective was about to start up the police vehicle when his cell phone rang.

Now what? he couldn't help wondering.

"Doyle," he announced as he opened his phone and put it against his ear.

Whatever else he was about to say died on his lips as he listened to what the person on the other end had to tell him.

Looking at the expression on his face, Cassandra couldn't begin to guess what he was being told. Something was obviously wrong. She did her best to piece things together from listening to his side of the conversation.

"When?" Danny demanded. His next question was, "How many? Are you sure?" That was followed up with a very deep sigh. "We'll be right there," he told the person on the other end of his phone call. "We're just leaving the hotel now."

With that, he closed his cell phone and slipped it back into his pocket.

Cassandra waited as long as she could without jumping out of her skin. The moment the detective stopped talking, she asked, "We'll be right where?"

"They found more bodies. This time, they were on the other end of the construction site," he told the two people in his car.

Travis leaned over toward the detective. "How many more bodies?" he wanted to know.

"Hard to tell," Detective Doyle answered honestly. "They just found the different body parts. According to what dispatch just told me, there were a whole bunch of body parts, not nearly as well preserved as the ones that were initially found. Whoever did this dismantling was not nearly as careful about preserving these parts as the other ones were. The killer was either in a hurry—or he didn't care nearly as much as he had earlier."

Travis hazarded a guess. "Maybe it's not the same person."

"Oh, it's the same person all right," Danny assured the other two detectives. There was no missing the conviction in his voice.

"What makes you so sure?" Cassandra asked.

"Because the killer carved what looked like initials into the bones. We need to have the pathologist examine them and draw whatever conclusions he can from them. The letters are hard to make out—but they are definitely letters," Danny said, assuring them.

Cassandra frowned. This could all be a tempest in a teapot. "What if the serial killer is dead by now?"

"It is a possibility," Danny agreed, then countered, "But what if he isn't? What if this turns out to be just another wave in this guy's killing spree? After all, until those first group of bones turned up, we didn't even realize that we were dealing with a serial killer."

"All the more reason for us to get some answers. The faster we get those answers, the better," Cassandra said with conviction. She looked at Danny. "All right, let's get going," she urged.

"Yes, ma'am," he murmured, pretending to be docile as he started up his vehicle.

Chapter Ten

"Doesn't take long for word to get around, does it?" Travis asked, looking out of the police car window at the crowds that were gathering on either side of the newly cleared construction site off the West Side Highway. Because of the isolated nature of this site, it was the perfect place to dump bodies, especially with construction happening. Someone was bound to find the gore and invite others to the party.

"People have a macabre sense of curiosity, I guess," Danny commented. He pulled his vehicle to stop as close to the scene as he could get.

Cassandra spoke up. "Not me," she said with feeling. "I don't get why anyone would want to get up close to human suffering."

Danny looked at her, highly skeptical of the sentiment that the sexy California detective had just expressed.

"You're not curious?" he said. It was obvious that

he didn't believe her. To him, curiosity was the very foundation of being a decent detective.

"No, not in the usual way. I just want this case to be closed and over. But I have to admit that I have this sick feeling this predator is going to keep on killing people until we catch him."

"Men," Danny said with emphasis. "This serial killer is going to keep on killing *men* until we catch him."

Danny had gotten Travis's attention. Up until this point, that idea hadn't occurred to either him or to his cousin. "You think this guy is motivated by some sort of feelings of jealousy?" Travis asked as he got out of the vehicle right behind Danny and his cousin.

"If I had to make a guess," Cassandra added, "I'd say that maybe it's more of a feeling of inadequacy than just jealousy," the California detective speculated.

"Why?" Danny said, challenging her thought process. Since the time he was twelve years old, he took nothing at face value.

She shrugged. "Why not?" she challenged. "There are an awful lot of possibilities here," she told the two detectives as the three of them walked over to the newly discovered burial site. "We just have to examine every one of them."

Cassandra shifted over to the side and then abruptly stopped walking as something on the ground caught her eye. "Hey, guys, I think I found something," she announced.

"Just one something?" Danny asked. There seemed to be bones spread out everywhere he looked. It had to mean three, possibly four more bodies.

But Cassandra had taken out her cell phone and was crouching over what appeared to be the bones, taking pictures. Closer examination indicated that there was a class ring on the ground.

Satisfied that she had captured the ring that had seemingly fallen off a finger by accident, she pulled out a handkerchief from her pocket and used that to pick it up.

Travis was looking over her shoulder. "Think that belongs to our killer?" he asked.

"Well, it's a man's university ring. That's about all I can see at the moment," Cassandra said. "You might be able to pull prints off it—if there are any—or find some kind of number inside, depending on the metal."

Danny was right next to her. "We can send it to our lab," he told the other two detectives. "See if we can find out who it belongs to."

Keeping it tucked into the handkerchief, Cassandra handed the ring over to Danny. "Could have belonged to the killer—or one of the victims," she said, theorizing as various ideas popped into her head, crowding one another out. "If they can lift a print," she said, watching Danny carefully tuck the ring away, "Maybe that'll get us closer to some sort of an answer."

"Maybe," Danny said, although he didn't sound very hopeful or convinced of the possibility. It was obvious that he didn't allow himself to get carried away until he could actually prove something.

"Hey, every little bit helps," Cassandra told the detective with unabashed conviction. "You've got to maintain positive thoughts," she said to both men. But it was obvious that she was really talking to the New York detective.

Danny shot a glance at the man next to him. "How does she stay so upbeat all the time?" he asked, then lowered his voice just a little. "Is she on something?"

"Just terminal optimism," Travis told him. "It's a requirement if you're a Cavanaugh. At least for most of us."

Danny read between the lines. "You mean there are a few of you that *aren't* so terribly chipper?" he asked.

Overhearing the detective, Cassandra added in her two cents. "One or two," she told the New York detective. For a moment, she pretended to be serious. "But we don't talk about them." She grinned at Danny. "We're waiting for them to come around and be like the rest of us." And then she turned serious. "In my opinion, I think that your forensic examiners should see if they can make any sort of identifications or if there's a way to compare these bones to your missing persons files from around that time."

Cassandra took in a long breath as she looked around the grounds, taking in the milling policemen and women. "We just need something to steer us in the right direction. I've got this gut feeling that these bodies are all connected in some fashion. We just need to identify one person, and that just might provide us with the key to all the others."

"You really think so?" Danny asked. He had the same skepticism in his voice as he'd had previously.

Cassandra shrugged her shoulders. It wasn't a helpless gesture; it was one open to suggestions. "There's nothing else on the table right now, we might as well give this idea a try." She saw the dismissive look on Doyle's face, which caused her to bring up a point. "If I recall correctly, the Son of Sam was finally caught because of a parking ticket. You just never know where your break might come from," she said. She shifted over to the side as Danny's people carefully loaded the newly discovered bones into a truck for transportation. They were on their way back to the precinct to work on assembling this latest jigsaw puzzle.

He blew out a breath as he looked at the support team that had been assigned to him and this case.

"You heard the lady," he told the staff. "Let's get this back to the precinct. We've got work to do, people."

DANNY HAD SOME of his people focusing on recon-
structing the scattered bones into a whole skeletal
structure and another team combing through the
missing persons reports, pulling those that had to
do with missing men of a certain age.

He was convinced that Cassandra was onto something. Or if for some reason she wasn't, then it was
up to him to find a way to disprove it.

Cassandra and Travis volunteered to be part of the
team reviewing the missing person's files.

The piles of papers they were going through had
been narrowed down to include good-looking males
between the ages of eighteen and forty. It seemed
like as good a place to start as any, he reasoned.
That idea hadn't been explored yet, and who knew?
It might just work.

IT WAS GETTING LATE, and one by one, most of the
people had left the department for the day. Danny
was growing bleary-eyed as he looked at the face in
the file that Cassandra had just pulled and brought
over to him.

"You think he's good-looking?" Danny asked her.
His tone told her that he didn't harbor those thoughts
himself.

She glanced at the photo in the file. "Well, he's not
about to stop any clocks, if that's what you're asking." She smiled at him as she placed the information in a small, growing pile. "Besides, beauty is in

the eye of the beholder. I can see another man being jealous of him," she told Danny. "Our serial killer might easily see this guy as being competition, one way or another."

Danny picked up the photo and studied it for a moment. The skepticism in his eyes grew. "One way or another?" he echoed, then looked up at the woman. "Just what is that supposed to mean?" he wanted to know.

"Competition when it came to the ladies—or to another man," she said expansively.

Danny rolled his eyes. He didn't see it that way. "If you say so," he said, his voice trailing off without any sort of emphasis behind it.

Danny's tone had caught her attention.

They were the last two people left in the conference room. Everyone else had already gone for the night. That included Travis, right after he had made Cassandra promise to either have Danny bring her to her room or to have her take an Uber as a last resort.

At the time when Travis had made his request, Cassandra had waved her cousin off, telling him that he worried too much and that she was perfectly capable of taking care of herself. That was when her cousin had turned toward Doyle, who needed no prompting.

"I'll see she gets to the hotel all right," Danny promised.

It was obvious that Travis didn't trust his cousin to

go along with this. Travis stifled a yawn as he looked at Cassandra. "I can stay," he told them.

"Go!" both Cassandra and Danny ordered in unison. Exhausted, Travis nodded as he stifled another yawn.

"I'll be back first thing in the morning," he promised, making his way toward the door and out of the conference room.

"And then there were two," Cassandra murmured under her breath as she heard the door close behind her cousin.

Danny made no response. He was busy reading the latest missing persons folder he had pulled over in front of him. Something within what he had read struck him. He had almost missed it on his first pass, but then he reread the passage.

"Hmm," he commented to himself.

Cassandra's attention was immediately aroused. Blinking, she looked up. "'Hmmm,'?" she repeated quizzically. "Did you find something, Detective?"

"It's probably nothing," he told her, dismissing his first reaction.

"But...?" she prompted, waiting for him to fill in the blank. When he didn't say anything, she pressed the point. "You never told me you were a tease."

That caught his attention. "A tease?" the detective repeated.

"Yes, you threw a statement out there, then didn't follow it up," she told him.

He frowned at her. "I'd say that you were the tease, not me."

"I'm just trying to gather all the information I can on these cases so we can finally catch a break and hopefully finally catch this guy before he strikes again."

Danny listened to what she was saying, then slowly nodded. The woman had a point. "You know, you really would be a very good addition to my team," he told her. This time, Danny allowed a drop of his admiration to slip through.

"*Your* team?" she repeated, surprised that he would say something like that to her.

"Well, it is my team," he reminded her. "And if you must know, you've displayed more enthusiasm for attempting to solve a crime than I've witnessed in a very long time. Ever think about staying and working in New York?" he asked.

She paused for a moment, looking at him. The man was actually being serious, she thought. "Now don't take this the wrong way," she began slowly, "but no. New York is a great place to visit, but I really couldn't live the rest of my life here," Cassandra told him.

His perfectly shaped eyebrows rose just a bit. "Mind if I ask why?"

She knew he was taking this to heart—which surprised her—but she had to be honest with him. Cassandra began to review her reasons.

"The heat in the summer, the cold in the winter, and I hear that you have very hungry mosquitoes that like to go to town, munching on people. I can go on," she said.

"No, that's not necessary," he told her. Danny shut her down. "I see you've given this a lot of thought."

"Actually, those were the first things that came to mind," she told the detective in all honesty. Just then, her stomach rumbled rather loudly. Cassandra flushed. "Sorry."

Danny immediately realized what the problem was. "No, I'm the one who should apologize," he told her. "I had all of you working straight through the late afternoon when I should have sent out for food." He actually looked somewhat embarrassed at his oversight. "I'm sorry. I just have a tendency to get caught up in what I'm doing, and I guess I forgot all about food."

She nodded, understanding the problem. "I think that's part of the reason why Travis left earlier. He and food can't stay apart for very long. He might not show it, but that very mild looking guy gets very grumpy if he and food are separated for more than a few hours." She grinned as she looked at Danny. "I take it that's not your problem."

"When I get caught up in a case, I totally forget about eating, sleeping—you name it," Danny confessed.

Cassandra gave him a once-over. "Well, that explains why you don't seem to have an ounce of fat on you."

"Thanks—I think," Danny said a bit uncertainly.

"Nothing to think about," she told him. "That was a compliment."

"Are California women always this outspoken?" he asked her. It seemed as if from the moment he had met her, the woman had spoken exactly what was on her mind.

"I wouldn't know about California women," she told him. "But we Cavanaugh women are—politely so," she said. "But we've also been known to speak our minds on occasion."

A smile played along his lips. "Yes, I've noticed." He exhaled as he closed down his computer. "Well, Detective Cavanaugh, I think maybe we should call it a night. We've made enough decent headway for one day," he said, nodding at the folders Cassandra had stacked on the desk she was using as well as the folders on his own. "Do you want to grab some takeout or stop at a pizzeria?" he asked, referring to what they had had yesterday.

"That sounds great, but to be very honest, right now I feel as if I'm just too tired to chew," she admitted. She stretched a little because she had gotten so stiff from sitting there and wound up yawning as well. "I think I'm going to call that Uber now," she said, pushing her chair back from the desk and rising to her feet.

"No, you're not," Danny told her.

She blinked. "Excuse me?"

"I said, you're not calling an Uber," he told her. "Not while I'm at your disposal." Danny rose and pushed his chair back under the desk.

"That would be imposing," she protested. Although not too stringently.

"No, that would refer to working as a team," he said, correcting her. "Team members are there for each other. Or don't you do things like that in California?" he asked.

"We most definitely do, do things like that in California," she told him. She blew out a breath. More than anything, she hated imposing, but she hated arguing about it even more. Besides, she was too tired to be making all that much sense at the moment. "Okay, you can take me to the hotel," she told Danny.

"Oh I can, can I?" he pretended to ask hopefully.

She found herself laughing, and it felt good. "You are crazy. You know that, don't you?" she asked, doubling up her fist and punching him in the arm.

She had a hard punch, he caught himself thinking, massaging his arm. "I'm beginning to realize that," he told her. "Okay, let's go, champ," he told Cassandra, ushering her out of the room.

Danny switched off the light before closing the door.

Chapter Eleven

It felt as if time had just stood still. Cassandra, her cousin and the New York detectives working on the newly formed task force that revolved around the bodies left behind by the serial killer were all back in the conference room again. They were going through the folders that had been compiled, searching for a common thread.

In truth, two weeks had passed by. And the only common thread that Cassandra and the others were able to find was that the victims they had been able to identify at this point were all males.

Good-looking males by most standards, Cassandra noted.

If this was a small town where a person's idiosyncrasies might stand out, or at least be a thing of public knowledge, this tendency for having handsome men of a certain age just disappear would be much easier to track down, Cassandra thought.

She could feel a headache beginning to build. She

massaged the bridge of her nose as she reread a paragraph for what felt like at least the hundredth time.

Closing her eyes, she exhaled impatiently. It was actually more like the third or fourth time, she admitted silently. But it certainly felt like the hundredth time. As it was, there were so many small details that had been compiled, and they had a tendency to swallow and obliterate some of the other facts.

God, her head was killing her, she thought—and her eyes felt as if they were going to pop out at any second. She closed them, willing her headache to go away.

It wasn't listening.

When she opened her eyes again, she found herself looking down at a bottle of aspirin that had been placed right in front of her. Momentarily bewildered, Cassandra slowly turned her head to see where the aspirin had come from.

Danny was standing not that far from her right side, smiling at her. He gestured toward the half-filled bottle.

"You look like you could really use a couple of those," he told her.

Cassandra picked up the bottle and studied it for a moment. "I could probably use the whole bottle," she quipped. "But I wouldn't want to steal your supply. If this is what you have to deal with on a regular basis, you'll probably wind up needing this a lot more than I do," she told the detective.

"It's not mine," Danny told her, not that it mattered one way or another to his way of thinking. "I got it from the clerk who delivers our mail."

She picked up the half-empty container of pills, looking at it for no apparent reason. This headache was really bad, she thought.

"The mail guy, huh?" she repeated. She thought for a moment, then realized who he had to be referring to. "You mean the guy who pushes that mail cart through here a couple of times a day? The tall guy with the bulging biceps?" she added. She had already decided that when he wasn't here, the guy had to spend the rest of his time in the gym. No one was born with biceps like that.

Danny nodded with a grin. "That would be him," the detective confirmed.

She looked at the small bottle, considering it. She could see the guy bringing mail and packages and even dropping off interoffice memos, but aspirin bottles? That seemed to be over and above the call of duty.

She handed the bottle back to Danny, who wouldn't accept it. "Isn't this rather a strange thing for him to offer you?"

"Take a couple," he urged, then went on to say, "It's all part of Curtis looking out for us," Danny told her.

"Curtis?" she repeated, surprised that the detective knew the mail clerk's name. Danny didn't strike her as the type to make note of something like that.

"Curtis Wayfare," Danny's partner, Lee, filled in. He looked at Danny for confirmation. "I've got to admit that the service has gotten a lot better since Wayfare started working here a couple of years ago. No wrong deliveries, everything delivered on time. The guy comes in early, stays late until the day's job is done. Everyone should take the kind of pride in their work that Wayfare does."

"And providing the aspirin is part of that?" Cassandra asked, having trouble hiding her amusement.

Danny shrugged. "Like I said, the guy watches out for us. The last guy we had used to toss things on our desks, usually the wrong desk," he specified.

"Between you and me," Lee confided, "I think that work—and working out—is all that guy has. He's kind of shy as well."

"What makes you say that?" Travis asked. He had picked up the thread of the conversation as he came over to grab another stack of missing persons folders.

"The guy likes to talk—mainly to my friend Danny here," Lee said, nodding at his partner. "I think if he wasn't so conscientious about doing a good job, he'd shoot the breeze all day with Danny."

Danny waved off the speculation. "I think that's just because my desk is the closest to the exit."

Cassandra supposed that made sense, but she wasn't 100 percent convinced of that, she thought.

The guy gave off a vibe that she couldn't quite put her finger on.

The next minute, she was opening the aspirin bottle and popping two pills.

Mentally crossing her fingers, Cassandra got back to work.

SHE WAS SO involved in what she was doing, she was oblivious to everything else. The next time that the creaky noise made by the mail cart's wheels penetrated her consciousness, Cassandra looked up, startled. Looking around, she zeroed in on the man's location.

She flashed a smile in the clerk's direction. "Your aspirin did the trick," she informed Wayfare once the man had drawn closer.

Wayfare dropped off a package on a nearby desk. He looked somewhat perplexed by Cassandra's reference. "Excuse me?"

She realized that the man had no idea what she was talking about. "Detective Doyle offered me the bottle of aspirin you gave him," she explained.

For a moment, Cassandra was unable to read the expression that came over the man's features. And then a spasmodic smile lifted the corners of his mouth as the man said, "Glad to hear that it helped. Headaches can totally disorient you and wipe you out."

She could have sworn that she made out what

looked to be disappointment pass over the clerk's features. His dark eyes clouded over and his jaw slackened. And then he pulled back his shoulders and told her, "If you'll excuse me, I have to get back to work. I don't want to fall behind." With that, he began to push the cart away from her desk.

Cassandra couldn't help wondering if he was holding on to the sides of the cart in what appeared to be a rather exaggerated motion as he walked by Danny's desk. When the detective didn't look up at him, she thought she heard Wayfare sigh to himself. But then, that could have very well been her imagination.

This case was getting to her, Cassandra told herself.

"Any word from that cousin of yours?" Danny asked right after Wayfare had gone on to another department.

Cassandra laughed as she looked up. "Detective, you're going to have to be a lot more specific than that. I have literally a *ton* of cousins," she said.

He frowned. There was only one of her cousins that mattered in this conversation. "I'm talking about the computer wizard."

Buried the way Cassandra was in the center of all this paperwork, she had all but forgotten the call she had placed to Valri.

A call that hadn't been returned yet.

"Thanks for reminding me," she said as she pulled

out her cell phone. She glanced at the screen to see if she had somehow missed a call, but she hadn't.

This wasn't like Valri, she thought as a wave of concern washed over her.

It took Cassandra three tries to get through to her. The call kept getting cut off with a strange busy signal. She had a feeling they had a bad connection.

But finally, her call went through.

"Valri, it's Cass. Are you all right?" she asked the minute she recognized her cousin's voice on the other end.

"Other than drowning in paperwork, yes, I am. Why do you ask?" Valri wanted to know.

"Well, you never returned my call," she told Valri.

"Oh, I thought you were just being nice and giving me some space," her cousin confessed. "Seeing how overwhelmed with paperwork you knew I was," she told Cassandra.

Cassandra sighed. She should have known better than to worry. Her cousin had a way of being able to bounce back no matter what.

"Val, when have I ever been nice?" Cassandra teased.

"Good point," Valri agreed.

Cassandra heard the rustle of paper and assumed that her cousin was retrieving some pages. From the sound of it, Valri went on to draw them over to the phone.

"I didn't find much," Valri confessed.

Cassandra tamped down the disappointment she felt rising within her. Maybe Valri was being modest. "What did you find?" she pressed. "Do you have any indication of who Nathan's friends were, who he hung around with, anything at all like that?"

"Well, what I have here is that when our wayward cousin wasn't hanging out with a whole bevy of sexy women, he liked to go to the gym to build up his body so he could continue attracting those women."

"And that's it?" she asked, unable to keep the disappointment out of her voice. "No names? Did he use a particular trainer or teacher?" she wanted to know. "C'mon, Val," she begged, "I need a name. Something to start me out."

"The only name I could find was this young guy, Carl Wilson," she told Cassandra. "He attended the gym at the same time that our cousin did. Nathan disappeared, and from what I can tell, so did this Carl guy. I know this doesn't exactly help," she told Cassandra.

"Well, we now know something more than we did before," she told Valri. As she spoke, a thought came to her. It wasn't anything concrete, but maybe it would lead to something. "They both belonged to that gym, didn't they?"

"Yes. I just said that," Valri reminded her.

"Can you get me the name of that gym and see if they had membership cards with their photos on them on file? I think that was about the time when clubs and corporations began to keep records like that."

"It's definitely worth a try," Valri agreed, then said, "That is, if the gym didn't close down or get replaced by some sort of other business."

"It might have just changed hands or even names," Cassandra said, reviewing the possibilities. "It's been known to happen."

"Okay, I'll check it out and get back to you," the woman everyone at the precinct thought of as "the computer wizard" told her.

"Great, but this time, do me a favor and try not to bury this," Cassandra requested.

By her tone of voice, it was obvious that Valri thought she had this coming to her. "I am really sorry about that," her cousin said. "It won't happen again, Cass, I promise."

"I guess you are human after all," Cassandra told her with a soft laugh.

"All too human," Valri admitted.

After another moment, the call between them terminated.

Tucking the phone away, she saw Danny and her cousin Travis looking at her. Danny spoke up first.

"Well?" the detective asked. "What did she have to say?"

"Valri promised to get back to me. She said she forgot to call us back because she just got buried in work and she didn't realize that we were in a hurry," Cassandra explained.

"How could she not realize that?" Travis wanted to know.

"The point is that she didn't. But we're not dead in the water yet," Cassandra told the two men.

"I'll believe it when I see it," Danny told her.

"Wow, talk about being a skeptic," Cassandra marveled, shaking her head.

"Hey, I'm a detective," he reminded her. "I'm supposed to be skeptical, not gullible."

"Nobody said anything about being gullible," she reminded him. "Valri is going to get back to me about the trainer or guy who worked out or trained with Nathan. Who knows, if we can locate the guy, maybe he can point us in the right direction. You just never know when one of these details could amount to something," she told the other men.

Danny looked far from impressed about the lack of information, but he had to agree that Cassandra might be onto something. In any event, it was a good place to begin the following morning.

"You're right," he said to Cassandra, reluctantly agreeing. "Okay, why don't we order in and get some dinner, then call it a night?" he suggested. "Requests?" he asked, looking around the room.

Cassandra held up her hand. "I want to know who's paying for all this," she asked. "We've been eating pizza, Chinese takeout and the like, and neither Travis nor I have contributed toward any of the cost. Are you going to hit us with a tab at the end?" she wanted to know.

"Don't worry about it. The NYPD's pockets are deep enough to cover a few sandwiches and take-out orders. Besides, it's the chief's way of saying thanks for the help."

Cassandra backed off a little. "Well, I've learned never to argue with authority figures," she told the New York detective flippantly.

Danny met her comment with a dismissive laugh. "Yeah, right. Like I believe that."

"You should," Cassandra told him. "Because I'm very serious. I don't argue with authority figures—I might, however, attempt to chip away at their armor with very small swings, but nothing that would crack their exterior," she told the detective. "At least, not all at once."

"Don't worry about it. Now, pizza or Chinese food?" Danny wanted to know, referring to the two items she had asked for during the week.

Cassandra answered without thinking. "Pizza," she told him. "It tastes good hot or cold." She thought for a moment. "You know, we need to find a way to solve these cold cases soon. Otherwise, I am going to wind up gaining an *awful* lot of weight," she confessed. Her mouth curved. "In case you haven't noticed, I just can't say no to pizza."

Danny looked at her, feigning an innocent expression. "Nope, did not notice that," he told her.

Travis, who had said very little up to this point, content with just observing his cousin, couldn't get over the difference he'd noticed in Cassandra. Usually, she was all business, applying herself to the evidence in front of her and exclusively attempting to solve the giant, disjointed jigsaw puzzle and nothing more.

Now, if he read the look in his cousin's eyes correctly, she was also involved in something beyond just solving the case.

The case, of course, was *always* exceedingly important to her; it always had been since she had begun working on the police department. However, he saw that there was room for something else, something more. She seemed to be very taken with the detective that she had—just a couple of weeks ago—locked horns with when she first arrived in New York.

Now, apparently, she had backed off.

It was going to be interesting to see where this was going to lead, he thought. But obviously not tonight.

Stifling a yawn, Travis hoped the food would get here soon.

Chapter Twelve

"You know, I get this feeling that we're missing something. Like we're circling around the solution, and it's right there in front of us, but we're just not able to put our finger on it," Cassandra told Danny. She was clearly frustrated.

Dinner had come and gone. When they were finished eating, Danny had brought the two Cavanaughs to their hotel.

Exhausted, Travis went to his room immediately, but when it came time for Cassandra to go in to hers, she and Danny both found that they weren't ready to call it a night yet, despite the late hour. They caught themselves talking about and sharing theories that struck them about the elusive killer who had robbed so many young men of their lives.

They were still talking when they finally got out of Danny's vehicle. Neither one hardly remembered taking the elevator to her room.

Cassandra stood by the door and turned toward the detective. "Would you like to come in?" she asked him. "They put in one of those cute little coffeemakers in my room. We can have coffee and brainstorm a little more."

The New York detective glanced at his watch. "Coffee?" he questioned. "At this hour? Don't you want to get *any* sleep?"

Cassandra was caught off guard by the detective's question. "Oh, coffee won't keep me up," she told him. Using her keycard, she opened the door and let the detective into the room.

Danny peered over the threshold, debating coming in. "Really?" He was looking at her skeptically.

"Really," Cassandra answered. "You could inject a mug of coffee into my bloodstream, and it really wouldn't have any effect on me." She saw the doubtful look on his face intensify and assured him, "I've been like this ever since I was a kid. But if you're too tired..." she said, her voice trailing off.

Danny gestured toward the opened hotel door. "Lead the way. I think I can keep my eyes opened long enough to learn something new," he told Cassandra.

That was when she had said to him that she felt as if they were overlooking something, missing something that was right in front of them. She went on to admit that she had nothing concrete to point to, that it was more of a feeling she had. A *gut* feeling, something some of her uncles and cousins were partial to pointing to.

Some of them, she went on to tell the detective, even swore by that feeling. She knew it sounded fanciful, but at the same time, she would have bet anything that she was experiencing the very same feeling that her cousins and uncles had right now.

The feeling just seemed to run too deep, too strong, to be fanciful.

"Okay, what do you think we're missing?" Danny asked her patiently.

Cassandra laughed softly. "If I knew that," she said with emphasis, "the pieces would fall into place instead of just floating around aimlessly in my head." With that, she tossed a rather thick folder onto her bed.

He looked at her in surprise. "You brought the folders to the hotel with you?"

That didn't seem like something that she would be inclined to do, not without asking permission and signing the folders out, at any rate.

"No, these aren't the actual folders. I made copies and brought those with me," she told the detective. Cassandra smiled at him. "I know better than to take the actual folders out of the precinct." Her eyes met his. "I wouldn't want to bring down the wrath of the New York Police Department on my head."

"No wrath," Danny told her with a straight face.

And then he grinned. "We would just hang you out to dry, that's all."

The corners of her mouth curved in amusement. "Well, no need for that," she told the detective. "We might be a little unorthodox where I come from, but we do make a point of following all the rules. Or at least the ones that make sense."

He nodded. "Never meant to suggest that you didn't."

Cassandra smiled at the man in her hotel room. "I appreciate that," she told him. "Would you like that coffee now?" she offered, then explained the reason for her question. "Your eyes look like they're drooping," she told him. "You're either tired, or I'm boring you."

"Absolutely not," he told her with feeling.

If anything, Danny admitted to himself, he was finding her increasingly stimulating. He had, of course, already noticed that she was a very beautiful woman. But beauty all by itself had never really moved the detective beyond a certain point.

There was something about the look in Cassandra's incredibly green eyes, something about the way her mouth curved at the corners when she was beyond amused, that he found almost hypnotically inviting.

It spoke to him, moved him.

At first, he tried very hard not to dwell on his reaction to her, but as time went by, he was finding that response far more difficult to bury than he had first thought.

She smiled at Danny's almost enthusiastic response to her question. "So, tell me out of sheer curiosity, do you have any theories about who this serial killer might be? Do you think he's someone who just randomly stumbled across these people, and for whatever reason, they brought out his killing instincts? Or was this something that the killer found himself planning because of his response to that person? Something that he felt compelled to carry out?" Asking the question, she studied his reaction to it.

She might have been studying him, but Danny caught himself studying her as well. He was caught up in watching the way her lips moved as she formed her questions.

With effort, Danny forced himself to look away from Cassandra. He couldn't allow himself to get carried away by this woman. There were far more important things at stake here than watching the way her lips moved as she worded her questions.

Danny thought for a moment, considering what she had just asked him. "I guess that's where the investigation comes in."

She thought of her own reaction to the situation. "You've got to have a gut feeling about it," she told him with simple solemnity.

"Maybe later," he responded. And then, to lighten the conversation, he just changed its direction. "Did you always want to be a cop?" he asked the attractive woman.

His question, without any preamble, caught her up short. In order to give the detective an honest response, she had to think about it.

When she finally did come up with an answer, it wasn't one that he was expecting.

"James Bond was my hero," she admitted.

His brow furrowed. That didn't make any sense to him. "But he was a guy," Danny said. "Fictional," he said, tagging that on, "but very much a guy."

"More important than that," Cassandra told the detective, "he was someone who righted wrongs, and I have to admit, that aspect always *really* appealed to me."

Danny laughed under his breath as he shook his head. "You are one very strange lady, Cassandra Cavanaugh."

The grin she flashed reached her eyes. "Not sure if you mean it this way, but I'm going to take what you just said as a compliment."

He pretended to assume a serious expression. "I suppose you can, in a way. You certainly are unique, I'll give you that," the detective told her. "So, I suppose my answer to your question is a very roundabout yes," Danny concluded.

"I suppose so," she agreed, nodding her head. "But then, I never saw any sort of other alternative," she told him, referring to her choice of heroes. "All my heroes were police detectives."

Danny thought of the era she was referring to. "Men," Danny said. Back then most of the detectives were men, he recalled.

"Except for the policewoman who was Uncle Brian's partner," she said. "The woman who he eventually went on to marry," Cassandra told him, then, seeing the confusion in Danny's eyes, she said, "It's complicated."

Danny laughed dryly. "I don't think that there's anything straightforward about your family," the detective told her. "At first encounter, they seem to be straightforward enough, completely down-to-earth and all that. But then, after listening to the details for a while, you realize that there is really *nothing* straightforward about any of your family members," he told her.

She grinned, ready to contradict him. "Yes, there is. You're just not accustomed to people like us," she told him matter-of-factly.

Her grin grew as a shine entered her eyes. "We're just different."

Danny shook his head and shrugged. That wouldn't have been his word for it, he thought, but she seemed to be rather comfortable with it.

"I suppose that's one way to describe it," Danny told her. "But then," he said, as another thought occurred to him, "maybe I'm just being jealous."

He had managed to surprise her again, she thought.

Cassandra blinked after she all but drained the remainder of her coffee. "Excuse me?"

"Maybe I'm admitting too much," he told her uncomfortably.

Oh, no, she wasn't about to have him back away now. "Sorry, you can't just stop now. *Why* are you jealous?" Cassandra wanted to know.

He had started this, but it was too late to back away now. Danny took a breath before launching into his explanation. "You have this really big family…" he began.

"There's no denying that," she said, the corners of her mouth curving. She had gathered that Danny's family was next to nonexistent.

He moved over to the window. It looked down at Sixth Avenue, six stories below. Danny had his hands wrapped around what was left of the cup of hot inky-black coffee. He could feel the warmth sinking deep into his soul.

"After my aunt just disappeared," he remembered, "there was just my mother and me. And then she came down with leukemia."

His voice grew still. "I just couldn't seem to spend enough time with her—at least not enough time to make a difference." He worked at keeping the sadness out of his voice. "Certainly not enough time to gather up into some imaginary mental sack that I could hold on to and occasionally peek into whenever I felt the overwhelming need to remember her."

He turned from the window and saw the startled way Cassandra was looking at him as she listened to what he was telling her.

Danny flushed. "Sorry, I think I'm just getting punchy," he said. He set his cup on the counter next to the coffeemaker. "I'd better get going."

He still looked rather bleary-eyed to her.

"I don't think you're in any shape to drive, Detective," she told him.

"Well, clicking my heels together and saying, 'There's no place like home,' isn't an option at the moment, so I guess that just leaves driving," he told her.

"No, there is another option on the table," Cassandra told him.

Okay, she had made him curious. "And that is?" Danny asked, at a loss as to what she was referring to. He really doubted that she was suggesting what he thought she was suggesting. She struck him as too straitlaced for that.

"You can sack out on the sofa," she told him matter-of-factly. "Or, if for some reason that isn't comfortable for your back, you can take the bed, and I can take the sofa," she told him.

He wasn't expecting that. Yes, he was tired, but spending the night in the same room with her struck him as far too tempting, exhausted though he was.

Danny shook his head. "That's okay," he began, only to have Cassandra cut him short.

"No, it's not okay," she informed him, her voice taking on an authoritative tone. "I am not having you fall asleep behind the wheel of your car."

"I just finished the coffee you felt you had to offer me." Danny nodded at the large mug he had put down. It was now all but empty.

"I can see that," she told him. "And for some reason, it didn't seem to kick in the way you thought it would," Cassandra said. "Now, you either get a room here for the night, or you take me up on my offer and my sofa and spend the night here."

She could see that Danny was about to argue with her, and she cut him off before he could get started. "I refuse to be responsible for them finding your body embedded in what's left of your vehicle. Now stop arguing with me," she ordered. "You know I'm right."

Danny sighed. "Yeah, I do," he said. "But even if I didn't, I've got the feeling that you wouldn't let me win this argument."

"And that's what makes you such a good detective," she told him with a wide smile.

He looked down at what he was wearing. "I don't have a change of clothing with me," he said.

"No go-bag in your trunk?" Cassandra asked him.

"No what?" he questioned.

"Never mind," she assured him, waving away the

term she had used. "No one is going to grade you on the fact that you are wearing the same thing two days in a row. The only thing that counts is finding this serial killer," Cassandra told him, then amended her statement. "Or at least getting close to solving this thing. I assure you that the people who work with you will take more note of the news headline in tomorrow morning's paper about the cold case detective who was found plastered against the inside of the windshield within his extremely mangled vehicle."

Tired, he still had to laugh as he shook his head. "You have a really colorful imagination."

"No, what I have is the memory of a friend who insisted on driving home when he shouldn't have—and the guilt of my not putting my foot down and insisting that he not drive in his present, drowsy condition. Now stop arguing with me," she said. "I need my sleep."

And with that, she gathered up a pillow and blanket, spread out the latter on the sofa, and then, satisfied that she had done her best, she turned around and laid down, fully dressed, on her bed.

She was asleep within ten minutes.

Chapter Thirteen

He frowned to himself as he stared up at the building.

He knew for a fact that Detective Doyle had ridden up with that two-bit California detective, and Doyle hadn't come down yet.

That meant that he was still up there with her.

His frown grew deeper. He had taken an instant dislike to her the moment he had seen her walking in through the door of the precinct. She had that know-it-all look about her, the kind he had seen on so many women's faces when he was growing up, he thought, his face growing darker.

The kind that made him angry.

Very angry.

As he felt himself growing progressively angrier, he decided to ride up to the visiting detective's floor. Every time he'd heard the elevator bell go off, he could feel himself growing increasingly more uptight. It took effort to control his breathing.

Getting off on the sixth floor, he was carefully

watching the signals that were coming from the state-of-the-art tracking device that he had managed to slip into Doyle's pocket earlier today. He had done it while he was distributing the mail.

A pleased smile lifted the corners of his full mouth. At the same time, he could feel himself getting angrier and angrier because that tramp was still in there with Doyle. Having her here could spoil everything.

It could lay waste to all his carefully laid plans, causing them to crumble.

Moving quietly, he made his way past the hotel door. Because of the late hour and the fact that it was the middle of the week, there was no noise coming from the room.

Any of the rooms, actually.

He stared at the door as if he could actually see through it and into the room. Detective Doyle and that worthless two-bit who had clamped onto him had worn themselves out. He could just *sense* it.

As he thought about the circumstances behind the silence, his face grew progressively redder and redder as his eyes all but bored holes into the door.

At that moment, he heard someone coming down the hallway. Instantly alert, he moved in the opposite direction, making his way toward the stairs.

He wasn't about to take the elevator and risk running into anyone. The chances were incredibly slim, but he knew that he *could* wind up running into someone from the precinct.

He supposed he could explain it away by saying that he was visiting someone here, but then he might be asked to identify that person, which meant that he might have to kill the person who was questioning him, because he didn't have a ready name to offer up.

He could feel his adrenaline rising as he made his way quickly down the stairs. Reaching the ground floor took no time at all. Neither did taking a side door.

The woman would pay, he promised himself, his fists clenched at his sides. Maybe not right now. But soon.

Very soon.

Envisioning the scene, he took comfort in that.

STIFLING A YAWN, Cassandra slipped out of bed, went into the bathroom and threw some cold water on her face.

It was time to start getting ready, she told herself. She and Danny had spent too much time together, talking as well as enjoying each other's company.

A couple of times she had even thought that the distance between them was going to melt away and that their lips would wind up making contact. Deep contact.

That was just wishful thinking, Cassandra told herself. She had no idea why her mind had even gone

that route. It wasn't as if anything even remotely romantic had passed between them except for that one
fleeting kiss she had delivered that first evening.

Last night she had just gotten punchy, she told
herself.

Splashing water on her face to wake up, she came
out of the bathroom and wound up swallowing the
scream that had instantly sprang to her lips. She had
walked out of the bathroom and directly into Danny.

Swaying, she appeared so startled, Danny grabbed
hold of her shoulders to keep her from toppling over.
Otherwise, he was fairly certain that she would have
wound up unintentionally hitting the floor.

"Hey, steady there," Danny said, just as startled as
she was. "I can't be that scary first thing in the morning—can I?" It sounded like a genuine question.

She could feel her heart pounding against her rib-
cage. It took her a moment to get her pulse to settle
down.

"You're not," she told him. "It's just that when
I left you, you were completely dead asleep, and I
walked back in less than ten minutes later, you're
wide awake and look as if you're ready to leap into
the fray."

His forehead furrowed. Maybe he was still dreaming. The woman wasn't making any sense. "You want
to run that by me again?"

But Cassandra shook her head, waving away her
words. "Never mind," she told the detective, then

suggested, "Why don't you take a shower and we'll get going?"

"Are you telling me that I smell?" he asked her, pretending to be offended while keeping an innocent expression.

"What? No," she said in vehement denial. "I just thought that since you slept in the clothes you had on yesterday, you might want to refresh yourself a little. But you don't have to," she told him quickly.

His eyes swept over her. For a moment, he could almost *see* her taking a shower. "How about you?" he asked. "Or did you already take a shower?"

"Actually, no," she said. "I wanted to make sure that you made use of the bathroom if you had to before I got into the shower."

"That sounds as if you had a couple of bad experiences," he said, amusement playing on his lips.

"I did. As a kid," Cassandra specified, "but it did make me very leery. Long story short," she told him, "the bathroom is all yours if you need it."

Danny nodded. "Be out in a few minutes," he promised.

And he was, she noted, amazing her, to say the least. Barely seven minutes had gone by, and Danny emerged out of the hotel bathroom, toweling his hair dry.

Cassandra looked at the man in unabashed surprise. Her brothers would have definitely taken longer, especially Campbell. "That *was* fast," she told him.

He laughed at her comment. At this point, Danny sincerely doubted if he knew *how* to take a slow shower. He had gotten into the habit of being speedy early on out of sheer necessity.

"When I was a kid, between my mother and my aunt and me, taking showers—quick ones, mind you—the hot water ran out really fast," he said. "I got really good at taking what I felt, at the time, were the world's fastest showers.

"When our landlord got around to replacing our ancient water heater and we actually had hot water for longer than three minutes at a time, I was already trained to take really fast showers."

The smile that lifted his lips was a fond one as he thought back to those days. "Anyway, it was a good habit to get into, I guess. It keeps my water bill down and within reason."

Cassandra laughed. "I wish you had been around to talk to my brothers back in the day," she told him. Glancing at her watch, she was ready to go. "What do you say we grab some take-out breakfast on the way to the precinct?"

Danny nodded. "Sounds good to me. Why don't you go and wake up your cousin?" he suggested, nodding toward the outer door.

His words were met with a wide smile from Cassandra. "You're beginning to get to know how we Cavanaughs operate," she told him.

"We New York cops are not known to be slow on the uptake," he told her matter-of-factly.

"Yes," Cassandra answered, her eyes slowly washing over the detective. She kept finding herself responding to the man. "I guess I am definitely beginning to see that."

Maybe, Cassandra silently lectured herself, she needed not to look at him so much. There was something about Danny Doyle that really drew her in, and the more she looked at him, the more drawn to him she was.

That wasn't usually the case for her when it came to men. The more she was around them, the less attracted to them she became. She found things that wound up turning her off.

But this was different, she realized. The more time she spent around Danny, the more she found herself liking him. Trying to understand why only made things more complicated, she thought.

The case, damn it, Cavanaugh. Focus on the case, not the man's compelling green eyes or his really muscular biceps, Cassandra said, scolding herself.

Taking their winter coats with them, they went out into the hall and stopped two doors down. Cassandra knocked on Travis's door.

There was no answer. She tried again.

It took three knocks, each progressively louder, on her cousin's door before it finally opened.

Her cousin, looking as if he were dead asleep on

his feet, mumbled a greeting at them as he took a step back, opening the door wider.

"Is it morning already?" Travis asked in a raspy voice.

"Yes, and you'd know that if you looked out your window," Cassandra told him, pointing toward the daylight that was just beginning to stream in.

Travis stifled a yawn. "I'm still on California time," her cousin told her. "Besides, windows are for watching pretty girls walk by, not for measuring the time," Travis said, stifling yet another yawn as he attempted to rub the sleep out of his eyes.

It didn't work. He still appeared to be very bleary-eyed.

"That would be a little difficult on the sixth floor," Danny said.

"I didn't say it was easy," Travis mumbled. He felt as if there was wad of cotton in his mouth. He rubbed his eyes again. "Just give me a couple of minutes to get dressed," he told Cassandra and the detective.

"Travis, you *are* dressed," Cassandra said.

Travis looked down at what he was wearing, more surprised than they were to find himself wearing clothes.

"Oh yeah, I am." Travis responded. "I can't remember if I tumbled into bed fully dressed or got dressed in my sleep this morning." He stifled yet another yawn. "I think I got dressed this morning," he said more to himself than to Cassandra and Doyle.

Cassandra leaned into Travis, taking in a long breath as she gave her cousin the once-over. "That would be my guess," she told him. "Now, are you ready to go, or should Doyle and I here each grab one arm and just drag you out into the hallway?"

Travis drew himself up indignantly. "I can walk on my own power," he told his cousin.

"Yes, Virginia, there is a Santa Claus," Cassandra declared with a laugh. She led the way back out again.

The trio took the elevator down to the first floor and then made their way out of the hotel.

"Do you remember where you left the car?" she asked Doyle.

"Always," he told her. "My basic survival depends on it."

He led the way back to where he had left his vehicle in the parking structure and drove it out onto the street.

Cassandra didn't say anything to either of the two men, but throughout it all, as well as the trip back to the precinct, it felt as if they had never left. And she just couldn't seem to shake the feeling that they or, at the very least, she was being watched.

Which just didn't seem possible, she told herself. *I really am getting paranoid*, Cassandra thought.

Even so, she could have sworn that she felt eyes all but drilling into the back of her head. Why? She hadn't felt that there was someone watching her yesterday morning. No, this feeling was definitely new, she thought.

"Something wrong?" Danny asked as he slowed down at a light and waited for it to turn green again. Glancing at her, he had noted the look on her face.

"You mean other than a madman running around killing people?" she asked him.

"Yes, other than that," he answered.

She debated telling the detective about the uneasy feeling she'd been struggling with, but she was fairly convinced that he would tell her that she was being paranoid, or something along those lines. Cassandra didn't want him thinking less of her.

"No, I'm just thinking," she told him.

"About?" Danny prodded. She couldn't tell if he was genuinely interested or just giving her a hard time.

She shrugged, avoiding his eyes. "Just stuff."

"Like?" he wanted to know. Then prodded when she didn't answer. "C'mon, out with it. What's on your mind? What's bugging you?" Danny asked point-blank.

She sighed. The man wasn't going to let up until she gave him something. And then she would have something new to regret, she thought.

"All right, if you must know," she told him in slow, measured words, "I can't shake the feeling that—" And then, at the last minute, she changed her mind, dismissing her feelings. "Never mind."

But Danny refused to back off. "No, you started this," he told her. "So, out with it. What's bother you?"

She closed her eyes and sighed, then, opening them again, she said, "All right, you asked for this," she told him impatiently. "I can't shake the feeling that there's someone watching me. There," she declared. "Are you satisfied? Go ahead. Say it."

He was driving again, so it took a moment before he could spare Cassandra a fleeting glance. "Say what?"

"That I'm getting paranoid or letting the serial killer get to me or something equally as critical of my thought process."

A serious expression slipped over the New York detective's face. "I can't, because I'm don't think that you're wrong," Danny told her in a quiet voice.

It was hard for Cassandra to keep her mouth from dropping open. She glanced over her shoulder to exchange looks with her cousin. For the life of her, she couldn't figure out if Danny was putting her on—or not.

But it didn't sound like it.

Chapter Fourteen

"Can you repeat that?" Cassandra said, looking at the detective.

She wasn't sure if Danny was actually being serious—or if he was just having fun at her expense. She would have liked to think that he was being serious, but in all honesty, she still didn't know him well enough to make that judgment call.

"You heard me the first time, Detective," Danny told her, certain that she had. And then, just to be sure, he repeated it. "I don't think that you're wrong."

He sighed, debating the significance of the admission he had just made. He might as well get all of it out, he thought. "Something keeps sticking in my craw," he admitted. "I would have said that you were being paranoid—that *I* was being paranoid," he underscored. "Except that…" His voice trailed off, and then he almost wound up saying the words to himself rather than to her. "Except that," he repeated, "I can't seem to shake the feeling that there is someone watching us.

"With a case of this magnitude, I guess that's not unusual," he went on to say softly, as if some invisible voice had whispered those words into his ear.

He had a point, Cassandra thought, focusing on what he had just said. But still, she couldn't separate herself from the feeling that there was something more to this whole set up, something they were all somehow missing.

She sighed. "We *really* need to get to the bottom of this," Cassandra said to the two detectives in the car as she turned in her seat to look first at her cousin, then back at Danny. "First thing I'm going to do once we reach the office is to call Valri to see if she's made any headway compiling that list of people that the victims were in contact with just before they summarily went missing."

She pressed her lips together, thinking. "Maybe that'll point us in the right direction so we can actually begin solving this thing and finally find that serial killer."

"Maybe you should make that the second thing," Travis said. "Don't forget, our computer wizard is three hours behind us timewise. She probably feels exactly the way that I do right now—punchy and sleepy." Cassandra's cousin punctuated his statement with a huge yawn.

"Punchy," Cassandra repeated. "Is that by any

chance the name of Snow White's eighth dwarf?" she asked, humor curving the corners of her mouth. "In any case," she told her cousin more seriously, "Valri's not like the rest of us. You know that," she insisted. "The woman runs on batteries and can multitask better than all the rest of us put together," she said, reminding Travis. "At any rate, the sooner we get our hands on this list once she puts it together, the sooner we can begin finding and investigating these people. And that, in turn, gets us closer to finding this fiend and putting him away. Permanently," Cassandra said, stressing that last word with feeling.

"You know, it might not be a man," Travis said.

He was wrong there, she thought. This could not have been the work of a woman for one good reason.

Cassandra smiled to herself. "If it's a woman doing this, then it's a woman who is capable of bench-pressing at least two hundred pounds, if not more. These are not skinny, underweight little men who are being hauled out and done away with," she said. "From the photographs I saw in the files, every one of the victims were all full-sized men. Dragging them out of sight, picking their bodies apart and then burying them—most likely quickly—required strength," she told her cousin. "A lot of it."

Listening to the conversation, Danny finally pulled his vehicle into the parking structure beneath the precinct. He parked it in his customary spot, pulled up the handbrake and then turned off the engine.

Staying in his seat, the detective turned around to glance back at Travis.

"This is the one time that I'm throwing my vote in with your cousin," he told Travis. Pausing, he cleared his throat, then continued. "Meanwhile, we track down any leads, however slim, however minor," he informed the detectives from California. "There has to be something that we're missing, something that will get us closer to an answer."

He saw Cassandra smiling at him as she got out of his car. That had to mean something.

"What?" Danny prodded, even as he caught himself thinking that maybe he really didn't want to know what was on her mind.

"Nothing," she denied, then went on to tell him, "You know, that's actually a very positive attitude." Her smile deepened. "I'm just surprised—and pleased—to hear those words coming out of your mouth, Detective."

She paused for a moment. There was a sparkle entering her eyes as she looked at him. "It looks like maybe I'm rubbing off on you," Cassandra told him.

Danny looked at her as they walked through the precinct's front doors and made their way to the elevator. The New York detective caught himself thinking that he would have welcomed having the woman actually rubbing off on him.

Or just simply rubbing, Danny mused for a moment.

The next moment, he managed to rouse himself again and focus on something more serious.

The New York detective cleared his throat.

He would have probably found himself getting slapped for the direction his mind was taking.

He attempted to berate himself but just couldn't get his mind to go that route. Instead, he couldn't stop smiling as he thought about the woman who had been assigned to his division.

This was not the proper attitude for an investigator of his caliber to assume, he told himself again, doing his best to pull back.

Danny could see Cassandra looking at him. Her expression was rather bemused. For a fleeting second, the detective thought that with his luck, the woman was probably a mind reader.

Drawing himself together, Danny quickly took refuge in the comment Cassandra had just made about rubbing off on him. "I guess maybe you are at that," he said, then commented, "Lucky me."

"Now that just sounds like sarcasm," Cassandra told the detective.

His mouth quirked just a little as his eyes washed over her almost in slow motion. "Well, you're a detective," he reminded Cassandra. "I'm guessing that you have the tools to figure that out."

He had just sent a definite warm shiver down her spine with that look of his, she realized. "I'll get back to you on that," she heard herself responding, uttering the words almost in slow motion. She cleared her head and went on to say, "Right now, I want to see if Valri came through with something."

With that, she all but marched into the office.

"Let me know if she has anything worthwhile to tell us," Travis requested, calling after his cousin.

"Will do," Cassandra promised, tossing the words over her shoulder.

At that point, she realized that she was not going to the conference room alone. She found that she was being shadowed by Danny.

She glanced at him just as she crossed the threshold. "Is there something you forgot to tell me?" Cassandra asked him.

Danny shook his head. "Nope."

"Then we just happen to be heading in the same direction at the same time?" she asked Danny skeptically.

Danny inclined his head. "Sure looks that way." And then he grew more serious. "Look, I want to know what you know as soon as you know it. Don't forget," the detective reminded her, "this was my case before you ever stepped one foot onto the scene."

Well, if he wanted to play it that way, she thought, she had something to counter him with. "Yes, but he was my cousin before he ever disappeared in your city."

Though she didn't have any knowledge of him.

It was like saying she was distantly related to Anne Boleyn. Sure, she could claim a personal need for information, but the case would officially belong to the authorities.

"Tell you what," Danny proposed. "Let's stop playing tug-of-war and just see what this brilliant cousin of yours can tell us about our serial killer."

She inclined her head. "Well, I certainly can't argue with your wording."

Walking into the conference room, she noticed that one of the members of Danny's team was already in the room, going over one of the files, most likely for the umpteenth time if one went by the papers that were all spread out on the man's side of the table.

Danny gave the burly man, Murphy, a dismissive look. "We need the room for a few minutes, Murphy," he told the sergeant.

The man rose from the table. "I think I'll go get some coffee," Murphy told them. "Can I bring back one for either of you?"

Danny reacted with total disbelief. "You've got to be kidding. I wouldn't drink that stuff if I was dying of thirst."

"That was a little drastic, don't you think?" Cassandra asked as the other man left the room.

Danny looked at her knowingly. "You've never tasted the coffee here at the precinct, have you?" It really wasn't a question.

"No," Cassandra agreed, "I haven't."

"Let's just say that I just saved your life," the New York detective told her. There was a laugh in his voice.

The man was steadily growing more animated, Cassandra thought, and that, in her mind, was a good thing. She could definitely deal with animated. *Animated* made the man more human in her book, and more human was always a good thing.

You need to stop focusing on the man and focus on the bigger picture, she told herself sternly. Heaven knew Detective Doyle was already stirring her in ways that she felt were not appropriate on the job—or off the job, for that matter, in her case.

She didn't have any time for all those stirrings that she had heard her friends talk about. At least no time while she was working, she thought—which seemed to be all the time.

And yet, here she was, reacting to being around the man. Reacting to the sound of his voice. Reacting even to the thought of their being together, and not just as a working couple.

Knock it off, Cavanaugh. You have a job to do. Just do it, she ordered herself.

Cassandra became aware that the detective was watching her. Blowing out a breath, she forced herself not to focus on the fact that his eyes were on her.

Picking up her cell phone, Cassandra called the number that she had used so often that it was all but permanently burned into her brain.

The phone rang a total of six times as she waited for Valri to pick up. She thought it was going to ring again. But then she heard a voice on the other end responding.

"Cavanaugh," Valri announced in a very clipped tone of voice.

Cassandra guessed that meant the computer wizard was already swamped at this early hour. Well, she knew that couldn't be helped as she drew back her shoulders.

"Hi, Valri. I'll make this fast," she promised the computer wizard.

"My mistake, I thought this was Cassie," she heard Valri saying to her.

"You know it's me, Valri. I was just trying to be thoughtful," Cassie told the computer wizard in all sincerity.

"Hence my confusion," Valri told her with a laugh.

"Is this a little preamble before you tell me that you unearthed something good in your search, or are you trying to entertain me before you pull the rug out from under me and tell me you have nothing to give me that would count as helpful?"

"Which would you like to hear, Cass?" Valri asked.

Cassandra instantly read between the lines and had her answer. "Okay, you have something," she declared happily.

Valri hedged her response. She never liked bragging. "Nothing great, but better than nothing."

She had forgotten that Valri never built things up and definitely did not like tooting her own horn. Out of all of them, Cassandra recalled, Valri was considered to be the most conservative one.

"I'm listening," Cassandra said quietly, waiting.

"Okay, I'm going to text you a couple of pictures."

Cassandra looked down at her phone screen. The images were not all that clear. "Who am I looking at?"

"Guys who were last seen in the company of some of the men who went missing shortly thereafter," Valri told her.

Cassandra continued to stare at the two photographs on her phone. "Valri, is it my imagination, or…"

She heard her cousin laugh. "So, you see it too I take it?"

Danny couldn't pretend not to be listening to this conversation any longer. He looked over Cassandra's shoulder at the photographs that had been sent to her phone. "What is it that you're looking at?" he asked.

The question was no sooner out of his mouth than he realized what the two women who were talking had meant.

He saw it as well.

There was a very strong similarity between the two people in the two photos that had just been sent.

Cassandra raised her eyes to Danny's face. "They could be one and the same person," she said.

"Or they could just be related," Danny said. "Working this job, I've met a lot of brothers who looked as if they were the same person," he told her.

Cassandra got back to asking her cousin questions. "Do you have names for these guys, Valri?"

"Do I have the names?" Valri repeated incredulously. "Are you doubting me this far into our relationship?"

"Nope, not me. I wouldn't dream of it," Cassandra told her cousin innocently.

"Good. Sending you those names now, but I don't have addresses yet. The first guy did give one, but following it would put him in the middle of the East River," she said. "Unless we're dealing with a comic book hero, that just isn't possible," she told Cassandra.

"Agreed, but send me anything you do have. I'll make sense of it as we go along. When were these two photos taken?" she asked Valri.

"As near as I can place it, about a couple of years apart. I'm still working on connecting other people who might have been associated with your missing hunks."

"Come again?" Cassandra asked.

"It has to have hit you by now," Valri said. "All these dead guys could have been used in an old-fashioned movie about gorgeous guys. Maybe even singing and dancing ones," she added with a laugh.

Cassandra exchanged looks with Danny. In typical Valri fashion, the computer wizard had put her finger directly on the most salient point, the main connecting factor.

Chapter Fifteen

"Well, actually it did," Cassandra said to the computer technologist. "I just didn't want to sound as if I was being shallow."

"Nothing shallow about being accurate," Valri told her. "To my way of thinking, I'd say that this is a very unique case," the Aurora Police Department's computer wizard said. "Okay, I'm in the process of exploring more names. Right now, there's just the two of these guys—and maybe not even that many," she said, still entertaining the possibility that this was one and the same man.

"Why would you say that?" Cassandra asked her cousin, wanting to explore Valri's thinking.

"Because these two guys look eerily alike, and as far as I can tell, they were never captured at the same time in the same place. I find that a little bit suspicious, but I could be totally wrong. However," Valri said, continuing on, "I haven't given up. There still might be more offenders on the list. Plus, these two could just look eerily alike.

"If there are any breakthroughs," Valri said, "I'll get back to you immediately."

"I'll be waiting," Cassandra told her cousin. "Meanwhile, please say hi to the rest of the family for Travis and me."

"Will do," Valri promised. And with that, the call ended.

Cassandra turned off her cell phone and put it away. She turned her attention back to Danny. "Call in your troops, and let's see if either one of these two guys can be found in the greater New York area," she told the detective. "I think it might be time to hit the bricks instead of sitting here and breathing in all this dust."

"Hit the bricks?" he echoed. "Is this an old Humphrey Bogart movie?" he asked, amused. He raised his hand as she began to answer him. "Doesn't matter. You're not going to get an argument out of me. Though I myself prefer Jerry Orbach in the original *Law & Order.*"

"That works for me too," Cassandra said.

"Like him, I actually prefer talking to people one on one," he told her.

Cassandra looked at him in surprise, but if he noticed, he gave no indication. He just continued with his explanation. "Looking into their eyes helps me see just how honest—or dishonest—they are being."

"Well, we certainly agree on that too," she told the detective. "I like hitting the bricks. A lot better than I like sitting in an office, pushing papers around and getting cross-eyed." She looked down at the address of one of the two suspects that Valri had given her. "Let's see what Rick Allen has to say about his friendship with Pete Wilson and if he has any feelings about the man disappearing the way that he suddenly did ten years ago."

THEY FOUND RICK ALLEN at home. The man lived in a one-bedroom walk-up that had seen far better days but was not as run-down as it could have been. From all indications, Rick Allen hadn't been able to hold a steady job since Pete Wilson had abruptly disappeared the way he had.

Suspicious at first of the two detectives' appearance on his doorstep, it soon became obvious that he was more than happy to talk about the missing man he claimed was his best friend.

"I can't tell you what a great heart Peter had. Maybe a little too great," Allen said sadly.

"Could you tell us what you mean by that?" Cassandra asked.

Rather than answer her question directly, Rick Allen seemed to only want to talk to Danny. "Well, if you ask me, Peter was far too trusting," he told the New York detective. "He felt that he could tell everyone anything and that they would be receptive of his words and honest in their response," Peter Wilson's so-called friend stressed.

"I kept telling him that someday he would wind up regretting being so damn trusting. Hell," Rick Allen said, frowning at the memory, "this is the big city, not some little farm in the countryside."

"According to our information," Cassandra told the older man, referring to her notes, "your friend was born and bred right here in the heart of New York City."

Rick Allen frowned darkly at her, then went back to looking at the detective who had come to conduct the interview with her. It was obvious that Allen preferred Danny, but this often happened in interviews with witnesses or persons of interest.

"That doesn't change the fact that Peter was way too trusting," he told her gruffly, then turned his attention back to Danny.

For a moment, Cassandra was about to say something about keeping a civil tongue in his head. But then she decided there was nothing to be gained by putting this bitter older man in his place or on the defensive. Not to mention, her role was to listen, observe and ask questions, not scold.

The man's behavior just gave her that much more insight into his character.

"Did you ever talk to him about that?" she asked. "About his being so trusting?"

Rick Allen avoided making any eye contact with

her. Instead, he shifted his eyes to look at Danny and gave his answer to him, as if it had been Danny who had put the question to him.

"I did," the man admitted. "Once—but I didn't want him to think that I was picking on him," Allen said with what passed for an innocent expression. "I got the feeling that it was hard enough for Peter to make ends meet and to just go about the business of living. I did lend him money, and very honestly, I didn't expect to ever see it again.

"After a while," Allen said, "I began to notice that he kept looking over his shoulder, as if he expected someone to just come pouncing out of the shadows and overtake him. Maybe even wind up beating him up."

Danny took his cue from the fact that Rick Allen was addressing his words exclusively at him. Glancing at Cassandra and mentally apologizing to the woman, the New York detective pushed ahead and asked, "Why do you think that he would he expect that?"

"Because we've got a serial killer loose in the city—or so the rumor goes," Rick said whimsically. It was hard judging by his expression whether he bought into that or not.

At this point, Cassandra couldn't help herself. She had to ask the man. "Are you afraid of a serial killer?"

He spared her a look and snapped, "No." Then

shifted to look at the very handsome detective before him.

"Why should I be?" he asked Danny. "It's probably all just a wild rumor that's been blown out of proportion."

"Bodies have been known to turn up," Danny said. He couldn't help pointing this out to the man.

"Hell, this is the big city. Bodies have been known to turn up all over the place," he told Danny with bravado. He went on to say, "Here. In Chicago. In Los Angeles. Hell, in any big city where people can get into an argument. But that still doesn't mean that there's a serial killer on the loose."

He laughed to himself, dismissing the idea. "If there was, I'd move back to my dad's farm and then just wait around to die of boredom."

Cassandra read between the lines and raised her eyes to look at the man who was talking. "I take it that you didn't like working on the family farm too much?"

"No longer than I had to," Rick answered honestly. "The second I could take off, I did," the man said, informing Danny proudly. "I didn't belong in the sticks. I was always meant to be where the action was."

He sat up straighter, his body language signaling that the interview was over, at least as long as the woman was here as well. He looked at Danny pointedly. "Is there anything else I can tell you?"

"No, not now," Danny answered. "If we think of anything, we'll get back to you."

Rick looked directly into Danny's eyes as he said, "I'll be sure to keep a candle burning in the window for you."

Cassandra walked out of the apartment first, moving quickly. She was eager to get a breath of fresh air, such as it was.

Danny joined her, and they walked down the metal stairs to the street. Only then did she trust her voice not to carry up to the man they had just left. She thought he might have been listening to anything they said to one another. He struck her as that type.

"I think someone has a crush," she said, glancing back mischievously. The man seemed to have strong opinions about her. It said a lot.

Danny shook his head. "Hey, if it helps move the case forward, I'm okay with that."

Cassandra nodded. "It's interesting. While sitting there, I had a hard time picturing Rick Allen as someone's son," she replied, barely stifling the shiver that had come over her. "Because of my large family, I usually envision people as being part of a family, large or small. But not this guy," she said with feeling. "He just makes me want to shiver. Like there's a creepy story there."

The NYPD detective laughed, then surprised her by agreeing with her assessment. "Yeah, me too," Danny said, then asked, "Are you up to trying to find and talk to the other potential suspect that your resident computer genius unearthed?" He glanced at her over his shoulder as he led the way back to his vehicle.

"Absolutely," Cassandra told him with enthusiasm. She paused as she got into Danny's car. "Maybe it's just my imagination, but I feel like this case is *finally* moving—hopefully in the right direction."

Starting up his vehicle, the detective smiled at Cassandra. "I really hope that you're right," he told her. And then he began driving. "I think your cousin managed to locate what looked like a current address for this guy who befriended the second victim on the list."

"Valri is very good at her job. She knows how to dig deep in places others might miss. I've never known her to make a mistake," she told the detective proudly. Cassandra watched as the streets went by and realized that she hadn't answered his question yet. "Let's go," she said.

He paused at the next light. "There's just one problem," Danny told her.

"Just one?" she said, kidding, then immediately realized that he was being serious. "What's the problem?"

He blew out a breath. He was definitely not happy about this, but he knew he had to own up to it.

"The place is listed as being off the island," he told her, then said, "I'm going to need to get directions."

"From me?" she asked him, completely caught off guard.

"No," Danny corrected. "From the GPS system that's attached to the dashboard." He pointed toward it. "It's positioned so that I can't readily make it out, and I don't want to fiddle with it. Just put in the address and read the directions to me."

"Won't the GPS give you a readout?" she asked. All the systems she knew of talked.

"It would if the volume hadn't somehow gone dormant and then shorted out," he told her.

She didn't understand. "Can't you just replace it?"

His brow furrowed. "I can and I will, but that doesn't do me any good right now, does it?"

The truth of it was that he meant to upgrade the GPS, but more important things got in the way. He hated that she noticed his subpar system and realized that he had snapped the answer. He immediately toned it down a little. "I know my way around this city—just for some reason, not in the particular neighborhood where this guy's apartment is located," he confessed. "So," he began again, "if you don't mind…"

"Nope, I don't mind at all," she told him cheerfully, looking down at the GPS as she typed in the address that was written in on the sheet. "You ready?" she asked.

"Yeah, I'm ready."

Cassandra noticed that the New York detective's voice was rather strained, but she ignored it.

Getting to where Roy Adams lived was a challenge. They drove to a secluded part of Brooklyn, in a neighborhood that was more residential, with gardens and patches of grass that could pass as a lawn. The gray winter light barely peeked through the clouds. Because some people had cars parked on the streets, parking was especially difficult.

Finding the man was even more challenging.

Luckily, both he and Cassandra had good eyesight and the determination to find Roy Adams. They knocked on doors and found a couple of his neighbors in, but no one had any idea where the man was.

Cassandra and Danny spent the rest of the day attempting to track Roy Adams down. They went into stores and showed pictures of him, even stopped people on the street. After a while, they sat in a café to regroup and go down another list of streets they could canvas. In the end, they got nowhere.

It was, Cassandra thought, as if they had used up their luck just by locating Rick Allen. Trying to find Roy Adams was a futile expedition.

When they went back to one of the neighbors who hadn't been there a few hours earlier, they struck potential gold. Lucy Valdez, a grandmother of three who worked as a nurse in a nearby hospital, suggested that the man was away, fishing. It was his favorite pastime, she confided.

"It's the middle of winter," Cassandra protested, pointing that out to the woman who had offered that excuse. The idea of fishing in what amounted to bitter cold had little to recommend it.

"Roy says, that way, he doesn't have to put up with any competition," the woman at the door informed them. She looked over her shoulder as she heard sizzling noises coming from the direction of her kitchen. "Look, I gotta go. I'm starting my dinner late," she complained.

Not waiting for any response from the duo standing in her doorway, the woman closed it on them.

Cassandra exchanged looks with the frowning detective at her side. "I think that's our cue to call it a night. Are people here always this friendly?"

Danny chuckled. "They don't want to get involved. Mrs. Valdez has enough on her plate than to find herself wrapped up in a bunch of homicide cases."

"I get it. But still, we've gotta find this guy."

Cassandra nodded, totally in agreement. The more time they spent together, the more he knew he would miss her when she went back to California. They'd had this easy way of working together, as if they'd been on cases before. It only seemed natural to continue into the night. "You want to grab some dinner?"

Cassandra realized that she was hungry and had been for a few hours now. All that walking around fired up her appetite. "You've twisted my arm," she told the detective.

"What would you like?" he asked Cassandra.

She smiled at him as they returned to his vehicle again. Cassandra slid into her seat. "Oh, I don't know. Why don't you surprise me?"

A thought flashed through his mind that had nothing to do with dinner or anything remotely practical like that.

Surprise her, he caught himself thinking. How he wanted to just lean over and kiss her again, right here in the middle of nowhere after a long day. The idea seemed natural to him, to look into her flashing green eyes and draw her closer.

This time, it took a great deal of concentrated effort on his part to rein in his thoughts and focus on something other than bringing her exceedingly tempting mouth up to his.

It was not easy.

"You in the mood for Chinese food?" Danny finally asked her.

"I'm in the mood for food," she responded. "Anything but three-day-old dirt at this point will do nicely."

He looked at her as he brought his car into a nearly packed parking lot that accommodated three restaurants. "That is an interesting choice of food."

"Just my way of letting you know that I'm up for anything," she told him.

He nodded. "I got that impression," he said. Stopping his vehicle in a small parking space, he got out first. It was really cold out.

Danny turned up the collar on his coat. Without thinking, when Cassandra got out, he put his arm around her back to keep the chill at bay as best he could.

"Walk quickly," he recommended. "The restaurant door is just up ahead."

"And here I was planning on dawdling," she responded with a laugh.

"You really are a wise guy, you know that?" he said to her.

Cassandra smiled up into his face, completely amused despite the bitter cold night. She could feel herself responding to him.

"I know," she answered.

He walked faster to get Cassandra in through the restaurant's door as quickly as possible.

As he did so, Danny noticed that the California detective kept up without any complaint.

When they walked in, the warmth inside the restaurant all but embraced them.

It was an exceedingly welcome feeling.

Chapter Sixteen

"I had no idea I was that hungry," Cassandra said, looking down at her empty plate. A plate that had been more than full just a little while ago with the most delicious orange chicken, sticky rice and stir-fried broccoli. They still had a great deal of food they could take home. Home. How easy it was to think of them together. Understandable, since they'd been working together every minute since they'd met. But disturbing too since she started to imagine how much it might hurt to leave.

She made sure to take mental pictures of Danny, how cute he was, especially now, when he was at ease, smiling and talkative.

Danny wiped his mouth, crumpled up his napkin and allowed it to drop down onto his own empty plate.

"You just got caught up in the case," he told her, supplying her with an excuse. "I've had the very same thing happen to me on more than one occasion. So," he continued, his eyes meeting hers, "do you want anything else?"

Cassandra paused for a moment, then told him, "No."

"If it wasn't so cold out, I would suggest a short walk to help kick-start digestion—we did have a lot to eat," Danny said, commenting on the portions they had just consumed. "But it really is pretty cold outside, so taking a walk, even a brisk one, isn't such a good idea." He grinned as he looked around for their server. Spotting her, he signaled for the check.

The waitress came over almost instantly and cheerfully handed them their bill. Glancing at the total, Danny proceeded to peel off a nice-sized tip to place on top of the bill, then left what amounted to the exact amount of the check to pay for their dinner.

"We'd wind up being popsicles before we ever managed to walk a couple of city blocks," he told her, returning to what he had mentioned earlier.

Walking out of the restaurant, his eyes met hers. "Unless you're interested in giving it a shot," the detective added as a postscript. His indication was that he would if she would.

Cassandra pulled her coat more tightly around herself. "Maybe tomorrow," she suggested, stifling a shiver.

His lips curved. "Tomorrow it is," he responded. "As for now, I think that I'd better get you over to the hotel."

Despite the hour, Cassandra realized that she didn't really feel like calling it a night just yet.

"Do you live close by?" she asked as she got into his car.

The question surprised him. "Close enough," he answered. Because everyone knew how pricey apartments so close to the heart of the city were, he felt he needed to explain why he had gotten so lucky.

"The apartment I live in belonged to the former detective who initially recruited and trained me. Stan Beal was a lifelong bachelor who went to live in Florida when he retired. He hated to see his apartment go to waste, and he didn't want to sell it, so his solution was to pass it on to me as a 'relative,'" he told her with a smile. "Stan was a real good guy." "Why?" he found himself asking in response to her initial question about the closeness of his apartment.

"No reason," she answered. "I just thought I'd like to see it, that's all."

"It's not all that exciting," he told her. It was actually rather drab by modern concepts.

Cassandra shrugged noncommittally. "I just haven't seen all that much of New York City except for the precinct and the hotel—and interviewing witnesses."

"And you want to go sightseeing," Danny guessed.

"Eventually," she agreed. "But right now, I just want to see something that isn't part of the case."

He laughed softly. "Never exactly thought of my

apartment as much of a tourist draw," he teased, "but you're more than welcome to come by and see it."

With that, he pulled away from the curb and drove to the apartment he had inhabited ever since his mentor had retired and taken off for Florida.

The detective's one-bedroom apartment, truly in the heart of Manhattan and not too far from the police station, was located on the fourth floor of a well-maintained prewar building. With only seven floors and five apartments per floor, it was the kind of residence where everyone knew each other's business—in the best possible way. Danny often found plates of cookies on his doorstep from one of his more grandmotherly neighbors. Now if only he could find someone to clean his apartment, he'd be in a better place to entertain visitors.

Unlocking the door, he switched on the light and immediately began to apologize. "Sorry, I wasn't expecting company," he explained as he moved about, picking up papers and cast-off clothing from the floor, stacking them together in a semblance of a pile on a love seat.

She grinned at the detective's apology. "No judgment," she said, trying to assure him. She looked around again and then smiled. "This is actually neater than the way my brothers lived until they found the loves of their lives, who accepted them 'for better or for worse.' Housekeeping fell under 'for worse.'"

His thoughts going back in time, Danny laughed softly to himself. "If she were here, my mother would have told you that she raised me better than that."

"She probably did, but right now you're as caught up as the rest of us are in this ongoing serial killer saga. Neatness has to take a back seat for the time being," she told him. "Trust me on that."

She was being awfully nice about this. A lot of women he knew would have been rather critical about the state of his living quarters, he thought. He rather liked the fact that she had given him a pass on his limited housekeeping abilities.

The more he got to know this unusual woman, the more he found to like. He couldn't help wondering if it was the ongoing case that was doing it—or if it was the woman.

Danny had a feeling that it was the latter since, sadly, this was not the first serial killer case he had worked on.

He gestured toward his kitchen. "Can I get you something to drink?" he offered. He knew that if he extended the offer to include something to eat, she might very well explode. He was pretty much stuffed to the gills himself.

"Do you have any diet soda?" she asked him. He didn't look like the type who favored diet drinks, much less anything carbonated, but she thought it was worth a shot.

"No alcoholic beverage?" he questioned.

She shook her head. "Not right now," she said. "I'd fall asleep right where I'm sitting."

"Can't have that," he told her. Walking over to his refrigerator, he opened the door and rummaged around for a moment. "You're in luck," he told her. "There's one unopened can left."

Taking it out, he offered the can to Cassandra. He fully expected her to pass on it, but to his surprise, she took it from him and popped open the top. A small fizzle showered down lightly for just a second.

Danny watched the woman close her eyes as she took a sip, savoring the drink. He found himself captivated for a moment.

"Never saw anyone enjoy soda quite like that," he told her.

She flushed just a little. "It's a guilty pleasure. Left to my own devices, I would probably drink four or five cans a day. I've had to cut back drastically in the last few years," she said.

"Never exactly thought of drinking soda as an indulgence," he said. He'd seen a lot of people on the force abuse alcohol, but diet soda never fell into that category. Every now and then, he liked a soda, but it wasn't his go-to, beverage.

She laughed. "I suppose it had something to do with the amount I consumed—it could have filled a small ocean at one point," she said.

Danny wound up shaking his head. "You really are a revelation, Detective Cavanaugh," he told her, amused.

"Glad I could entertain you," she told him as her eyes met his.

Cassandra had no idea exactly how they had come to be sitting so close to one another. And how that close proximity managed to stir her up the way that it did.

She could feel her pulse speeding up—just like her heartbeat.

I need to be careful, Cassandra thought, silently lecturing herself. Otherwise, she had a feeling she would wind up going a step too far.

But even as she issued that warning to herself, Cassandra could feel the effects that the detective's blue eyes were having on her, could feel herself growing warmer than the temperature warranted.

It didn't really help matters any to have the man take a sip from the can she was holding. Nor did it help to have him slowly run the tip of his thumb along her lips.

Cassandra swallowed. She was growing progressively hotter and could have sworn she heard a rushing noise in her ears.

Breathing took effort.

Cassandra hardly remembered Danny removing the can from her hand and placing it on the coffee table before them. What she found herself suddenly aware of was the detective leaning forward, taking her face in his hands and then softly pressing his lips against hers.

Her heart suddenly slammed against her ribs, completely stealing away her ability to breathe. Cassandra hardly remembered the detective taking her into his arms.

All she was really aware of was the end effect.

And the fact that everything inside of her was reduced to a single puddle.

The next moment, Cassandra caught herself returning the handsome detective's kiss. Over and over again, her mouth slanted over his, each kiss growing more ardent, more passionate. And each and every time she did, the fire within her only grew more.

Danny pulled her onto his lap, and she sat above him on the sofa. He kissed her with an intense passion he had no idea existed within him until it was suddenly there, dictating his every move.

But even so, he drew back just for a moment. "Are you sure you want to do this?" he asked her in a quiet, husky voice. The last thing he wanted was for her to feel as if the situation she found herself in had been forced.

Cassandra blinked, looking at him in slight confusion. "Are you trying to back out of this?" she asked the detective.

There was no way he wanted that, but he didn't want her feeling any sort of pressure either. "No, but—"

"Then shut up and kiss me, Detective," she told

him. Without waiting for him to take his cue, she sealed her mouth to his.

The rest happened so quickly, it seemed as if it were all transpiring within the blink of an eye.

They did make it to the bedroom, but just barely. Clothes went flying in all directions, littering the floor and leaving them both nude and eager. Their bodies heated against one another, the flames rising higher and higher with every long, soulful kiss that passed between them as well as each long, loving caress.

Danny was eager to hurry through the lovemaking, to have the final moment explode within him and fill every empty, wanting crevice within his body. But at the same time, he wanted to savor every moment, to hold on to it and treasure every second he was experiencing, because it was so wondrously fulfilling.

Danny lovingly slid his hands over every curve, every tempting inch of her palpitating body.

Locked in a torrid embrace, he kissed Cassandra over and over again, each kiss growing more and more pronounced until he had her, willingly and eagerly moving beneath him, hungry for the wondrous feeling he seemed to be able to create within her.

When Danny finally entered her, Cassandra caught her lower lip between her teeth, stifling a cry. A soulful moan managed to escape, surrounding them.

United, they moved as one being, going faster and faster until the explosion overtook them, shaking them both down to their very souls.

And when it was over, they fell back, still wrapped in each other's arms, hardly able to draw in enough breath to sustain themselves.

She could feel her heart pounding against her rib-cage and thought it was never going to subside. But eventually, it did.

That was when she felt Danny looking at her. "What?" she questioned.

"I've got to admit, that was certainly a surprise," he told her, brushing his lips against her forehead.

"Why?" she asked, confused. "You didn't think I had it in me?"

"No," he laughed, drawing her closer to him, tucking his arm around her body again. "I didn't think that *I* had it in me," he told her. Danny kissed her forehead again. "No doubt about it, Cavanaugh," he said, lowering his voice. "You do bring out the very best in me. A 'best' I never even suspected I had."

A sparkle entered her eyes, teasing him. "Would you like to do it again?"

He could feel his heart beginning to race again as a smile curved his mouth. "Hell yes. But I think it's only fair to warn you, this time I just may expire."

She could only shake her head. "You do know how to turn a girl's head," she told him just before she brought her mouth up to his.

"I do my best," Danny answered, his warm breath teasing her just before he began to kiss her with every ounce of passion he had within him.

IT WAS THE man's third time around the block. With each pass that he made, the images he envisioned within his mind's eye grew more vivid, taking on form and breadth—and stoking what felt like a deep, inner rage within his chest. One that threatened to completely undo him.

This feeling was nothing new to him, but the extent to which it filled him was. He had never felt this intensity before.

He had found out about Danny Doyle and that little tramp's rendezvous in Doyle's apartment completely by accident. He had followed the detective's vehicle, waiting for him to be done with that little California witch and bring her back to the hotel.

He had even sat outside the restaurant in his car, waiting for them to be done and come out.

But instead of taking the woman and leaving her at her hotel, the detective had taken her to his place.

His place, damn it!

The very thought filled him with red-hot fury that he couldn't even put into words.

It made his blood boil.

They shouldn't be together, he thought darkly.

Doyle shouldn't be spending time with her. If anything, the detective should be giving *him* his atten-

tion. He had been cultivating the man for almost a
year now, bringing him coffee just the way he liked
it, finding topics of conversation that helped to make
the detective's job more tolerable. He knew that for
a fact.

That awful woman had no place being there with
him, doing heaven only knows what.

He set his jaw hard. So hard he felt that it was
close to snapping.

She'd pay for this, he promised himself. By God,
that two-bit little whore was going to pay. He'd see
to it.

He circled the building one last time, looking up
to where he knew the detective's windows were located.

And then he made his way to his car and drove
away.

Soon, he promised himself. He'd seize the opportunity for revenge very, very soon.

Chapter Seventeen

A new warmth had generated between them and continued to thrive even after the other night, but Cassandra and Danny were both determined not to allow that feeling get in the way of their working well together.

More importantly, not get in the way of their catching the serial killer they were pursuing and doing their best to bring to justice.

When they walked into the precinct the following morning, the first person they ran into was Danny's partner, Simon Lee.

When he saw them, the detective looked as if he were barely able to contain himself.

Danny was well acquainted with the signs. Something was definitely up, and by the look on his partner's face, it wasn't good.

"Okay, Lee, what's up?" the detective asked before he even took off his overcoat.

The man's eyes swept over the duo as the words

fairly exploded from his mouth. "They found more bodies!"

Cassandra's heart sank. She might be in the business of solving murders, but she ached every time a person was killed. "When?" she asked.

"Half an hour ago," Danny's partner told them.

"Was it recent?" Danny asked. Just what had set this killer off on his latest killing spree, he couldn't help wondering.

"That's the odd part," Lee told them as he followed behind the pair into the squad room. "It looks like these people have been dead for about a year or so. The bodies were just taken into autopsy, so we'll know more once the ME gets done.

"It's like the killer has been saving them somewhere and then for some reason decided that now was the time to release them." Lee told them his theory. "The city is just catching up and coming back to life after experiencing a two-year paralyzing hiatus," he said, referring to what New York—and the whole world—had endured with the pandemic. "There's been a lot of construction going on all over the place in an effort to get back to normal." He shrugged, sitting down at his desk. "I guess no one noticed these bodies being planted."

"Or if they did, they pretended not to," Danny said, hanging up his overcoat as he shook his head.

The information was not computing as far as Cassandra was concerned. Taking off her own jacket, she blew out a frustrated breath.

"How can they do that?" she asked.

He knew she was referring to the fact that the citizens were deliberately trying to ignore what was going on right in front of them. But he could also see the other side of the picture.

"It's called survival," Danny told her.

"Maybe," Cassandra agreed. "But at what price?" To her, the people who cast a blind eye to what was happening were sacrificing their humanity.

"Why don't we get philosophical *after* we solve this mystery and catch this cold-blooded killer?" Lee suggested.

At bottom, Danny's partner was right, Cassandra thought. She caught her lower lip between her teeth as she tried to make sense out of all this.

"It's got to be someone who's in the heart of things. Someone who can easily blend in without being noticed or calling attention to himself," she said, thinking out loud.

Lee inclined his head, agreeing with the detective from California. "Kind of like 'Where's Waldo?' right?"

"Yes, except in this case, Waldo is a lot less friendly," Cassandra speculated, a deep frown transforming her features. She only wished this situation was like that lighthearted challenge, but it obviously wasn't. Waldo had never left a stack of bodies in his wake.

"How many bodies did they find?" Danny asked.

"I haven't seen them for myself," Lee admitted. "But I was told that there were three."

"All good-looking men between the ages of twenty to forty?" Cassandra guessed, mentally crossing her fingers that she was wrong about that this time.

Lee looked at her and sighed. This was definitely the work of the same person. "It's like you were there."

She blew out a frustrated breath. "Only in my nightmares," she told the two men. The fact that it was the same person doing the killing meant he was getting braver. Hopefully, he was also growing more careless since he hadn't gotten caught yet. "Can we go to autopsy?" she asked Danny.

"Not yet," Lee told her. "From what I heard, the medical examiner was just getting started, and she has a reputation of not liking having anyone looking over her shoulder until the autopsy is completed. So it's going to be a while."

"There are probably no surprises. I mean, it's got to be the same guy, right?" she asked, looking from one man to the other.

Danny nodded. "That's the option that gets my vote," he answered. "Do we know who these latest victims are?"

Another member of Danny's team, Eduardo Suarez, walked in just in time to hear him ask the last question. He had an answer for the team leader.

"We've managed to get IDs on them," Eduardo said as he joined the group. He had brought in three photographs and now hung them up on the bulletin board. "I've got to say that this guy's got great taste," he commented.

"For a crazy person," Travis said as he joined the group.

"They found three more bodies," Cassandra told her cousin.

"Yeah, I just heard," Travis replied. "Maybe the city can call a moratorium on construction for a while," he said.

She looked at Travis. He was joking, right? "You really think that's going to stop this guy from killing people?"

Travis shrugged. "Wishful thinking."

Cassandra turned toward Danny. They needed to get busy. "Where would you like us to start?" she asked him.

"We talk to the families if there are any in the area, try to reconstruct the dead men's lives. Working backwards, we'll focus on both the similarities and the differences in all three cases. Maybe that'll wind up pointing us in the right direction," he told the rest of his team. Several more members had walked into the squad room and had gathered around him.

Cassandra nodded, agreeing with Danny's assessment. "All we need is just one break," she told the others gathered around them.

"That's good in theory," Lee told her. "But…" His voice trailed off.

She knew where Danny's partner was going with this. "I know, I know," she agreed. "We need to make that theory a reality."

She definitely didn't want to step on Danny's toes, especially after the night they had spent together, so she proceeded with utter caution, taking nothing for granted. "What do you want us to do?"

Danny distributed the copies of the photographs of the latest victims who had been discovered. He gave one to each of member of his team, including Cassandra.

"Go talk to the dead men's friends, employers, landlords—anyone who might have seen them before they disappeared off the face of the earth," he instructed. "The serial killer has to have quirks we can track down and use. Something that can pinpoint him, however small and initially insignificant," he told his team. "It's only hidden from us at the moment because we can't see it."

That sounded like a saying, Cassandra thought. Unable to help herself, she asked, "Can I embroider that on a towel?"

"You can do anything you want once we catch this SOB. Until that happens, I want all of our attention to be directly centered on this guy." His eyes swept over the people on his team, taking each and every one of them into account. "Have I made myself clear?"

A sea of heads bobbled up and down. "Absolutely," several members told him.

Another one gave him a smart salute. "You got it."

"Uh-huh," another member responded.

Danny looked over toward Cassandra. She hadn't responded yet. "Detective Cavanaugh?" he asked, waiting for her answer.

"You were never clearer, Detective Doyle," she said to him cheerfully as her eyes met his.

"Then let's get to work," Danny said, encouraging his team.

THE DISTINCT SQUEAK of the mail cart as the delivery clerk made his way through the squad room seemed particularly grating on her nerves this morning.

Cassandra paused what she was working on and looked up to find Curtis Wayfare approaching their work area.

She could see the look on the clerk's face as he pushed the mail cart in front of him. He was looking in Danny's direction. Cassandra could see the man's features softening.

The man was seriously interested in Danny, Cassandra thought. Whether it was just a harmless man crush or something more remained to be seen.

When his glance shifted toward her, for just a second, she felt a really cold shiver zip down her back.

Maybe it was just her imagination, but even so, she couldn't shake the feeling that the mail clerk just didn't like her. She was more than a little convinced that for whatever reason, the man was harboring a strong grudge against her.

"I hear that more bodies turned up, Detective," Wayfare said, directing his words toward Danny. "Think it's the same killer?" Wayfare asked him. He appeared to be genuinely interested in Danny's opinion. He also sounded as if the conversation was just between the two of them, excluding the others in the room.

"They did," Danny answered, keeping his tone matter-of-fact sounding. Then, because he felt it was warranted, he added, "The ME will undoubtedly be able to tell us if it's the same serial killer."

"I bet it is." The clerk almost sounded cheerful as he made the pronouncement. "Some puzzle, eh, Detective?" Wayfare spared a glance in Cassandra's direction. His smile faded almost completely, and then the clerk resumed his route. "Well, good luck, Detective Doyle. I've got mail to deliver. Call me if you need anything. I'm working a full day today. Just like you," he added happily.

Squeaky wheels marked his departure.

Cassandra said nothing until Wayfare had left the area on his way elsewhere. The clerk sent shivers down her spine and it was not the welcomed kind, she couldn't help thinking.

"You know, if I were you," she told Danny, "I'd make sure that my sidearm was always on my person."

Danny looked at her. "You mean because of Curtis Wayfare?" he asked her. "Oh, the guy's harmless enough."

"If you say so," Cassandra responded. It was obvious that she didn't agree with the detective. "But there's something about the way he looks at you that would definitely give me pause if I were you."

Danny waved a hand at her statement. "Curtis is just grateful. When he first came here about two years ago, he was like a lost puppy. I felt sorry for the guy, so I just spent a little time with him, pointed him in the right direction. He's been thankful ever since." Danny raised his shoulders in an absent-minded shrug. "That's all."

"Uh-huh. And here I thought that you New Yorkers were supposed to have been born suspicious."

He laughed and shook his head. "We just have a bad reputation. Who knows how it started. You won't find nicer people than in this city, especially in a crisis—of which we've had many."

Cassandra nodded her head and smiled. He was so cute, the way he defended his city. She understood the impulse since she loved her home fiercely. Aurora had sheltered her, had revived her after painful assignments and had shown her the meaning of love and family. She could never leave the Cavanaugh kingdom, even though this handsome detective had her thinking traitorous thoughts.

She watched him browsing through folders and notes. And then he looked up suddenly, directing his gaze at her. "I think I just found something."

"What?" she asked, trying to direct her vision toward what he was looking at.

"This must have gotten mixed in with the wrong papers," he commented, holding up a page. "It's information on your cousin."

Wayfare was immediately forgotten, and renewed interest about the case they were dealing with entered her eyes. "What kind of information?" She guided her chair in closer to Danny's in order to get a better look at what he had found.

"It says here that just before he disappeared, Nathan intended to apply to the police force. That he was no longer interested in leading an aimless life but had decided to make something of himself— like the rest of his family. He was planning on taking a police aptitude test and had high hopes he was going to do well."

"And?" she prodded, hoping there was more to it.

"And nothing," Danny told her. "There's nothing more in the folder or on the misplaced page I found stuffed inside. There's nothing more about your cousin at all," he said. He turned the page, examining it more closely and thumbing through other pages but didn't find anything else.

She looked at the page. There was no more information to be gleaned from it, "We don't know how he did," she said sadly.

"We don't even know *if* he did," Danny said. "There's no official mention of his taking a test to get into the police academy or anything like that."

"Is there any way we can find out if he did take the exam to get into the police academy?" she asked.

"The papers regarding that might have been warehoused," Danny suggested.

"Warehoused?" Cassandra echoed, immediately interested. "Warehoused where?"

"It's an old building located downtown," he told her. "If I remember correctly, it's by the river," he told her.

"Can we get into the building and access those old files, or would we need to have someone's permission to get us in?" Cassandra wanted to know. She followed that by making the detective understand why she was pushing this the way she was. "I know that my Uncle Brian wants to bury this heretofore missing family member in the family plot.

"It would just make him feel better," Cassandra explained. "I get the impression that he feels guilty about what happened to Nathan. That if he hadn't lost touch with him, then maybe he would still be alive."

Danny shook his head. "There's no point in the man beating himself up for that," Danny told her. "From what you said, your cousin's mother wanted to cut off all ties to the family."

"She did," Cassandra said, and confirmed with a sigh. "But Brian Cavanaugh is the chief of detectives. He takes *everything* upon himself. The only thing I can do to make things somewhat easier on his conscience is to at least solve the riddle of what happened to Nathan after Uncle Brian lost track of him."

Moved, Danny nodded. "Okay, let me see what I can do," he told her, heading for his captain's office.

"Want me to come with you?" Cassandra offered. She was already half out of her chair and rising to her feet.

But Danny shook his head, putting his hand up to stop her. "No, you stay here. When it comes to the captain, I really do better when I approach him on my own."

Cassandra smiled as she inclined her head toward the detective. "I bow to your wisdom," she told him.

He paused for a moment, waiting for the inevitable punch line that he felt was going to be coming.

Danny was really surprised when it didn't. He decided not to make any sort of a reference to that effect. He saw it as progress on her part.

"I'll be right back," Danny said, leaving the squad room quickly.

"I'll be here," she said to the detective with a resigned sigh. After a moment, she got back to looking over the folders that were spread out on the desk she was using.

Chapter Eighteen

Cassandra would read a couple of words or so—none of which had any sticking power when it came to her brain—and then look up, waiting for the door at the far end of the squad room to open again.

But it didn't.

Doyle was taking a lot of time to talk to his captain. Maybe the man didn't want to be convinced.

And then, finally, the door opened again. Cassandra gave up all pretense of reading the file before her. Getting up, she crossed over toward the detective.

"So, what did the captain say?" she asked the second that she was within the detective's earshot. "Will he release my cousin's body and have it sent back to my uncle?"

He hated to disappoint her, but he wasn't about to lie. "Not yet, but soon," Danny said quickly as he saw her expression fall. "The captain wants to give it a little more time. He feels that we might be on the brink of getting some answers."

For once, Cassandra found that she had to dig deep to find some optimism. She sighed. "I hope that he's right and something comes of this."

"I've known the captain for a while now, and while he's not the world's friendliest man, he does have good instincts and is usually more right than not about things," Danny said. "And no," he added with a small laugh, "In case you're wondering, I'm not wired."

She looked at him in surprise. Why would she even think that? This was not an overly trusting bunch of detectives, she decided.

"That never even crossed my mind," Cassandra told him. She sighed again, looking down at the file she had been going through. "I am getting cross-eyed from reading and rereading these files, trying to find the one salient point that I might have missed before. The one thing that might wind up pointing us to the killer."

Danny frowned, looking at the folder she was reading. "If it's even there."

"It *has* to be," Cassandra said, insistent. "The guy's human, and all humans have a habit of slipping up somewhere along the line. Some more often than others, but they all do it," she told him. "We just have to be patient and find just where this guy made a mistake."

She had an idea. Cassandra pulled out the two photos she had had blown up—the two that Valri had forwarded to her phone—and placed them side by side. They were as clear as possible but still fuzzy.

"Maybe we can try to locate some of the remaining friends or relatives of the serial killer's victims. One of them might remember seeing one of these guys lurking around our victims, trying to spend time with them," she said hopefully.

"It's definitely worth a try," Lee agreed. "We're not getting anywhere this way," he said needlessly.

Danny pulled up the list he had put together on his computer. He didn't need to count them. The names were imprinted on his mind. "All told, we've got fifteen victims."

"There might be more," Lee said to his partner.

Danny closed his eyes for a moment as he sighed, searching for patience. It was in precious short supply—even less than usual. "I realize that, but let's focus on the ones we know about at the moment," he said, instructing his partner.

Lee nodded. "How many is that?"

"Not nearly enough to answer our questions," Danny told the man, less than happy about the results.

Cassandra drew the sheet of paper closer to her. "All it takes is just one," she said, staring at the names on the list as if doing that would somehow emboss them on her brain. "Question is, which one is it?" she murmured to herself, looking at the list of names and the photos that went with them.

Nothing stood out or spoke to her. But then, that was to be expected.

"Let's see how many of these people are still living in the immediate area, or at least the state," Cassandra said, thinking that was as good a place as any for her to start.

As IT TURNED OUT, there were nine friends or relatives of the deceased men still living somewhere in the general vicinity. One had moved to Manhattan, while the other eight were somewhere within the other four boroughs.

Cassandra began to grow hopeful again.

Danny split the names up, handing them out to his team. The accompanying words were not exactly brimming with hope, Cassandra couldn't help but notice.

"I really don't hold out that much hope of finding anyone who can wind up pointing us in the right direction," he told his team.

Second verse, same as the first, Cassandra couldn't help thinking. "I keep telling you, Detective, you need to think positive."

Danny sighed, doing his best not to let what she was saying get on his nerves. There was such a thing as baseless optimism.

"Okay," he agreed. "I'm *positive* that none of these people are going to point us in the right direction." There was a slight edge to his voice.

"You really have to work on improving your attitude, Detective," she said.

"This *is* my improved attitude," he said to the woman.

All Cassandra could do at the moment was shake her head. She needed some fresh air, no matter how cold it felt going into her lungs. "Well, I'm going to go and interview my two people to see if there's anything they can tell me that'll point me in the right direction."

It was a long shot, but at least it was something, she thought.

A weary smile rose to his lips as Danny shook his head. "It never rains on your parade, does it, Cavanaugh?"

"Oh, sure it does," she said, contradicting him. "I just make sure to always keep an umbrella handy."

Danny caught himself laughing. "Let me see the two names that you have."

"Why?" she asked. Did he think she wouldn't be able to find the addresses? "I'm not going to get lost." She had a decent sense of direction, and she had also scrutinized online maps of the area. "Unlike you, I have a very sophisticated GPS."

Okay, maybe that was a low blow, but it irritated her that he would think she needed a chaperone. This wasn't nineteenth-century England—at least, she hoped it wasn't.

Some men she'd worked with felt she needed constant protecting. More than once, she'd had to explain that her training had been thorough and that she could take care of herself. Could Danny be another obstacle in her path to solving this case?

"That's not what I'm worried about," he told the woman from Southern California. "I just figured that we can combine our lists and go question these people together."

Her first thought was that he wanted to hide his feeling that she couldn't hack it as a detective. He didn't want to be liable if anything happened to her while chasing down this killer. She could feel her back going up. "You know that I can take care of myself."

"I know. I was just worried about the people you're going to be questioning," Danny told her with a wink. "Besides, I figure that two sets of eyes and ears are always better than just one."

She was not about to waste precious time arguing with the detective. If this was the way he wanted to play it, so be it. She couldn't shake the feeling that they couldn't afford to lose more time than they already had.

A gut feeling had taken hold, driving that point home. The kind of gut feeling that her uncles and occasionally her cousins like to talk about having.

The kind that she instinctively knew she couldn't afford to ignore. She couldn't explain the feeling; she only knew that if she ignored it, she might very well wind up regretting it.

"Fine, we'll join forces. You'll probably strike fear into their hearts, and we'll get our answers—if there are any answers to get," she added, thinking about what he had said earlier.

He looked at Cassandra in surprise. "You're not arguing with me?"

The smile that curved her lips was an amused one. "I get the feeling that in this case, arguing with you wouldn't do me any good. Besides," she said, not able to help herself, "if I was intent on opposing you, I wouldn't tell you. I'd just do it and let the pieces fall where they may."

"Now you have me worried," the detective said, only half kidding.

An easygoing grin quirked her mouth as a smile entered her eyes. "Sorry, that wasn't my intent."

The hell it wasn't, Danny thought. Just when he felt he finally had a handle on the woman, she threw a curve at him. It was obvious that she liked keeping him on his toes. To be honest, he couldn't really say that it bothered him.

He had a genuine question for her. "You want to call these people first, or just surprise them?"

Cassandra was startled that Danny gave her a choice in the matter rather than doing something that he had decided was set in stone.

She gave him an honest answer. "I've always had better luck with surprises."

Danny, on the other hand, liked to have things as predictable as possible. But he supposed he could see the advantage on having surprise on his side. For now, he nodded his head.

"All right," he said agreeably, "then surprise it is."

Standing behind her as she sat at her desk, Danny indicated the list before her. "Pick one of the people on the list. We'll go see if we can find that person at home or maybe even at work."

Looking at the list, she printed out information on the first four people that were on it, then circled them.

Danny frowned a little as he took in the names of the places. "Isn't that biting off a bit more than you can chew?" he asked.

"We're not showing up at all these places. We have no way of knowing if we're going to find *any* of these people where they're supposed to be. I know all the names on the list were initially researched, but things do have a way of changing, not to mention that people do just pick up and move. This, at least, allows us to gather some sort of information about one or two of the victims." She turned in her chair. The detective was standing much too close and generating all sorts of feelings that had nothing to do with tracking people down. Her throat felt dry as she formed the words. "I'm just attempting to cover all our bases."

Danny nodded. "I get that and appreciate the way you're thinking." He moved back so that she could push her chair away from the desk and get to her feet. "Let's go."

The detective paused for a moment to tell his partner just where he and Cassandra were going.

"Detective."

Curtis Wayfare's deep voice called out just before Danny managed to reach the squad room door.

He recognized the voice. The detective stifled a sigh as he turned toward the man who had called to him.

The mail clerk pushed his cart toward the man he clearly seemed to idolize. Wayfare was holding out a coffee container. "You forgot to take your coffee with you."

Danny was caught off guard. "Oh, right. I did." The detective took the container from Wayfare. "Thanks."

The mail clerk was beaming at him, as if he had just done something really noteworthy as well as personal. "You know you have trouble functioning without coffee, Detective," Wayfare told him knowingly, as if their so-called friendship went way back.

"Yeah, thanks," Danny said to the mail clerk, feeling somewhat awkward for the first time in the man's presence. He looked at Cassandra. "Like I said, we'd better hit the road."

Wayfare paused and looked after the departing detective. "Good luck," the mail clerk called out. His attention was exclusively directed toward the New York detective.

Cassandra waited until the clerk was out of earshot. "Your fairy godmother must have oiled the wheels on his cart. I didn't hear him roaming around the squad room this time."

Danny's frown went clear down to the bone. "He's not my fairy godmother," the detective told Cassandra.

"Oh, I beg to differ. I think Wayfare certainly thinks he is," she contradicted. "I think he would have carried you into the elevator if you would have let him."

Danny's frown deepened. Her comment made him uncomfortable. "You're exaggerating, Detective," he said.

"You didn't see the way he looked at you. I would say that look is nothing short of idolizing you." She grew serious. "I don't know if you're just his hero, or if there's something else involved."

"Speak plainly," he said to the woman. "Are you suggesting that Wayfare is the serial killer?"

Danny didn't know whether to laugh or take her seriously.

"What I'm suggesting is that there are eight million people all crowded into this little island of a city, and who knows what some of these people might be capable of?" she said to Danny. "I just think that we should keep our options open.

"By the way," Cassandra said as they walked out to the elevator, "do you know anything about this mail clerk? What his background is, things like that?" A lot of questions popped up in her mind when it came to Wayfare.

"I know next to nothing about the man," Danny said admittedly. "The only time I pay any attention to him is when he comes squeaking in and drops off a piece of mail or a package on my desk."

She pushed the down button, waiting for the elevator to arrive. "His cart stopped squeaking," she said, "right after you made a comment about the noise the wheels made."

"Are you saying he did that for me?" he said in disbelief. "That was just a coincidence."

"All I'm saying is for you to keep your mind open to the possibility that he's trying to please you. At this point, we don't know why."

He looked at her as the elevator arrived, opening its doors. "I think we both could use some fresh air," he suggested. She was letting her imagination run away with her, he thought.

"In the city?" she questioned, barely hiding the grin that overtook her face.

At that point, Danny laughed. "You work with what you have."

Pressing for the ground floor, the detective waited until the car went down to its destination. When it reached the lobby, the elevator doors opened.

Danny waited to comment until they were leaving the building. "You're wrong, you know."

"About?" she asked, not really sure what the man was referring to.

"About the mail clerk."

"You mean Wayfare?" Cassandra said.

"Yeah, him. He probably thinks that being friendly with me might help him get a raise, or at least not laid off," he said.

Cassandra shrugged. "You might be right."

He looked at her before they reached his vehicle, making a judgment call. "But you don't think so."

"Right now, until proven otherwise, everyone is a suspect in my eyes," she said.

"And you seemed like such a trusting soul," Danny said with a laugh. He liked that underneath her cheerfulness lurked an aggressive and observant detective. How he felt sorry for future perpetrators who were caught by her. They didn't stand a chance. And neither did he, come to think of it.

She reached out and touched his shoulder, a quick and flirtatious impulse. It reminded him of the previous night, what they meant to each other for a few precious hours.

"You know, Danny, we're just as suspicious in Aurora, California, as you are in New York City. We're just better at hiding it. We smile more. Between you and me," she said, getting into his car and reaching for her seat belt, "that's how we wind up catching the bad guys—by acting as if we don't suspect them—until we're snapping the handcuffs on their wrists."

"Ah," he nodded, starting up his vehicle. Excitement brewed within him, and not just for solving this case. He began to think his feelings had everything to do with his budding infatuation for this California detective dynamo. "Mystery solved."

Chapter Nineteen

"And you're looking into my cousin's background, why?" Denise Wilson, the woman standing in the doorway, asked. Less than thrilled about being questioned about her annoying cousin, she hadn't been quick about responding to the detective's urgent knocking on her door.

For her part, Cassandra was about to walk away when no one responded the third time around. But because he could faintly detect the sound of a TV, Danny was fairly certain that there was someone in the apartment. So he knocked again, more urgently this time.

When she pulled the door open a crack, the gray-haired, slightly disheveled woman did not look happy about being disturbed. Her eyes narrowed as she regarded these people with suspicion.

"What do you want?" she demanded in a less than friendly voice.

Danny immediately held up his badge and ID for

her benefit. "We'd like a few words with you about your cousin, Ms. Wilson. Pete," the detective said.

The woman's face darkened. "Maybe later," she said, trying to close her door again.

Danny was not about to move. He kept his foot in the doorway so that the woman wasn't able to push it closed. "Now would be better," he told her in a no-nonsense voice.

"This will only take a minute," Cassandra said, attempting to soften the woman.

"Yeah, right." The woman rolled her eyes and sighed dramatically. "Oh, all right. C'mon in," she told the duo. But as she opened her door further to admit them in, she looked at her watch. "You got ten minutes," she said, putting them on notice. And then ordered, "Talk fast."

"No problem," Danny responded.

The entrance to the apartment was narrow and extremely cluttered. The woman was obviously a hoarder. Danny focused exclusively on the annoyed woman.

"Our records indicate that you're related to Pete Wilson," Danny said.

Denise Wilson appeared less than pleased about the connection. A thin, angular woman, she raised her chin defiantly as she asked the two detectives, "And you're looking into my cousin's background, why?"

"We're conducting a routine questioning," Danny

informed her. "According to the information we've managed to gather, your cousin, Pete Wilson, was friends with Claude Jefferson, whose body was recently found intermingled with five other skeletons."

It was obvious that the woman had absolutely no intention of being helpful. "So?" Denise said in a challenging way.

"So," Danny continued, "we were wondering if you had ever heard the two of them arguing or having any sort of a disagreement."

She seemed almost insulted by the question. "Look, I've got better things to do than to hang around paying attention to who my cousin argues with. For your information," she said to the two detectives, "we don't even get together around the holidays." Her voice grew even colder. "Are we done?"

At this point, he saw no advantage in pushing the woman. Not until they had something to actually go on. "Unless you have anything to add, Ms. Wilson, I suppose we are," Danny told her. For now, this was going nowhere.

"No, I don't have anything to add," the woman answered, striking an almost antagonistic attitude. "Other than the fact that Pete thinks he's such a big deal, doing what he does." There was nothing but contempt in her voice. "Like that makes him special."

"And you don't think he's special," Cassandra concluded. A sliver of a premise occurred to her, and she focused on expanding it.

The woman glared at her, stunned by the question. "Special?" she repeated with more than a little contempt. "Have you *met* my cousin? He thinks he's such a big shot because he doesn't have to work if he doesn't want to."

"And why doesn't he have to work?" Danny asked. He hadn't gotten that impression when he examined the man's records. There wasn't all that much there. Still, he could have missed something.

"Because his parents died and left him a boatload of money, that's why," the woman said with contempt. It was more than obvious that she resented her cousin. "You'd think he would be happy—but he's not."

"Why isn't he happy?" Cassandra asked. Maybe they were finally getting somewhere, she thought, mentally crossing her fingers.

Denise Wilson shook her head as she shrugged. "Something about not giving him the true worth of his parents. They were both killed in a boating accident." She sighed, not about to elaborate any further. "If you ask me, I'd say that Pete was a little off, spouting gibberish." Her expression softened as she looked more closely at Danny. "My guess is that this is one case that isn't going to be solved for a very long time—if ever. But the good thing about wanting to solve a murder is that if you can't find the answers to one, there'll be another murder coming along soon enough."

And then Denise looked at her watch. "Looks like you're out of time, detectives, and I've got somewhere else to be," she announced.

In Cassandra's opinion, Denise Wilson looked far from dressed for any sort of an occasion. But she also didn't sound as if she were about to volunteer anything further at the moment.

Danny found that he had to struggle to hold on to his temper. He could feel himself on the verge of losing it and telling Wilson's cousin that she was deliberately throwing up roadblocks, but that was not going to get them anywhere in their investigation. He had half a mind to take her into the precinct for further questioning. But for now, he let that go.

With effort, Danny stiffly thanked the woman for her time. She closed the door before he could get all the words out.

"And another friendly, concerned person heard from," he murmured. Taking Cassandra's arm, he left the building.

"Well, that was a depressing waste of time," Danny commented in disgust.

"That doesn't mean the next one will be," Cassandra told him, sounding a great deal more upbeat than he was.

Danny stopped for a moment as they approached his vehicle. "You really are optimistic, aren't you?"

"I have found that it's the only way to survive," she told him. "And the minute we get that serial killer off the street, all this running around will all turn out to be worth it."

Danny could only shake his head incredulously. A smile curved his lips. For a second, he was taken back in time. "My mother would have loved you."

Stunned, Cassandra looked at him in total wonder. "That has to be just about the nicest thing you've ever said to me," she told the New York detective.

Danny lifted his shoulders in a vague, dismissive shrug. "Guess I must be slipping." He spared her a glance as he unlocked his car. "So, are you game to question the next person on the list?" He wouldn't blame her if she wasn't.

But there wasn't a moment of hesitation on her part. "Absolutely," Cassandra told him with enthusiasm.

THE NEXT PERSON they questioned was another one of Pete Wilson's acquaintances. Unlike the woman they had just spoken to, Dwight Jorgenson found Pete Wilson to be a very intriguing man.

Jorgenson had nothing but nice things to say about Denise Wilson's cousin, although their friendship did not go back very far. It seem to encompass only the last two years, roughly the space of time, it turned out, that Wilson had been working delivering mail at the precinct.

Cassandra realized that Valri had mentioned to her that a Pete Wilson had worked out at the same gym that her cousin had before both had just vanished. It seemed like an odd coincidence to her. Could this Wilson be the same person? Had he turned up again? She wanted to make sure before she ran any of this by Danny. She didn't want to look like a fool, jumping the gun.

"He's an avid bridge player," Jorgenson told them, then said, "I'm in awe of the way his mind works. It's like he's about twelve moves ahead at any given time—and a totally different person."

Danny exchanged looks with Cassandra. "What do you mean by 'different'?" he asked, unclear as to what the man was attempting to convey.

"Well, when I try to talk to him about anything else, he just reverts to single-word answers. Like he has no interest in anything that doesn't challenge his mind.

"You can tell the difference," Jorgenson said. "When you mention something that Wilson's keen about, you can see this light entering his eyes. Like he's suddenly come to life." Continuing, the man shrugged. "When he's not interested in something, it's like the power was suddenly shut off." Jorgenson looked frustrated. "I'm not explaining this very well."

"No," Cassandra contradicted, determined not to lose the man. "I think that you're explaining the situation *very* well. Most people at least pretend to listen or be accommodating to the other person. It sounds like Mr. Wilson was laser-focused on his own life and whatever interested him. Nothing else."

The fact that the man lit up like a Christmas tree was not wasted on Danny. Cassandra knew how to communicate with people, he thought, how to get them to talk.

She had turned out to be an asset.

They talked to two other people who knew or had known Pete Wilson at some point or other. Living in different parts of the city, it took a bit of doing to find them. It was telling that other than Wilson's cousin, the three people they found to talk to were all men. No women seemed to populate Wilson's inner sphere.

By the time Danny and Cassandra had finished questioning the second of the two people who knew this "Pete Wilson," it had grown dark.

It was definitely time to call it a day, Danny thought.

"Tomorrow is Saturday," Danny told her as he walked Cassandra back to his car. "And unless the captain calls us in for some reason, how would you like to play tourist?"

Cassandra looked at the man at her side in utter surprise. She wasn't sure that she had heard him correctly. "Are you offering to take me sightseeing, Detective? While we're in the middle of hunting down a serial killer?"

He inclined his head, a warm smile curving his

mouth. He had never been one for going the tourist route. But suddenly, it was sounding very appealing.

"Sometimes, taking a break makes you think more clearly. So, are you interested?" he asked.

The wide smile on her face gave him his answer.

They stopped at her hotel room to pick up a change of clothes for her, then went on to his apartment, where they spent a glorious evening making one another forget that such things as serial killers existed and lived among normal, peaceful people, disrupting their lives whenever a whim moved them.

They made unabashed, reckless love on the bed they'd messed up the night before.

The second time around, Cassandra discovered, much to her surprise and happiness, it was even more glorious and exciting than the first time had been.

They lay side by side, breathing erratically and marveling at what adrenaline could do. Cassandra turned over on her side and stared at her partner in more than one arena.

"Let's pretend that this is our lives. Just this night and this bed."

There was a pause where Danny ran a hand through his hair. He then turned to face her and grinned. "I'm right with you on that."

His blue eyes glinted with mischief as he pulled her back to him and kissed her.

Eventually, exhaustion came to claim both of them, and they wound up falling asleep in each other's arms.

STILL SOUND ASLEEP, Cassandra felt something stirring beside her. Slowly opening her eyes, she realized that it was Danny. She felt lit up from the inside.

Sliding a finger lightly down her nose, he whispered, "Open your eyes, Cavanaugh. Time to wake up."

She struggled to clear her mind. It wasn't easy. Danny had managed to tire her out more than she had thought possible. She was still half asleep but oh so happy.

"Another body?" she murmured, asking the first thing that came to her mind as she dragged herself up into a sitting position. She desperately struggled to wake up.

"Right now, the only bodies around are yours and mine." He kissed her shoulder, sending arrows of warm desire shooting through her. "Time to get ready to go sightseeing," he told her, brushing his lips against hers. "This might be the only opportunity that you get to be able to do that. With the team picking up some of the questioning, we get a little break. Granted, there's too much to stuff into even a week, much less a day of sightseeing, but we'll give it our best shot," he promised. "You snooze, you lose."

The urge to sleep was beginning to slip away as

the world around her came into focus. Cassandra
blew out a breath.

"Then I'd better get ready," she said. Turning to
look at the man in bed beside her, she asked, "You
want to shower first or second?"

"How about simultaneously?" he suggested.

She had a feeling that this way would take longer
than having them shower separately, but today—and
possibly tomorrow—was about them. That meant
doing things at their own pace.

Who knew if that could even happen again?

She grinned, running her hand along his face.
"Works for me," she announced as she tossed off the
sheet that had been tucked around her body.

As SHE HAD SURMISED, it took longer to get ready
showering together, but it was also a great deal more
rewarding and fun.

It was still early by the time they wound up hitting
the road, but they did it fully prepared and looking
forward to whatever lay ahead of them.

Danny decided to bring her to Rockefeller Center
and then follow that experience up with going on an
abbreviated tour of the Museum of Natural History.
Because of its size as well as its composition, there
was just too much to take in at the museum, but they
held hands under the giant shark hanging from the
ceiling, strolled casually past dinosaur bones and
kissed in the hall of gems and minerals. Cassandra

had a feeling that they had barely scratched the surface before Danny had even told her as much.

She could probably spend a month wandering around here, she surmised. Except that she didn't have a month, Cassandra reminded herself.

They ended their little trip with a walk in Central Park, where families were doing their best to play winter games in the fields. Despite the cold, the sky was bright blue and made for a cheery picture.

"This is breathtaking," Cassandra said to the detective.

"I agree."

She realized that Danny was looking directly at her, not at the park. She laughed and shook her head. "You can't possibly compare me to what there is right in front of you," she told him, waving her hand around.

The detective never tore his eyes away from her. "That depends on your definition of *beautiful*."

"This is," she told him, once again waving her hand at the area that surrounded them.

Danny merely smiled at her. "You have your definition of *beautiful* and I have mine," he told her.

Putting his arm around her shoulders, he drew her closer to him. "Are you in the mood to take in any more landmarks?" he asked her. "Or have you had your fill for the day?"

She would have wanted to go on touring the city endlessly, but she really couldn't manage that. "I think you've officially exhausted me," Cassandra told the detective.

"Oh, I certainly hope not," Danny said with genuine feeling. Pressing a kiss to her temple, he told Cassandra, "I know this great little crepe place we could go for dinner. You'll really like it."

"I'm all yours," she told him.

His eyes were saying things to her that made her pulse beat fast. "I certainly hope so," he told her.

She really wished that she could believe him. What he said sounded absolutely wonderful, but she was convinced that it was one of those spur-of-the-moment responses that rose to a person's lips and was only true for the time being. In the long run, the actual truth of the matter faded, leaving only broken fragments of possibilities in its wake.

"READY TO GO HOME?" Danny asked her after they had finished eating dinner an hour later.

Home.

Danny had said "home." Cassandra knew that she should point out to him that it was his home, not hers.

She should.

But just for tonight, she accepted the use of the term and allowed it to warm her clear down to her toes. How she relished the idea of seeing this wonderful guy every day, every night. They never needed to search for topics to discuss, and the more she learned about him, the stronger her feelings became. It would sting to leave him when this case ended.

No, not sting. *Hurt.*

There was time enough to come to terms with the actual truth of the situation tomorrow. Tonight was for wistful dreams. For forgetting about how they lived on opposite coasts.

"Ready," she answered Danny.

Danny slowly drew back her chair for her, helping her rise to her feet. He had to admit, if just to himself, that he was already anticipating the night that lay ahead.

Chapter Twenty

She was so beautiful. Even though he wasn't looking directly at her, Danny could feel her presence near him. Her concentration was intense and so was his, usually. Today Danny was having a hard time coping with his wild, out-of-control attraction to her and the idea that she would leave. They had been together for an incredibly short time, Danny thought as he looked up from his work at Cassandra. If he was being honest with himself, the time they had spent together could be thought of as existing in the blink of an eye.

And yet, life had laid itself out for him as existing BC and AC. Life before Cassandra had entered his life and life after she had entered it.

Looking back now, he understood that he had just been going through the motions, that in reality, he hadn't really been living at all. And now, even sharing a sandwich with her took on a whole new meaning.

The detective caught himself smiling. Suddenly, the very simplest of things meant so much more now than they had before. It occurred to him that prior to Cassandra entering his life, Danny hadn't really been living at all. At least not in the true sense of the word. Without realizing it, he had secretly been waiting for life to catch up with him.

To actually *mean* something.

Yes, Danny quietly acknowledged, he was dedicated to catching the bad guys, to ridding the world of these people who had no regard for life in any sense of the word. But somehow, that wasn't enough. Bringing them to justice didn't make him feel like smiling, like he had done a good job. It was just something that was an offshoot of his having worked a case and doing a decent job.

It wasn't until he had opened himself up to what Cassandra added to his world that he discovered himself finally coming to life. Until that point, he had just been coasting.

Cassandra put down the file she had been going through and working up. For the last hour, she had been compiling more witnesses for them to question and talk to. They had many blocks to walk before this case ended. Keeping herself focused on this killer had to be her number one priority.

But at the moment, the pensive expression on Danny's face had completely captured her attention.

"A penny for your thoughts," Cassandra told him. "Or, judging from the look on your face, my guess is that a dollar fifty would probably be more appropriate."

Caught off guard, Danny blinked. "What?" he asked, clearly confused.

"You look very pensive," Cassandra explained, the file temporarily forgotten. "I was just wondering what you were thinking about."

The corners of Danny's mouth curved. He had been smiling a lot more lately, and that was all thanks to her.

"I'll tell you later—over dinner. Or afterwards," he added sensually.

She could feel herself responding to what he was saying. This man knew how to stir her more than any other man she had ever encountered. Just the way he looked at her excited her. It had been a while since she'd felt any kind of connection to someone. And this guy pushed all her buttons in the best possible way.

Who would have thought that tracking a serial killer could have had this sort of a reward attached to it?

"I plan on holding you to that," she told Danny.

His eyes slid over her, undressing her in his mind. It took him a moment to focus on what she was telling him.

"Deal," he promised. He drew over the file she had been working on and glanced at the names that she had listed. It looked rather complete—for now. "Ready to go out and question more people?" he asked, nodding at the newest list of friends and relatives his team had managed to put together.

Cassandra was already on her feet, reaching for her jacket. "It's what I live for," she told him with a touch of mischief in her voice.

Danny led the way out.

As Cassandra hurried after the detective, the mail clerk, Curtis Wayfare managed to angle his cart so that her path out of the squad room was cut off.

"Sorry," Wayfare apologized flatly, looking anything but repentant. "My bad."

His cutting into her exit had been deliberate, Cassandra thought, frustrated. She couldn't help thinking that she was right. The Wayfare and Wilson were one and the same person She needed to find a way to pin him down and be sure.

"No harm done," she told him after a beat.

They had just entered the hallway. Wayfare was blocking her way to the elevator with his cart.

Okay, enough was enough. "You need to move back," Cassandra told the mail clerk when he just remained standing where he was.

The look in his eyes darkened. "And you need to remember your place," he told her, his voice low, menacing.

Cassandra tossed her head. He was brazen, she'd give him that. "And where would that be?" she challenged.

"Back to where you came from," he told her nastily. His pasty skin wrinkled in a grimace. "We don't need you parading around here, acting so high and mighty and getting in everyone's way," Wayfare informed her. "The department was doing just fine before you ever came on the scene to stick your nose in all this."

"And just between the two of us," she said, knowing she was pushing his buttons, "I don't think that Detective Doyle shares your opinion about the matter," Cassandra told the mail clerk, aware that the remark would set him off.

Infuriated, Wayfare's complexion turned a deep shade of red. "Of course he does," he all but shouted. And then, regaining his temper, Wayfare lowered his voice as he added, "He's just too polite to say so."

Danny chose that moment to come back, looking for Cassandra.

"What happened to you?" he asked, striding back toward the hallway entrance. "Did you get lost? I thought you were right behind me."

Cassandra saw the nervous, wary look that had come over the mail clerk's features. "I was," she told the detective. Slanting a glance toward Wayfare, she explained, "But then I realized I had forgotten to take something with me, so I had to double back for it."

The expression on the detective's face said he wasn't buying her story. She was up to something, but they were losing time, so he felt he could pick this point up later, when there was more time to explore the various points that needed to be touched upon.

Nodding at the mail clerk by way of taking his leave, Danny took Cassandra's arm and hurried her along.

It wasn't until the detective had her alone in the elevator that Danny finally asked Cassandra, "What was that all about? And don't tell me, 'Nothing,'" he warned. "The look on Wayfare's face said that this was definitely about *something*."

Cassandra debated brushing the detective's question aside, then decided that Danny was not about to let the matter drop easily. Until she was sure, she wasn't going to tell him about her suspicions about the mail clerk.

"He was just being protective."

That didn't make any sense to him. "Of what?" Danny asked.

The elevator opened up and they walked out across the ground floor. "More like of who," she corrected.

"All right," he said gamely, deciding to go that route. "Of who?"

Okay, she thought with an inward sigh. The man had asked for it. Her eyes met his. "You."

Eyebrows drew together so closely, they all but made a single arched, dark brown line.

"Me?" he questioned, clearly stunned. "Why was Wayfare being protective of me?" It just didn't make any sense to the detective. She had to be mistaken.

She bit her tongue. "To save you from me, I would imagine," Cassandra answered.

Danny shook his head as he began walking again, heading toward the parking garage. "You've lost me, Cass. What are you talking about?"

He didn't see it, she thought. But then, that would take his admitting that he was the object of the mail clerk's affection, and Danny clearly didn't think in those terms. That sort of blatant adoration was hard enough for the detective to accept, much less admit to himself that he had somehow managed to miss all the signs.

Cassandra gave the detective a good onceover. She could easily see why the mail clerk had been drawn to Danny. Not only was the man easy to be around, but he was also kind to everyone. His team-mates respected him and sought him out through-out the day, not just to discuss details of the case but just to talk. And while Danny may have been an astute detective, he downgraded his own influ-ence on others.

Still, she felt she had to at least make Danny aware of the situation with Curtis Wayfare. "For lack of a better word right now, I'd say that that Wayfare and

Wilson are one and the same person. And he apparently has some kind of attachment to you." She slanted a look in his direction. "I vote that we begin gathering more information on him. It could be entirely benign, but I think we really need to check him out."

It made the detective uncomfortable to admit it, but she just might have a point, Danny decided. Still right now they couldn't just drop everything else to exclusively focus on only Wayfare/Wilson, because they could be wrong and the real serial killer could go scot-free.

Danny did make a mental note to look into the matter further. He couldn't afford to just shrug the matter off. Cassandra wouldn't push the matter to this degree if she didn't believe that there was something there.

For now, he thought, he and the team would continue to focus on the new list that had been compiled. There was no shortage of people to visit and interview.

Distributing the list, the detective made sure that each member of his team had the same number of people to talk to and investigate.

"You know, I'm really beginning to feel like a dog that's trying to chase its own tail," Cassandra said as she got back into Danny's car. They had just finished talking to someone professing to be a close friend of one of the newest victims that had been discovered.

He looked at her for a second. "Now that's rather an interesting image to consider," Danny commented, pulling out of the parking that was located across the street from the person they had been questioning.

As always, there was traffic. He made his way slowly down the block and back onto a bustling avenue. "Care to explain why?"

"Because no matter how much energy is used, all we seem to be able to do is go around in circles—which wind up taking us absolutely nowhere."

"Not all of the cases we work are going to be neatly wrapped up in a bow," he told her, then sighed, struggling to keep the disappointment out of his voice. "A lot of these cases are *never* solved."

She nodded. He was not telling her anything new. "I know, but I still can't seem to shake this feeling that we're overlooking something. That we're staring at the answer right in the face and just not seeing it."

He shrugged, allowing his vehicle to idle as he waited for the light to change. "Maybe you're right." And then he added, "Hang on to that feeling."

"Oh, I fully intend to," Cassandra told him. She hadn't flown three thousand miles from one coast to the other just to fail.

"Okay," he said, resigned to continue going down the list. "Who's next?"

She had held on to the list and glanced down now. "Albert Walker. He's a retired engineer who lives in Queens." She ratted off the address that was written right next to the man's name.

Danny nodded, familiar with the area. At least, he had been when he was younger.

But when they finally arrived at a crumbling single-family home that looked as if it had been constructed just at the end of the Civil War, it was nothing like he had remembered. The painfully thin woman who came to the door in response to his knock told them that Albert Walker had recently sold the house and had moved to Florida.

"Did he give you a number where he could be reached?" Danny asked her.

The woman, Gloria, shook her head. "I think he was afraid that I would call him to say I changed my mind and ask for my money back." She smiled, showing off her brand-new dental work. It was clear that she was very pleased with herself. "He didn't know about the developer who was buying up the entire block. His loss, my gain," Gloria declared triumphantly.

"And you're sure you don't know how to get in touch with Albert Walker?" Cassandra asked. This could be the one person who mattered, she couldn't help thinking.

"Perfectly."

With that, Gloria closed the door before they could ask any more questions.

Danny blew out a frustrated breath as they made their way back to his vehicle. "Okay, next person," the detective said wearily. He noticed that Cassandra seemed to fall back before they reached the automobile. "Something wrong?" he asked, looking around the general vicinity.

Cassandra pressed her lips together, wondering if she should say anything to him. He would probably think she was just imagining things or being paranoid. Maybe she was, but for the past day, she couldn't seem to shake the feeling that they were being watched—and most likely followed. At first, she was certain it was all in her head, but the gut-wrenching feeling continued, growing more intense as the day grew longer.

"I don't know. Maybe it's nothing," she responded.

"But?" Danny prodded, waiting for her to tell him what was really bothering her. "C'mon, Cavanaugh," he said, unlocking the doors to the car. However, for now he remained standing next to the vehicle. "Out with it."

"You're going to think I'm being crazy. Again," she added since she had already admitted to having this feeling before.

"I'll let you know if I do—or not," he told her.

Cassandra blew out a breath. "All right, you asked for this." She drew in a breath, then said, "I think we're being followed. It's a gut feeling more than anything else," she admitted. "But every time I turn around, I could swear I just missed seeing the person who's following us."

To her relief, Danny didn't laugh at her. He listened to her elaborate a little on her admission, then said, "The next time you feel like someone's watching us, give me a signal." Then, before she could ask what sort of signal, he told her, "Take my hand."

"All right," she agreed. "But this just might be you, getting a little spicy on me."

"Hey, I have to find a way to break up the monotony somehow," he deadpanned.

For a second, she felt as if the tension had dissipated to a degree.

But only for a second.

The next moment, that tense, uneasy feeling that haunted her returned to continue to shadow her.

When he brought his vehicle to a stop at a red light, Danny glanced in her direction. He noticed the way Cassandra was covering the sidearm at her hip with her hand. He sensed that she wanted to be ready, just in case.

"You can feel him, can't you?" he asked.

"It's probably just my imagination," she told him with a shrug.

"I know it's only been a short while, but I've learned to trust your imagination," Danny told her.

"You'll have two sets of eyes on the alert and watching instead of just one set," he told her.

She was not sure if he was just humoring her or not, but the detective knew how to make her feel better, Cassandra thought, taking comfort in his assurance.

THEY WENT ON to another name on the list, making a real effort to find and question the person.

Edward Heller turned out to be exceedingly cooperative. A librarian by trade, he gave the impression that he was very aware of his surroundings.

But in the end, after questioning the man, they were no closer to solving the puzzle they were attempting to reconstruct than they had initially been.

And the feeling, of someone following them, refused to abate.

Cassandra comforted herself with the thought that this could mean that they were getting closer to finally finding the serial killer. It was just a matter of time, she promised herself—and hoped that she wasn't wrong.

Chapter Twenty-One

"Don't take this the wrong way, but the streets of your city really make me nervous after dark," Cassandra told the detective walking at her side.

"You're just not used to them. Don't believe the hype."

"Yeah, but dark city streets are still great places to commit crimes."

"We are trained to deal with them, remember?" Danny said with a teasing light in his eyes.

"Thanks for reminding me." She hoped she conveyed sarcasm, but maybe he really believed that she might be afraid. Not afraid, just on her guard. It wasn't the worst quality to have in a detective and had saved her butt on numerous occasions.

Danny leaned in closer as they made their way up the street. The temperature had dropped again, the wind had picked up, and it was practically close to freezing.

They had one more person to talk to on their list

for the day. Could this be the one who would break open the case for them? That was always the question and why they kept going for hours on end.

Danny had come close to calling it a night right after they had finished interviewing the previous person, Raul Chan, but Cassandra wanted to talk to this last witness.

"This way, we can start fresh in the morning," she told him.

The detective had a different view of the situation. "Maybe we'll get lucky, and Jason Bradford won't be home," Danny said as he led the way to the unlit apartment building.

Cassandra kept looking around, memorizing her surroundings. She was trying to remain alert to any sort of possibilities that might wind up transpiring.

As she and Danny drew closer to the building, she could feel her pulse quickening in anticipation. No matter what Danny said, she could sense something was up. It could very well be her imagination. Cops often had a sixth sense about upcoming scenes and this was one of those times. She knew they wouldn't go home so quickly after this next visit.

"Funny how the lack of light can make some places appear absolutely creepy," Cassandra couldn't help commenting.

Danny totally agreed with her insight. "No argument there. City funding when it comes to better lighting in all neighborhoods has been slow going.

In the meantime, I like the summers here. It might be hot and sticky, and at times a total mosquito-fest, but at least the light does last longer. Cuts down a bit on the creepiness," he added. "So, I guess in a way, it's a tradeoff."

"Are you trying to distract me, Detective?"

"Hey, if it helps…"

The detective glanced down at his cell phone. The last address on their list had been sent to him by an assistant a few minutes ago.

He frowned as he read the address and then looked up at the building they were standing in front of. It resembled a neglected Gothic hotel, with shadows, faint lights in windows and the promise of cobwebs and creepy corners inside.

"This is it." Danny glanced at the woman accompanying him. "This doesn't look very hospitable, does it?" he asked, commenting on the way the building looked. "Would you rather come back tomorrow morning instead of going in tonight?"

Just as they had approached the building, Danny had noticed that the lights corresponding to Jason Bradford's apartment were not on. For the second time, the detective thought that it might be a better idea to approach Jason Bradford's apartment when they were all fresh.

But Cassandra didn't share his view of the matter. "We're here. We might as well see if the man is in."

Danny sighed, nodding. "I had a feeling you were going to say that."

Amused, Cassandra glanced at him. "Am I really all that predictable?"

"Just to me," Danny told her with a broad wink. With that, he proceeded into the building and up the elevator to the right floor. The decor didn't get any less creepy with its peeling paint and patchy carpeting on the floors. Danny leaned forward to ring the outdoor apartment's doorbell. When there was no corresponding sound, he decided that the doorbell was more than likely broken, so he knocked instead.

Twice.

No one answered.

Danny decided that there was no one home, or at least no one who was willing to answer at this hour. Either way, he felt that there was only one course open to him.

"Looks like we're coming back in the morning after all," Danny said.

But just as he was about to turn on his heel to walk away, Cassandra caught him by the arm, holding him in place. When he looked at her quizzically, she nodded toward the apartment. "Did you hear that?"

"Hear what?" Danny asked.

"I could swear there was a sound coming from the inside the apartment," she answered, then urged, "Listen."

Danny was inclined to dismiss her words as being

the product of her imagination when he took a closer look at Cassandra. More to the point, he saw the expression on her face.

"You're actually being serious," the detective realized.

"Of course I'm serious," Cassandra insisted, lowering her voice. She nodded toward the door, then repeated, "Listen."

So he did, cocking his head and concentrating. This time, Danny thought he picked up a very faint noise coming from inside the apartment.

"Maybe a window was left open," he theorized.

"And maybe someone isn't answering for a reason," she countered. Specifically, she thought maybe whoever was in the apartment didn't want to talk to anyone.

"There could be a lot of reasons for that," Danny told her.

She saw no reason to argue the point. "True," Cassandra agreed, then completely threw him when she said, "Could be a thief, ransacking the place. I'd say it's up to us to check it out."

Danny was beginning to know her looks. "You're not going to give up until I agree," he surmised. "We'll have to bring in the landlord so they can use their keys."

"No need," she informed him as she took out a long, thin sliver of metal and proceeded to utilize it. The next thing Danny knew, she had managed to unlock the front door of Jason Bradford's apartment.

As he had already determined, there were no lights on, but from the sound they had detected, there was definitely someone there.

Danny took the lead, motioning to Cassandra to follow him as he slowly made his way toward the next room and the source of the noise.

Everything happened lightning fast from that point on.

There was a tall, thin man in the shadows. He was bending over Jason Bradford, the prone figure on the floor and was obviously startled as he jumped.

Cursing, he shifted his attention from what he was doing to the two people who had caught him at it. Even in the dim light, the hatred in his eyes was definitely noticeable.

"Damn it!" the man cried, following the exclamation with a number of other, far more ripe expressions of vile anger. It was then that Danny noticed the man was holding a knife in his hand. The sharp weapon was bloodstained.

The next second, he lunged at Danny, determined to sink the knife into his flesh.

Horrified, Cassandra recognized the mail clerk just as she attempted to stop him by pushing him out of the way. The killer tossed her aside as if she were a mere rag doll. Landing, on the floor, she wound up hitting her head against a cabinet.

Dizzy, she tried to clear her head while she was still on the floor. Every bone in her body ached as she reached for her weapon. Cassandra was very aware of the fact that she had only a few seconds to stop this man from committing yet another murder.

Or two.

Infuriated, Curtis Wayfare had raised his knife high in the air, determined to do the maximum amount of damage when he wound up making contact with Danny's body.

Only he didn't make contact.

At the last possible moment, Cassandra screamed out a warning, then as the serial killer spun around, about to plunge the knife into her, she fired.

Discharging her weapon rapidly, she managed to hit Wayfare/Wilson in the chest, in his left shoulder and in his head.

The killer fell with a thud at her feet. His last conscious act was to attempt to grab her in order to remain upright.

There was a scream, and it took Cassandra a moment to realize that the sound had torn from her own lips, encapsulating the horror she had just experienced.

Danny seized his weapon, pointing it at Wayfare/Wilson, ready to shoot. But there was no need to discharge it again.

The serial killer was dead, as was his latest victim.

Danny's eyes swept over Cassandra, more concerned than he had ever been in his life.

"Are you all right?" They asked the question simultaneously, then laughed as their voices, still mingling, replied, "Yes."

Lodged protectively in the detective's arms, Cassandra cast an uneasy look at the man on the floor, blood pooling and swiftly leaving his body.

"Are we sure he's dead?" she asked, staring at the killer and watching for him to make a move—*any* move.

"Unless he belongs to one of the undead, I'd say, yes, he's most assuredly dead."

Reluctantly releasing Cassandra for a moment, Danny took out his phone and quickly called for an ambulance, giving his badge and ID number to dispatch, along with a quick summation of what had happened.

Ending the call, he put his cell phone into his pocket. "The ambulance should be here soon," he told her.

Cassandra looked down at the deceased serial killer and his victim. "I don't think that'll make much of a difference to either one of them."

"The ambulance is for you," Danny told her, then watched as Cassandra's shoulders stiffened.

"I don't need an ambulance," she said to the detective despite the fact that her head insisted on spinning.

Taking out his handkerchief, Danny wiped away

the blood on her forehead. She had managed to hit it in two places. Holding the handkerchief up for Cassandra to see, he said, "I beg to differ with you, Detective Cavanaugh. You most definitely need to be checked out. I'm not letting anything happen to you on my watch," he told her. "Now stop arguing with me and just rest until the ambulance gets here." He could hear the siren in the distance. "Which, from the sound of it, will be any minute now."

Woozy, Cassandra blew out a breath. She hated having a fuss made over her. "This is a waste of time." Although, to be honest, her legs started to feel weak, not to mention that her head was still spinning.

"And it's my time to waste," he informed her. "I thought you California girls were supposed to be easygoing."

"We are," she responded in a crisp voice.

"Arguing is not easygoing," Danny said.

Just then, they heard the ambulance pulling up. The next moment, there was a knock on the door, and two paramedics came in, pushing a stretcher between them.

Danny felt it only fair to warn the ambulance attendants, "She's going to tell you that she doesn't need to go to the hospital. Don't listen to her."

And then he pointed toward the dead serial killer and his victim lying on the ground. "No hurry with them, they're both dead. But FYI, that one," he indicated thedead mail clerk, "is the serial killer everyone's been living in fear of ever since those bodies were found buried within the construction site."

The shorter of the two paramedics crossed over toward the dead serial killer. "Doesn't look all that the scary now, does he?"

"He was scary enough to kill all those people over the years and get away with it," Cassandra said, her voice fading a little. "He had been slaying men for much too long. Someone should have caught on before now," she told them. "But the trouble was that this guy looked almost harmless and much too fussy to represent the kind of danger that he was actually capable of."

That was when the paramedic waved over his partner, who brought the stretcher over toward Cassandra. "Time to take you to the hospital to check you out, Detective." He indicated that she needed to get onto the stretcher.

Cassandra tried one last time. "I'm fine," she protested.

"The rest of us want to make sure that's the actual case. You're not going to deny that to us now, are you?" he asked Cassandra.

She was of a mind to go on protesting that she was fine, except that she suddenly became really dizzy.

The sensation only grew stronger, and rather quickly at that. She caught herself clutching at Danny as her knees began to buckle, threatening to make her collapse.

That was when a pair of strong arms caught her, then gently put her onto the stretcher. Things began to grow increasingly distant as well as blurry.

And then suddenly, everything shrank down to the size of a pinprick, after which it completely disappeared.

WHEN CASSANDRA CAME TO, she found herself lying in a hospital bed. Not only that, but she was wearing a hospital gown. Sunlight streamed through the window blinds.

Danny was sitting beside her. When he saw her opening her eyes, he was instantly on his feet, relieved to see color coming back to her face. "Welcome back," he told her.

"Where are my clothes?" she asked, uncomfortable to find herself like this.

"We held a raffle," he told her.

She blinked, attempting to focus. "What?"

"Don't worry," he told her, taking her hand. "Your clothes are in the closet." He indicated the closet next to the bathroom in the front of the hospital room. "But they're going to be taking you to get some X-rays and an MRI shortly, so you won't be needing your clothes for a while."

Danny could see the protest forming on her lips. He fell back on the logical excuse. "They have to check you out, Cass. They don't want to risk being sued because they merrily sent you on your way," he told her. "And as for me, I want to be able to continue making love with you without worrying that you're suddenly going to expire on me in the middle of it all."

She put her hand to her forehead, as if that would help her make sense out of what she had just heard. "Continue making love?" she repeated, mystified.

"Well, yeah—unless you've already grown tired of me," he said, hoping that hadn't become the case.

"No, I haven't grown tired of you," she said, not really believing she was having this conversation with him. It all felt rather unreal to her. How was it that she wound up here with Danny at her side?

"Good, because the minute they give you a clean bill of health, you can show me just how not tired of me you are," he told her with a warm grin.

"Okay," she said just as a nurse came in to take her down for her workup.

Cassandra found herself clutching to the arms of the wheelchair as she prepared to be pushed out of the room. This was not the time to point out that with this serial killer put out of the city's misery, she and Travis would be on their way back to Aurora, most likely very soon.

But that was still in the future, no matter how close that future might be. Moreover, for now, she needed to focus on not having the world dance around in her head. Even the light in the room seemed a little too bright.

"Will you be here when they bring me back?" she asked the detective as the nurse started wheeling her out of the room.

He laughed at the question. "Like you could dynamite me out of here."

Cassandra nodded. "Good. Definitely not planning on doing that," she told him. She didn't like not being in good enough shape to walk on her own. But even she could admit that she needed some help and a whole lot of TLC.

Chapter Twenty-Two

It continued to be the story of the hour. Coupled with the human interest angle that finding their cousin's killer—Nathan could finally be sent home to rest—was ending the threat of a serial killer roaming the streets of the most exciting city in the country, possibly the world, brought with it a huge collective sigh of relief.

Cassandra could almost swear that she was able to hear it as she lay in the detective's arms a week later. There was a constant lull of city noise and cheering around the police precinct that had cracked the case. Every now and then, members of the team, with chests puffed out, would go outside to give interviews about the work involved in tracking this killer.

As for Cassandra, she had been released from the hospital with a clean bill of health, then had spent the rest of the time dodging eager reporters who were looking to write the next Pulitzer Prize winning story based on the capture and elimination of the serial killer who had been haunting the city for such a long time. A few reporters asked for details of Nathan's life, something she felt was too private to talk about even if she were so inclined. There was even talk of a limited series starring several promising actors.

"You know, you're missing a great opportunity to be immortalized as the detective who rode in from California on a surfboard to save a bunch of New Yorkers from suffering at the hands of a deadly, cold-blooded killer."

Cassandra curled up against the detective. "It's not as if I didn't have help. A *lot* of help," she emphasized, looking up at him from her vantage point.

But he shook his head. "I just got into this after you saw what was going on. You were the one who honed in on Wayfare with that gut feeling of yours."

"What can I say?" she asked, smiling at Danny. "You bring out the best in me."

This was a truth she'd come to accept. Working with Danny had helped her delve more deeply into a case, scout out every possible clue no matter how obscure. It made her feel…creative. In a family of law enforcement, one could easily fall into a way of operating that was the opposite of creative. But Cassandra knew her gift was imagining scenarios that might not be likely but could be. This was how she knew to follow her gut on this case…and work with Danny.

"Ditto. You've helped me be a better detective,

that's for sure," he told her with a smile. And then the smile faded a little as he thought about the near future. "You're going to be leaving soon, aren't you?" The words tasted extremely bitter on his tongue. "Going back to Aurora, right?"

Without realizing it, her arm tightened around his chest as she attempted to deal with the situation. "That was the plan, yes," Cassandra responded. Now that this was all over and the killer had been caught, she and Travis were supposed to be scheduled to go back home. Nathan's remains has already been shipped, preceding them.

So, why did going back to the West Coast, back to everyone she had ever loved and cared about, feel so wrong to her right now? Every time she tried to envision leaving her family, she forced herself to ditch the idea. But leaving Danny seemed just as ludicrous and, yes, wrong.

Cassandra let out a long, shaky sigh, which encouraged the detective to continue talking, continue voicing the idea that had been forming in his head for a while now. It hadn't jelled until just recently, spurred on by seeing Cassandra lying in that hospital bed and realizing that he could have very well lost her permanently. And what that would have felt like if he had.

He saw himself wandering city streets like a zombie and going back to coasting through life. He could make a life solving case after case and obeying the needs of his work. But something had changed in such a short time. Was that even possible?

The idea of going through the motions for the next forty years was suddenly unacceptable. No way could he do this without Cassandra by his side, her upbeat attitude nudging him into the day.

"Would you happen to know if there's any place in that precinct where you work for another cop, or more to the point, perhaps another police detective?" he asked.

Cassandra felt her heart suddenly flutter as she drew herself up to look at the man beside her. Was he saying what she thought he was saying, or was he just extrapolating on information he had just happened to hear? Maybe her injuries had taken a toll on her.

She would hate to ask and put herself out there only to be disappointed. The smart thing would be just to coast and let him keep on talking, eventually getting enough information to draw a conclusion.

But she didn't feel like being smart or cautious. Coming face-to-face with an actual serial killer and surviving that encounter had a way of negating all her previous underpinnings of caution. There was only this life, and she wanted it to be with him.

"Are you asking for yourself?" she asked.

"And if I was?" he posed.

He *was* asking for himself, she thought, everything within her rejoicing.

"I'd find a way to get someone to retire in order to

get a good position for you," she told him. Cassandra sat up, looking at him. "I am sure that you would be a welcome addition to the Aurora police force. Uncle Brian is always looking for a good man to join up." Excitement had caused her mind to scramble and fog up. It took her a second to be able to get her thoughts in order. "As a matter of fact, I know of at least two positions that are due to open up when Hotchkiss and Evans retire."

"Hotchkiss and Evans?" Danny repeated slowly.

"Two long-time detectives who have put in their papers and are set to retire," she told him. And then she realized that she was getting ahead of herself. "You *are* thinking of something permanent, right? Or is this just a passing fancy that you're thinking of exploring in the short run?"

His eyes were already making love to her. "That all depends."

She ordered her heart to settle down. It didn't listen. "On?"

He lightly kissed her temple. "On whether or not I can get a certain very sexy homicide detective to tell me how she feels about the idea of having me transfer to her precinct. I don't want to intrude if you just want to keep all the Cavanaughs to yourself. I mean, I get it if this is too sudden and you—"

"Sexy?" she repeated, surprised. "You think I'm sexy?"

"Oh, hell yes," Danny answered. "I might have

missed all those initial signs pointing to Wayfare being the serial killer we were hunting, but that doesn't mean I'm totally blind."

She laughed, throwing her arms around Danny's neck. "You really have the strangest way of complimenting a person, but I will definitely take it," she told him happily just before she sealed her lips to his.

It took her a while before she was able to draw her lips back again, as well as catch her breath so that she was able to put a question to him.

"So, I take it you'll be transferring to the Aurora Police Department?" she asked him hopefully.

"As soon as I can put in my papers," he said.

It all sounded wonderful, but she had been taught a long time ago not to count her chickens before the eggs were at least laid, much less hatched.

"What if you don't like it there?" she questioned, then felt herself start to babble excitedly. "I mean, Aurora is like a paradise with mountains in the north, both urban and rural delights, good restaurants, lots of Cavanaughs, of course. But I'm sure New York is way too exciting to leave even though you have these really cold winters and probably not a lot of tanning opportunities."

"You're going to be there, right?" he said to Cassandra.

It seemed like an odd question to ask her, but she answered anyway. "That's a given."

"Then I'll love it," he assured her.

"But—"

"Cavanaugh," he said, drawing her back into his arms and nibbling on her ear.

She breathed, her pulse racing madly. Dreams did come true. Who would have thought? That's why it paid to be an optimist. "Yes?"

"Stop talking. I've got much better things for your lips to be doing," he told her and then proceeded to show her exactly what he meant.

Her heart pounding hard, she found herself agreeing with him totally.

* * * * *

COMING SOON!

We really hope you enjoyed reading this book.
If you're looking for more romance, be sure to
head to the shops when new books are
available on

Thursday 2nd March

To see which titles are coming soon, please visit

millsandboon.co.uk/nextmonth

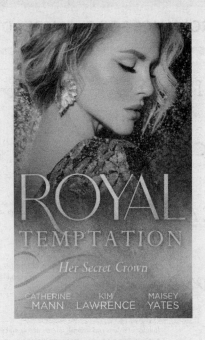

LET'S TALK
Romance

For exclusive extracts, competitions
and special offers, find us online:

JOIN US ON SOCIAL MEDIA!

Stay up to date with our latest releases, author news and gossip, special offers and discounts, and all the behind-the-scenes action from Mills & Boon...

 @millsandboon

 @millsandboonuk

 facebook.com/millsandboon

 @millsandboonuk

It might just be true love...

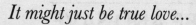

GET YOUR ROMANCE FIX!

Get the latest romance news, exclusive author interviews, story extracts and much more!

MILLS & BOON
Desire

Indulge in secrets and scandal, intense drama and plenty of sizzling hot action with powerful and passionate heroes who have it all: wealth, status, good looks…everything but the right woman.

MILLS & BOON
MODERN

Power and Passion

Prepare to be swept off your feet by sophisticated, sexy and seductive heroes, in some of the world's most glamourous and romantic locations, where power and passion collide.

MILLS & BOON
MEDICAL
Pulse-Racing Passion

Set your pulse racing with dedicated, delectable doctors in the high-pressure world of medicine, where emotions run high and passion, comfort and love are the best medicine.

MILLS & BOON
True Love
Romance from the Heart

Celebrate true love with tender stories of heartfelt romance, from the rush of falling in love to the joy a new baby can bring, and a focus on the emotional heart of a relationship.